NOVA PRAETORIAN

N.R. WALKER

COPYRIGHT

Cover Artist: Humble Nations
Editor: Labyrinth Bound Edits
Publisher: BlueHeart Press
Nova Praetorian © 2018 N.R. Walker
First Edition 2018

BLURB

Quintus Furius Varus is one of the best lanistas in Rome. Tall and strong in build, fearsome in manner, and sharp of wit, he trains the best gladiators bound for the arenas of Rome. When Senator Servius Augendus seeks personal guards, he attends the Ludus Varus to purchase the very best. He puts to Quintus an offer he cannot refuse, and Quintus finds himself in Neapolis, contracted as a trainer of guards instead of gladiators.

Kaeso Agorix was taken from his homelands of Iberia and delivered to Rome as a slave. Bought by a senator to be trained as a guard, his fate is handed to the man who would train him. Absent free will, Kaeso knows his life is no longer his own, though he soon realises the gods have favoured him when he learns his new master has a kind heart.

Quintus and Kaeso forge a bond that far exceeds the collar at Kaeso's neck, and together they discover the senator's move for promotion has an ulterior motive. Thrown into a world of politics and conspiracy, of keeping enemies close, they move against time to save Rome before traitors and the gods themselves see to their end.

And in doing so, see the dawn of the nova praetorian—the new guard—rise.

INFORMATION AND GLOSSARY

PRIOR TO READING

Cast of Characters

- Quintus Furius Varus
- Kaeso Agorix (pronounced Ky-so)
- Doctor Oscilius
- Senator Servius Atrius Augendus
- Senator Marcus Cornelius Maternus
- Emperor
- Fleet Commander Linus Jovian
- Praetorian Guard Tiberius Hirrus
- Guards: Gallio, Oppius, Mettius, Decius, Lucan
- Gladiators: Appias, Caius, Lars, Paullus, Arruns, Pellio, Artamo, Messenio, Harpax, Phaidon
- Gladiatrix: Salonia, Varia
- House slaves: Helier, Benedictus, Matalia, Petilia, and Cythereia

Locations

- Neapolis: City of Naples
- Roma: City of Rome
- Rome: Italy and lands conquered by the Roman Empire
- Puteoli: City of Puzzuoli

Glossary and some Latin explanations:

- Ludus: Gladiator school
- Ludus Varus: Gladiator school owned by Quintus Furius Varus. Best ludus in Campania, southern region of Italy.
- Villa: Roman home on large lot/rural area
- Domus: Roman home in city
- Dominus: Owner or master (male)
- Domina: Owner or master (female)
- Doctor: Trainer of Gladiators. Not to be confused with Medicus
- Medicus: One who practises medicine/treatment of injury
- Quaestor: Official in charge of revenue/accounting
- Stipator: Slave bodyguard who carries weapons
- Sicarii: Assassins. Literally means "daggermen"
- Vilicus: Slave who is in charge of other house or villa slaves
- Prima pilus: First Centurion (high ranking officer)

* Sesertii: Type of coins
* Magus: Magic
* Jocus: Joke
* Priapus: Roman god with huge penis

Clothes and weapons

* Pugio: Dagger
* Rudis: Wooden practice sword
* Palus: Wooden pole/stick
* Strigil: Scraping tool to oil/clean the body
* Subligaculum: Soft cloth underwear, tied on with straps
* Pteruges: Skirt of leather straps
* Pauldron: Leather shoulder guard
* Manicae: Arm or wrist padding
* Clipeus: Round (small) shield
* Galea: Helmet
* Caliga: Sandal boots
* Pallium: Cloak over toga

DATE AS CE:

Common Era. As in 62CE, being the secular equivalent to 62AD

Author Note/Disclaimer:

While this book stays true to Roman culture and way of life, and there are some historical events/factors, a lot of creative licence has been taken. The emperor and all senators are fictional.

SPECIAL THANKS

A special thank you to Alyson Roy who helped with the detail of Roman customs, politics, vernacular, and everything in between.
These boys wouldn't be half as good without your knowledge and expertise. I'm so grateful for your time and patience.

These boys are for you.

NOVA PRAETORIAN

N.R. WALKER

INTERLŪDIUM

OPLONTIS, CAMPANIA. 62CE

LUDUS VARUS, one of the most prestigious gladiator training schools in all the lands of Rome, sat nestled between green fields of grain and the blue of the Bay of Neapolis in the seaside village of Oplontis. On these sands, gladiators trained under the watchful eye of *Dominus* Caius Furius Varus and beneath the hard hand of their *doctor*, Oscilius.

Men with the strength of mountains and the will of the same sought glory or freedom in the arenas. Some earned it. Most lost blood and limb, or head, in a vain attempt.

The men within the *ludus* walls were owned, slaves to the house of Varus. Gladiators who trained and the men who tended them all pledged their lives to Caius Varus. He was a kind master, fair and swift with both punishment and praise. He kept his word, and he kept his reputation with the hierarchy of Rome.

Oscilius bore a whip in his right hand, his face scarred from temple to jaw. He had fought undefeated and, as such, earned his place as doctor at the ludus, shaping the men he now taught. Those who fell onto the sands beneath his whip would not have agreed, but Quintus, son of Caius, adored him. And Oscilius, a man of otherwise hard lines and fierce temper, held a soft affection for the boy.

Quintus Furius Varus, just seven summers old and son of Caius, would watch the men train each day. He took expert note of defence, offence, footwork, and skill, and would stand with Oscilius. He would wield wooden practice daggers, mimicking the men, and Oscilius would correct him with feigned orders, withholding a smile as Caius, approving and proud, watched on.

"Rest assured, Dominus," Oscilius had said to Caius. "Your legacy is steadfast with him. Quintus will make a fine man."

Caius gave a slow nod, his eyes and lips lighted with good humour. "If this ludus falls to ruin, I shall meet the gods knowing he'll earn good coin on the sands of the emperor's arena."

Both men laughed, for it seemed so unlikely, so ludicrous, to dare imagine. The gods had favoured them. Ludus Varus stood in wealth: gold silk-adorned doorways, lush gardens, fresh meat and wine served by the best slaves. Caius gave Mira, his wife and Quintus' mother, the best milk baths, the best oils, the finest clothes and jewels. They held good standing in Campania. Emperors and senators alike came from Rome to their ludus to select the finest gladiators and guards. To visit Caius and Mira and holiday by the sea with them, hold alliance with them. It was oft spoken that when Quintus was of age, he would succeed the ludus, and Caius would take position in politics.

Yes, the gods had favoured them. Shined upon them, blessed them.

And as the men's laughter quietened, as if the gods had heard and answered, the earth began to shake.

The fighting men stopped, looking aghast on unsteady ground. Weapons fell to the sands, soon followed by tumbling walls. Slaves screamed, men scrambled, and somewhere in the courtyard, a small boy, just seven summers old, with dark curly hair and fearful eyes, called out. "Father! Father!"

CAPITULUM I

SEVENTEEN YEARS LATER...

SENATOR SERVIUS ATRIUS AUGENDUS stood at the balcony, observing the display of skilled men on show for him. His white, curled hair was not marred by the heat, for his entourage of slaves beside him waved fans of feather and frond, offering water and wine.

He had travelled from Neapolis to Oplontis, to the Ludus Varus, for one purpose.

Rome had become uneasy. Times of unrest were looming, the state of the Empire on a blade's edge. He lived in the port city of Neapolis, close to the naval command port of Misenum. Naval generals acted upon the emperor's word, but Servius had his eye on becoming a prefect over the navy. While he revered his senatorial standing and the tidings that came with it, he wanted his own command. Under the emperor, of course. With the prestige of his position came too, the threat on life and property.

Servius was no fool. He knew the men under rank from him watched with keen eyes, waiting for his misstep. His house was grand, his wife beautiful and loyal, his slaves submissive and pliant. Of course he had his *stipatores*, his slave-bodyguards, but with his increased wealth, he sought more protection.

The ludus of Varus was the best gladiatorial school, in reputation and in honour, and so, he stood watching. Gladiators in training squared off, practising technique and showing skills. They wore only loincloths and leather guards upon wrists. Their bodies gleamed with sweat and battle scars. The constant strikes of wooden practice swords on shields echoed around the courtyard. There were many good fighters amongst them, but Servius only had his eye on one.

Quintus Furius Varus stood alongside the doctor, giving direction and orders the gladiators wouldn't dare defy. He looked a brute, tall and physically strong. His tunic barely concealed his muscled arms and thighs. He had short curls of black hair that shined with the blue of his eyes. His gaze was sharp; his mind even more so. He would have made a great soldier, Servius mused, quickly rising through rank to general if he was not bound to his father's ludus.

After the quake that killed his parents, Quintus was raised by the house doctor, the man who stood beside him now, the teacher of gladiator slaves. Unusual as it was, that he be raised by his own slaves, fate had nonetheless been kind. The villa, once grand, had been rebuilt, and Servius would commend Quintus for his success in the face of such adversity. Now the dominus of his house, his ludus, he had not only maintained his father's reputation, he exceeded it.

Servius watched as Quintus barked orders at the biggest fighter in the yard. The doctor held his whip at the ready, but Quintus picked up a practice sword and took his place against the gladiator. He instructed as he deflected wayward strikes, and the gladiator did not hold back. He was a mountain of a man, though not bigger than Quintus, and he was no match. The other gladiators all stopped to look on as the biggest man amongst them struck against their master, his temper flaring with each mistake. Quintus was agile, with more speed and wit than his student. He countered a forward strike with a knee into his off-balanced opponent and sent him sprawling to the sand. Quintus held the wooden sword to the man's throat. "Your temper will see your blood spilled. Keep your focus or lose your head," Quintus said.

The other men laughed and applauded, and Quintus withdrew his sword only to offer the prone man his hand. He pulled him to his feet, the doctor ordered the men to keep fighting, and Quintus raised his eyes to the senator. Servius smiled from the balcony, and Quintus replied with only a small nod of gratitude.

Yes. The senator had chosen his man.

"SENATOR," Quintus said, joining him in the grand hall of the ludus' villa. Quintus knew the senator was used to more luxurious surrounds, but Quintus was proud of his house. He had, after all, helped rebuild it with his own two hands. "I trust you are pleased with the men. They show great discipline, strength, and skill."

"You've taught them well," Servius replied smoothly. "The legacy of your father lives on."

Quintus bowed his head. "Gratitude. Though I would like to think he would say I have more to learn."

Quintus' banter had the desired effect because the senator smiled. "We all should strive to best our fathers."

Quintus gave a nod. "And in doing so, honour them."

The senator smiled, then looked to his slaves that stood

behind him, waiting for such a moment that he might need them. "Please leave us," he instructed. The two women closest to him gave him their absence without looking up, and one male slave met his master's eye, as if asking a silent question. Servius gave him a nod. The slave glanced, for the briefest moment to Quintus, then disappeared out the door.

The two men were alone. "Senator?" Quintus asked. It was rare that a senator would seek absence from his slaves. Most men regarded their slaves with as much concern as they would a piece of furniture and had no qualm in speaking their mind in their company. The fact the senator asked for privacy made Quintus uneasy. "Is there a matter of concern?"

"Yes," the senator replied. The older man observed Quintus for a quiet moment. He bore the blue eyes of his mother yet had short dark hair and skin browned from too many hours spent in the sun training his slaves, much like his father. He smiled kindly. "You are your father's son."

"You knew him?"

"Yes." The senator waved his hand toward the court-yard beyond the door. "When he started this ludus, when you were just a boy."

"I remember such days with fondness."

The senator's eyes narrowed. "Less troubling times. Which is what brings me here."

"If you wish to purchase any of my men, you only need say. Tell me which you favour, and I will make it so."

"The biggest of your lot."

"Appius," Quintus replied. "Very good selection. Strong and able in the arena. The crowds favour him."

The senator smiled, belying the pointed edge in his eyes. "Yet he was no match for you."

Quintus bowed his head slightly before holding the

senator's gaze once more. "No slave would dare beat their master. None even more so with Oscilius standing near, whip in hand."

"You outmatched him in every way," Servius stated.

When the senator didn't continue, Quintus said, "Then perhaps another. I can most certainly recommend any man who trains here."

Servius raised one eyebrow. "And if I do not want one who trains here?"

"Apologies, Senator, but I do not follow your meaning. If you do not seek any man trained here, then whom do you seek?"

"You."

Quintus stared at him for a time longer than was considered appropriate with a senator. "You seek me?"

"I seek my own guard," Servius explained. "I have reason to fear troubled times ahead, and I wish to take on personal security."

"Do you not have stipatores?" Quintus pressed. "Slave-bodyguards?"

"Yes." The senator studied Quintus for a long moment, as if trying to decide whether to place trust in him. "I am seeking someone from outside the house."

Quintus was taken aback. "If you have no trust in your own house, then what do you have? No offence intended, Senator, but you speak of a greater issue."

"I speak of concern yet to come to pass. I trust my slaves. I treat them well and expect as much in return, and they have been with me for many a year. Yet, if I take on a personal guard, I need reassurance that he holds no favours amongst my slaves. That he be known to none of them, that he be a man I can trust." The senator looked around the great hall. "I have known your father. He was a man of moral fibre and sound business sense. You are cut of the same cloth. You are of sharp mind and have the skill to back it."

"I..." Quintus stopped and took a breath to keep anger from the words that would follow. He kept his eyes cast down, his voice much the same. "You ask me to do the work of a slave?"

"I will pay you handsomely."

Quintus shot the senator a disbelieving look. "Senator, I cannot leave my ludus. I—"

"If you seek written authority from the emperor, I shall get it," the senator said simply. Quintus froze and Servius smiled, much the way a hunter would smile when he came upon a trapped rabbit. "Would you dare defy an order from Rome?"

"No, never." Quintus bristled and struggled to tamp it down. "You are removing my choice."

"But I am not," Servius said coolly. "You either agree and are rewarded with good coin. Your ludus will profit and you stay in good standing with Rome. Enough for a year's taxes." He tilted his head, just so. "Or you refuse, and I serve you with an order in which you will do as I bid, for no coin. You would be taken against your will, your men would no doubt retaliate and would, therefore, all be executed for rising against the word of Rome. So, my dear Quintus, as you can see, you *do* have a choice."

Anger flared in Quintus' blood; his muscles trembled with the need to expel energy. Like crushing the senator's skull with his bare hands. "That is no choice."

The corner of Servius' mouth curled upward. "I agree. Not one a man of sound mind needs to consider. I am so glad you see reason."

Quintus' jaw ticked. His hands were fists in his lap. The

senator was forcing his hand, and Quintus could think of no rebuttal. There was no way for this to end in his favour, not without losing more than his own blood.

"State your terms," Quintus said through clenched teeth.

"As I said, a year's taxes. And tell no one the purpose of your service. I would rather have the element of surprise on my side if someone thinks of attack."

"For what length of time?"

"Until I determine no threat remains."

"That is not determinable."

"If you wish to come back to your ludus, then you best be good at your job."

Quintus' nostrils flared, and he didn't care if the senator disapproved. "If I do this, I remain my own man. I am not owned by you. I shall not pledge the oath of a slave to you. I will give you two full moons, then I shall return to my ludus, as free as the day I leave it."

"And if the threat still remains?"

"Then you best be good at making friends over enemies," Quintus dared reply.

The senator's sneer almost became a smile. "I will give you one day to put your house in order. Then you shall be expected, as a guest, in my house. You will be granted your own sleeping quarters and slaves. No need to bring your own." He sniffed. "I shall leave half payment now, the remainder to be paid upon receipt of threat against me extinguished." Servius took a purse from the folds of his toga and threw it on the table, its contents spilling.

Quintus eyed the gold coins that slid from the pouch and exhaled with defeat. It would be enough money to acquire meat and grain for his house for a year. He didn't want to accept this path the gods had chosen for him, but what choice did he have? The senator was right on one thing: this was no choice at all. "Know this, Senator. I do not do this for you. I do this for Rome."

The senator eyed him earnestly, his voice amused and musical. "Are we not one and the same?"

Quintus made no attempt at reply, though his *no* rang loud in the silence.

The senator rose to his feet with a flourish, smiling now the deal was done. "Do not be late, Quintus. I do not tolerate being made to wait."

Quintus did not see him out. He refused to even stand. Not long thereafter, Oscilius found Quintus still seated in the great hall, surrounded by silence and fading sunlight. "Dominus," Oscilius said quietly. "The senator left without purchase?"

"If only that were true," Quintus answered.

A look of confusion crossed Oscilius' face. He looked from the coins still spilled across the table, then back to Quintus. "If not gladiators bound for arenas, then what?"

Quintus took a deep breath and lifted his chin. "The one thing I never thought bore price." He looked to the man, the slave that raised him. "He bought me."

SENATOR SERVIUS ATRIUS AUGENDUS' house was stately. High stone walls wrapped around its borders, and Quintus had to wonder if this defence strategy was to keep people out. Or to keep them in. The house itself was a sprawling villa, larger than Quintus' by half again and made of marble, whereas Quintus' villa was made of stone.

He dismounted his horse and knocked on the hulking wooden door and was met by a guard. The guard wore leather *pelmets* over a white tunic, armed with a sword and dagger, though his weapons were of little significance. Quintus stood a foot taller, broader, and when he barked out, "Quintus Furius Varus to see the senator," the guard took one step back in fear, then scurried toward the house.

Patterned tiles covered the entry floor, running seamlessly through to the impluvium and atrium in the centre of the house, built for the purpose to catch both sunlight and rain. Male slaves wearing tunics and female slaves wearing transparent silks flitted with purpose about the hallways, holding trays or pitchers. Some wore a tin band around their wrist or neck, more decorative than actual collar. Some wore jewellery; some did not.

Quintus took note, though. The slaves were smiling, as if their purpose to serve the senator gave them joy. He had said he treated them well, and Quintus could not deny it. The sound of shoes on tiles and the swish of fabric and quiet chatter could be heard before the senator appeared through a doorway. He wore a less formal tunic this day, no overcloak. His curled, grey hair looked neatly washed, his face bright, smile wide.

He opened his hands. "Quintus Furius Varus, welcome," he said, as if he had extended invitation instead of threat.

Though his eyes darted to the guard who had fetched him, and Quintus was quick to play along. *No one could know.* "Gratitude, Senator."

"Come, come," he said, ushering Quintus inside. The guard ran back to his post at the gate. "Tend to his horse and bring in any belongings," Servius said to one of the male slaves, and the man left with no more than a nod.

Servius led Quintus through the atrium to a grand stairway, along a hall to a private office. The room was empty of house slaves, and none followed them. A large oak desk took pride of place, positioned, Quintus assumed, to best use the sun, in front of large windows, the shutters opened wide.

The house overlooked the Bay of Neapolis. Blue water shone under the sun, boats and ships were tethered, and naval men scuttled about like hundreds of sand crabs on docks and decks. He could cast his eye across the bay toward his home of Oplontis, to the great mountain that posed as backdrop, and out to the unending ocean. It was an impressive vista, Quintus could not argue.

"Such a view would inspire poets and artists alike," Quintus allowed.

Servius glanced out, as if seeing it for the first time. "Quite. One gets complacent with it," he said, then sat at his desk, his back to the window, to the view. His focus was on stacks of papyri of both words and numbers, ledgers perhaps; important letters, Quintus deduced. A stylus lay askew from the inkwell as if thrown in haste, and Servius picked it up, dabbed it neatly in the black ink, proceeded to sign his name at the bottom of the top two pages, then sat the stylus upright in its stand.

He only then seemed to breathe and relax, sitting back in his padded chair. Quintus had remained standing, and only when the senator waved to the chair opposite his own did Quintus sit.

A female slave came in, wearing transparent silks and beaded jewellery, her dark hair in luxurious waves to her pert nipples. She slid a tray with a pitcher and cups onto the edge of the desk. "Thank you, Matalia," the senator said. The woman bowed her head and backed out of the room. "You must need refreshment," he furthered to Quintus. "After your travels."

The subterfuge confused Quintus. He was being treated as a long-lost friend, not as a man in the senator's employ. "Are we afforded privacy to speak on matters at hand?"

Servius held his gaze, unblinking. "Of course."

"I am here for a service."

"You are."

"Yet am treated as an invited guest."

Servius waved his hand, as if to shoo away the bad blood between them. "That was but politics, Quintus. There was no harm intended."

"There was harm in idle threat."

The senator's eyes hardened. "The politics of men do not keep company with alliances. If your father had lived to educate you in such affairs, he would have told you that matters of business and personal matters do not mix."

Quintus ignored the mention, the jab to his chest, of his father. "This is business?"

"Strictly." Then his face softened. "I trust your house is well prepared without you?"

"As can be expected," Quintus replied. "Oscilius is a good man. Capable, and the men respect him."

Servius appraised him a moment. "You told him what of your departure?"

"That I had extended business of confidence and would send word when able."

Servius studied the papers in front of him, frowning. "You trust him."

"With my life. With my house, my ludus."

"He is your slave."

"He raised me in my father's absence."

"Hmm," the senator hummed. "Not an easy life, one would imagine."

"I fared well. Well enough to be here as your guest in service." Quintus couldn't help but prod a little. He assumed it would push Servius to talk of his purpose here. He wasn't wrong.

"Evidence is apparent." Servius stood and poured two cups of water, handing one to Quintus. "We should discuss your service. You are familiar with security, personal and property."

It was not a question. "I am. I will start with the perimeter guards. The man at the gate was inadequate. Not through fault of his own. He has never been taught. If you want me to work with the men you already have, I will train them. That is my area of expertise. If anyone dares to gain access, they will not get far."

"And when I travel outside of the gates, you will accompany me. Even if you can train them well, you will still shadow me."

"Has a threat already been made upon you?"

"Indirectly. The way whispers threaten. When you can feel eyes upon you and your skin prickles with unease." The senator glanced at the door, to the window behind him, or more to the naval base. "The fleet is expanding, and news of it does not please all who hear it."

"Political rivals?"

His eyes shot to Quintus'. "Those with political agendas fuelled by jealousy of all I have accomplished. All that I have. And my connections in Roma. I worked hard for this pedestal upon which I stand, but a pedestal from which they believe I can fall."

"When is your next planned trip to Roma?"

"At month's end. Ten days from now."

"Ten days?"

"A date I cannot influence. It will have to be enough."

Quintus sighed. "Then I shall start today. First, I meet the men I will train. And Senator?"

Servius paused in waiting, though he didn't speak.

"If you have asked me here for my skills, I trust my method of training will not be questioned." Quintus let his demand hang between them. "If you expect men the calibre of gladiators to defend your house, there will be those who may not be of worthy stock."

Servius thought about this for a moment. "The men I have here might not meet this standard. I will let you decide. Though it may be of interest to you, I am expecting a shipment of slaves in two days. There may be some fighting stock amongst them."

"From where do they hail?"

"Iberia. Possibly some from Gaul."

"Hmm." Quintus didn't hide his disapproval. "Unlikely. I will study the perimeter today, become versed in entries and flaws. I will need to see all quarters, the layout complete. Then I will meet your current bodyguards and such, and see which I can sharpen to blade point. And see which of them will break."

Servius gave a solemn nod. "Let me show you to your private quarters first."

HIS ROOM WAS long and narrow, twice the size of his own back at the ludus. It held patterned tiled floors, plastered walls painted red and gold, a bed against the far wall underneath a high window. A small table graced one corner, a pitcher of water atop it. Folded bedding sat at the foot of the bed. The leather sack of belongings that had been strapped to his horse's saddle lay neatly on the mattress.

"I trust this will be adequate," Servius said.

"More than," Quintus replied. The truth was, it was more comfort than he had ever allowed himself. In his house, he would never afford himself such luxuries while his men slept on thin mattresses of straw.

He wasn't sure how he felt about it now. Sleeping in such quarters while his men slept in rough housing still. Though he wasn't afforded time to dwell on it. The senator quickly moved him on. Quintus was shown the *culina*, where slaves stood cooking over stoves and loaves of baked bread sat on counters of mason. The *latrinus* and bathhouse, the slave quarters, the other bedrooms, dining rooms, the senator's private bedroom.

At the outside gardens, Servius called a slave over. A young man by the name of Helier. He was perhaps twenty, had dark hair and eyes, pale skin, wore a loincloth and sandals, kept his head bowed but a pleased expression on his face. "Yes, Dominus," he said, the perfect submissive.

"Please show Quintus the gardens and animal stalls and what have you..." Servius waved his hand dismissively as though the mere idea of animal stalls was offensive. Or the stench, at least. "Show him all he asks to see, and answer any questions."

Helier bowed his head again. Servius left, leaving Quintus with his slave. Quintus stood a head taller and double the breadth of Helier. Quintus wondered what Helier's role was in the villa, for he had not the build of a man who was accustomed to menial labour.

Helier, head still bowed, extended his arm toward the far end of the garden. "This way."

The boundary walls were of stone, tall and plastered a ruddy white. The villa was encased by walls, and like most Roman houses, there were no outside windows that Quintus could see. No way for marauders to gain access. Not from outside the villa walls, at least.

There were trees that bore apples, plums, and pears, stalls for pigs and horses. His horse stood amongst them, his saddle astride a short wall. There were rows of vegetables and men that tended them. It was a very large parcel of land, securely fenced and maintained. Quintus stood for a moment and took note. "The senator supplies his own foods," he said, aimed at Helier but not a question.

Helier nodded. "He will make purchase at markets if

need be, for fish and crab, but prefers not to be reliant on others."

"I would not have thought him short on coin."

Helier met Quintus' eyes before quickly lowering them again. "The purpose is not for less coin. Dominus does not trust food from merchants."

Quintus considered this. Did the senator truly believe there was threat of poisoned food from a market? Was there legitimate chance of conspiracy? Was the senator's cause for concern true, or was he imagining it?

Quintus knew only time would tell.

"The senator treats you well," Quintus said, plucking a damson plum from a tree. "His house slaves appear in high spirits."

Helier bowed his head and replied quickly. "Yes. He is a kind dominus." Then Helier looked up and Quintus could see honesty in his eyes. "I am proud to serve the senator. A slave, yes, but we are elevated from most."

"Agreed. You are treated better than most slaves I have seen." It was true. They had bedding, food, and hot baths; more than most free citizens. It was quite an honour, indeed. Quintus bit into the plum, and for a brief moment, he was lost to its sweet flesh. "Your duties here, what do they include?"

The question clearly made Helier uneasy. "I serve the senator."

"Ah. A body slave in his chambers?"

Colour tinted Helier's cheeks. "Not in that regard. The senator favours women."

"And his wife?" Quintus pressed. "Does she take bed slaves?"

Helier glanced at the house nervously, then spoke to his feet. "If you will, I can refer your question to Dominus. He bade me to answer you, but perhaps not in such a personal nature."

Quintus chuckled and clapped Helier on the shoulder, the gesture surprising Helier. Despite the difference in stature—a free man to a slave—Quintus liked him. "You are loyal to the senator, and you do well to honour his wife. I care not who is invited to her private chambers, only that they are invited."

This seemed to please Helier. He nodded, but Quintus saw the hint of a smile. "She has her favourites, approved by the senator." Then Helier looked up, meeting his gaze. "You are a guest here for some time?"

"Yes."

"Then you shall witness with your own eyes. They do not hide it."

Quintus smiled. "Very well."

Then Helier said, "My duties are to see my dominus has all he needs. I run errands and do his bidding. I accompany him most everywhere. If he calls for someone, it is usually me." Helier said this with great pride, and it made Quintus happy.

They continued to walk the perimeter, and Quintus took note of the gate in the back corner for the slaves to enter to and from. They walked in otherwise companionable silence, Helier a fraction of a step behind with subservience. After the inspection was done, Helier stood before him with his head bowed. "If that is all," he said, seeking absence.

"One more thing," Quintus said. "Which of the senator's men are his personal guards?"

Helier kept his head down so Quintus could not see his eyes, but his brief pause did not go unnoticed. "His bodyguards... The gateman. You have met him. And you will find two men aside his office door."

The gateman had trembled like a child: there was no man at the entrance door to the villa, no man at the gate behind the property. Quintus was certain he could stop the two men at the office door with little more than a look. Perhaps the senator was overreaching with his threat of conspiracies, but his security was lacking regardless.

THE NEXT MORNING, Quintus met all the house slaves and those who tended to the land. They stood in the outside courtyard, were quite large in number, and though some eyed him with strange curiosity when the senator made vague introductions, most cared little of his presence.

Once dismissed, Quintus called for the men to remain. They stood in an uneven line, and Quintus reminded himself that these men were not soldiers; they were not gladiators. They were common house slaves. Some bigger than others. Those who worked the gardens or tended animals were stronger than the likes of Helier. Even those who called themselves guards were not men of any stature.

It was little to work with.

Quintus stood before them, as if he were in his ludus and these were his men. "I ask you to remain for one purpose. There will be the matter of training. Regardless of your duties in this house, you will become well versed in security. Should the senator need defending, should this house come under threat, you are the front line. I expect not to make gladiators of you, but I do expect effort in the attempt."

The men became nervous, glancing at the house, as if in search of their master.

"The order comes direct from the senator and shall be treated as such," Quintus added. "I am but an extension of the senator's hand, of his will." He let his authority settle over them. "You will attend your duties until after the midday meal, when you shall meet behind the stable away from prying eyes. Bring with you any tool you use in duty which may be used as a weapon. One you have near at all times."

Quintus dismissed the slaves but held the three body-guards. "You three remain." They reformed into a line before him, nervous but chins raised. They wore leather pelmet skirts over tunics, sandals, and small breastplates, fit more for decoration than to quell injury. Quintus stood before them like a mountain, his hands clasped behind his back. "Your training starts now."

He led them to the patch of dirt behind the stable, and though their efforts were commendable, their skill was hopeless. He allowed them to use a *palus*, wooden poles, or sticks in lieu of actual weapons to stem needless injury. They practised moves in attack, thrusting, cutting, slicing, how to stand in readiness, and how to counter attack in defence. It was rudimentary, at best, and not without fault, but when Quintus called a halt to training, the three men were sweating, panting. Smiling.

There might be hope for them yet, Quintus thought.

The rest of the slaves were a different story. He would imagine Oscilius would call them a 'herd of sorry fucks, good for nothing but the spilling of tears and blood.' Quintus refrained from such words. Barely.

They were a test to his patience as both man and trainer.

They stood in disorganised lines of formation, holding the tools they considered weapons. Some were useless but well intended, much like the men who held them. But not all hope was lost.

One man who tended the gardens, lacking both youth and strength, brought with him a long-handled digging tool. Another man, who tended animals, brought with him a hammer. One man, who cut meat and fish, brought with him a sharpened cleaver. Helier brought with him a metal rod used for poking fire, and the *vilicus*, the slave supervisor who was but a slave himself, carried a whip.

And so Quintus drilled them with technique and practice. It would take time and much effort, and although at times he thought the task before him was too steep, at the end of the first day, he was pleased.

"How do you fare?" Servius asked him after their evening meal.

Quintus gave a small smile and nod. "If a slave represents their master and his house, then you are well respected."

This pleased Servius, as Quintus knew it would. The senator beamed. "I treat them well."

"Evidence is apparent."

It was then the senator's wife bid him goodnight, with her two closest body slaves close on her heel. Her sultry smile over her shoulder left no mystery as to her intention, and Helier's words came back to him. *They do not hide who they bed.* So, the *domina* took women to her bed, Quintus realised.

Servius sipped his wine and watched Quintus for his reaction. "Do any of my slaves catch your eye?" he asked. "You are welcome to choose, as a guest in my house. Though I would warn you off any of my wife's chosen women. We care to enjoy their loyalty in private, if you take my meaning."

Quintus gave a nod. The slaves whom the senator and his wife chose to bed were not on offer. "Understood."

Servius raised his eyebrows as if a sudden thought occurred. "You have not sought a wife in marriage?"

"No woman," Quintus replied. Then he added, "Nor man," to clarify his preference.

"Did you leave behind a lover?"

"No." Quintus shook his head. "The ludus and a lover would compete for time I have not to spare."

Servius gave a smile, resigned to lose the argument. "Then perhaps one of the slaves that arrive on the morrow will be more to your liking."

CAPITULUM III

THE DAY of training went as expected, with little ground gained. The bodyguards, or stipatores, continued admirably, if not comically. Quintus fought not to show disdain for their efforts, but his disappointment was apparent in the orders he barked.

He feigned attack and defence against them, armed only with a pole against their wooden swords, and he still defeated them without effort. They were covered in sweat and dirt, and Quintus appeared unperturbed.

As it stood, in that instance, if they were attacked by soldiers—or worse, gladiators—they would be dead before they could raise their weapons. Quintus pushed them harder, allowing sparks of his anger and frustration to fuel their efforts. He attacked them with more brute force, driving them to defend on instinct, making proper guards of them yet.

His lesson with the house slaves went as expected. He weeded out those with skill and gave them more advanced tasks than the others. But not all skill was physical, Quintus knew. And so, he noted those who could read and write, those who could count, those who could converse with proper etiquette.

Probable attack against the senator could come from any angle, and Quintus needed to prepare the slaves accordingly. As they were done with training for the day, and as the slaves went about preparing for the evening meal, Helier fell into step beside Quintus. "You have a plan not yet disclosed," Helier said.

Quintus almost smiled at him. "The plan is disclosed to those who need know it."

Helier did not hide how this pleased him. He was attractive, Quintus admitted only to himself, in a way that a slave could be. And Quintus was free to act upon any inclination, if he so wished; the senator had given permission. But he withheld such need, now, as he always did. He was master of his own body, and there was strength in practised restraint, evident in how he ran his life, his ludus, his gladiators.

"The house is abuzz for this evening," Helier said as they walked inside.

"What is this evening?" Quintus asked.

Helier slowed his steps and spoke as if this was news Quintus should have known. "The new slaves arrive for viewing. There will be a feast and wine to honour their arrival."

"To honour them?"

"To honour the senator's wealth," Helier clarified. "New arrivals are to enter in full view so we are reminded of his power. The new arrivals are fed meat and wine so they know their compliance will be rewarded. The senator will read the placards around their necks and decide where to send them. The *vilicus* then replaces chain for collar. It is quite the affair."

Quintus took this news in without comment.

"Helier, how long have you been in the senator's house?"

He smiled serenely. "I was ten when I joined."

Helier was called away, and Quintus went to bathe and prepare for his evening. He was grateful for Helier's warning of the feast, because he was called to the dining hall early.

It was more formality than Quintus was accustomed to, and he was grateful, again, to Helier, for forewarning him. Quintus wore his heavy woollen toga, and Servius greeted him warmly. "Please, sit. Enjoy the spoils of my good fortune." He motioned to an empty chair at his right.

Quintus nodded respectfully to the senator's wife before taking his seat. He was offered wine and fruits from trays held by smiling women, which he took with a nod of thanks to the senator. Helier appeared with a tray adorned with slivers of spiced meat and flatbreads, and when it was Quintus' turn, Helier leaned a little close. "Gratitude for the warning to wear suitable dress," Quintus said.

Helier bowed his head without a word, though his smile was evident, and when Quintus looked back to the senator, Servius gave him an approving smirk. "Are you certain you do not favour him? From the display I just witnessed, I can assure you he would not oppose."

Quintus sipped his wine to give pause for embarrassment. He risked a glance at Helier, who had tinted cheeks and a demure pose, but Quintus turned his attention back to Servius. "He is loyal to you."

"And to you?" Servius pressed.

"Amicus."

"Ah," the senator crooned. "Let us see if any of the new acquisitions are of interest." Then he winked at Quintus. "I should hope they spark interest in some form for the denarii they cost."

Then, with some loud voices and a crack of a whip, the vilicus entered the room. "Dominus, Domina," he greeted his owners. "May I present to you your newest purchase."

Then, naked but for the chains around their necks, six slaves were walked into the room. Three men, three women, all in need of a bath, stood before them. They each had dark hair, long and unkempt, their heads slightly bowed. Their skin was tanned, and without closer inspection, Quintus could see no other visible marks. No scars, no brands or tattoos. The women had pert breasts and smooth, rounded hips. Quintus estimated none of them older than twenty years. The men, of similar age, looked strong and lean, able-bodied, and would make good workers.

They would make good soldiers.

Quintus was used to seeing naked men. His gladiators bathed, changed, stripped without judgement. Though seeing the three men now, with their cocks on display, stirred his own blood. He sipped his wine and studied them. If he had been at his ludus, he would have the men thrown into the training arena to see which would hold their ground. But this wasn't his ludus. These were not his men.

They each had twine around their neck and a small scroll of papyrus threaded upon it, and as all the house slaves came in to bear witness, the senator stood and made an audience of them. He started with the first girl, feeding her slivers of meat and fruit, sips of wine, all of which she took eagerly. It was apparent they had been without food and drink.

"You will be looked after here," Servius made a show of announcing. "Care for your dominus and domina, and the house shall care for you."

Then he lifted her hair, gently brushing it from her face and lifted her chin. She could be beautiful, Quintus mused. Servius took the papyrus from the twine around her neck and read the list aloud to the room. "She is called Petilia. Can sew and weave fabric."

Servius looked impressed and waved his hand around the audience of the room, and she was received well with whispered chattering and giggles. The senator's wife was particularly interested, and with a subtle lift of her finger, Servius smiled.

Bed slave.

Then he moved to the next woman and repeated the ritual. Fed her, gave her wine, inspected her face, read her inscription. Then repeated this again for the last woman. Then it was the first man.

He was of decent build but mild of manner. He had been a farmer in Iberia and would make a sound addition to the house. Then the next man. Slightly bigger than the first, also a farmer.

And then the third man. Also Iberian, he was smaller in stature and his skin was a rich warm brown, but his dark eyes held fire the first two men had lacked. He could be no older than twenty. His long, dark hair fell past his shoulders, and when Servius lifted the man's chin, he snarled.

Quintus was on his feet and beside Servius before anyone could blink. "If you seek the biggest threat in this room, slave, look no further than me," Quintus ground out. His bulking size, his deep voice commanded respect, and the slave met his eyes and did not look away.

Servius was clearly pleased with Quintus' immediate

defence and ripped the slave's papyrus inscription from around his neck. "He is called Kaeso. Shows some defiance, though is able with a sword. Can read."

Servius looked up to Quintus, then, still on display for his audience, said, "What shall we do with them?"

Quintus looked over the six of them, his eyes lingering on Kaeso. "Have them bathed to be rid of their stench." Kaeso held his gaze, daringly.

Servius, oblivious to the slave's defiance, smiled. "Agreed." And he simply waved them away. The vilicus held out his whip in indication of the direction in which they should go, and the six slaves were walked out of the room.

Quintus watched them leave, taking in the back and buttocks of Kaeso as he walked. He was offered more wine, but Quintus declined. "I shall stand guard while they are bathed and have their chains removed."

The senator lifted his wine in reply, as if caring neither here nor there. "As you see fit."

Quintus followed the slaves to the bathhouse. It was a singular room with a large tiled basin in the centre, the water fed by hot springs. Surprise coloured the slaves' faces as they stepped into it. "*Thermae*," one muttered. They each sank into the water, eyes closed, followed by quiet sighs of relief.

"Yes. The water is warm," the vilicus said harshly. "Your new master, Dominus, is senator to Rome. That you step foot in his house means the gods have shined upon you, and you will do well to remember it. You will find luxury here the likes of which you do not deserve." He glared at Kaeso. "But hear me this: one misstep, and you will find yourself in the mines."

The slaves had their chains removed. The men had

their long hair cut short; the women had theirs washed. They were sponged, oiled, and scraped with *strigils*, their tanned bodies glowing in the flicker of oil lamps, and when they were done, they were wiped down. As they stood in line once more, Quintus admired all their forms, naked and in their prime, but one even more so. Kaeso stood with chin raised and eyes narrowed, his pride defying his position. The shorter hair suited him, and it allowed Quintus to best see his finer features. And the rest of his form was not a hardship to look upon. His cock hung half hard; the warm water and bodily touches had aroused him. Quintus' own body reacted, desire licked at him, warming his pulse.

Kaeso turned to look at Quintus then, perhaps feeling eyes upon him. Quintus looked from Kaeso's cock to his face, and Kaeso's nostrils flared with a small pull of his lips, before he turned to look directly ahead once more.

Was that interest shown in return? Or was it daring?

Quintus ignored his own need, as he was accustomed to doing. He stepped in front of them and spoke, his voice as commanding as his height. "You will do as you are bid. The senator's word is final. In his absence, you will answer to the vilicus, for his is the word and will of your dominus." Quintus nodded pointedly to the man beside him with the whip. "You will now face the senator once more, where you will be donned with collar and duty. You will not cause a scene. Defy me, and it is not the mines I will send you to, but the afterlife."

The six slaves, heads bowed, understood. And so, they were led back to the feast and everyone gathered around once they had entered. From the colour of cheeks and volume of talk and laughter, there had clearly been more wine consumed, more food laid on the table.

Servius raised his arms, wine in one hand, and called for

silence. The slaves knelt before him, and as though a common house ritual, the vilicus told them, "When a collar is placed upon you, you will pledge yourself to Dominus. Your life is now his."

The room was silent and still, and the senator made a show of taking each collar, holding it aloft in two hands, then ceremoniously placing it around the neck of the slave and fastening it at the nape. Like the collars of all of the senator's slaves, these were of fine tin. More ornamental than the common iron band worn by field slaves, but the significance was the same.

The first slave, Petilia, bowed her head. "Dominus," she said.

Then the next two women, then the two men. When it was Kaeso's turn, he barely concealed his distaste, but when the collar was clasped, he raised his eyes to meet the gaze of Servius. "Dominus," he bit out.

Deepened silence fell over the room at this blatant show of disrespect. Servius stared at Kaeso, and Quintus took long strides to stand beside him. They both stared down at Kaeso, who still held his chin high, his eyes sharp and wild.

"What shall we do with this one?" Servius asked. "Quintus, what would you have done to this slave?"

Quintus stared into the eyes of Kaeso and was met with further fury and defiance. "Flay the skin off his back until his manner improves," Quintus replied simply.

The vilicus stepped forward, whip at the ready, but the senator raised a hand to stop him. "An example is to be made here," Servius said. He looked down at the slave, his voice gone cold. "The next insult from you will see your slave kin"—he pointed to the five slaves kneeling beside him —"tied to a post and flogged."

Servius took one step back. "Stand!" he demanded loudly.

Every slave flinched at the harsh tone, and the six new slaves were quick to their feet. Servius smiled serenely, as if he had not made the room uneasy, in a show that made Quintus realise the man was capable of being both kind and cruel. In his two days here, he had almost forgotten the senator's blatant threat that brought him here, but the sinister smile he wore in that moment was a swift reminder.

Servius ordered five of the slaves to sit on a floor mat near the fire. Kaeso was ordered to kneel, apart from the others. They were given bowls of fish, beans, and bread, yet Kaeso could only watch. From the manner in which the bowls were emptied, Quintus could only imagine they had gone some time without food.

Yet Kaeso knelt, his hands behind his back, eyes forward, unmoving. His hair was dry now, black and shining in the light of the fire and candles. His skin was golden brown, rich and warm. His jaw was strong, his nose fine, his cheeks high. Still naked, on full display, his cock hung gloriously, and Quintus couldn't deny the gods had favoured the man with design.

"Your earlier words that no one has yet caught your eye proves false," Servius said, startling Quintus. So lost in thought, he had not heard his approach.

"Apologies, Senator." Quintus bowed his head once. "Not false at the time the words were uttered."

Servius smiled. "It seems your eye is drawn to the defiant one." They both watched Kaeso a moment as he stayed knelt, stoic. "In curiosity? Or in desire?"

"Apologies," Quintus gave him a look of uncertainty. "Clarify your meaning." Quintus was almost certain he knew what Servius was alluding to, but he didn't want to give an answer that would implicate his intention.

"Do you wish to beat him for insubordination? Or do you wish to fuck him?"

Kaeso's gaze shot to them, having heard the words spoken. Clearly alcohol loosened Servius' tongue. Quintus didn't have time to answer, because the senator put a hand on his arm and led him toward the kneeling slave. Servius touched Kaeso's head, traced a line down the side of his face to his mouth, which he forced open. "Slave. If Quintus wants to fill your mouth or arse with his cock, you will allow it."

Quintus wasn't overly happy with the senator's turn in behaviour, and apparently neither was Kaeso. He pulled his head back and bared his teeth in distaste.

"Quintus," Servius said loudly. "If this was your slave and he raised temper to you, what would you do?"

Everyone watched them, listening for his reply. "I would send him to the afterlife, absent eyes and tongue," Quintus answered.

Kaeso's nostrils flared, but he lowered his gaze.

"Then it is settled," Servius announced. Quintus was sure the senator was about to order the slave be killed. But fate was not so kind. Because instead, he lifted his wine to Quintus, in a manner of celebration, and claimed for all to hear. "This slave is yours. For the duration of your stay, he will answer to you. Any disrespect he bestows is a reflection upon you, and any insults in this house are against my name."

"Senator," Quintus said, unable to keep alarm from his tone.

Servius moved to turn away, then stopped. "Oh, and Quintus," he said as if an afterthought. "If you wish to part the man of eyes and tongue, please advise me. We shall put on a show."

———

KAESO SWALLOWED BACK HIS ANGER. He breathed through his rage and kept his gaze fixed to the floor. Just weeks ago, he had been hunting on his father's land and he had paid no mind to whispers of how the Romans were moving in, taking everything in their path. It seemed so unbelievable to be true. His homeland of northern Iberia, of mountains and green valleys, was a world away from the brutal sands of Rome.

Just weeks ago he had been free.

But the Romans had come. They took his parents' land, then they took his parents' lives. Kaeso had tried to fight them. He had bested a few, but they were too great in number and he was overcome, beaten, and thrown into that ship. A pit of darkness and horror that caused a tremor to run through him even now, weeks later.

Now, he knelt on the cold floor with two collars around his neck. Owned by two men, for twice the shame, he was a slave. His life no longer his own. If his fate had rested in the senator's hands alone, Kaeso would favour his odds at escape. But the giant man with striking features and cutting eyes sealed Kaeso's fate.

He was now a slave.

Once he had been a free man, to do as he pleased. Then, all because the Romans thought it their right to take all they desired, Kaeso's life now held no value.

Worthless.

"Move closer to the fire," the man called Quintus said to

him. Then he motioned to one of the house slaves. "And get this man something to eat and drink."

Kaeso dared to look up at him. Quintus wore a serious expression as he stared right back at him. "Do not mistake my kindness for weakness."

But then Kaeso was offered meat and bread, and he was so hungry, all he could do was nod.

CAPITULUM IV

MORNING CAME EARLY FOR QUINTUS. He had
barely rested at all. Caution for the senator's gift robbed him
of sleep, yet he was still first to the training arena. He had
lain awake, troubled, giving thought to reasons behind
Servius' purpose. After Quintus' surprise and anger, he saw
the senator's act for what it was. Handing Kaeso to Quintus
would ensure compliance. The slave was prone to defiance,
and if he did so now, responsibility for it would land on
Quintus' shoulders.

Servius was ensuring the slave's submission.

Quintus would make it so.

Surprising him even more was Kaeso, the first to arrive
for training. Still with defiance in his eyes, pride in his
raised chin. But regardless, there he stood. He wore a loincloth and leather sandals, and a leather band now entwined
with the senator's tin collar around his neck.

The leather band that now bound him to Quintus.

For his time under the senator's roof, under his bidding,
at least.

The other men filed in line, turning to face Quintus

with the rising sun at their backs. The new slaves, the Iberian men, had some training, or perhaps they had learned quickly after being enslaved. Either way, evidence was clear within the first few orders given. They held good line, responded to orders as a soldier should, and were familiar with handling weapons, even sticks instead of swords.

Quintus ceased all training, allowing them to catch their breath and perhaps learn more of the men and where their strengths lay. The two taller Iberians, Gallio and Oppius, were once farmers with strength and endurance, Quintus confirmed. Kaeso, it appeared, had better training.

"And you," Quintus said. "From which lands do you hail?"

Kaeso, breathing hard from his training, stood tall. He stared direct ahead as he spoke, "From the valleys of Asturias."

"You are trained in weapons, more so than your slave kin," Quintus stated.

Kaeso clenched his jaw. "I hunted on my father's land."

A hunter. Quintus was not surprised to hear this. "Evidence is apparent. You fight well and are disciplined in skill and movement." Kaeso remained still, save only a brief glance to Quintus as if not expecting praise or accolade, a reaction Quintus did not miss. Then he spoke to all six men. "A good swordsman knows when to strike. A great swordsman knows when *not* to strike. Reading an opponent's intent will gain you the upper hand."

He had the men pair off to practise, and as the sun reached its peak in the sky, the men were sweating and showed signs of fatigue. "Halt," Quintus ordered. "Enough training. Drink water." He motioned to the barrel of water and wooden cups in the shade beside him. The six men did as told, the three guardsmen worse off than the three new slaves, falling to the grass with barely withheld groans. Quintus laughed. "You will be hardened yet. These three men," he motioned toward Kaeso, Gallio, and Oppius, "have barely broken sweat. The senator's gentle hand has weakened you, but fear not. It is an issue I have been set to rectify."

None of the men raised questions and they knew well enough not to complain, though Kaeso spared him a curious glance. Quintus didn't press for answers, and he did not make issue of the slave's eye contact or unasked question. If one of the training gladiators in his ludus had given him such a look, he would learn a harsh lesson from Oscilius' whip. Instead, Quintus ordered the men to the slaves' quarters to eat and rest.

Later that afternoon while the other house slaves came to the yard for their training, the guardsmen had gone to their posts for duty. Gallio, Oppius, and Kaeso had joined the lines of other slaves for more practice, where the other bedraggled slaves held their household weapons and awaited instruction.

Quintus reminded them, "To ward off attack on this house, you are the first line of defence. You will use whatever weapon is at hand to protect and defend against any intruder whose intent is to bring harm. I need not remind you, if you intend on using weapon or skill against this house—" He gave pause with his gaze upon Kaeso. "—I will have you scourged and, while you yet cling to this life, fed to wild pigs."

Kaeso kept his eyes ahead, though his nostrils flared a little. His defiance would see a purpose of two ends. It would either see him be the best guard of the house, or it would see him killed.

Quintus couldn't help but bargain a mental wager on the latter.

After the men had run through drills of strike and defence and performed as well as they had before—Quintus allowed, though it was by no means to a military standard—he took a *rudis*, a wooden practice sword, and called a cease to their training and stood before them. "To enhance practice." He turned to Helier in the front row, holding his metal fire prod. "Come forward."

Helier's eyes widened, his face paled, but he did as ordered.

Quintus braced his stance, held his rudis in defence, and said, "Come at me as you would an intruder."

Helier did not move.

Quintus stared at him. "If you wish to live, should you come under attack, you will need to practise. Now, hold your weapon and come at me."

Helier lifted the metal rod above his head and lunged at Quintus as if to strike him down. Quintus countered easily, holding his rudis to meet the iron rod and, deflecting, he thrust downward. Helier dropped the metal rod and he stepped back, a look of horror on his face, before bowing. "Apologies. Apologies."

Quintus surprised everyone by laughing, a loud hearty sound. He clapped Helier on the shoulder. "No apologies. You did as I instructed. Now, pick up your weapon and try again."

And so they did, and then the remaining men against each other, until their slave duties called. Gallio, Oppius, and Kaeso all remained, and instead of letting them rest, he furthered their training. They lifted heavy wooden rails onto their shoulders or pushed large wheels that ground grain. It was hard work, but Quintus knew such exercise built strength and grit.

As the sun got lower when their day was done, the senator met Quintus near the yard. He watched the three slave men drink water and take rest in the shade. "What yet comes of my newest purchase?" Servius asked.

"They hold well," Quintus allowed. "They come with some skills already learned, which I assume you already knew."

Servius almost smiled, giving himself away. Of course he knew the slaves he had bought had some training. If the painting of the senator's purpose was uncertain, Quintus could see it was now fully formed.

"Because why pay heavy purse for trained gladiators when you can pay a few denarii and have me train them," Quintus answered aloud.

Now Servius gave in to his grin. He aimed it at Quintus, followed by a hand on his shoulder. "You begin to under-stand politics."

"I understand it all too well."

Servius hummed, then his gaze fell upon Kaeso. "And of your man? The defiant one. Is he worth his trouble?"

Quintus looked at Kaeso and spoke, knowing he could hear. "He is the best amongst them. His boldness may be of favour yet."

The senator cocked his eyebrow at Quintus. "You would offer praise within ear?"

"I give praise to whomever deserves it." Quintus looked at the three men, Oppius, Gallio, and Kaeso, before turning back to Servius. "And if they are to act as guards, they should dress as such. Shall we talk about uniform and armour?"

Servius turned and motioned for Quintus to join him

on his walk back to the house. "Do you believe it wise to do so soon?"

"If you seek guards to attend you in Roma in eight days, then they should look the part. If you arrive with six men uncomfortable with armour and sword, they will appear weak, easy to defeat, and you will look a fool."

Servius stopped walking, and Quintus considered apologising for his choice of words but held his tongue. It was the truth, and it warranted being said. Quintus continued, "And if someone, as you so believe, wishes harm upon you, is it not best to be prepared?"

It was reason the senator couldn't argue with. "I can see your point is valid." Then he scowled at Quintus. "Though your delivery was careless."

Quintus bit the inside of his lip to withhold his smile. "And swords. Two small daggers each should suffice."

Servius' reaction was cool but alarmed. "You would have them act as stipatores? Or *sicarii*?"

"Any armed guard can be a stipator, as the name would have it," Quintus said. "The sicarii are trained with daggers, with purpose."

"With the purpose of an assassin," the senator hissed.

"With equal purpose to defend you from such. Is this not what you requested upon my employ?"

Servius released a sigh. It was, and both men knew it. "It sounds far reaching when it is brought to light," he said.

"Do you still believe a threat is made upon your life?" Quintus pressed.

"I do."

"Then my training these men to be as skilled as sicarii, to be *your* sicarii, is not without purpose."

The senator gave a grim nod. "Yes. I shall make enquiry for your requests. See me tomorrow." He left then, and when he was but a few steps away, a line of slaves filed in behind him, Helier at the lead.

But one slave remained, standing a cautious distance. Kaeso stood, not as a submissive but more as a waiting acquaintance. "Kaeso," Quintus addressed him.

He nodded as though it caused him physical pain. He was without injury, he was simply unaccustomed to having superiors. Quintus admired the man's form, all muscles and strength contained by golden skin, dark hair, dark eyes, full lips. They stood inside the house where the dining room met the garden courtyard, where other slaves busied themselves with duties toward preparing the evening meal and cleaning.

Kaeso remained silent though that curiosity was back in his eyes, and Quintus found himself smiling. "You would raise question?" When Kaeso still did not speak, Quintus furthered by saying, "You have the eyes of a rabbit. Big and brown, seeing everything, on keen alert for danger. That might serve you well in your old life, but here it leaves you vulnerable. I can read your intent." Quintus stepped in close, their faces almost touching. Quintus was much taller than Kaeso, but the slave simply raised his chin. There it was, that defiance. It was fire and anger, barely contained. "You struggle with your new-found position," Quintus mused. "You are not accustomed to being a slave."

It seemed to remind Kaeso of his place. He looked down, his brow furrowed. "No. I am not."

"I would ask the gods to deliver a swift lesson," Quintus said, almost smiling. "If you wish to stay of this world."

Something flashed across Kaeso's face, but before Quintus could lay name to it, it was gone. Kaeso spoke more mildly. "If it is a lesson the gods deliver, then I ask for the grace to learn it."

Quintus liked this response and waved his hand in the direction he wished to walk. "Come. I need to clean up before the evening meal." Kaeso followed him dutifully but stopped at the door when he realised Quintus had entered the bathhouse. Quintus noticed his unease and met him with a smile. "Fear not. I will not ask for something not willing to be given. I need to clean, and I would caution you to do the same if you intend to sit with me at the table tonight."

Kaeso's gaze flicked up to Quintus. "I would sit with you?"

Quintus untied his *caliga* and slipped his foot from the boot. "You are my slave, are you not?"

"I wear the leather band to prove it," Kaeso replied. "Atop the metal band of the senator." He gave pause, his eyes full of uncertainty. "Is it customary for Roman slaves to have two masters?"

Quintus smiled as he pulled off his second boot. "No, it is not."

Kaeso took tentative steps to sit next to Quintus. Not close enough to touch, though. An arm's length; a cautious distance. He untied one of his sandals.

"You are under my name here as guarantee for compliance," Quintus said. He stood and undid his belt.

"He said for as long as your duration," Kaeso pressed warily. "What was his meaning?"

Quintus pulled off his tunic then. As he undid his *subligaculum,* he answered. "I am here to train his men. I am the dominus of my house, a ludus. A school for gladiators. I take ordinary men and make them gladiators." He pulled away the cloth of his subligaculum and tossed it upon his discarded tunic, and he stood there in front of Kaeso, completely naked.

Nakedness amongst and in front of slaves wasn't a strange thing, though this felt more personal to Quintus than perhaps it should. Kaeso took in his form, his gaze raking down his body, taking pause at his cock before he looked away. A blush coloured his cheeks, another reaction that did not go unnoticed by Quintus.

"Does something you look upon appeal to you?" Quintus asked with a grin as he stepped into the hot bath.

"You have the body of a gladiator," Kaeso replied, not strictly answering Quintus' question. Not looking at him either. "Your tunic hid the true result of your training."

Quintus laughed as he sank into the water, which became a sigh as the heated pool engulfed him. "Many years training. The ludus is in my blood."

A naked Kaeso slipped into the pool, again at safe distance from Quintus. He was quiet a moment, and Quintus watched him until he spoke. "Slaves here are allowed warm baths and food to eat. It comes as a kind surprise."

Quintus gave a nod. "The senator treats his slaves well. As do I. The well-being of a slave is a reflection upon the owner."

"You treat your gladiators well?"

"As I would a guest in my house. Meat and grains to eat; they even sleep on beds. I treat them well, they return the favour." Then Quintus smiled. "I have not the luxury of hot springs though. Our water needs heating."

Kaeso's lips twitched, and he was quiet a while. Though his questioning eyes told Quintus more words would come. "There are many masters who would rather see slaves starve than feed them." Kaeso frowned, as if his statement came from firsthand knowledge.

Quintus took a deep breath. "A master who starves his

slaves forces them to steal, and for that the owner should face penalty alongside their slave. To make slaves beg so they barely cling to this world is not acceptable. Some beat slaves for no more reason than sport. Such men should not have the privilege of keeping swine, much less a human slave." Quintus washed his chest and arms. "Though have it be known, I give respect and expect the same in return. If a slave should disrespect or defy me, I would part his head from his neck."

Kaeso was silent, though his eyes spoke words his tongue could not. Quintus smiled. "If you have question, rabbit, ask it."

Kaeso's gaze shot to Quintus. "Rabbit?"

Quintus chuckled. "Your eyes remind me of such a thing."

Kaeso's jaw ticked, his dislike apparent. "A rabbit is easily snared."

"So quick to take insult," Quintus mused, shaking his head. "Rabbits are quick and cunning. They outwit both fox and hunter, do they not?"

Kaeso's brow narrowed with thought. "I had not given mind to such a view before."

"Your question. Put tongue to it now, or let it remain unasked," Quintus said, washing water over his arms.

"You train as a gladiator. Have you stood in an arena as one?"

Quintus found himself smiling. "Do you ask to determine odds against me in battle?"

Kaeso quickly dropped his gaze. "Of course not."

Quintus looked at him, how his shortened hair glistened black, how the leather strand around his neck—the very leather collar that bound them as slave and master—lay against his skin. How his dark eyes told stories, and how his lips parted just so.

Quintus could not deny his attraction to him. Though he would not allow himself to act on impulse. He was schooled in discipline; he had spent his life embracing it. He wouldn't allow himself to be spoiled with the comforts of another man now.

"I have never stood on the sands of an arena to fight," Quintus admitted. "Though I have bested many a man who has."

Kaeso looked upon Quintus then, a smile pulling at his lips. "You gave praise to us when speaking to Dominus," he said. There was almost a shyness to him now, but curiosity also.

"Yes. And so deserving." Quintus stood and took a swathe of linen to dry himself. "But heed caution, rabbit. Praise should not keep company with complacency."

"Yes, Dominus."

Quintus gave pause. "Reserve that address for the senator."

"Is the second collar around my neck not for you?"

"It is. And its worth should not be diminished." Quintus tied his subligaculum. "Let it be known to you, that your service to me was not expected."

"Apologies to be of disappointment."

Quintus slid his tunic on. "I am not displeased. I am your master, but this house is not my ludus, therefore I am not called Dominus here. I would think it disrespectful to the senator if you address me as you would him. I am born Quintus Furius Varus." He tied his belt and watched Kaeso step out of the bath and waited for the slave to meet his eye. "You may call me Quintus."

WHEN QUINTUS TOOK his seat at the table, Kaeso sat beside him without so much as a murmur. He sat back a little, ate gratefully, eyes downcast, hands in his lap when he was done. Though Quintus could see Kaeso was observant: a keen eye, a sharp mind.

Talk soon turned to the men's training, and Quintus explained his progress, feeling ever under the scrutiny of Servius. When the night drew to a close, Quintus bade the table goodnight, and he stood. "Kaeso," he said when his slave made no move to stand beside him.

Kaeso shot to his feet. "Quintus," he said, in the way he might have said *Dominus*. He took a step back, his head bowed.

But Servius did not miss the salutation. He raised his brow in surprise. "He calls you by your *praenomen*?"

Quintus gave a nod. "At my request. He may wear a collar of the Varus name, but the title of Dominus in this house is spoken for."

Servius gave a sly smirk behind his wine goblet. "That it is." He looked around Quintus to where Kaeso stood in his shadow. "I see the defiant one finally bears some manners. Have you taken full advantage?"

Quintus declined to answer. In place of words, he gave a polite smile and bowed his head. "Goodnight, Senator."

Servius chuckled and raised his wine goblet as Quintus and Kaeso left the room. Quintus walked to his private quarters, Kaeso one step behind him. Quintus pulled back the curtain and gave pause. "You need not follow me here," he said. "I hold true my words spoken earlier. I do not take that which is not freely given."

Kaeso baulked, as if he did not realise he had followed Quintus to his chambers. He bowed his head. "Apologies."

"None required. Sleep. And tomorrow we will see plans come to light."

———

KAESO LAY ON HIS BED, a mat of reeds with a coarse linen blanket, and stared at the wall. It was a large room with many beds, and he was thankful for the oil lamp near the door, so he was not in complete darkness. Some of the other slaves in his quarters were sleeping. Some were fucking while those still awake pretended not to notice.

Kaeso was made well aware that slaves were used for sex, and the senator had warned him if Quintus wanted it, Kaeso was to give it. The other slaves told him of awful things they had seen, heard, or had been done to them, of parties the senator would sometimes have where slaves were handed around like wine.

Kaeso shuddered at the thought.

Yet Quintus did not want him. Perhaps men were not his preference, even though he had looked favourably upon him in the baths. He said he would not take what was not freely given. He wouldn't take Kaeso to bed unless Kaeso offered. And that was a welcome surprise. As was his kindness to the other slaves, how he spoke to Kaeso as though he was just a man, as though his collar didn't make him lesser. He had offered praise to him in front of the senator, and Kaeso might have been new to slavery, but he knew that was not the done thing.

He had asked Kaeso to call him Quintus.

Kaeso smiled in the barely lit room. Quintus was a mountain of a man, and Kaeso would never dare doubt

Quintus' temper or skill in a fight. But there was a kindness to him that drew Kaeso in like a moth to a flame.

Kaeso no longer held any power, nor his own free will. Yet he would do all he could to keep in favour with Quintus. Kaeso wanted to show him his worth. Because if Quintus could look upon Kaeso and see him as more than just a slave, then Kaeso would honour that respect and see it returned.

And perhaps Kaeso would get to see Quintus smile again.

CAPITULUM V

KAESO WAS AGAIN the first to arrive in the training yard, and this pleased Quintus. "I trust the morning sees you well."

Kaeso acknowledged this with a nod. "And you?"

"Quite." Quintus held back the smile that threatened his lips and threw a rudis to Kaeso. "Do you favour odds against me when it is us alone? A practice round, perhaps?"

Kaeso caught the wooden sword with ease and smiled. "I have no coin and can wager only pride."

Quintus grinned at his offer accepted. "Pride is a price we both can afford to pay."

They stood facing each other, practice swords at the ready. Circling at first, daring to see who made move to strike. Quintus could see strategy in Kaeso's eyes, and as the smaller man lunged at him, Quintus laughed as he deflected easily, rounding upon him to make contact at his ribs. "Leave your side open for attack like that and your innards will find the dirt at your feet."

They circled each other again, Quintus seeing every

move of foot, every flinch of muscle, every intent in Kaeso's eyes. They struck again, countered, attacked, and defended, and Kaeso kept favouring a rounded strike. Again and again he made the same move, and just when Quintus was about to reproach him for a foolish tactic, he sidestepped, feigned defence, then moved to attack as Quintus was caught off guard.

He struck the rudis to Quintus' ribs without force. It was a fair strike. A good strike.

Kaeso stood back, wary and fearful, and he lowered his weapon. Quintus was surprised to be hit, yes. But also pleased. He let out a laugh. "The rabbit shows cunning."

"You are not offended?" Kaeso asked.

"Offended only at my own mistake." Quintus' grin widened as he raised his rudis and resumed position. "Again."

By this time, the other five guards had appeared. Upon seeing the two men fighting, they were alarmed but soon realised it was only sport. The more the two men lunged and struck, parried and deflected, the more Quintus laughed and Kaeso smiled.

"You hold back," Kaeso said, easily deflecting a move.

"How so?"

"If you held true concern, you would be absent a smile."

Quintus lowered his rudis and stood to his full height, their sparring over. "And I would be a fool to think you showed full force in return also."

Kaeso lowered his head as if to hide the beginning of a smile, but he did so without answering.

Quintus welcomed the other men to their training and set them the task of fighting with odds stacked against them. Each man would defend against two attackers, and they took turns in rotation until the sun almost met the highest point of the sky.

Servius walked from the house to the training yard, catching the end of the training session. "All is going well," he said smoothly. The men in the yard stopped practice and stood in a neat line facing their dominus.

"Yes," Quintus replied. "Today we learn defence with greater odds against us. It is best to assume a single attack comes from many swords."

Servius made a face. "I fear you may be correct." Then he eyed Quintus. "You do not train with them?"

Quintus first thought Servius spoke in jest but soon realised he was serious. "My training is with men twice their size and number. With weapons of blade and bludgeon, not a wooden rudis."

Servius looked at the six men in the training yard, then back to Quintus. "You could best all six of them at once?"

Quintus met Servius' gaze without fear, without doubt. "Without weapon."

Servius' smile grew wide, and he waved toward the training yard. "Then please," he said smoothly. "Show me what my purse has paid for."

Quintus entered the yard, the six guards watching him warily. He stood before them, rolled his shoulders and stretched his neck. "Your aim is to see my face meet the dirt. Use your wooden swords however you wish." He held up his hands to show he held no weapon. "To hold back is to show dishonour."

Five of the six men shifted their weight with unease. Kaeso did not. He settled his stance, raised his rudis, and eyed his opponent. Quintus grinned at him, then made short work of the first two men, deflecting their jabs and sending them sprawling to the dirt with no more than a flick of his hand. "You lunge too soon and offer an easy opening," Quintus said, eyeing the four remaining men. The gateman made a gallant but feeble attempt, attacking and warding off Quintus' first strike of his fist. But his execution was slow, and Quintus had him disarmed and thrown over his shoulder and was facing the three remaining Iberian slaves before the gateman had hit the dirt.

They spread out, widening their attacking front. Quintus smiled. "Good," he said, still smiling. They attempted to circle around him, but Quintus moved also, away from the stable and yard gate.

"He moves to keep a wall from his back," Kaeso said to the other two. "So he cannot be cornered."

Quintus grinned but did not break his defensive stance. "He speaks the truth. He is wise to the tactics of battle. You would do well to seek his instruction."

And, just as Quintus predicted, one of the men, Gallio, risked a glance to Kaeso. Quintus struck him swiftly, batting the rudis from his hand and kicking his foot out from under him. He landed on his back, the wind knocked from his lungs.

"Your first distraction in battle will be your last," Quintus warned, now facing the two remaining men, Oppius and Kaeso.

"We attack together," Kaeso said to Oppius. "Move to his side. He will need to face one of us."

Quintus' grin grew wider and they circled, moving around him like he stood as the sun. With a nod from Kaeso, Oppius lunged. With Oppius' rudis aimed for Quintus' chest, Kaeso struck low, aiming for his legs. But Quintus was familiar with such tactic. He turned, pushing his fist into Oppius' arm and kicking the heel of his boot into Kaeso's arm.

Oppius' rudis went soaring, and Quintus took the opportunity to send Oppius to the dirt. While Kaeso had been knocked off guard, he had yet to fall, and he took opportunity of his own. He somersaulted, rolling neatly away from Quintus, and when he found his feet once more, Quintus saw that Kaeso now held two wooden swords.

So, of course, Quintus grinned. "Odds are still in my favour, rabbit."

Kaeso almost smirked. "Let the gods cast the die."

They each took a step closer and began to circle. Kaeso held two swords by way of the *dimachaerus*, a gladiatorial style of fighting with which Quintus was well accustomed. Though being unarmed, he would show patience and wait for Kaeso to strike first.

He did not wait long.

Kaeso kept one blade across his body, protecting, and raised the other to strike. Quintus leaned away, feeling the breeze of the wooden sword brush against his skin, and while Kaeso had overstepped, Quintus pushed him.

Though he did not predict Kaeso would sweep the second blade up and under his arm into his path. The rudis scraped up the inside of his arm, and if it had been a blade, it would cause decent injury. But the manoeuvre left Kaeso with his back to Quintus and he was quick to take advantage. He grabbed his dominant arm, bringing it down and forcing the sword from his hand. But instead of resisting, Kaeso rolled into the momentum, pulling himself free and somersaulting again away from Quintus. But this time when he found his feet, he was holding only one sword.

Quintus grinned again, and Kaeso held the sword down by his thigh, not upward, which Quintus had not expected, and Kaeso ran at him. But instead of attacking him, he slid on his knee, lower than Quintus' defensive strike. He slid with ease and, like a thief, plucked his discarded sword from the ground. He faced Quintus again, armed with two swords once more, and it was Kaeso who smiled.

Tired of games, Quintus' smile was gone. He ran at Kaeso, who raised both swords, and a lesser man might have found himself parted from life and limb. But Quintus moved like water despite his size, fluid and fast. He struck with forearm, fist, and foot, and in less time than it had taken the watching men to blink, Kaeso was on his back. Quintus stood over him, pointing two wooden swords to Kaeso's neck.

The tension and silence were broken by slow applause. Quintus, with swords still at Kaeso's neck, looked toward the sound. It was Servius, his smile gratified and self-serving. "You put on a decent show."

Quintus turned back to Kaeso, whose eyes burned with the rage of defeat, and pulled the swords away. "You surprise me, rabbit."

Kaeso got to his feet, his nostrils flared, eyes wild, and it was apparent he had much to say. Before he could further disrespect the senator, in his company no less, Quintus cautioned him. "Choose your words with care," he said, glancing briefly toward where the senator stood.

Kaeso took much needed deep breaths and calmed himself. He bowed his head, just a little. "You honour your ludus."

Quintus grinned. There may be hope for this wild rabbit yet, he thought.

"Quintus," Servius said. "I would have you accompany me to the docks." Servius spared a glance to Kaeso, with barely contained distaste. Then he gave Quintus a curt smile. "If your man can be trusted, have him join you."

Quintus stood tall and met Servius' eyes. "Trust given is trust earned. He will be with me."

QUINTUS WALKED alongside the senator as they left the villa gates. Kaeso followed directly behind Quintus, Helier followed Servius, the two armed guards at the flank. Given the villa's elevation above the city, the path was downhill and relatively short.

The people of Neapolis were quite wealthy, by civilian Roman standard. The port allowed for naval fleets and trade ships, so work was plenty. There were brothels, inns, taverns, and markets.

As they strode the stone streets, by high stone walls, Quintus noted how the people looked upon the senator. Most were favourable, offering smiles, bowed heads, and pleasant greetings. Some less so. Quintus noted it was the poorly clothed, less fed people who offered only hardened glares.

And as they arrived at the docks, naval men leered warily. Some feigned nicety. Some attempted to hide their disdain. "When you speak of likely threats upon you," Quintus murmured as they entered a narrow alley. "You said political persuasion. These civilians and fleet men pose a threat also?"

The senator waved his hand and sighed with short temper. "They are quick to moan of taxes but make no complaint of quality roads and baths. They have the best *latrinae* outside of Roma. I would like to see their complaint if they were still expected to dump bed pots of shit out of their windows."

It was clear to Quintus that this was a sensitive matter

to the senator. But Quintus sided with him on this issue and could easily see his standing. Quintus was happy to pay taxes if his daily standard of life was improved.

Servius stopped at a door. His two guards entered first, then Servius and Helier. Quintus gave Kaeso a dubious shrug but followed directly after, though Quintus knew from the smell and the heat in the small room that they had entered a blacksmith's. It was dark and narrow, with poor air, and the man who stood awaiting them was grimy. Quintus wondered if the man had ever seen sun or bath.

But it was obvious they were expected because the man retrieved a tray with a swathe of old linen on top. He lifted back the fabric to reveal a supply of daggers. A handle wrapped in leather, a blade the span of Quintus' hand. They were high quality, double-edged *pugio*. Single edge blades were of use only as direct offensive weapons. But a twin-edged blade worked just as well on defence.

Quintus took one, holding its weight, testing its balance. He gave an approving nod to Servius. "Quality."

"Tests would make certain," Servius said with little regard if he insulted the blacksmith.

The blacksmith dragged out a sack stuffed with sand and straw, with a centre mark painted in tar. He leaned it against the far wall, some six strides distance, then scampered quickly out of the way. Quintus held the knife handle, judging the weight again for the distance required. Then with no practice aim, with no preamble, he flicked the blade outward from his chest, and the knife sliced into the bag. He had missed the centre mark, favouring rightward half a hand.

It was still a fair shot. If aimed at a man, it would see them fall from this world. Quintus made a thoughtful face to show he was pleased enough with his effort, but he caught a quiet huff from Kaeso who wore a smug smile.

"Care to be bested twice in one day?" Quintus asked him. "Favour your odds to do better, rabbit?"

Kaeso looked Quintus dead in the eye. "I would."

Servius made to disapprove, but Quintus always found the sport in a challenge. He picked up another pugio and handed it to Kaeso, then waved his hand toward the target. "Perhaps you will fare better with the dagger over a practice sword."

Kaeso took the knife, smiling at Quintus. The senator and Helier took a step back, clearly not wanting to stand near an angry slave with a new weapon. Kaeso, not breaking eye contact with Quintus, not even sparing a glance at the target sack, pitched it sideways and struck the black circle. Dead on centre.

Quintus could not attempt to hide his surprise, and he found himself grinning. "I consider myself schooled."

Kaeso gave a genuine smile and it struck Quintus with its purity, but Kaeso glanced at the senator and his smile died and he bowed his head. Quintus turned to Servius to raise a question, but he didn't have to.

"You offer praise to a slave?" Servius said with disbelieving anger in the tic of his jaw.

"Well deserving, I might add." Quintus felt a little protective of Kaeso. He had been placed into his welfare, and he would treat him as such. He nodded toward where the blade still stuck from the target. "Not many could make that shot."

The blacksmith, absent from the conversation, came back to them carrying a leather-and-pressed-metal chest plate. Quintus soon realised that it was not only a guard's uniform, a large guard's uniform, but it was *his* uniform.

Servius seemed to find pleasure in reminding Quintus of his position. "See that it fits and retains its purpose."

Quintus bit back his contempt at wearing the uniform of a slave and forced a smile upon his lips. "As you wish."

The chest plate covered his torso, leaving his arms free to move. It was strapped at his ribs: brown leather and senatorial red fabric held it fast. He had a leather-and-pressed-metal *pauldron*, a shoulder guard to complete the torso. Leather *manicae* protected his forearms and greaves of pressed metal and leather were bound to his lower legs.

Quintus looked down at himself. It was a sight to behold, he could not argue. He filled the uniform well, his figure an imposing one in the narrow room. "I assume a *clipeus* is forthcoming and a *galea*?"

Servius raised a humoured eyebrow. "You required neither today against six men."

But sure enough, the blacksmith returned with a small circular shield and a helmet with a red plume of bristles standing proud from forehead to nape. Once Quintus wore the outfit complete, he looked even more fearsome.

The blacksmith was agog. "You will need only but one. The man is his own army."

Servius shot him a look because he dared speak out of turn, and Kaeso fought a smile. Quintus saw, of course, and gave him a nod. "See this man uniformed as I. Then see if he still finds humour in it."

Within the moments that followed, Kaeso went from slave in bare garments to a senator's guard in full uniform, and the transformation made Quintus' pulse quicken. Quintus noticed Kaeso might have stood a little taller, but the edge of defiance in his eyes remained.

"A Roman will be made of you yet," Quintus said.

Kaeso cast him a scornful look. "Dress me as the emperor, should you wish, but it will not make me so."

"Fair statement," Quintus allowed. "Though your allegiance now falls to Rome, does it not?"

Everyone in the room watched and waited for his response, the Senator most of all. Quintus hoped Kaeso would know better than to insult Rome in front of Servius. The senator met him with cold eyes. "Yes, Iberian. Where does your loyalty lie?"

Kaeso's jaw ticked. "I am loyal to my dominus."

Well answered, Quintus thought. He took two of the daggers and offered them, handle first, to Kaeso. "How would these be best cloaked?"

Kaeso took the knives. He slid one into the leather sleeve on his wrist and one into the leather belt. Quintus asked if he could still move, free of restriction or injury. "You can be armed without delay?"

Kaeso smiled, and in one swift movement, he had both daggers out and in hand, raised in defence. The other men became alarmed, but Quintus only grinned, pleased. The order of weapons and armour was finalised, a large purse of gold coin was given, and they took their leave.

They stepped one foot in the alley when Servius raised his hand. "Is it wise to arm him so soon?" He sniffed at Kaeso, no care given that he could hear him. "He has proven both skill and defiance, and you would see him bear arms? Amidst the good people of Neapolis?"

Quintus squared his shoulders. He had been raised, first by his father and then Oscilius, to respect those who had earned it, so he was cautious of the direction he aimed his next words. "I trust this man. He has sworn allegiance to you as a slave, as have I as a citizen of Rome. I have seen hundreds of men sworn to bleed for these sands, and if you hold my word with any regard, know these are men of honour no matter if they wear the armour of a gladiator or guard."

Servius' eyes hardened. "You would raise word with me in defence of this slave?"

"Do not underestimate the weight of the collars upon his neck," Quintus warned. "It may be of insignificant tin or leather to you. But to those who wear them, it bears more meaning than you or I could dare measure."

Servius spared a glance at Helier, who lowered his gaze as though he thought Quintus' words profound. His tin collar caught the sun as though the gods agreed with Quintus and wanted to prove his point.

"I will hold your word with regard," Servius replied. "As I will hold your name in restitution for your slave's actions."

Quintus smiled with his jaw clenched. "As you wish."

"I have business I must tend to," Servius said, and from his tone, it was clear to Quintus his attendance was not required. The senator turned on his heel and gave an order. "I trust you will not keep my house slaves late for your training. The sun is getting low."

Quintus looked skyward. Yes, he should return with haste. "We should not wait."

Before he could turn, Kaeso put his hand on Quintus' arm. "I owe you gratitude."

"For?"

"You defend me. My dominus voices concern, and you rebuke him. He, a Roman senator, and me, a slave."

Quintus met his eyes. "Yet both are just men."

Kaeso stared, countless emotions warring in his big brown eyes. "Do not fall out of favour with the senator for me."

"I will fall in and out of favour with who I see fit,"

Quintus said with a smile. "Now..." He turned toward the end of the alley. "We must return to the villa. I am expected at training, and I have one expectation of you."

Kaeso bowed his head before looking back up to Quintus. "Of course."

"You will teach me how you can strike a blade with perfect aim without even a single glance."

Kaeso followed dutifully through the city with cautious eyes and vigilant feet. And an upward curve of his lips that Quintus wished to see a lot more.

KAESO FELT CONFLICTED. He had been given the prime opportunity to escape—to walk through the city with only Quintus. No other guards, no other witnesses. He could have easily slipped through the crowd and disappeared. He would be faster than Quintus, and he could give his name of rabbit a better meaning.

But he knew Servius would then hold Quintus responsible, accountable. And Kaeso did not wish for Quintus to suffer because of him.

He had been nothing but kind.

If Rome was full of conceited men and greed, then Quintus was the one good man amongst them.

Kaeso had enjoyed the challenge in the training yard. If there was one place where all men stood on equal footing, it was in battle. Wealth and status meant nothing when a slave had more skill. And Quintus treated all his training men as equals. He showed no favours and expected none in return. Quintus had declared to Servius his trust in Kaeso, and it plucked at his heart like a seamstress picking at tapestry gone wrong; one thread at a time would see it all undone.

Kaeso respected Quintus, and he had not expected that. He had not expected to forge any kind of bond with a Roman. Kaeso had every intention of leaving this place at his first opportunity, being free of his binds, free of Rome.

But he had not expected Quintus.

And as they walked back to the villa, Kaeso's chance for escape was gone. Still, he walked beside Quintus, and he couldn't bring himself to be sorry.

CAPITULUM VI

QUINTUS TRAINED the house slaves as planned, and when they were called to evening duties, leaving him and Kaeso alone, he dragged a target sack of straw to lean against the stable wall and handed Kaeso a knife. "Teach me how to better my aim."

So Kaeso did.

"Take weight," he said, balancing the knife on the palm of his hand, then handed it to Quintus. "Feel its centre?"

Quintus nodded. "I can."

"See the distance to the target and close your eyes."

Quintus cast him a look of disbelief. "Close my eyes? How am I expected to see the target?"

Kaeso levelled his stare. "You seek my advice only to question it?"

Quintus bristled. "It bears no reason to seek a target absent eyesight."

Kaeso bristled right back. He was much shorter than Quintus, but he was not intimidated. His jaw bulged, his eyes hardened to black. "How many days until we leave for Roma?"

"Seven."

"Then you will do well to listen when taught," Kaeso said, his anger evident in his tone of words and the flare of his nostrils.

"And you will do well to not raise your hackles with me," Quintus barked.

Kaeso growled in response, and in one fluid movement, he took the blade from his belt and the blade from his cuff, and without sparing a single glance toward the target, he spun and flung the knives toward it.

He straightened to his full height, facing Quintus. He need not look behind him, because he knew he had hit his mark.

Both blades had struck the bullseye.

Quintus' eyes grew wide and his mouth fell open, too stunned to offer a reply.

Kaeso pointed his finger at him. "When you are ready to learn, you will listen."

So Quintus did.

FOR THE NEXT six days that followed, the house was busy. Everyone was preparing for the departure to Roma, which was quite the procession. There would need to be horses, accompanying personal slaves, the senator's wife and her entourage, plus carriages for clothing and personal effects that Quintus had not even considered.

Quintus trained the guards, then the male house slaves, and then he and Kaeso would practise with blades and targets until the sun drew low to the horizon. His aim with the knives was much improved, to which he owed Kaeso full credit.

He had been taken aback by his quick temper at first, but Kaeso had proven to be a good mentor. Once Quintus had settled into the role of student, Kaeso was patient and calm in his instruction, and by the day before they took leave for Roma, Quintus' aim was almost as good as Kaeso's.

Almost.

"You still favour your own strength," Kaeso admonished him. "The blade will respond more to gentle touch than a brute one. Watch."

Kaeso held the blade handle with the barest of touches, and with no more than a flick of his wrist, the blade sliced the air before finding the bullseye with pure ease.

"You still force the blade from you," he continued, "yet the harsh movement calls for the blade to travel in a harsh arc. And you miss the target."

"I barely miss."

"Yet a miss is still a miss. Be gentle in the hand, and the knife will favour you."

"How can I be gentle yet still throw with force?"

Kaeso put the blade handle in Quintus' palm and folded his fingers around the leather. "Gentle," he whispered. Then, still holding the knife in Quintus' hand, Kaeso moved to stand beside him. Quintus could feel Kaeso's breath on his shoulder, his body heat at his back. Kaeso's hand felt good wrapped around his own. "Draw it into your body," Kaeso murmured. He still held Quintus' hand, his arm now wrapping around Quintus. He liked it more than he should. "Close your eyes," Kaeso said quietly. "Can you see the target in your mind?"

Quintus could barely find his voice. "I can."

"Breathe out when you throw," Kaeso whispered. "With force, well contained. Like a lover's touch."

Quintus took in a sharp breath, and together, with Kaeso's hand still around his own, he threw the knife.

He heard the blade strike the target but kept his eyes closed. He dared not move, not even to breathe, for fear that Kaeso would step away. Kaeso's touch, his gentle words, the rise and fall of his chest against his back was a pleasure too long absent from Quintus' life.

But Kaeso didn't move; his hand, his body remained.

Quintus could so easily turn and take him. He could slide his hand along Kaeso's jaw and bring their mouths together. He could demand it if need be, but he refused to take anything that was not freely given.

"You repeat those words for my benefit? Or to remind you of your own?" Kaeso asked. He let go of Quintus' hand and stepped away.

Quintus shook his head, clearing it. "Repeat words?"

"That you will not take what is not freely given."

"I said no such thing just now."

Kaeso almost smiled. "I beg to differ. You spoke just now, as if in prayer. You will not take what is not freely given."

Quintus huffed indignantly. "As if in prayer?"

Kaeso's eyes sparkled with amusement. "To which gods do you pray?"

"To any that can give me enough self-control not to send you to the mines."

Kaeso laughed. "It did not sound as such. Self-control, maybe. But not to send me away."

Quintus' cheeks flamed with embarrassment. "You speak out of turn."

Kaeso returned his look with a full grin, the kind that made Quintus misstep. He nodded toward the target. "Your aim with a blade is improved."

And it was true. Quintus had thrown the knife dead centre of the target.

Kaeso pulled the knife from the sack and handed it to Quintus. "Yet your aim with words still needs much effort."

"My words?" This conversation was courting around a subject with which Quintus was not familiar. It made the air heavy, and his lungs squeezed with effort.

Kaeso stood before him, unmoving, unblinking, though his cheeks were painted pink. "If you will not take what is not freely given, perhaps you should seek permission."

Quintus' heart thundered and his stomach tied itself in knots. His mouth was dry and his tongue struggled to find words. "Would permission be granted?"

Before Kaeso could answer, Helier ran down to the training yard, interrupting them. "Quintus," he called. "You have been summoned by the senator."

Quintus looked to the sky, unaware the day had grown long. He hurried inside the villa with Kaeso close behind and made his way past the two guards at the door and into the senator's office. "Apologies."

The senator looked up from his papers and dropped the stylus into the inkwell. "I trust all last-minute matters for our trip to Roma have been attended to."

"They have," Quintus replied. "I believe us ready."

The senator let out a relieved breath. "I have been largely absent here with many business matters needing my attention before we leave."

"You're a busy man," Quintus allowed.

The senator almost smiled at his attempt to pander. "I wanted to give you this," he said, producing a folded piece of papyrus and sliding it across the desk to Quintus. "It arrived this afternoon."

Quintus picked it up and opened it to see familiar hand-writing. "It's from Oscilius," he said quietly.

Quintus had sent word back to his ludus that he was well but would be away for another week, at least, while he tended to the senator's request in Roma.

"Everything well?" Servius asked, though he had no doubt read the letter.

Quintus scanned over it.

Dominus Varus,

All is well and in good standing.

Your keen eye and rule are missed by your house.

Your laughter is missed by me.

We look forward to further word, should it come before you.

In trust, in servitude, Oscilius.

"Yes, everything is fine."

"Do you wish to send reply before we depart for Roma?"

"Not yet," Quintus replied. "I should send word when I know more of my length of absence."

The senator considered this. "Fair point." Then he cast a somewhat pleased glance at Quintus. "I see the guards are well-fitted for their uniforms. They look the part, though their improved talent is yet to be seen."

"I should hope you do not need to bear witness to hours spent in training, for that would mean a threat is upon us. I should hope this trip to Roma be as uneventful as your talks of politics." Quintus gave him a smile to emphasise his jest.

"Yes, we should hope so," the senator said, amused.

"Put worry for own duties ahead of concern for mine," Quintus furthered. "We are ready."

The senator nodded, appeased. "Good, good." He dismissed him, saying he was too busy to join them for dinner, but stopped him as though it was an afterthought. "Oh, Quintus?"

Quintus stopped at the door. "Yes, Senator?"

Servius glanced briefly at Kaeso before looking back up at Quintus. "I note that your slave is yet to share your bed."

Quintus blinked. "Senator?"

Servius took his stylus and began to write, not even looking up as he spoke. "When we travel, he will be confined to your quarters to sleep. I trust there is no problem with that?"

Kaeso would be in his room, sleeping next to him. Quintus' stomach filled with jitters and his skin grew warm all over. He swallowed hard, though he dared not look at Kaeso. "No, Senator. No problem at all."

KAESO SAT beside Quintus during dinner, as always. He sat back, his arms resting in his lap, ate quickly and neatly, and when he was done, he kept his head bowed. The senator and his wife weren't at the table, and Quintus felt he had more rein to be himself.

"Have you eaten enough?" Quintus asked. "Kaeso?"

Kaeso's head shot up in surprise. "Oh, I have. Gratitude."

"There are apricots and grapes," Quintus suggested, moving the plate toward him. "You can eat what you like."

Kaeso looked around the table, and seeing no other eyes

upon him, he took a slice of apricot. He bit into it and his eyes closed for a brief moment of pleasure at the taste, and Quintus smiled.

He told himself he didn't notice how long Kaeso's lashes were or how his tongue caught a wayward drop of nectar. He didn't notice how full his lips were or the straight line of his nose.

He didn't notice Kaeso's gaze upon him. "You should not look at my mouth like that in the company of others," Kaeso whispered, his cheeks tinted pink, then he glanced around to see if any other slaves had noticed.

Quintus looked straight ahead and sipped his wine to hide his embarrassment. "The apricot," he said. "Is it favoured by you, or does it provoke memories you hold dear?"

Kaeso's eyes shot to his. He took a moment to collect his thoughts and put his words in order. "My mother would give me apricots when I was just a boy," he admitted softly, glancing to his hands neatly folded in his lap.

"As would mine," Quintus said. "Where did your memories take you just now?"

Kaeso looked at him then, his big brown eyes wide and imploring. "To the fields of my father's farm. The valley green, the sky blue, the air fresh."

"You were happy as a boy?"

Kaeso nodded. "Yes."

"Are your parents yet of this world?" Quintus asked.

Kaeso frowned. "No. Taken but too soon by Roman hands."

Quintus frowned at this. "Mine were taken too. Not by Roman hands, but by the gods. But my mother was kind of heart, and she would fetch apricots for me."

"And of your father?"

Quintus smiled. "Big and strong. Fearless."

The corner of Kaeso's lips turned upward. "I can see that," he said, glancing at Quintus' size.

Quintus turned the wine goblet in his hand. "I was a boy when they joined the shades. But I was raised to be a man by Oscilius. He is doctor of my ludus, first to my father, then to me. But he taught me, he said, as my father would have wished. He is a good man."

Kaeso's big brown eyes filled with questions, but instead of giving them voice, he lowered his gaze.

"Speak your mind," Quintus said. "You have questions yet asked. I can see them in your eyes, rabbit."

Kaeso almost smiled at the pet name, but his eyes gave seriousness to the words that would follow. "Oscilius is your slave?"

"Yes." Quintus put the wine down and turned in his seat to face Kaeso. "Oscilius was a gladiator many men feared in the arena. He was injured in the arena which saw his fighting days end, but he yet lived. My father saw honour in him, and he became doctor at my father's ludus and soon saw many gladiators to victory in Rome."

Kaeso nodded as though deep in thought. "It would explain your ways," he murmured. "That you are kind to slaves because you were raised by one."

"I am kind to slaves not because of Oscilius, but my parents before him. My mother believed people were like the apricot trees. Show them kindness and their fruit will be sweet and plentiful. My father ran his ludus in a similar vein. He gave his gladiators much, and they gave much in return. Cross him once and punishment was swift and final, but honour him and you would be richly rewarded. He manumitted many gladiators, giving them their freedom."

Kaeso studied Quintus, searching for something in his

eyes. "Not many in your place would show such kindness to slaves."

"Slaves are but people, are they not?" Quintus mused. "Jupiter himself stands apart, but mortal men are one and the same, favoured only by the name unto which they are born. A child has no say if he is born to a slave or an emperor. It is decided by the fates."

Kaeso gave a gentle smile. "The senator would not agree."

Quintus grinned at him. "Most certainly not. It is just as well he is absent from the table tonight." He drained the rest of his wine in one mouthful. "I know not if it is the wine that loosens my tongue or the melancholy that follows the memories of my parents. But I believe my chambers call me."

"I shall see you to them," Kaeso said, and the smile he gave made Quintus' blood quicken. Kaeso helped him to his feet. "I see the wine also makes for unsteady feet."

Quintus stood before him, swaying a little. Almost a head taller, almost twice as broad, he traced his thumb across Kaeso's cheek; his skin kissed by the sun, his lips drawn by Venus herself, and those eyes... "My rabbit," he murmured.

Just then, Petilia entered to clear the table. Upon seeing her interruption, she quickly bowed her head. "Apologies."

Kaeso, with reddened cheeks, turned Quintus for the door. "Come. We have a full day's ride tomorrow." He walked Quintus to his room, pulled back the curtain, and helped him to sit on his bed. There, he knelt at his feet and untied his boots and slid them off.

Quintus sat, looking down at the beautiful man who tended to him. The vision of Kaeso kneeling between his legs made his cock fill, and when Kaeso looked up at him with those big dark eyes and licked his lips, Quintus was almost brought undone.

Kaeso stood. "Do you require anything else of me?" he asked, his voice a rough whisper.

Oh, Quintus required much more of him, but he would abstain. "I have told you, rabbit. I do not take anything which is not freely given."

Kaeso's chest rose and fell with harsh breaths, his cheeks tinted the most glorious hue of pink, and he wet his lips once more. He swallowed hard, and Quintus longed to hear permission given.

Instead, Kaeso inhaled a jagged breath and bowed his head. "Sleep well, Quintus."

Quintus watched him retreat, then fell back upon the bed. His body craved release but his mind swirled with wine and memories of pink lips and how, when Kaeso said his name, it sounded as though Apollo, the god of music and poetry, had spoken.

RABBIT.

Quintus' pet name had grated on him at first, yet now Kaeso liked it. It was said with affection, with kindness, and how Quintus had looked upon Kaeso when the wine had gone to his head... Kaeso rushed from Quintus' room with his blood pounding in his ears and desire pooling in his belly.

Quintus wanted him, that was clear from the heat in his eyes, and Quintus could demand Kaeso to his bed if he wished. Yet he held fast to his integrity, and that appealed to Kaeso even more. And if there could be good found in these unfortunate circumstances, in being forced to Rome and made a slave, then perhaps Kaeso should be so bold as to take that one good thing with both hands.

If Quintus would not take what was freely given, then Kaeso would have to be the one to offer it. He would prove how bold he could be, cunning and luring, just like the rabbit Quintus called him.

CAPITULUM VII

QUINTUS SADDLED his horse before the light of day with a heavy gut and aching head. He was still cursing the wine when his six trained guards met him at the stable, Kaeso at the fore. In full uniform, they stood proud, awaiting Quintus' orders.

"We shall lead the caravan and flank the senator. You will protect him at all cost. Expect to ride hard for two days. Tonight we sleep in Frusino and make for Roma tomorrow." Quintus scowled, his ill from wine sat well with ill temper. "We must be ever vigilant. I fear the journey may be an easy task compared to what awaits us in Roma. Strap your helmets to your saddles; we only wear them into Roma. Be ready, we ride at first light."

The men nodded and set about saddling horses, and seeing they were alone a moment, Kaeso went to Quintus. To see him in full armour, wearing leathers and pressed metal, with the red fabric and plumes, Quintus could not deny his attraction. His body reacted whether his mind cared or not.

"I see the wine has left its mark," Kaeso said, low enough so only Quintus could hear.

Quintus' dark mood worsened. "I trust your words hold purpose."

Kaeso ignored his biting tone. "I also trust you to seek duty before nourishment." He pulled out a crust of bread and two dates from the folds of his uniform. "For you."

Quintus heart squeezed, touched by Kaeso's offer, and he felt remorse for his sharp tone. He took the offered food, but before he could offer gratitude or apology, Kaeso turned and tended to his horse. Quintus ate the bread and dates, feeling the grain and sugar restoring him directly. He hated that he had let himself be ill from drink, and he hated that Kaeso had known it. Most of all, he hated that Kaeso was right.

By the time the caravan was ready to take leave, Quintus had fitted his helmet to his saddle, as the expected heat would make it unbearable to wear for two days, and mounted his horse. The six guards followed his lead, and he gave them an approving nod. The horses were uneasy, and Quintus turned his horse in a tight circle in front of his men. He controlled his huge horse as if he and the animal were one, and the horse yielded to his command like the gladiators in his ludus.

From there he gave his final instruction. Lucan and Decius would hold the rear of the caravan, Mettius behind the senator's carriage, with Gallio and Oppius flanking the sides. Each man nodded at their order. Then Quintus looked Kaeso dead in the eye, his gaze never faltering even as his horse moved underneath him. "You, you will ride with me."

THE FIRST DAY'S ride was long and hard under the summer sun, the second not much better. Clouds offered no reprieve; the sky was endlessly blue. The ride might have even been pretty, and Quintus might have enjoyed riding alongside Kaeso through the hills and valleys of Rome, if not for the constant threat of possible attack. They rode at the head of the caravan. Quintus kept his eyes sharp, and he noted with something akin to pride that Kaeso did so as well.

He would have made a fine soldier, Quintus allowed. No, not just a soldier, but a *prima pilus*, at least. It was a cruel blow by fate to see him standing as a slave when he could have led a cohort in the army.

They were otherwise silent, not a word between them spoken. Their lax conversation of days before was replaced with duty.

And as the sun sank lower in the afternoon sky, they rode on. Green fields of wildflowers and swaying grasses gave way to villages, to roads and houses, narrow streets filled with onlookers, and just before the fall of night, they rode past the *pomerium*, the formal boundary of the city of Roma. Gates were opened, foot soldiers lowered their spears, and Quintus led them through the stone streets to the *domus* where the senator resided when he was in Roma.

As they rounded the final corner, a man stepped onto the street and grabbed for Quintus' leg. Kaeso charged his horse at the attack, his pugio in hand, pointing the blade at the man. "Halt, or die where you stand," Kaeso ordered.

The man wailed and raised his hands, and it was then they could see the man was a blind beggar. He was no threat, and the procession moved forward without incident, though Quintus' pulse thundered along with his heart.

It wasn't the beggar reaching for him that caused his

blood to quicken. It was Kaeso's immediate reaction, his impulse to protect him, to put himself between Quintus and possible attack.

Quintus found himself smiling as they made their destination. His body ached from riding two days, his muscles strung tight as if he had trained in the ludus with the gladiators from sunup until sundown. And yet, he still smiled.

As soon as they stopped, Servius climbed out of the carriage as fresh as he went into it. Not a hair misplaced, not a sweat broken. He gave Quintus an acknowledging nod as he approached. "Helier will show you to your quarters. Have your horses fed, then meet with me in the atrium to discuss our stay."

What Quintus wanted most was to find a hot bath and a plate of food, and maybe take a moment to rest his eyes, but he nodded in return. "Yes, Senator."

All the house slaves were quickly dismantling the carriages of clothes and food, Quintus and the guards saw the horses were tended to, and no one rested for a moment. Helier waited impatiently for him to be done, then led Quintus into the domus at a pace; Kaeso followed behind Quintus.

"Apologies if I kept you from your task," Quintus said, his good mood still carried.

Helier almost stumbled a step, and he cast a surprised look. "You would apologise to me?"

"No doubt the senator will set duties for you long into the night in preparation for tomorrow. I did not intend to keep you from them." Quintus looked around the lavish domus as they walked, noting rooms, the baths, but also points of entry and stairs, means for escape if needed. "If the senator seeks explanation, send for me."

Helier bowed his head, a mix of confusion and gratitude

on his face. "Your quarters are this way," he said, extending his arm. He led Quintus to a doorway with a heavy curtain, and he pulled back the fabric to reveal a small room with one bed. "Instruction from Dominus: you are to share quarters."

Helier had ignored Kaeso until now, when he risked a glance toward him. Was he searching for a reaction? That look, that twist of his lips. Was he jealous?

Kaeso brushed past and entered the room. "One bed," he said, turning slowly to cast a look at Quintus. He had mischief in his smile that Quintus found amusing. "I would hope you do not mind sharing."

Helier's mouth fell open, his shock apparent that a slave would speak to his dominus in such a way. His wide eyes turned to Quintus to wait for his reply. And if Quintus' mood had not been so lifted, he might have rebuked Kaeso, but instead he smiled. Before he could speak, Kaeso shot Helier a pointed glare. "Quintus seeks a hot bath and warm food."

Helier lowered his eyes. "Of course. Though I would caution against time wasted in the baths. The senator did request a meeting."

Kaeso gave Helier a pleasant smile that belied the words he implied. "It will not be time wasted."

Helier nodded in understanding—that Kaeso's and Quintus' time spent naked together in the baths would not be wasted—and with a final bow of his head, he ducked out of the room.

Quintus fought a smile. "Leave the poor man alone."

Kaeso growled in distaste. "He has eyes for you."

Quintus didn't miss the jealousy in Kaeso's tone, and he was unable to stop the grin. "And this concerns you, how?"

Kaeso eyes sparked with familiar defiance. "Well, you

claim to refuse what is not freely given. You would have no concern from Helier."

Quintus barked out a laugh. "I will also refuse what I do not want. And by the gods, I do not want him."

This seemed to appease Kaeso, his defiance and temper waned, and in its place was a gentle curve of his lips. "What is it you want?"

"A hot bath and warm meal, apparently," Quintus replied. "Or was that order given to Helier because you so desired it?"

"Possibly." Kaeso had the decency to look embarrassed. "I assumed it would be so desired after a long day's ride."

Quintus nodded toward the bed. "You also assumed I would share a bed."

Kaeso's gaze shot to Quintus before he lowered his gaze to the floor. "Assumed only to put Helier in his place. Apologies if offence was taken."

Quintus smiled at Kaeso's sudden servile demeanour. "A bed, I will share. A man, I will not."

Kaeso looked up then, their gazes meeting. Neither man uttered a word, perhaps the smile Quintus gave him said enough, when they were interrupted once more. Upon seeing it was Helier, Kaeso made no attempt to hide his irritation. He growled and turned away, but Quintus could only smile. He knew Helier had seen them look upon each other, caught in private smiles and conversation.

"The baths have been heated," Helier said, then backed out of the room without casting another look toward Kaeso.

Quintus undid his chest armour and threw it on the bed, his smile barely contained. Then he lifted one foot onto the bed and untied his shin guard, then the other one. "Does your contempt for the man make his words unheard?"

Kaeso shot him a confused look. "Unheard?"

Quintus made short work of his other shin guard and threw it on the bed. "The baths have been heated," he repeated. "The senator does not appreciate being made to wait. And trust me when I tell you, rabbit, neither do I."

He turned and walked out, knowing Kaeso would scramble to follow. And he did. When he entered the baths, Quintus stood beside the bath. He had untied his manicae and pulled the leather wristbands off, then rested his foot on the seat and untied his caliga, pulling the boot off, while Kaeso undressed without a sound.

When Quintus unclasped his *pteruges*, Kaeso held his breath. Quintus pulled the skirt of leather straps from his body and tossed it to the floor, and when it was time for Quintus to untie his subligaculum, his last remaining thread of clothing, it seemed Kaeso's own clothes were swept from mind.

The soft cloth fell away to reveal the naked form of Quintus. His big cock hung heavy and full, and Kaeso's cheeks grew red, his lips parted, his eyes darkened. Quintus stood tall, without shame, allowing Kaeso's gaze to rake over him. With a smile, Quintus stepped into the bath and lowered his body into the hot water. He leaned back and closed his eyes, allowing himself to revel in the pleasure of the bath.

Only when the water splashed did he open his eyes. Kaeso now sat beside him, and as he sank into the hot water, he seemed unable to contain the groan that escaped him. It was a sound Quintus imagined Kaeso might make in the throes of passion, perhaps when he slid inside him. It was a sound that made Quintus' insides curl in a carnal way.

Quintus was caught staring at him, uncertain if Kaeso was sent to him from Cupid himself. Or from Discordia.

Kaeso, eyes closed and lips parted, rocked forward in the hot water, arched his back, and breathed out a sigh, and Quintus' suspicion was confirmed. It was most definitely Discordia. The goddess of strife surely made mockery of him. To bring this man to him, to bring unwarranted complication in already complicated times. This man, this slave was his, belonged to him, belonged with him.

"Your gaze falls upon me, yet your brow is marred with worry," Kaeso said.

Quintus snapped back into the moment, unaware he had been caught staring. "My mind turns in circles."

Kaeso frowned at that. "Perhaps if you give them voice, together we shall see your worries straightened."

"I am not convinced giving voice to concerns will lighten the load when the one who lends his ear is the cause."

Kaeso recoiled. "I am the cause?"

Quintus shook his head and smiled. "You confound me, rabbit. That is all. It is no great concern."

"How so?"

"I deny myself many things to keep tight rein on control of my mind and body, yet the gods mock me by sending you. It is a test I doubt I will be able to pass."

Kaeso stared. "Perhaps the gods have a higher purpose," he whispered. He licked his lips, his dark eyes were pools of desire, and Quintus lifted his hand to run his thumb across Kaeso's jaw.

"If I were to seek permission," Quintus murmured. "Would it be granted?"

"Apologies," a voice said from behind them. Both Quintus and Kaeso turned to the interruption to find Helier standing, head lowered. "Quintus, you have been summoned by the senator," he said, then quickly made his exit.

Kaeso growled again. "If that man should lose his footing and fall on my blade—"

Quintus laughed as he stood. "Do not speak of such things," he said, stepping out of the bath. Ignoring his rigid cock, he quickly dried himself and began to re-dress. Though Kaeso looked upon him with keen eyes, not hiding his disappointment when Quintus tied his subligaculum, hiding his erection from view. Quintus smiled. "Go eat, then sleep. I know not how long I will be."

He collected his other clothes and got to the door when Kaeso stood. His hard cock jutted proudly from his body, and the sight alone almost stole Quintus' breath. "Sleep where?" Kaeso asked.

It took every ounce of self-control Quintus had not to go to him. To take him and have him. "My bed," he replied and, with that, turned on his heel and walked out.

THE SENATOR'S meeting was long drawn, and as Quintus stood with his feet apart and hands clasped behind his back, he found his mind wandering. If it was the subject matter he found tedious or made so by knowing Kaeso was waiting in his bed, he was unsure. Regardless, Servius was pleased with the journey from Neapolis, and he was pleased with how his new guard had formed. He explained the Senate would meet at sunrise to debate and discuss matters until sundown, and he expected Quintus to be present.

Servius didn't have to voice a reason, though Quintus could see it in the flinch of his eyes. To speak such things out loud could prove treasonous, but Quintus was now certain Servius believed the threat upon his life would come from within the Senate.

"Would you have the full guard attend you to the Senate house?" Quintus asked.

Servius seemed to ponder this, as if weighing up whether the spectacle of arriving with bodyguards would outweigh the risk of a threat. "To and from, yes. Only you and your best guard should remain for the duration. It will cause enough tongues to wag, I am certain."

Quintus' reply was simple. "Better to let them talk than to act."

Servius gave a grave nod. "The hour has become late," he said, drawing their meeting to a close. Quintus turned to leave, but Servius' voice stopped him. "And Quintus?"

"I assume you intend to have the defiant Iberian as your accompanying guard tomorrow?"

Quintus gave a nod. "You requested the best."

"You trust he will act without incident?"

"I do."

Servius hummed, then brightened. "His behaviour is your reputation. So might I suggest you teach him a lesson in submission while he shares your quarters." He gave a smile Quintus didn't exactly care for. "If you know what I mean."

Quintus forced a smile before ducking out of the room, and he seethed with every step to his room. The senator was playing some kind of game with him, he was certain of it. But to what end?

Yet when Quintus pulled back the curtain to his room, his anger fell away. Kaeso was asleep, facing the wall, the blankets pulled to his ribs. Quintus watched the steady rise and fall of Kaeso's ribs, and while he was disappointed the senator's meeting had taken so long that Kaeso fell asleep, it was hard to stay upset. Because watching Kaeso sleep struck something inside Quintus, as plucking the strings on a lyre, attuned and resonating.

He stripped down to his subligaculum and slid into bed. Kaeso shot up, awake and startled, but Quintus soothed him. "It is only me. Go back to sleep. Morning comes early." Kaeso settled back on the mattress, shuffling over to allow for Quintus' huge frame. The bed was warm, Kaeso's body even warmer. The comfort Quintus received from such an innocent touch warmed him from the inside out. Kaeso fell fast asleep, and Quintus tried to turn his mind to the senator's motives, but he was too weary, too comfortable. He allowed himself to rest his face against Kaeso's shoulder, marvelling at the closeness, the contact, and sleep soon took him to places of green fields and warmest sunshine, perfect pink lips, and apricots.

QUINTUS WOKE, taking a moment to recall his place. Then he remembered. He was in Roma. In a strange bed, and he was not alone. Kaeso. He had shared a bed with Kaeso, and now the smaller man was curled into him. Quintus' arm was his pillow, his back pressed firm to Quintus' front. They aligned like cogs, every hill and valley of firm muscle slotted together with a precision Quintus had never known.

His cock was long awake to such sensation, hard and filled with need, pressed snug against Kaeso's arse. He let out a steady breath and willed himself control, partitioning off pleasure from his mind, not allowing the seed of desire to sprout.

But then Kaeso's deep breaths stilled, as if his senses were roused from sleep. And he moved, not away from Quintus, but into him, as if his body chased desire absent of thought and reason. As desire was wont to do.

Quintus sucked back a breath, and with a hand on Kaeso's hip, he stilled him. "My control hangs by but one thread. I would ask you to refrain."

Kaeso breathed out a huff of sleepy impatience. "For fear of what?"

"For fear we would not leave this bed for days." Quintus pulled away and sat up, feet to the floor. He repositioned his cock and willed desire away, focusing on the duties at hand. "The house is already awake. We cannot be late."

Kaeso sat up on the bed; the blankets pooled at his waist. His hair was mussed in a way that made Quintus' heart ache, his fingers burned with the need to touch. The metal and leather strands around Kaeso's neck twisted something inside Quintus that he could not lay tongue to. He wanted to see Kaeso a freedman, ruled by no one, free of bindings and slavery. Yet he longed for that leather strand to remain for always.

Those two strands around Kaeso's neck left Quintus conflicted in ways for which he was not prepared.

Even as they dressed in silence, donning armour and weapons, Quintus' eyes were drawn to the collars.

"Is something amiss?" Kaeso asked, raising his hands to touch his neck.

Quintus pulled on his wrist guard, then gently stroked the leather strand that bound Kaeso to him. "This appears absent under chest and shoulder guards."

Kaeso's smile had an unhappy twinge. "Would you rather it be worn on the outside?"

"I would rather it not be worn at all," he replied, the words out before he could stop them.

Kaeso raised his chin and defiance flamed in his eyes. "Apologies if my presence falls under obligation. You state that I confound you. Well, you take fucking honour. Your eyes speak of your desire even though your words do not. Your body longs for it, the evidence pressed hard against me all night, yet you refuse me."

"I have not refused you. You speak of things not yet offered." Quintus pointed his finger at him. "And you will do well to still your tongue should its barbs be aimed at me."

Kaeso dropped his gaze, and Quintus cooled his temper before he spoke again. "I would rather see you wear but one collar. It would be an untruth if I said my leather upon your neck does not appeal to me. But I will not seek desire with a man if his presence in my bed falls under obligation."

Kaeso kept his gaze low but his words were clear. "And if obligation was removed and he yet found himself in your bed, would you seek desire then?"

Quintus knew what Kaeso was asking. "If his will and offer are his own."

Kaeso's gaze shot to Quintus', and for a time it was as though the sun stilled in the sky. Neither of them spoke, only stared. Until movement and sound outside their door caused them to turn. The house was indeed awake, for Servius was readying for the Senate.

"We must leave," Quintus said. They slid blades into hidden places, grabbed their helmets, and left.

CAPITULUM VIII

QUINTUS HAD NEVER SEEN a senate meeting before, nor had he given thought to any expectations. He was not surprised to see so many togas with senatorial purple stripes worn by grey-haired men filled with self-importance.

He was surprised, however, to find the emperor himself in attendance. He understood the emperor had a civic duty to attend, but he was astounded at finding himself in the same room as the leader of Rome.

Quintus and Kaeso stood at the furthest wall, aiming for anonymity, though the red plumes atop their helmets weren't helpful. They drew the attention of a few curious eyes when they had first arrived, but as the day wore on and the senators, consuls, and other magistrates debated, no one spared them another look.

Except for the *praetorians*.

Dressed in full armour with helmets adorned with plumes to match the red of their capes, six of the emperor's personal bodyguards stood in military formation at the emperor's door. They cast curious and cautionary glances toward Quintus throughout the morning.

"The lead guard keeps you under watchful eye," Kaeso whispered. He kept his gaze directly ahead as he spoke. "Is he assessing a threat? Or perhaps he shows interest and he would like a more private meeting."

Quintus fought a smile. "He is of no concern to me."

"Perhaps you could sit for a portrait," Kaeso added, his tone cheerful. "It would save him time and effort."

Quintus covered his laugh with a cough. "Perhaps his neck causes discomfort. It would explain why he stretches it in our direction."

"If he extends even a hint of a threat to you, I will see his neck stretched so it bothers him no more."

Quintus risked a glance at Kaeso to find him still focused ahead with a serious expression. He smiled without care for who saw it. "Waging a war with the praetorian guard would see us outnumbered a thousand to one. These six we could best, but not the thousands that would follow."

"I would still favour us to victory," he replied. "Replace the queen bee with another and the drones will follow, regardless of who wears the crown."

Quintus frowned at him. "You speak dangerous words."

"I speak honest words. The praetorians are loyal to no one. They honour their own purse and care not who pays the coin. Their reputation far precedes them, even to my homelands."

Quintus was quiet again, and he gave reasoning to Kaeso's words. He had heard countless rumours of the praetorian guards, and what Kaeso implied was not wrong. Over the course of history, the elite guards had been the spring of discord more than they had prevented it. But Quintus couldn't deny that that truth also applied to himself. "Would you say the same of me?"

Kaeso turned his head, his eyes afire beneath his helmet. "How so?"

"I am loyal to the senator because he pays me."

"You are loyal because he threatens you. One begets the other." Kaeso stared straight ahead once more. "Above all, you are loyal to Rome."

Before Quintus could reply, the magistrate called for recess and the senators broke for food and drink. The large hall echoed with quiet chatter amongst the senators, some laughter, some heated banter, and it took Quintus a moment to scan the crowd and lay eyes upon Servius. He stood with three other men, and their conversation appeared amiable.

Just as he relaxed, he felt Kaeso stiffen beside him. "Company."

Quintus turned to find two of the praetorian guards approaching. Their armour pressed with the praetorian scorpion, a fitting emblem, Quintus mused. Their faces stoic.

Quintus whispered to Kaeso. "Still your blade. And your tongue. I know not which inflicts deeper wound."

Kaeso smiled at that, and Quintus turned his attention to the guards. "Greetings."

They nodded and the leader spoke. He was smaller than Quintus, and Quintus could see he had a scar above his eye. He smelled of sickly sweet mastic gum. "You wear the crest of Senator Augendus."

Quintus had no need to look down at the embossed emblem on his chest plate. He knew to whom the sails upon water related. "We do."

"Augendus must believe his status rivals the emperor?" the guard asked.

Quintus replied. "Status, no. There can be only one emperor. Threat upon life, perhaps."

The guard scoffed. "Threat? To what end?"

Quintus answered coolly. "Threat upon the Senator Augendus, or any senator, is to make threat upon the naval fleets of Rome, is it not?"

The guard's gaze hardened. "I shall press the matter with the emperor. If the senator lacks faith in the emperor's legions and commanders to defend the fleet, I am sure the emperor would be interested to know."

Quintus gave him a polite smile. "The emperor does know. The fact that you do not is the matter of interest, is it not?"

The guard's nostrils flared, and Quintus could see the insult burn in his glare. He spoke with barely concealed contempt. "Your name?"

Quintus met his gaze with unflinching nerve. "Is of no concern to you." Quintus was bigger than him, and there was no way the guard would cause a scene in front of present company.

The guard raised his chin, turned on his heel, and went back from where he came. Only now he stood in formation, his cold eyes trained on Quintus.

"If he could kill with but a look," Kaeso murmured.

"He would still lack aim and skill," Quintus replied. "He is nothing but piss and wind."

Kaeso chuckled beside him, and they watched as the guard's jaw ticked. Kaeso smiled and said, "And you caution me to not take aim with words."

Quintus shrugged. "I have dealt with the likes of him before. When a fair-sized dog is challenged by a bigger dog, it may bare its teeth, but soon turns with tail between its legs."

Kaeso snorted a laugh. "Tell me, Quintus. At your ludus, do you school your gladiators in diplomacy?"

"No."

"Thank the fucking gods for that."

Quintus laughed, and the watching guard across the floor seethed.

PROCEEDINGS BEGAN and continued well into the afternoon. The attention and posture of the senators waned as the day drew on, though Quintus and Kaeso stood vigilant. And it was toward the close of day when Servius took the floor to speak.

He addressed the emperor, magistrate, consul, senators, and the good people of Rome, and several things became clear to Quintus in the moments that followed. The first being, Servius was seeking election into a magistrate office, as well as taking on role of naval prefect; a position higher than his current standing, and one closer to emperor. He gave reason that an elevated position at Rome's naval base in Misenum was born of logic and necessity, that the emperor's will would be his command, and the majority of senators nodded—if they agreed or simply did not care, Quintus could not discern. However, several senators around the hall took vocal offence to his proposition, and Quintus quickly identified four of the loudest. Lastly though, and perhaps most important, was the reaction of the praetorian guard. Their collective demeanour changed from watchful and passive to what could be best described as scathing.

The emperor raised his hand and silence fell across the men. "The matter will be deliberated upon," he declared. "Verdict to be given when we reconvene next month."

The meeting was closed, and the hall gave way to the shuffling of feet as senators departed with harsh whispers and angry glances. Quintus half expected the lead guard to charge through the crowd toward him and draw his weapon, but as the emperor and leading consuls left, the guards obediently surrounded their leader and disappeared.

"Did you know of the senator's intentions?" Kaeso hissed beside him.

Quintus looked him square in the eye. "Not even a hint of it."

His eyes were dark and hard. "What does this mean for us?"

Quintus answered honestly. "I do not know." Then he spotted Servius in a sea of grey hair and moved through the crowd toward him, with Kaeso on his heel. "Senator, I would have you leave without delay."

They escorted him out, Quintus at the fore, barrelling through the small stone streets to the domus. It was not a great distance, yet the senator puffed for air and even asked to slow the pace, but Quintus ignored his requests.

Quintus led them to the slaves' gate at the rear, and once they were behind secure walls, Quintus turned to Servius. "May I request a private ear, Senator?"

Servius fixed his toga, still trying to catch his breath. "In my office."

The senator led the way, Quintus followed, and when Servius sat at his desk and Helier appeared with a jug of water, it was Quintus who spoke. "Leave us."

Helier's gaze shot to Servius' and the senator waved him away. Helier scurried off, and when Servius saw Kaeso stood beside Quintus, he raised a questioning brow.

"He stays," Quintus said. He stood before the desk, hands clasped behind his back, his size and anger a formidable presence in the room. "You seek a magistrate's position. Did you not think it of enough importance that I might be forewarned before you announced it to all of Roma?"

"I do not care much for your tone," Servius said coldly.

Quintus' reply was delivered with equal frost. "I do not care much for deceit."

The senator's eyes flashed with disdain. Then, like the flipping of a coin, he smiled and waved his hand as if explaining to a child. "Deceit in Rome is called politics. It is not trickery when used to gain the upper hand. I seek a traverse promotion, only to lessen time wasted awaiting written orders from Rome. If I can hold naval command from Misenum, then I shall. Naval prefect is a direct representation of the emperor."

"And this traverse promotion, as you so call it, leaps you ahead of the senators who stand in line before you," Quintus countered.

"If they are fool enough to delay their own advancement, then they deserve their position beneath me." He wore a patronising smile. "I was not aware you cared for political games."

"I do not care for political games or gain," Quintus replied. "I care for the target now put upon your back by your own hand."

Servius waved away his concern like it was nothing. "Those who voiced complaint today make complaint at every turn. That rain falls, that the sky is blue. The subject is irrelevant but to hear the sound of their own voices."

"And the praetorian guard?" Quintus shot back. "Trust their reaction was not a welcome one, and neither will be their course of retaliation."

Servius floundered for a moment. "The praetorians—"

Quintus spoke over him. "The praetorians have

executed emperors before to see their own put into power. And also, do not assume a senator poses no threat."

Servius sighed. "I saw Tiberius Hirrus approach you."

"The lead guard? Is that his name?" Quintus snarled. "I do not expect to break bread with him any time soon."

"Be wary. He bears the scorpion upon his chest and has the sting to match it."

"His sting now points at you," Quintus furthered. "The look he cast at me pales in comparison to the loathing he bears for you. Your announcement to sidestep positions and move closer to the emperor has gained you no favours from Tiberius."

The room was quiet a moment as Servius considered Quintus' words. Then it was Kaeso who spoke. "May I raise a question, Dominus?"

Permission was sought from Servius and he gave a wary nod. "Proceed."

Kaeso kept his eyes directly ahead, his tone polite. "The name of the senator with darker hair, curled at the back and eyes of a hawk?"

"I do not recall such a man," Quintus replied with a frown.

Servius gave a slow smile. "I know to whom you refer. Senator Marcus Cornelius Maternus. You noticed him, slave?"

Kaeso gave a firm nod. "I noticed his manner toward you. Others voiced their opposition to your proposal with pomp and ceremony, yet he sank low and silent. If his loathing alone could have launched daggers at you..."

Servius snarled and made a sound of distaste. "He slithers like a snake through the ranks of Rome and hisses his forked tongue at my success." Then he turned an ill-favoured stare at Quintus. "How is it your slave notices my enemy, yet you do not?"

"Quintus took note of four senators and six guards," Kaeso defended quickly. "I took notice of one."

Quintus raised his chin and spoke loud and clear. "As I have said before, and if it bears repeating, I chose Kaeso to attend me today because you requested the best."

Servius gave pause to look upon each of them. "Well, you best hope his talent is unsurpassed, because the high society of Rome is expected here as the sun sets."

Quintus' gaze shot to Servius. "For what purpose?"

"I intend to use this night as honey to sweeten my promotion. Magistrates, consuls, and even the emperor himself may attend," Servius said. "Which means Marcus Maternus will slither in, if there is any chance to oil the emperor."

Cold realisation dawned on Quintus. "And if the emperor attends, the praetorian guard follows."

Servius gave a nod. "They will. Which is why I would have you both not dressed as guards tonight. Carry concealed blades if you wish, but best not appear offensive to the praetorians. We will strike the hornet's nest only if our hand is forced."

Quintus scowled. "At risk of being stung first."

CAPITULUM IX

WITHOUT TIME FOR A BATH, Quintus requested a tray of personal effects be brought to his quarters. He began to undress, ignoring Matalia as she entered and set the tray on the floor by the bed.

Kaeso waited for her to leave before he spoke. "Apologies, Quintus. I did not intend to speak out of turn."

Quintus placed his chest plate on the floor by the wall. "Apologies for what?"

"When speaking to Dominus. I asked for the name of the senator with the scathing look. He rebuked you, and that was not my intent when asking."

Quintus put his foot on the bed and untied his boots. "I know. I care not for Servius' accolades or reprimands. Only that this Marcus has shown his hand." He smiled at Kaeso and started on his other boot. "Gratitude for your keen eye."

Kaeso blinked. "You are not mad?"

Quintus was now all but naked, save his subligaculum. He straightened to full height and met Kaeso's eyes. "I am not mad. Yet, if you remain in full armour or give us cause to be late, I will see my mind changed."

Kaeso noted the slight curve of Quintus' lips but he still hurried to undress. He left his armour on the floor beside Quintus' and took his place beside him by the bed. Quintus handed him the oil, and they both stood in only undergarments and scraped themselves, then doused the linen swathe in water to rub down. Neither man spoke, though each stole glances at sculpted forms and certain hands on skin.

Wearing only a soft loincloth did little to hide where Quintus' mind had gone. Yet he had neither the time to act upon the impulse, nor the time to do his desire justice. If the gods were willing, he would need more than a rushed attempt.

Needing distraction, Quintus pulled on his tunic and toga, then his sandals. He still ached with need, but at least his clothing hid it well. Yet Kaeso still wiped himself down, still appeared golden in fading daylight. It took the control of Jupiter himself to stop Quintus from touching Kaeso. He fisted his toga at his thighs and stepped away. "I should check the perimeter," Quintus mumbled. "And confirm Gallio and Oppius have their instructions."

He slipped out of the room, both desperate and remorseful for the distance from Kaeso. He required a clear head for this night. Which proved a sound and decent plan for the purpose of securing perimeters and ensuring all guards stood familiar with protocol. All house slaves were busy preparing food and wine and private rooms for entertainment.

All was as it should be.

Until Quintus cast his eyes upon Kaeso.

He stood guard by the door to the courtyard, his posture perfect, defiance alight in his eyes. He also stood wearing nothing but his loincloth. And his two collars, of course.

Quintus' step faltered, his heart thundered, and his skin flushed hot. He made strides toward him, yet could not meet his eye. "Your attire raises questions," Quintus said, his jaw tight.

"I have only my guard armour as an option," Kaeso replied. "Upon strict order against it, my choice was removed." He was quiet, staring straight ahead. "I wear the only other clothes I have, which are those I arrived in. Apologies you do not approve."

Quintus put his fingers to Kaeso's chin and forced his eyes upon his own. "It is not a matter of my approval that raises concern. But the matter of my distraction."

Kaeso's rabbit eyes darkened and his lips hinted at a smile, yet in that very moment, the gateman announced the first guest's arrival. The house was soon a hive of important men and painted women. Their wealth and status dripped from jewels and fine fabrics; they wore arrogance and ego as if it were brocade.

Quintus' guards stood at the far walls near the entries. They wore their guard uniforms, stood silent for the purpose of appearance. Most dignitaries expected guards, and while Quintus could see why Servius had insisted he not appear dressed in his armour—that the praetorians might see him as potential threat—Quintus cared not one bit if it was a blow to Tiberius' ego. It was evident to anyone who looked that Quintus was bigger and better than Tiberius. No uniform would mask that.

It also rankled with Quintus that Kaeso was forced to wear his slave garb. He had stood with honour beside him in the senator's forum, with no difference in status between them. Yet now Kaeso stood behind him, head bowed, his slave status on full display in loincloth and collars around his neck.

The emperor arrived with all the pageantry that his title afforded him. Having him accept the offer was quite the honour, and Quintus could see the pedestal it put Servius on over and above his peers. And of course, with that admiration came envy and the resentment that followed. Senator Maternus wore his false admiration for Servius like a cloak; free-flowing yet shrouding the antipathy he wore underneath.

Quintus paused to sip his wine, and Kaeso stood at his side. He turned into him, Kaeso's lips at his shoulder, and whispered, "The senator with the eyes of a hawk and tongue of a snake struggles to contain his contempt."

Quintus smiled into his cup. "You notice."

"It is difficult not to."

"Tiberius, the lead praetorian, has not recognised us," Quintus said into his wine with a pointed glance at the uniformed guards behind the emperor.

"Perhaps Dominus was wise to suggest you distance yourself from your position," Kaeso said. "Another guard Tiberius could confront, yet not a guest of the senator."

"Perhaps," Quintus allowed. "I believe Servius to have hidden motives at every turn. He appears to have Rome's best interest at the fore, though I would not discount a politician to see his own needs met first."

Kaeso's gaze narrowed, and he glanced up at Quintus' before lowering his eyes once more. "You do not trust him."

"No." Quintus looked around the crowd and noticed a few eyes upon them. It was not custom for a man to have close conversation with his slave in the company of elite. "We are causing raised eyebrows," Quintus whispered. "Play your part in my game."

Then Quintus raised his wine to Kaeso's lips, tilting his head back with a gentle touch, affording him a sip. "Drink."

Kaeso did.

A slave with a tray of fruit happened past, and Quintus took grapes and sliced fig. He put a grape to Kaeso's lips. "Eat."

Kaeso did.

Then a slice of fig, Quintus slid it into Kaeso's mouth, his thumb pressing his bottom lip. Kaeso's eyes darkened and his nostrils flared, and a dangerous warmth pooled in Quintus' belly, sinking to his balls and cock.

"Ah, I see you brought your pet with you," a voice said beside him. Quintus turned in surprise at the sound and was shocked to see it was the emperor who had spoken.

"Emperor," Quintus said with all the respect he could muster, his mind reeling. "Yes. My pet," Quintus said, motioning toward Kaeso, who had once again moved behind him, his head bowed.

It was quite common for slaves to be called pets and treated as such. It was the ruse Quintus had been aiming for so the prying eyes in the room would think nothing of his and Kaeso's closeness. He just had not expected it to garner the attention of the emperor.

The emperor smiled. "I know your face."

Quintus blinked, not expecting this conversation, then kept his eyes down. "Apologies, but I am only in Roma for business on behalf of Senator Augendus."

"From where do you hail?"

"Campania."

The emperor brightened. "I spent many summers in Campania before the duty of Rome called." He studied Quintus' face. "Who might your father be?"

"My father was Caius Furius Varus."

"Ah, of the Ludus Varus."

Quintus dared look at the emperor then. "Yes. I am Quintus Furius Varus."

The emperor gave him a warm smile. "I was very regretful to hear of your father and mother. Parted from this world too soon."

"Gratitude, Emperor. Though time eases the ache of loss."

"I knew your father well from my days as senator and called him amicus. You are the image of him."

Quintus bowed his head. "An honour."

"Tell me, as a *lanista*, what business does the senator have with you? I was unaware he held interest in gladiators."

"Gladiators, no. More a matter of reassurance."

The emperor almost smiled. "Assurance from injury or threat, I assume."

Quintus found himself cornered by his own doing. He wanted to keep the business of the senator private, but he would not lie to the emperor. He smiled and gave a nod. "The good senator believes there is a need."

The emperor sighed, not unhappily. "It is becoming more familiar. Senators and magistrates are not immune to the dangers of their position. Bodyguards are common. Tell me, are you here to train the guards, or do you take role as *privus securitas*?"

"Both. Until no longer required."

The emperor's eyes gave a curious edge. "Most take the gladiator, not the lanista."

"Why have the student when you can have the teacher?" Quintus said. "I would imagine you yourself wouldn't take a simple foot soldier as guard, but a valiant commander?"

This brought a smile to the emperor's lips. "Perhaps this

begins the dawn of the nova praetorian. Perhaps I should make my own inquiries."

"The dawn of the *new guard*," Quintus mused. "A suitable name for one who can best any of Rome's gladiators or a valiant commander. Should they be fool enough to attempt."

The emperor smiled genuinely. "I see your father taught you well. Ludus Varus was the best."

"And it remains so," Quintus returned.

Two senators drew near and the emperor gave them a nod, then turned back to Quintus. "I must attend business matters," the emperor said. "Extended gratitude for the conversation absent of political manoeuvring."

Quintus bowed his head. "The gratitude is mine." When he raised his head, the emperor was gone, and in his place stood his lead guard. Tiberius wore full armour and a scowl worthy of some merit. Quintus gave him a smile and could see his stare harden.

"Nova praetorian," Tiberius spat the words with disgust. Quintus wondered how he could manage words with that foul mastic gum in his mouth. "There will never come the day."

Quintus held his gaze and gave him a mocking smile. "You would need be absent eyes or a fool not to see the sun already risen on that day."

"Tiberius," the emperor called him to follow.

For a praetorian guard to be reprimanded in public, by the emperor no less, was quite a scandal—a hush fell over the room. The emperor may have well slapped him.

Quintus grinned. "Run along."

Tiberius snarled but did as he was instructed, and the noise in the room returned. He took his place behind the emperor but spared Quintus a parting glare.

Kaeso spoke from Quintus' other side. "If he had not marked you with a target before, he has now."

Quintus turned to face Kaeso, giving Tiberius his back. "Then we shall see how well he aims."

Kaeso looked up at him. "You are not concerned at all?"

Quintus shook his head. "What he lacks in threats, he makes up for with piss and wind."

"I do not trust the praetorian guard," Kaeso whispered.

"Nor do I. From your words earlier today, I assumed you would favour our odds against them. Was not I the one to caution you?"

"Their lack of loyalty makes it difficult to see from where the attack might come. There is a good chance many of the people in this room line the praetorian purse. In the company of men without honour, who do you believe who do you believe to be amicus? In whom do we trust?"

Quintus almost smiled. "We stand in a room of politicians, Kaeso. The answer is easy. Trust none of them."

AS THE NIGHT WORE ON, wine was drunk, meats and fruit were served with breads and oil, and Quintus was happy to distance himself from conversation. He had neither the inclination nor the need for political games. The fact the emperor had approached him for idle chat earned him curious assessment from the senators, and Quintus assumed his place in such company confused most of them.

But he took up a post near the doors to the courtyard, appearing casual while he surveyed the room. Servius was indeed doing the rounds, charming his acquaintences to vote in his favour, and his plan seemed well thought out and well executed.

Senator Maternus was the snake Servius had said he was, and Kaeso's description of hawk eyes was exact. Even his nose resembled a beak. He watched Servius, and he watched the other senators, and he watched who had given Servius favour and who perhaps had not. And Quintus watched him.

Tiberius never left the side of the emperor again, though his line of sight rarely strayed too far from Quintus. And every time, Quintus returned his stare until Tiberius was the first to look away. As the emperor announced he must return to the palace and gave a small speech of thanks to Servius for his hospitality, Tiberius gave Quintus a scathing look that said, *until we meet again*, to which Quintus smiled and raised his wine, a gesture that replied, *I look forward to it*."

At the departure of the emperor, it appeared social graces left with him. With the pouring of more wine came more laughter and loud conversations of ego and status, and a kind of depravity and debauchery Quintus had only heard about.

It was common knowledge that senatorial parties included orgies and other uninhibited desires of men with power. It was another thing for Quintus to see it.

Two women body slaves, Matalia and Petilia, were made to fuck while senators stood and watched. Another woman was laid upon a table and offered to any man who wished to have her. And they did.

A male body slave, Benedictus, was ordered to his knees with his mouth open for any man to fill with his cock. And they did.

Quintus could hear laughter from one of the private rooms, though he dared not think about what he could not see. The smell of sex was ripe in the room, of moans of men and women, pleasure and mirth, and more wine, and other house slaves moved through the room with trays of more food and drink as though all too familiar with the scenes before them.

It was dizzying and horrible, yet Quintus could not deny his body reacted. Watching men fuck and be fucked to completion, being surrounded by sex, made his cock fill and his balls ache.

One senator led a male house slave past Quintus and took him to the courtyard outside, and Quintus averted his eyes. "I am grateful for your collar upon my neck," Kaeso said from behind him. "Or I would be in his place."

Quintus turned to find those big rabbit eyes upon him. "As I have said, I do not take that which is not freely given."

Kaeso held his stare, though his words were a nervous whisper. "And I am grateful. Fate's cruel hand saw me collared yet delivers me instead with kindness to you."

"I could say the same for myself," Quintus replied. And suddenly the wine he had drunk so sparingly made his head swim. Or was it the sounds of sex all around him, with Kaeso so close and near naked, that sent his mind spinning? Or perhaps he had forgotten to breathe. And why was his mouth so dry? "I think I need water," he mumbled.

Kaeso smiled. "Allow me to get it for you. For a man of your size, you do not suffer wine too well."

Kaeso put his hand on Quintus' arm as he stepped around him, and his skin burned at the touch. Desire was already licking at his bones with the room around him full of grunts and groans, and he made up his mind to ask Kaeso if his permission was granted. They had skirted around the subject several times before, and Kaeso tempted him time and again with the look of desire in his eyes, a hint of tongue at his lips. And this morning, Kaeso had grown angry when

Quintus had denied him when they awoke in bed. Quintus had argued that permission was not given, and Kaeso had countered he had not been asked to give it.

So tonight Quintus would ask him.

Determined now, Quintus turned to look for Kaeso, but he was not at the table with pitchers of water. He searched the room and, with a rising panic, could not find him. He moved then, toward the crowds of men, and he saw familiar golden skin being cornered by two men. They were not senators, but from their clothes, perhaps socialites, and Quintus heard what they said.

"Servius did say we were free to enjoy any of his wares," one said. He was tall and wiry, and Quintus could snap his spine without trying.

"And this one looks fresh," the other man said, admiring Kaeso as if he was something to eat. He was short and stout, and Quintus imagined gutting him as he would a fish. "Is that not Servius Augendus' collar you wear, slave? Speak!"

Quintus appeared in the middle of them. His imposing height made both men have to look up. His voice was low and seething. "Lay one finger upon him, and I will see it removed from your hand. Dare to even cast gaze in his direction and I will take out your eyes."

Both men blinked, duly offended, yet clearly intimidated. The tall one managed to speak. "Who thinks he can make idle threat—"

"Threat is not idle," Quintus cut him off, growling the words. "Continue to raise question and I will part you of your fucking tongue."

Both men paled, one grabbed the other and they backed away. It took a moment for Quintus to calm his breaths, to unclench his fists.

"Apologies," Kaeso whispered behind him.

"None required," Quintus replied, turning to him. "From you, at least. Are you unharmed?"

Kaeso nodded. "You would cause scene for me?"

"I do not take what is not freely given, and I will not have what is mine taken from me."

The way Kaeso looked up at him... Those wide brown eyes made Quintus' heart too big for his chest. "Quintus, I—"

"I have asked for your permission, yet you withhold reply," Quintus whispered. He closed his eyes, unable to bear those damned rabbit eyes. "I fear I will lose my fucking mind if I am to stay in this room one more second, with the sound and smell of sex, and not know your answer."

Kaeso poked Quintus in the chest with his finger, not the reaction Quintus had expected. He looked at Kaeso then to find him smiling. "If you hold your tongue while I speak, you would find your answer. Yet you interrupt with stubborn pride."

"Stubborn pride?"

Just then a burst of laughter made them both turn. It was Helier; he stood talking to a senator with a wine goblet in his hand. He covered his mouth to stop from laughing, and the senator took the wine from him. Helier leaned in and whispered something, and the senator took his hand and led a very smug Helier to a private room.

"Hades and the Underworld mock me if Helier gets his cock touched yet I do not," Quintus grumbled.

Kaeso laughed and took Quintus' hand. "Take me to your quarters and let us see if Hades mocks you then."

Quintus did not need telling twice. He slipped through the crowd, past scenes of sex and naked people, the sounds of their pleasure lost to the sound of his blood pumping in his ears. He pulled back the curtain to his room and dragged

Kaeso inside, lit only by faint candlelight. He turned and cradled his face in his hands.

"Is this your permission?" Quintus asked in a whisper.

Kaeso swallowed hard. "It is."

Quintus leaned down and almost pressed his lips to Kaeso's, but he paused. "Answer me this, and give me only truth," Quintus murmured. "Do you grant me consent because my collar sits upon your neck?"

Kaeso pulled back. "You kill my desire to remind me I am a slave?"

Quintus found Kaeso's arm, now his eyes had adjusted to the low light. "That was not my intent. I ask so there is no doubt from where your consent comes. I need to know if you would bed me because it is something you want. If it is out of duty, then I would decline."

Kaeso took Quintus' hand and slid it over his loincloth, letting him feel his hard erection. "Does that feel like duty to you?" Kaeso asked, his voice rough. "Insult me again and consider permission revoked."

Quintus thought for one moment his blood might catch fire. Kaeso's hard cock made his knees weak, and he couldn't resist another second. He pulled Kaeso against him, crashing his mouth to his, and let desire take control.

Their tongues met and it tore the breath from Quintus' lungs. Kaeso pawed at Quintus' clothes, pulling in a vain attempt to reach bare skin underneath. Quintus broke the kiss and pulled at his toga, then his tunic underneath, and flung them to the floor. Kaeso was panting, his lips wet and swollen, and he pulled at the strap of his loincloth, letting it fall away.

Quintus sucked back a breath, and his head spun. "One sight of you and I forget to breathe," he whispered.

Kaeso smiled and put one knee on the bed. "And you forget to undress. Your subligaculum. Take it off."

Quintus chuckled, then pulled at the cord, and his undergarment slid to the floor. "You give orders now?"

Kaeso's gaze fell to Quintus' hard cock and his voice was just a breath. "If they need giving."

"See something you desire?" Quintus asked as he stroked himself, long and slow.

Kaeso met his gaze. "I see something I am not certain will fit where you intend to put it."

Quintus chuckled and slid his hand along Kaeso's jaw. The frantic urge from before was now a constant pressure, a fire more contained. Quintus pulled Kaeso's face upward so he could capture his lips, and he kissed him with a tenderness that belied his size. "I will take you to such heights, the gods themselves will envy you."

Kaeso let out a breathy laugh, but Quintus soon covered his mouth once more. Quintus held his face, then pulled his body close and lowered him to the bed. Kaeso moulded to him, every line, every curve, and he held onto his broad shoulders. He writhed, rubbing his cock against Quintus' hip, seeking pleasure.

Quintus took Kaeso's hands and pinned them above his head, causing him to gasp, and Quintus devoured his mouth once more. But soon Kaeso struggled against his hold and whined, so Quintus pulled back to let him speak. "Please allow me to touch you. How will I know this was not imagined if my hands cannot remember the touch of your skin?"

Quintus' cock throbbed at his words. "Your body will remember me."

But he released Kaeso's hands, and Kaeso was quick to touch everywhere he was able to reach. His fingers threaded through Quintus' hair, down his back, over his arse. He lifted his hips and wound a leg around Quintus' thigh, grinding and writhing. "Quintus, I would have you inside me now. I am short on patience and ache for release."

Then Quintus remembered the oil Matalia had delivered to their room for them to cleanse with before the guests arrived. He pulled away so he could rest on his knees, then reached beside the bed, retrieving the small vial.

"What have you there?" Kaeso asked.

When Quintus looked down at him, he was on his back, his legs spread, thighs over Quintus' and he pulled on his own cock. He was a sight to behold, and Quintus' heart thumped so loudly he thought Kaeso smiled because he could hear it. "Oil," Quintus answered as he poured a drop onto Kaeso's sliding hand.

Kaeso moaned as his hand found slickness, tight and desperate. "Oh, fuck the gods," he breathed. "If you do not act right now, you will be too late."

Quintus poured oil over his own cock and returned the vial to the floor. "What you lack in patience," Quintus said, leaning over him now, "you make up for with temptation. I have never seen a man lying before me look so beautiful."

Kaeso's hand stilled on his cock. "You would call me beautiful?"

Quintus smiled at him, kissed him tenderly, then spread Kaeso's legs wider, lifting Kaeso's arse up to meet his eager cock. "To all who would listen."

Quintus put his hand over Kaeso's, linking their hands around his cock, then fondled his balls, earning him delicious moans of encouragement. Then he moved lower until he ran his oil-slicked thumb over Kaeso's hole.

"What are you doing?" Kaeso asked.

"Readying you for my cock," he replied, slipping his

thumb inside. Quintus thought Kaeso might have appreciated his efforts, but he was mistaken.

His eyes were wide and furious. "You would tease me? You promise me cock, then refuse to give it?"

Quintus grinned at him. He lifted Kaeso's thigh and leaned over him, pushing the head of his cock to Kaeso's hole. "My impatient rabbit," he whispered, then pushed all the way inside him.

Kaeso's eyes went wide, his mouth open, his breath caught. He was struck without ability to speak, move, or breathe. Quintus held still, reeling in the intense pleasure, refraining from his carnal urge to thrust.

"Breathe," Quintus whispered against Kaeso's lips. Kaeso sucked in a breath, and Quintus rewarded him with a soft kiss. "Breathe."

Kaeso closed his eyes and his chest heaved with ragged breaths, and still Quintus did not move. Kaeso's arms were splayed outward, and he drew them in slowly. Quintus thought he might push him away, that it was too much, but he put his hands to Quintus' chest, to his neck with gentle fingers, and when he opened his eyes again, a new fire burned within them.

So Quintus pulled out a little and slid back in, and Kaeso's eyes rolled back in his head. He groaned, a deep resonating sound, so Quintus did it again, and again, and soon Kaeso was rising to meet him. He moaned louder, and he held onto Quintus with each thrust. Quintus had never felt anything like it. Never this hot, never this tight, never had his heart beat like this.

Kaeso took hold of Quintus' face and pulled their mouths together. But their joining, added with the mingle of tongues and whimpers and grunts, became too much for

Quintus. He broke the kiss to tell him, "You will bring me undone too soon."

Kaeso arched his back with this new angle, pleasure stricken on his face, and when Quintus took hold of Kaeso's cock, he cried out. Quintus thrust harder, pumped harder, and Kaeso went rigid and cried out as he spilled his seed. His arse gripped Quintus' cock tight, and Quintus drove deeper, thrusting his tongue into Kaeso's mouth as he emptied his cock inside him.

It took a time for the room to stop spinning, and it took even longer for Quintus' senses to return to him. Kaeso was drawing patterns on his back; Quintus was still inside him, and might have presumed he had arrived in the afterlife if he didn't know better.

"Am I crushing you?" Quintus asked. "I have not the strength to move."

Kaeso hummed, a happy sound. "I would have you never move. From atop me, inside me. Your weight, your cock, is a pleasure to which I could become accustomed."

Quintus buried his face in Kaeso's neck to hide his embarrassment. Though his own thoughts echoed Kaeso's. He loved how Kaeso's body moulded to his when he lay on top of him, and he loved being buried inside him. Even now, half spent, he could already go again. "I do not wish to move."

Kaeso brought his hand up to run it through Quintus' hair. "You promised to deliver me to heights the gods would envy."

Quintus pulled back and rested his head on his bent arm. "Did I see you delivered?"

Kaeso laughed and his body moved in a way that made Quintus buck his hips. They both could feel Quintus was most definitely ready for more. It drew another groan from Kaeso. "Delivered in capable hands," Kaeso said, writhing a little. "You will see me delivered again if you continue this path."

Quintus put his hand to the side of Kaeso's face and studied his features. His cheeks were flushed, his lips swollen and wet, and those dark eyes. Quintus had never seen a man so striking. "Tell me your name. Your whole name."

"Why?" Kaeso asked, almost smiling.

"Because I wish to know the full name of the man who has captured me so completely."

Kaeso's breath caught, his eyes swam with emotion. "Kaeso Agorix."

"The gods designed you with me in mind, Kaeso Agorix," Quintus said, kissing him, thrusting in slow and deep. "I am sure of it."

Kaeso pushed his head back, his neck strained, a groan low in his throat, and it seemed he could only speak after he had become familiar with Quintus' cock once more. "And you for me, Quintus," he breathed, rough and writhing. "Though Priapus was the god who answered."

Quintus barked out a laugh and he stilled his thrust, his cock buried to the hilt inside him. "And yet you can take it."

Kaeso stared up at him, smiling, daring. He looked at Quintus with reckless abandon, freshly had, and yearning to be had again. "I can think of a better purpose for your tongue than talking," he said. "Now show me what Priapus gifted you with."

So Quintus gave Kaeso his tongue and his cock until he wrought pleasure from Kaeso's bones, until he was wracked with tremors and sated, and fell asleep in Quintus' arms.

KAESO WAS UNABLE TO MOVE. Even if he had wanted to, he could not. Quintus lay over him, his weight pinning him to the bed. He had been so thoroughly pleasured, he fell asleep in Quintus' arms and that was where he woke. Strong arms encased him, holding him close, protecting him, Quintus' cock pressed hard against him. Kaeso ached in all the right places, a swift and pleasant reminder of Quintus' skill as a lover. He never wanted to move.

But he could hear the sounds of the house awakening and their room was lit with early morning light, and Kaeso considered rousing Quintus from sleep with his body, when the curtain to their room was pulled back.

Helier couldn't hide his shock, or his dislike, and Kaeso couldn't withhold his smirk. "You come bearing a message?" Kaeso asked. He stretched a little so the blanket would slip to reveal his nakedness, if the clothes strewn on the floor weren't evidence enough. He wanted Helier to know Quintus had bedded him, chosen Kaeso over him, but the movement stirred Quintus and he tightened his hold on Kaeso protectively until he looked up and saw it was only Helier and fell back with a groan.

Kaeso smirked behind Quintus' arm.

Helier lowered his eyes. "The senator requests your presence in his office," he said before disappearing and the curtain fell back into place.

Quintus groaned. "I would rather stay here."

"As would I. We have matters unfinished," Kaeso murmured and wiggled his arse against Quintus' erection. "Though I doubt the senator would agree."

With another groan, Quintus rolled off him. "You are a dangerous one, rabbit."

Kaeso picked up Quintus' undergarment with a smile and tossed it to him. "You best hurry."

"As should you. I would have you come with me."

"To see the senator?"

"To all places," he said, getting dressed. "To all places one requires a dangerous rabbit."

CAPITULUM X

"EXPLAIN WHAT BECAME of you last night?" Servius was at his desk under a heavy cloud of too much wine.

Quintus stood in the senator's office, feet spread wide, and his hands clasped behind his back. Kaeso stood beside him, though Servius had not even looked at him. He spoke only to Quintus. Memories of the night before were fresh in Quintus' mind, of being in bed with Kaeso, being inside him, of fevered mouths and desperate hands. But surely this was not what Servius referred to. "Clarify, please, Servius."

"I saw you break words with the emperor," Servius said coldly. "To what purpose?"

"If you bore witness, then you saw the emperor approached me."

"What in Jupiter's name would the Emperor of Rome find common thread about with you for conversation?" The senator was clearly curious, and jealous. "He is the emperor!"

Quintus ignored his temper and foul mood. "He knew my father."

Servius' eyebrows drew in. "And he recognised you?"

"The emperor has a keen memory." Quintus wasn't sure what else he could say. "He found my presence curious. After all, what would a trainer of gladiators be doing standing as guard for you?"

Servius' gaze narrowed, sharp as a dart. "You told him?"

"I confirmed only what he already assumed. He was neither surprised nor troubled at the news and admitted to other senators acquiring their own guards."

"It was not your place to divulge."

Quintus took care with his tone but little else. "I will not bear false witness to the emperor. To lie to Rome is treason, and no amount of coin promised will buy that from me. Do not mistake where I stand on this matter."

Servius stared at him, then did that cold shift in demeanour and gave a pleasant smile instead. "Of course. I also noted that his guard Tiberius received caution for harsh words with you."

Quintus withheld a sigh. "Tiberius might bark as a savage dog, but I am yet to see his bite."

"Be watchful of him," Servius said. "And the two city merchants? Acilius and Ramirus, what could they have possibly said to warrant threat of grievous injury?" Servius sighed now and looked upon Quintus as though chastising a wayward child.

"The two civilian men in vermillion cloaks?" Quintus asked. He knew it was the two men who had cornered Kaeso but thought it best to clarify.

Servius gave the smallest of nods. "Yes. Two of the wealthiest men in Roma."

Quintus ignored the slight change in Kaeso's stance. Instead, he stared at Servius. "They may hold wealth, but they lack manners and etiquette. I gave swift and final lesson in attempts to covet what is not theirs to take."

Servius' eyes darted to Kaeso for the first time since they had entered, then turned his focus back to Quintus. His expression was not pleased. "Well. Not a lesson they'll need to learn twice, I am sure."

"I should hope not."

Servius was quiet for a moment. "My mind turns back to your words when we were at the docks on Neapolis. You noted the public did not hold favour with me."

Quintus gave a nod, uncertain of the senator's purpose in recalling this conversation. "You cited taxes as a valid reason."

"I did," he added casually. "Yesterday my announcement for promotion to prefect was met with uncertainty, but last night's celebrations secured votes in my favour. I believe the Senate will see my rank of magistrate to fruition when it is voted upon next month."

"Then I offer my congratulations," Quintus said, his tone neutral.

"Yet I still need to secure the voice of the people of Neapolis." Servius made a thoughtful face. "Taxes must remain as they are, but perhaps I can give them something in return."

Quintus stared. "Such as?"

"I shall hold games in the city's arena. Free to all the good people of Neapolis, with invitation extended to the Senate and Emperor, of course."

Quintus' mind galloped at the realisation of what this meant. "Games?"

"Yes," Servius replied, smiling. "Chariot races, gladiatorial contests. Wild animal hunts, pompa, and re-enactments. Theatre for comedy. Public Executions. It will be celebrated, as will be the senator who gives such a thing."

Quintus closed his eyes and took a deep breath. "When?"

"Three weeks."

Quintus' eyes went wide. "Three weeks? You expect me to organise matters of security and personal guard for thousands of spectators and hundreds of contestants in just three weeks?"

Servius' smile was smug. "And I expect it done well."

What Quintus wanted in that moment was to see the senator's head on a fucking spike. Instead, he calmed his temper and spoke with as much restraint as he could summon. "When do we depart Roma for Neapolis?"

"Tomorrow."

Then Quintus knew what he must do. "And the day after we arrive, Kaeso and I will ride for Oplontis."

The senator blinked in surprise. "Under whose command?"

"Mine," Quintus replied sharply. "We will ride for my ludus, where I will secure a band of my best gladiators."

Servius looked confused. "For the games?"

"To act as guards." Quintus refrained from calling Servius a fool, but only barely. "I would have a cohort of five hundred men if I were able, but ten of my best men will have to suffice. If I am to have trusted guards, then they will be of my choosing."

"You would trust enslaved gladiators with my life?"

"I would trust them with mine," Quintus spat out. "And if you lack trust in my judgement, then our deal is worthless."

Servius eyed him, though took his time to form response. He waved his hand toward Kaeso. "And this slave goes with you?"

Quintus replied without hesitation. "Yes."

"And I have your word you will return?" Servius raised a cold eyebrow. "Or should I keep him here to ensure you keep your word?"

Quintus' anger took him a step forward. "He rides with me."

Servius gave a smile that Quintus did not care for. "Very well," he said easily. Too easily.

Quintus briefly considered taking off the senator's head but abstained. "You will pay increased price for the time and effort of my men."

"You bargain with me?"

"There is no bargain here. Your choice is removed." Quintus' voice gave no room for recourse. "We will ride for Oplontis and return with ten men. They will be trained, fed, housed, and you will have armour and weapons made for them. They will be under my command and will not answer to you."

Servius stared at him for a long time, which Quintus returned, and it was Servius who looked away first. "Under your command, and there so falls their actions. You best hold tight rein on them, for your own sake."

"I do not need to demand their respect," Quintus replied, his voice low. "They give it, without hesitation or question, because I have earned it."

Servius sneered then, and Janus-faced—as if he bore a face like two sides of coin—his expression changed once more. His smile was alluring and pleasant. "I accept these terms. But know this, if I am to pay for gladiators, I will have them in the games as well."

Quintus replied with, "How do you expect both guard and gladiator of the one man?"

Servius' answer was simple. "If you are as good as you

claim, you will find a way." With that, he waved his hand to signify their meeting was done.

Quintus turned and walked out, fuming with rage, and headed for the courtyard in need of fresh air. Kaeso followed and Quintus turned to him. "That man is a fool."

"Shhh," Kaeso urged. "Or he will hear."

"I care not if Jupiter hears," Quintus replied, stomping to the slaves' gate at the rear of the domus. Once they were in the cobbled streets of Roma, Quintus pulled at his hair. "He is driven only by power and greed. I question my ability to defend the man when I would rather see his head used for sport in the games he now organises."

Kaeso smiled. "You will defend him because you gave him your word. You value honour more than he does, and it is evident to all who see."

Quintus let out a long breath. "My honour might see the death of me."

"Not if I have fair say," Kaeso said. He wore a smile that made his eyes shine. "Do we really ride for your home the day after we arrive at Neapolis?"

"We do." Quintus let his anger drain away. "A bright moment on an otherwise dark day."

"Dark day?" Kaeso asked. "I would have said the day was cheerful. It certainly started that way when I woke in your arms, for me at least. But if you would call it a *dark* day..."

Quintus found himself smiling now, and he put his hand to Kaeso's cheek and pressed him against the wall. "The night was one of the best of my life, I will have you know. It fell dark when we were summoned to the senator's office and we had to leave our bed. I would rather have stayed as we were and had you again."

Kaeso grinned and leaned up to kiss Quintus. "I would

rather you have me all day long but for fear of the saddle I must ride in the coming days."

Quintus bit his lip. "Then I will abstain so as not to cause you discomfort."

Kaeso laughed and slid his hand over Quintus' subligaculum, gripping his cock. "You will do no such thing. I would rather bear the discomfort of a sore arse from having this inside me," he said with a squeeze of his hand, "than the discomfort of not having it."

"The discomfort of not having my cock in you?" Quintus asked, kissing Kaeso, pressing him hard against the wall.

"An ache of need and desire I cannot put a name to," Kaeso said. His ragged breath lent him a coarseness to his words. "Quintus, my blood burns for you."

Quintus couldn't resist one more moment. He took Kaeso's hand and pulled open the door to the courtyard. "Where are we going?" Kaeso asked.

Quintus paused to give his reply. "To our bed. Or would you rather I have you here for all to see?"

Kaeso smiled and asked no more questions. He gave nothing but moans and cries of pleasure as Quintus bent him over the bed and took him once more. Too impatient to undress fully, he simply lifted his tunic and moved his undergarment aside and drove his cock into Kaeso's tight arse. The oil made it slick and painless, and when Kaeso's knees gave out, Quintus gave him pleasure he had never imagined.

They collapsed on the bed, Quintus atop Kaeso and still inside him, trying to catch their breath. "Do you think all of the house heard us?" Kaeso mumbled.

"I hope so," Quintus whispered, planting kisses along

the side of Kaeso's head. "Let them all know who claims my bed."

Kaeso sighed happily, then he wiggled his arse, seeking life from the cock still buried in it. "You yet want more?" Quintus asked.

"I will take all you have to give," he answered. "You honour the gods with your skill."

Quintus chuckled and rolled his hips, thrusting his cock in deeper. "You flatter to get what you want."

Kaeso gave a half laugh, half groan and lifted his arse for more. "Still your tongue and send me once more to the heavens."

Quintus gripped his hip and drove home, hard, causing Kaeso to cry out. Yet the master of the slave did as the slave ordered him to do. He uttered not one more word and delivered Kaeso to the heavens, where Voluptas herself, the goddess of pleasure, soared with him.

Afterwards, Kaeso could not form words or even move. He was pliant and spent, though his lips curled in a smile, and he blinked slowly as if drunk.

"Do you dare to give me orders again?" Quintus asked, kissing Kaeso's temple with smiling lips.

Kaeso hummed. "If that is my punishment, I think I will."

Quintus chuckled and tightened his hold. "I think I shall be disappointed if you do not." Quintus wrapped him up in his arms and they dozed, regardless of the busy house outside their room.

THEY LEFT Frusino for Neapolis at first light the next day. Quintus was relieved to have left Roma the day before, and he was happy to ride with Kaeso by his side. When he had arrived at the senator's villa two weeks ago, he had not imagined the possibility of finding anyone he could care for. A slave, no less.

But Kaeso had unearthed something within him. A lyre's string struck with resonating aim. Quintus was born in a world where he saw blood spilled by sword and spear, given to honour the gods, where injury took the will of men long before it took their life. In a world where it was not women who turned his head, but men, he was resigned to solitude in his ludus, with no hope of a child to call his own, to carry on his name. And he loved his life training gladiators, living in his parents' house, continuing his father's ludus, his legacy.

He had not imagined finding someone who might share his life with him. He had not thought it even possible.

But now the smallest flame of hope flickered. Quintus was careful of it, cradled it in his chest somewhere akin his heart. Afraid if he fanned the fire, it would rage and burn him alive. Afraid if he snuffed the embers, it would never light again.

"You are distracted," Kaeso said.

They rode at the front of the caravan, guards behind them and astride of the senator's carriage. "My thoughts are many," Quintus answered, not wanting to give himself away.

"Thoughts aimed in many directions rarely hit but one mark," Kaeso said with a smile.

They wore their full guard uniform, and Quintus rather appreciated how Kaeso looked in his. "You keep concern for your own thoughts. I will have concern for mine," Quintus replied, though he smiled. Then he noticed Kaeso shift in his saddle. "You have discomfort?"

Kaeso shot him a look. "I do not. And even if I did, blame would rest with you."

Quintus withheld his smile. "I would blame he who begged for it twice yesterday. My warnings went unheeded."

Kaeso glanced over his shoulder in case others might hear. Then he hissed at Quintus. "Your warnings were uttered between groans and pleadings."

"They were not."

"What your eyes say and the words you speak are like night and day."

Quintus laughed. "Then be assured, there will be no utterances tonight, by eye or tongue, for we spend tomorrow on horseback as well."

Kaeso grumbled and ignored him, yet as they rode and as the day grew late, he shifted in his saddle, and Quintus noticed him wince a time or two. "You have been too long in the saddle," Quintus said. "Would you have us stop for a moment?"

Kaeso glared at him. "I will have you do no such thing on account of me. Neapolis draws near, and the promise of a warm bath will suffice."

"Are you sure?"

"Certain." He looked ahead as they rode. "Though I would kindly ask one thing of you."

"Name it."

"No matter how much I beg when I am in your arms tonight, do not give in."

Quintus laughed, and he smiled still as they rode through the city to the villa.

QUINTUS SAT in the hot bath and watched as Kaeso sank slowly in beside him. "Do not say it," Kaeso said, his eyes closed.

"I promised I would not utter one word," Quintus replied.

Kaeso moaned as the water soothed his aching body. "And yet, if you were to offer..."

Quintus laughed. "If I were water, you could drown and still die of thirst."

Kaeso sank low in the water and smiled. His eyes were full of mischief. "If you were water, I would not ache as I do now."

"Well, there will be no 'water' tonight. You have my word."

Kaeso sighed and let his head fall back. "I will lie with regret later tonight."

Quintus chuckled. "No, you will lie with me." Kaeso looked at him then, and Quintus raised his hand. "I will keep my promise, but I shall still have you in my bed. I know of other means to an end you will enjoy."

Kaeso's smile became a grin. "I look forward to being schooled."

Quintus laughed and his chest warmed, though it had little to do with the heated baths. They bathed and re-dressed, and at their evening meal, they sat separate from the others in the courtyard. The summer nights were warm, coupled with pleasant food and pleasant company, and Quintus allowed himself to be happy.

"Returning to your home tomorrow lifts your spirit," Kaeso said.

"It does. I long to see familiar walls and faces. Oscilius will be pleased to see me return."

"And I am pleased to accompany you. To see your home and your ludus."

"Have you laid eyes upon a ludus before?"

Kaeso smiled and shook his head. "Far be it for me to see a school for gladiators when I am yet to see a gladiator."

Quintus' eyes widened. "You've never?"

Kaeso chuckled, embarrassed. "No. I hail from a quiet life of fields and valleys, and when I was of age, I took up arms against the Romans who stole my father's land. So, I have seen battle and borne witness to fights between men, but gladiators, they were not."

Quintus sighed, his high mood dampened. "The reach of Rome is long. That cannot have been easy for you."

Kaeso met his gaze. "Imagine men from foreign lands came to your house and claimed it as their own."

Quintus had to look away. "I cannot."

"Those who protested were slain, no regard given to man, woman, or child. My father fought with honour, and my mother was—" His voice cracked.

Quintus reached over and took his hand. "Kaeso, I..." What could he say to soothe when such words were not possible? "Your loss brings me sorrow. I cannot... I do not..." He sighed. "I struggle to convey adequate words, but know if I could carry your burden, I would."

Kaeso squeezed his hand in return and gave him a saddened smile. "Your words are adequate, and I am grateful for them."

Quintus put his free hand to Kaeso's cheek and kissed him on the mouth—he cared not who saw it—and let the moment of peace settle between them. "Have you eaten enough?"

Kaeso nodded and looked at their joined hands. "I have. And I have sullied your mood. Apologies, Quintus. It was not my intention, but our thoughts turned to home and unpleasant memories followed."

"Apologies are not required." Quintus stood. "Come. The day has been long and morning comes early."

When Quintus climbed into bed still wearing his undergarments, Kaeso gave a confused look. "You said there would be other means to an end. A lesson I would be happy to learn," he said.

Quintus snorted a laugh. "There will be time for schooling when we are in my bed, in my house. Tomorrow night, I promise." He lifted the blanket and extended his arm in invitation. "Though I would still have you in my arms."

Kaeso slid into the bed and settled in close, with Quintus' arm as his pillow. He was so much smaller that Quintus could easily wrap his arm around him, and after a few moments, Kaeso sidled in closer still. It made Quintus smile, and he kissed the top of Kaeso's head. "My rabbit burrows against me," he whispered.

He expected a short reply, for he knew the pet name annoyed him. But Kaeso was still and quiet, and when Quintus pulled back a little, he found him already asleep.

Quintus kissed his forehead, tightened his hold, and whispered, "Sleep well, and may Morpheus grant you pleasant dreams."

KAESO HELD no trust or even liking for the senator. He had cold and calculating eyes, as though menace and deception lurked behind them, and Kaeso was always nervous when Servius called for Quintus, and this time was no different. They were readying to leave for Oplontis when Servius summoned him, and Kaeso dutifully followed. Servius sat at his office desk, surrounded by scrolls of papyri despite the sun barely rising.

"You asked for me," Quintus said.

Servius glanced at him briefly, then went back to his reading. He didn't acknowledge Kaeso, and Kaeso did not expect him to. "I did. You remember our deal?"

"Of course. I assume you recall it also."

Servius looked up then, his stylus paused. "Of course. I expect you back by sundown tomorrow."

"A tight deadline, but not impossible," Quintus replied.

"I will have two rooms made to accommodate your men," Servius said, his gaze flat. "And I expect them to be worth the coin they cost me." He threw a purse onto the desk. "I could buy slaves for the same cost as what I pay to hire yours. Do not disappoint me, Quintus."

Quintus took the purse. "It is not in my nature to either disappoint or fail."

Servius went back to his work, so assuming they were dismissed, Quintus and Kaeso left. Kaeso knew Quintus was eager to leave, feeling the call of home in his bones. They made their way directly to the courtyard, and Kaeso snatched up an apricot, throwing it to Quintus, who caught it easily. "So you eat something in your haste to leave," Kaeso said.

Quintus smiled at him. "You read me easily."

Kaeso rolled his eyes. "The gods may as well write your moods in the sky."

Quintus laughed. "My good mood makes me forgive any lack of manners, though I shall commit it to memory to call upon should punishment seem fitting."

Kaeso led the way to the stables. "If the punishment you deem fitting takes place in your bed, you will hear no complaints from me."

Quintus laughed some more, and as they mounted their horses and rode through the stone streets of Neapolis with sights set for home, Kaeso's spirits continued to rise. They kept a fair pace, mindful of the horses, and rode until the sun was well past the midday.

Quintus cast his gaze around. "These hills are known to me. This road, this air. My home is not far now."

"I can tell. Your smile grows, the closer we draw near." Kaeso sat higher in his saddle, his big brown eyes bright in the sunlight.

"Oplontis is like no other place I have been," Quintus said. "And I have seen much of the lands of Rome. I have travelled with my gladiators, to arenas near and far. Yet there is nowhere that compares. The air is fresh off the ocean. The fields grow the sweetest grain. Even the birds sing happier songs."

Kaeso snorted and shook his head. "You are yet mistaken. You describe my own Iberia."

Quintus let out a surprised laugh. "You speak of impossible things."

"I will be judge when I see it."

"Then let us not waste time in proving a point," Quintus said, then dug his heels into his horse, let out a cry, and set off at a gallop. Kaeso followed suit, but Quintus' horse was faster, bigger for the bigger man, and he led the whole way.

Kaeso didn't mind. He rode like a freedman. When he was with Quintus, he *was* a freedman. Despite the collars around his neck, he felt free from bindings and burden. Quintus was like an armour to the lurid life he found himself in.

Maybe the gods took pity on him, for the wrongs done to him, to his home. Maybe they had shown mercy. Yet as he rode his horse and the wind carried their laughter, Kaeso couldn't help but think the gods had done more than that. They had shined on him.

He knew not how long it would last. He dared not to question it. Being ripped from his homelands and collared like an animal, he found himself worth less than the sand under his feet. A slave, yet handed to a man who treated him with kindness. Who treated him like a man.

He doubted he would ever be equal. Even with the collars removed, Quintus was a man of moral standing that was innate, not learned, and Kaeso could only stand in his shadow. So perhaps not equal. But when he was with Quintus, he could be himself.

And that was the very best of freedoms.

And so he followed on the hooves of Quintus' horse through foreign hills to a foreign town that met a familiar ocean. And atop a hill stood a villa, with grey stone walls and a guard who, upon seeing Quintus approach, opened the gates with a grin and a celebrated, "Dominus!"

Quintus slid from his horse, so Kaeso did the same, and found himself in a courtyard area of grass and fruit trees. Another smiling slave greeted Quintus warmly and took their horses, and Kaeso followed Quintus through a door and into his villa.

There were tiled floors, plastered and painted walls, long seats and carpets. Not as grand as the senator's house, but grand nonetheless. Quintus turned to him with pure happiness on his face. "This way," he said.

They walked through the reception to the atrium, past private rooms, to another large room that fronted a balcony. Quintus came to a stop at the railing, and when Kaeso stopped beside him, what he saw made his mouth fall open with surprise.

Quintus gave a nudge with his elbow, his grin the widest yet. Below them was a large area with stone walls on three sides, filled with sand, wooden striking beams, and targets well used. Men stood in military lines, wielding wooden swords and shields, wearing protective leathers, covered in sweat and determination. They struck, parried, struck again, while a huge man with a scarred face and greying black hair hurled orders for perfection and persistence.

Kaeso had never seen anything like it.

Quintus extended both arms and raised his voice. "What say you, Doctor," he yelled. "Do these men deserve your time?"

The doctor stopped and spun to face the balcony, and the moment he laid eyes upon Quintus, he grinned. "Dominus!"

All the fighting men stopped also and followed his line of sight. Then, as one, they raised their swords and shields and chorused, "Dominus!"

Quintus let out a laugh, then ran to the end of the balcony, to a stairwell Kaeso had not noticed. Kaeso remained on the balcony, not sure if stepping foot on grounds where gladiators trained was permitted. But Quintus ran through the men toward the one he called doctor. They gripped each other's forearm in welcome.

Kaeso had thought the doctor to be huge, but now standing by Quintus in comparison, they were of equal stature, as were their smiles. The doctor turned and raised his whip. "Your dominus has returned!"

The men cheered again, and Quintus clapped a few of their shoulders in pleased response. Then, he turned as if looking for someone, and upon glancing toward the balcony, Quintus saw who he searched for. Kaeso thought he might call him down, yet instead, he turned to the doctor. "Oscilius, come. There is someone I wish you to meet."

Oscilius gave orders for the men to break and rest, and they did so without hesitation before Quintus and he ascended the stairs. The grin Quintus wore was contagious, and Kaeso found himself smiling. "Oscilius, the man who joins me from Neapolis is Kaeso Agorix. Kaeso, meet Oscilius, the greatest doctor in all of Rome, and the man who raised this boy to become a man."

Oscilius bowed his head. Not to Kaeso, but in response to Quintus' words. "The making of a man was always there," he said. "I barely made sure you stayed fed and clean."

Quintus laughed. "Not always an easy feat."

The bond between them was apparent as the sun in the sky, and despite Oscilius being twice Kaeso's size and covered in scars and absent one arm, Kaeso liked him. "It is an honour. Quintus speaks highly of you."

"Gratitude," Oscilius said, then turned his focus to Quintus. "It pleases me to see you return. This ludus has missed you."

"Momentarily. I am here for but one day."

Oscilius gave him a curious frown. "For what purpose? What does the senator require now?"

Quintus sighed and put his hand on Oscilius' shoulder. "Come. Let us discuss."

Kaeso followed as Quintus led them to an office where he told Oscilius his plans to return the next day, taking ten men with him. Kaeso sat in silence as Quintus explained the senator's plans to host games and the need for additional security.

"I would go with you, to ensure the men are compliant and that you are safe," Oscilius said.

"I wish it were possible, but I need you here," Quintus replied. "To run the ludus in my absence. I would trust no one else with my house or my men."

Oscilius gave a nod. "As you command."

Quintus pulled the purse Servius had given him from his belt and placed it squarely in Oscilius' hand. "Please see there is enough food for the men and new weapons for the arena as they need."

Oscilius bowed his head once more. "You are kind, Dominus. Your men know the gods showed mercy when they led them here. They are grateful."

"My men honour the gods," Quintus replied. "Their

blood is spilled in arenas to please the gods, and in doing so, they honour me. In return, I am grateful for them."

Just then, a female slave of fair age, wearing a modest linen dress, entered the room with a tray holding a jug and cups. "Dominus," she said, her smile genuine as she placed the tray onto the desk.

"Cythereia," Quintus said, greeting her warmly. "Gratitude for the water."

"Your return brings lifted spirits," she said. Then she spared a polite glance at Kaeso. "I shall ready another room for your guest."

"No need," Quintus said. "Kaeso shall stay in my quarters."

Cythereia paused ever so briefly before she nodded. "Of course."

Kaeso pretended not to notice the double take Oscilius was not so adept at hiding, though his face grew warm and he was secretly pleased.

"I would have the baths prepared though," Quintus said, "if you would be so kind. And a dinner to celebrate before we leave again tomorrow."

Cythereia nodded again and left quietly, and Quintus poured three cups of water. He handed one to Kaeso, who took it gratefully, then one to Oscilius, before taking one for himself. He gave Kaeso a pointed nod. "Even the water is sweeter here, is it not?"

Kaeso sipped it again. "Sweeter than that of Neapolis or Roma, agreed."

"But not of Iberia?" Quintus asked with a laugh. "Your memories are tainted with longing."

"Perhaps," Kaeso replied. "Though one day you shall stand in the mountains of my home and drink fresh from the springs. There you can give apology, but until then, we wait."

Quintus laughed again. "Apology? Unlikely." Oscilius cast them both a strange look, yet Quintus made no further comment on the matter. Instead, he cleared his throat before bringing the topic of conversation back to hand. "We are to have gladiators at the games the senator plans."

Oscilius nodded. "If ten return with you now, it will leave ten to train for the games."

"I would have it so," Quintus said with a hard nod. "Then when this nonsense with the senator is ended, we can return together. Now, let us decide which men leave with me on the morrow."

QUINTUS SIGHED as he sank into the warm bath and his look of contentment made Kaeso smile. "There is nothing quite like the comforts of home," Quintus said. "Agreed, the senator's villa is more lavish, but the familiarity of one's home, the scents, the sounds, the feel of it, make it grander than all the wealth in Rome."

"You are a different man here," Kaeso said. He undressed and silently slipped into the bath with Quintus. "You are happy here."

"I am."

Kaeso was quiet a moment as he considered all the questions he was hesitant to ask. Quintus sighed. "You have something on your mind, rabbit."

"May I speak freely, Quintus?"

"When it is just you and me, have you ever not spoken freely?"

Kaeso made a face. Quintus had a fair point. "I am allowed comforts with you."

"Comforts?"

"To speak my mind."

"I prefer honesty as long as it is married with respect."

"It's what makes you a good dominus."

Quintus raised one eyebrow. "Do you think of me as your dominus?"

Kaeso's heart beat out of time. "Of course."

Quintus scoffed out a laugh. "You cannot lie."

Kaeso sighed and his cheeks warmed. "I think of you as a leader, not a dominus. Not a man who owns and forces his will, but a man who leads by example. When I am with you, sometimes I forget the collars around my neck." He reached up to touch them, checking they were still there.

Quintus made a thoughtful face. "I am undecided if that is a compliment to me as a man or insult to me as a dominus."

Kaeso's stomach dropped. "I would never insult you. If a dominus were to command a hundred men to war, he would need to threaten and beat them to comply with his order. But you, a hundred men would follow you willingly. There is no greater compliment."

Quintus smiled. "Then I thank you. But tell me, what did you wish to speak freely about?"

Kaeso looked down. His cheeks and ears grew hot. "It is of no matter."

Quintus reached over and slid a gentle finger under Kaeso's chin to have him meet his eye. "I wish to hear it."

"Oscilius," Kaeso started, then swallowed hard.

"What about him?"

"His scars? On his face, his arm..."

Kaeso was certain Quintus knew this was not what

Kaeso wanted to know, yet he answered anyway. "He was a gladiator. He took hot tar to the side of his face and his chest, and a sword took proper use of his arm. Though I would caution any man who favours odds against him because of injury. I have seen him best three men at once. He might have only one arm, but he has the heart of a lion and the temper to match."

Kaeso smiled as he remembered Oscilius' reaction to seeing Quintus. "He looks upon you as a son."

"And I look up to him as one."

"He was surprised to hear I would share your room," Kaeso said, looking away.

And there it was. Both men knew that was the true question he sought answer to.

"I have never before allowed anyone to share my room," Quintus admitted. He reached out and put his hand to Kaeso's cheek, using his thumb to free Kaeso's bottom lip from his teeth. "I have had the company of men before."

"The evidence is apparent from your skills in such matters," Kaeso whispered quickly.

Quintus drew a slow smile. "Company, yes. Lessons in pleasure, yes. Had a man stay, invited a man, or trusted him to sleep beside me, no. You are the first."

Kaeso's mouth fell open; his chest rose and fell rapidly. He stared, unblinking, and he blushed. "I am honoured." He put his hand to his forehead. "I would feel sympathy for the poor men who weren't permitted to sleep in your bed if I was not so prideful to be the first."

Quintus chuckled and he leaned over in the water to kiss him. It was with open lips and a taste of tongue, and when he pulled back, Kaeso followed his mouth until he had climbed over and straddled him. "You take liberties," Quintus said.

Kaeso rubbed himself against Quintus' erection, splashing water out of the bath. He pressed their chests together and spoke against his lips. "Your quarters, these baths, are they private?"

"You have a day's ride in the saddle again tomorrow," Quintus reminded him.

Kaeso kissed him deeply, grinding on his cock. "You promised to school me on other means to an end in the ways of pleasure."

Quintus grinned and took hold of Kaeso's hips. "Hold on to me, rabbit," he said, standing up. Kaeso wrapped his legs around Quintus and held onto his shoulders before Quintus stepped out of the bath and carried him to his bed. He lay Kaeso down, and for a long moment, they kissed and writhed, still wet from the bath, and when Kaeso was aching with the need for release, Quintus pulled away. "I will have you in my mouth," he said. "And you will take me in yours."

Kaeso blinked, his mind fogged with lust. "You would have me like that?" It was not common for men to take their slave's cock, and Kaeso was stunned by the offer.

Quintus licked his lips. "And I will savour it." Then he manoeuvred their bodies so they were both on their sides, Quintus' cock at Kaeso's mouth, and Kaeso's at his. He fisted the base and sucked the tip into his mouth, and Kaeso cried out, but he was quick to take Quintus into his mouth, and soon they found a rhythm. Rocking and moaning, and Kaeso was lost to it. The wet, the warmth, the sucking. Quintus pulled off Kaeso's cock. "You make quick work of me," he panted.

"Let me taste you," Kaeso whispered before taking him in deep again.

Quintus attempted to slow their pace, in a clear attempt

to stave off his release, but Kaeso pulled Quintus' hips closer, taking his cock into the confines of his throat, and Quintus gave him what he so desired. Kaeso groaned and swallowed, and he thought, for a blissful moment, he saw Elysium. Never before had pleasing a lover felt so good.

While Quintus was lost to his pleasure, Kaeso's need was too hard to ignore so he stroked himself and when Quintus opened his eyes, he was quick to take charge. He batted Kaeso's hand away and fisted the base again and licked the tip. "I will taste you as well," he murmured before taking him all in. Quintus fondled his balls, the sensitive line that led to his hole, and Kaeso moaned, flexed taut, and gave Quintus what he had asked for.

Quintus righted himself on the bed, and Kaeso burrowed into his side. Quintus kissed his forehead, and they lay like that for a long moment though Quintus wore a stunned expression, and it made Kaeso smile. "Tell me your thoughts right now," Kaeso whispered. "You look upon a familiar ceiling in a familiar room, as though seeing it for the first time."

"You read me well," Quintus chuckled. "I have never seen this with a man in my arms, and it surprises me how it appears different. How nothing in this room has truly changed, yet everything is unlike it used to be."

Kaeso hummed happily. "I like it here."

"As do I," Quintus said. "And though I would rather stay as we are, if we do not make an appearance soon, someone will come looking."

Kaeso leaned up on his arm. He drew a finger along the fine hair on Quintus' chest. "Promise me we will lie as we are now later tonight."

Quintus pulled him in for a kiss. "I would be nowhere else."

They dressed, and Quintus led Kaeso out to the main reception area. There was noise in the dining area, then further off in the kitchen, but Quintus smiled as he went to the balcony. "I wish you to see this," he said and went down the stairs.

Kaeso followed and could see then the arches that spanned the back of the house. As if it were built into the side of the hill, they had entered the house at ground level but there was a level underneath, which led to the sandy training arena he had seen from the balcony. There were grey stone walls, and one side led to a grass courtyard filled with fruit trees until the land became rocky ledge that dropped to the ocean.

"It is magnificent," Kaeso said. "I can see why you long for it when in Neapolis."

Quintus grinned. "Better than your Iberia?"

Kaeso rolled his eyes. "A close second."

Quintus laughed at that. "The stables are there," he pointed to the side of the villa. "But come, this will interest you."

He led Kaeso back to the sandy training grounds, to the grand arches and porticos, which afforded shade to tables and long seats, and then to a door that appeared to go under the main floor of the villa. He could hear voices, murmurs, laughter, and Kaeso knew then he was where the gladiators lived.

A stone hall lined with small rooms with metal bars for walls housed the men. They each had a bed and small table with a cup and bowl, bedding of blankets and pillows. They wore codpieces and were all huge. Not as big as Quintus, but bodies of muscles and scars. When they saw Quintus, they each stood near their bars as though greeting an old friend. Cries of "Dominus" rang out and cheers, and it was very clear that Quintus was adored by them.

Some of them eyed Kaeso with curiosity, but Quintus made no attempt at introductions. "Your doctor tells me you honour me in my absence," he said. "As gratitude, evening meal tonight will be a feast."

Loud cheers went up and it was contagious; both Quintus and Kaeso were grinning when Quintus led the way back to the portico. "I would show you where the gladiators' baths are, but I will spare you the stench."

Kaeso laughed. "Gratitude."

Quintus stepped onto the sands and took a few measured steps and stopped, as though he was committing this moment to memory.

Kaeso gave him his peace and noticed the finer detail of the stone walls that framed the training arena. Uneven lines ran through the grey stone, newer stone on old. Then he noticed the same on another wall and the back wall of the house, patches of stonework; evidence of repair. "These were once fallen," Kaeso said.

Quintus walked over and stood near him, then ran his finger along the zigzag of mortar. His voice was quiet. "Yes. Seventeen years ago the earth trembled and buildings toppled. The gods took more from me than stone that day."

"Your parents were taken from this world when their house shook?"

Quintus sighed. "Yes. Many lives in Oplontis were lost that day. The walls inside have been replastered, but like these walls out here, my heart still bears the scar." He turned back to face the house. "My father here on this very ground, my mother in the house."

Kaeso looked up at him, his eyes full of concern. "You were with them?"

Quintus gave a sad smile. "I was playing in the orchard, climbing trees. I was but seven summers old and yet I can recall that day as if it were yesterday. It is strange what one notices at times such as those, but you know what I recall the most?"

Kaeso shook his head and waited.

"The silence. There was noise of men training, but I was used to that. Yet underneath that was silence." He took Kaeso's hand. "Come with me."

Quintus led Kaeso through to the orchard and he kept his hand tight until they had walked to the centre, and they were surrounded by trees. "Tell me what you hear."

Kaeso closed his eyes and listened. "I can hear the ocean. But loudest are the birds."

Quintus smiled at him. "Agreed. The birds. I would climb trees and pick apricots or pears and sit high in the branches and listen to the birds." He looked up at the sky as the sun began to set. "That day, the day the earth shook, the birds did not sing."

"Do you think they somehow knew?"

Quintus shrugged and sighed. "In the way that nature does, yes." He reached up and snapped a pear from the tree and handed it to Kaeso. "We best go inside. Cythereia will be less than pleased should we be late."

CAPITULUM XII

KAESO WAS SURPRISED to find Quintus ate his meals with the house slaves. He understood Oscilius and Cythereia had raised him from the age of seven, but for a man to dine with his slaves—as if they were equal—certainly was not the Roman way.

The gladiators ate downstairs at the long tables in the porticos near their quarters. They didn't enter the house unless summoned, but Kaeso could hear their laughter ring loud from below. The feast of fish and meat, breads and olives lifted spirits. "The men are happy tonight," Oscilius said, looking fondly upon Quintus.

"They have earned it," Quintus replied. "I will make announcements after they have eaten."

Oscilius gave a nod before returning his attention to his food. Though throughout the meal, Kaeso could sometimes feel Oscilius' eyes upon him. No doubt he wondered what Quintus might find appealing in him, and for that, Kaeso couldn't blame him. He wondered that too.

Kaeso looked on with great affection as they all talked around their tables, and stories and laughter filled the air.

And when Quintus slung his arm around Kaeso's shoulder, he was struck with a rush of warmth that was new and strange, yet wonderful and welcome. He also noticed an exchange of glances between Oscilius and Cythereia when Quintus did this. Cythereia smiled fondly and Oscilius may have smiled too, though it was hard to tell behind the bread he shoved in his mouth.

What Kaeso was certain of was that, though there was not one drop of blood between any one of them and regardless they were slaves and a master, Quintus' house was a home. And within the walls a family.

If it were possible, if Kaeso's heart did not swell with affection for him already, it most certainly would now. To sit beside Quintus, as if he was part of his life, his home—his family—was perchance to dream.

Quintus tightened his arm around Kaeso's shoulder and leaned in close. "Your mind is troubled," Quintus whispered.

Kaeso startled a little, and when he looked at Quintus, he saw concern in his eyes. "Not troubled. My mind was elsewhere. Apologies."

Quintus leaned into him, first his shoulder, then his forehead. "You are thinking of home."

Kaeso tried to smile, and he slid his hand onto Quintus' knee. "In part."

Then, at the same time, they noticed all eyes in the room were upon them. "Gratitude for the meal," Quintus said loudly, which apparently meant the meal was over because people stood and tables were cleared and the room soon emptied. All who remained was Quintus, Kaeso, and Oscilius.

Kaeso looked up at Quintus. "Would you like me to bring you wine from the *culina*?"

Oscilius answered. "Wine? Quintus does not drink wine."

Quintus turned to him. "I will have you know, I have had it twice now," he said defiantly, the way a young man might admit such things to his father.

Oscilius was shocked, but it was Kaeso who laughed. "That would explain his inability to stand after just two cups," he said.

Oscilius laughed as well. "I would imagine so. And how did he fare?"

Quintus chuckled. "Like the gods had split my head the next day."

Kaeso laughed again. "He found comedy at the bottom of every cup, yet his humour was lacking when the sun rose."

"My humour is rarely lacking," Quintus replied. He met Kaeso's gaze and they smiled at each other, a tender moment passing between them.

Oscilius cleared his throat. "Would you have me gather the men?"

"Yes, gratitude," Quintus said. He watched Oscilius disappear out onto the balcony then turned to Kaeso, his eyes filled with warmth and joy. Then, with his fingers under Kaeso's chin, he lifted his face and pressed his lips to Kaeso's. It was a soft kiss, warm and lingering.

"You would kiss me where they might see?" Kaeso asked.

"This is my house. If I cannot kiss you here, then where?" he replied, kissing him again.

Kaeso opened his mouth for him, and their gentle tangle of tongues was slow and sweet. They never rushed or moved to deepen their kiss. There was no pulling at clothes, no frantic desire. Only gentle affection.

Quintus hummed to end the kiss, his forehead pressed to Kaeso's. "Will you tell me where your mind went earlier? I suggested home, and you answered in part."

Kaeso was still aloft from that kiss, and it took a moment to feather back to earth. "Your mouth is a potent kind of *magus*."

Quintus chuckled. "And you mock me for being drunk on one cup of wine."

Kaeso let out a dreamy sigh. "Your kiss alone could bring me undone."

"We shall attempt such undoings later," Quintus said against Kaeso's lips.

Kaeso had moulded himself to Quintus' side, draped like human fabric. He had not given mind to do so; his body acted without thought. "Do you want to know where my mind is now?" he purred.

Quintus groaned out a laugh and pulled Kaeso even closer, almost dragging him onto his lap. He was kissing down his slender neck when the crack of Oscilius' whip broke his trance. He chuckled and dragged himself away. "Come on. The men must be restless."

Quintus walked to the balcony with Kaeso by his side. "Your dominus," Oscilius announced his arrival. On the sands below stood twenty men, all looking up at them in the early night, lit only by oil lamps upon the stone walls.

"The senator has called for a duty to Rome. At first light tomorrow, I will be leaving once more for Neapolis, and ten of you will attend me. You will act as stipatores; a guard who is permitted weapon." A quiet whisper spread amongst them, and Quintus raised his hand for quiet. "You will pride yourself on the good name of this ludus—my name— and you will honour me. Do I have your word?"

Their cry was united. "Yes, Dominus!"

Quintus gave an approving nod. "Stand behind your doctor: Appias, Phaidon, Harpax, Messenio, Caius, Lars, Paullus, Arruns, Salonia, and Varia."

Ten figures moved out of formation to stand behind Oscilius. Kaeso could not make out features well in the dark, but he could see well enough to know they stood tall and proud.

Quintus turned to those still in line. "Those who remain will continue to train for the games in three weeks. Oscilius has my word and my will, and if you disrespect him," he said, "he can punish you how he sees fit." Kaeso doubted any of them would dare disrespect Oscilius. Then Quintus gave a nod to Oscilius, and the doctor dismissed them back to their quarters. Quintus went down the stairs, and this time Kaeso followed.

Quintus stood before the men he had selected. "You are chosen because you are my best. You will travel with me back to Neapolis tomorrow, and you will stay at the senator's villa. I answer to him; you answer to me. My order is final. If he puts demands upon you, you will come to me." Then Quintus paused and looked to Kaeso. "In my absence, you will seek answer from Kaeso."

Kaeso felt every eye upon him, and though he wanted to spare a questioning glance to Quintus, he kept his gaze fixed straight ahead.

Quintus turned back to his men. "Something amuses you, Appias?"

"I expected a general to be taller," he replied, and a few others laughed.

It was common knowledge that gladiators heckled and goaded. And Kaeso knew confidence was better than armour, and a hint of doubt would see a man killed. But Quintus clearly did not care for words spoken about Kaeso that way. He raised his chin and smiled at Appias. "Go stand before the target."

Appias' smile quickly faded. "Dominus?"

Quintus stared at him, unblinking. "Now."

Appias walked to where he was told. It was a large square of pressed and bound grasses with a target painted on it. Quintus went to the arsenal and took out four daggers. Metal, not simple wooden rudis, and he dropped the blades randomly across the training field, some thirty or forty paces from where Appias stood.

Quintus waved his hand toward the sands. "Kaeso, please give Appias a lesson in manners."

Kaeso's eyes widened. He wouldn't dare question Quintus in front of his men, but he knew what point Quintus was trying to make. He just doubted skill to see it made without injury. "It is dark," he said.

So Quintus turned to Appias. "Then I suggest *you* do not move."

All eyes were wide upon him, Oscilius smirked at Quintus, Quintus fought a grin back at him, and Appias looked bewildered. Kaeso took a deep breath and calmed his racing heart. He centred himself, then in one fluid movement, he somersaulted to the first knife and flicked it toward the target. Then he leapt and rolled to the second, then the third, then again to the fourth.

Appias stood at the target, eyes squinted shut. He had a blade under each arm, one between his legs, and one split the hairs atop his head.

All eyes, wide and stunned, went from Appias to Kaeso. Even Oscilius could not hide his disbelief. Kaeso rose slowly to his feet and dusted himself off, hiding his smile, and Quintus stood before his men as though not surprised one bit. "Anyone else wish to doubt him?"

They answered as one. "No, Dominus."

Quintus walked to Appias, who still had not moved. Quintus pulled out each dagger and handed them to him, and he spoke in a hushed tone. "All *jocus* aside, laugh at him again or look at him in a manner I do not care for, and I will send you to the afterlife absent your fucking skin."

Appias paled. "Dominus."

"Get back in line." Appias was quick to comply, and Quintus turned to face his men. "Rest well. We travel at first light."

They made a quiet line back to their barracks and Oscilius followed them, with a parting smile and nod to Quintus and Kaeso. Quintus looked up to the stars above, and when they were alone, Kaeso slid his hand into Quintus'. "Now it is you who is troubled."

Quintus looked down to him. "I am not troubled. At day's end, I am blessed." He smiled at him then. "Even more so with you by my side."

Kaeso's chest expanded, blooming with a warmth that coloured his cheeks. "Your words take place in my heart."

Quintus lifted his hand and drew his fingertips down the side of Kaeso's face. "You are striking in this light. Under these stars. In my house." He blinked slowly. "As a younger man, I never dreamed I would have a man who captured me as you do. Foolish dreams that I might stroll through my orchard and kiss a man under the leaves and stars."

Kaeso pulled him close. "No dream is foolish." And with that, he took Quintus' hand and led him through to the orchard. It was dark, only half a moon to guide them, so Kaeso didn't venture too far. He stopped under the trees and, still holding Quintus' hand, faced him. He could barely stand how his heart thundered. "Is this what you wished for?"

Quintus gave a nod. He looked at Kaeso in a way that stole his air and scrambled his thoughts. He cupped Quintus' face as tenderly as he dared, and kissed him. The wind caressed them, the ocean applauded, the night sky winked, and Kaeso's heart soared.

They stood there, in each other's arms, tangling tongues and breathing each other's air until Quintus broke the kiss. "I cannot decide which I want more; to have you against the tree or to take you to my bed."

Kaeso chuckled, his lips plump and wet. "I do not care too much for splinters."

Quintus laughed. "To my bed, it is."

QUINTUS DID NOT WANT to move. He lay in his bed, in his house, with a man in his arms. One he favoured dearly, one who burrowed into his side. He would have rather stayed in bed all day and do to Kaeso again what he had when they fell into bed. He would do it a thousand times. Yet the sun rose with purpose and would not be stilled.

With a parting kiss to Kaeso's sleeping head, he rose and dressed, then slipped from his room. He sought rations for his men who would accompany him, and he was found in the culina by Oscilius. "You greet this day before the sun," he said.

Quintus smiled at him. "Much to do before departure."

Oscilius took a pear from the basket and inspected it. "The look of joy upon your face is because you leave your ludus or because of who shares your bed?"

Quintus couldn't stop his smile from widening. "I do not wish to leave. I do so only at the senator's request."

"So it is Kaeso who puts the spring in your step?"

Quintus rested his hands on a basket of bread and sighed happily, though he was afraid to voice matters of the heart so prematurely.

"Oh, Quintus," Oscilius admonished. "I see it in your eyes, how you look upon him."

"I never thought it possible," he admitted in barely a whisper. "That I would find such a thing."

"Are you not deserving?"

Quintus met his eyes. "It is not a matter of my worth but a matter of my duty to my house, to my ludus."

"You can have both, can you not?"

"Before him, I would have thought not. Now I dare to think maybe..." Quintus had always been honest with Oscilius, in all matters, but he had never had to broach the subject of affections because Quintus had never found himself in such a position.

Oscilius slid the canister of olives toward him. "From the way he casts eyes upon you, I would say he *dares to think maybe* also."

Quintus grinned. "You noticed?"

"As anyone with eyes could."

Just then, Kaeso appeared half-dressed and with a look of panic in his eyes. "Oh, there you are," he said upon seeing Quintus. "I awoke and found you gone. I thought perhaps..."

"That I would leave without you?" Quintus almost laughed. "Unlikely. I awoke early to attend to matters before we depart."

Kaeso was wearing his guard pteruges, a skirt of leather straps, but was holding the chest plate. He pulled it on and fastened the straps at his sides. "Give instruction and I will see it done."

Quintus reached for him and planted a soft kiss on his lips. "See to the horses. Artemo should be in the stables already. Twice the hands should halve the work," Quintus said, and as Kaeso turned for the courtyard, Quintus stopped him. "Kaeso?"

"Yes?" he asked.

"Gratitude," Quintus said.

Kaeso blushed and his lips twitched with the beginning of a smile before he turned. Quintus chuckled and lifted the basket of rations, but Oscilius put his hand on Quintus' wrist. "He wears a collar?"

Quintus' smile faltered. "He does. In fact, he wears two."

Oscilius was taken aback. "Two? How can one man be a slave to two masters?"

"Servius bought six new slaves, Kaeso being amongst them. Though quite skilled, he showed temper and defiance, and Servius put him in my charge to ensure compliant behaviour. He wears my collar for the duration of my stay."

Oscilius' eyes narrowed. "If he is your responsibility, that means his actions are too."

Quintus nodded. "Servius is sly. He does nothing without calculated measure."

"His cunning may prove a double-edged sword."

"How so?"

"Responsibility is one edge. But knowing you hold affection for Kaeso allows the senator a hold over you."

Quintus frowned. "I had not seen it from that angle."

"And what is to become of Kaeso when your duty to the senator is at its end?"

Quintus' jaw clenched. "I... I will speak to Servius upon my return."

Oscilius gave Quintus' arm a gentle squeeze. "Withhold such talks too soon. Do not show him you have a weakness. If he is as cunning as you say, he will only use it to his favour."

Quintus met Oscilius' gaze and nodded. "Sound advice, well given."

Oscilius' eyes softened. "Tread carefully."

"I will."

"And be sure when you return that Kaeso is beside you."

Quintus gave him a nod, though his heart now felt heavy. "I dare to hope. Though now a pebble of doubt spreads ripples where before there were none."

"Doubt and fear not, Quintus," Oscilius said. "Put your mind to the task to make it so, and you will see it done. If anyone can find a way, it is you."

"Gratitude," he replied. "And know if you need for anything in my absence, send word. This ludus, this house—you—is, was, and will always be my first concern."

Oscilius gave him a warm clap on the shoulder. "Let us get the men in order."

They carried the baskets to the stables and found the sun had begun to lighten the sky. Kaeso and Artemo had the horses ready along with the carriage to transport the men. Oscilius slid the baskets into the carriage. "I will see to the men," he said, then disappeared back through the training square.

Quintus watched Kaeso tighten the iron lever in the drawbar. His arms flexed and bulged, his shoulders too, though the determination on his face made Quintus smile. Oscilius' warning now weighed heavily on his mind, but

Quintus would set it aside for now. He had more pressing matters to tend to first.

Kaeso looked up, and seeing Quintus, he smiled. "If you wish to stand and stare all day, we will see the senator's deadline pass. I would not see cause for concern, but the senator might strike issue."

Quintus chuckled. "We are well for time. But first, I wish to give you a parting gift in my room."

Kaeso looked around to see they were alone before he spoke. "Then we will surely miss the deadline, though you will hear no objection from me."

Quintus snorted. "Not that kind of gift. Though you flatter to imply it is."

Kaeso stepped in close and, with a devious smile, whispered, "A gift I am only too happy to receive. I will be happier when there is no horse riding so you can see the gift delivered directly to where I crave it."

Quintus barked out a laugh. "You are without shame." Then he pulled Kaeso's chin upward so he could kiss him before murmuring, "Tonight, you will have the gift you so desire, as deep as you can take it."

Kaeso drew in a sharp breath, his rabbit eyes darkened, and his nostrils flared. "A promise made, and one I will not allow you to forget."

Quintus kissed him again, then stepped back. "To my quarters, please. If you will." He turned and walked, knowing Kaeso would follow. When they stepped into his room, Quintus said, "I recall for the senator's party you had no clothes other than your subligaculum when you do not wear your guard's uniform."

Kaeso stopped near the bed. "Not by my choice."

Quintus turned to him and sighed. "A fact I know too well. Which is why I offer you mine."

Kaeso titled his head. "Yours. An offer I am not ungrateful for, but surely one tunic of yours would dress two of me."

Quintus chuckled as he rummaged through his clothes. "I have remnants from my adolescence." He pulled out a tunic he wore maybe ten years prior. "I outgrew many tunics before the fabric wore through. So much so it made Cythereia suggest to stop feeding me so I would stop growing." He smiled as he remembered. "Before she could sew me a new one, I'd have outgrown it."

Kaeso stood, his gaze down and filled with sadness.

Still holding the tunic, Quintus dropped his hand. "Apologies if clothes already worn offend you."

Kaeso's head shot up. "The opposite, Quintus. That you would offer me anything to wear, to own as mine is... is humbling. I am but a slave, yet you would dress me as equal."

Quintus took two long strides to stand before him and he slid his free hand to hold Kaeso's face, making him meet his eyes. "You are but a man, and you will do well not to insult one I care for."

Kaeso's eyes widened and his lips parted, shocked at Quintus' words. "You care for..."

Quintus ignored the heat in his cheeks, in his chest. "Will you take the clothes?"

Kaeso nodded quickly. "Of course. With gratitude."

Quintus stepped back. He felt if he didn't, he and Kaeso may not leave his room this entire day. "We should leave. You can put your new tunic in the carriage with the other wares."

Quintus walked to the doorway, and Kaeso's voice stopped him. "Quintus."

"Yes?"

Kaeso stood with the tunic draped in his hand. "Gratitude, for bringing me to your house, for showing me..."

"Showing you what?"

"Showing me this side of you," he answered. "For showing me there is good in Rome."

Quintus' heart squeezed. "I know your life here has not been favourable. But not all of Rome, or the men in it, are errant. At least I would like to think it so."

"If we had not crossed paths, if all I had known was the senator and his men, Rome to me would be a fate worse than death. Yet you have changed all perception."

Quintus walked back to him, took Kaeso's face in his hands, and kissed him softly and slowly. Then he said, "I wish it were not so, but we must leave."

KAESO DIDN'T wish to leave either. If it were up to him, he would stay here with Quintus for all his remaining days. Though he knew they had to go.

They went down through the training square to the stables where Oscilius stood with ten tall figures. They were in formation, and Appias, who Kaeso had thrown daggers at the night before, deliberately did not make eye contact with him, and it made Kaeso smile. Then Kaeso noticed something about the ten men he had not noticed the night before.

Two of the gladiators were not men at all.

They were tall and thin, with warm dark skin and shaved heads. And they were, Kaeso allowed, strangely beautiful. He had never heard of female gladiators, but there they stood in armour that declared them to be exactly that.

"You are ready to join me," Quintus said, his voice loud and commanding.

"Yes, Dominus," they replied as one.

He gave Oscilius an unspoken command and Oscilius ordered them into the carriage. Then Quintus and Oscilius embraced, in the way a son and father did, and bid farewell, and then Oscilius turned to Kaeso.

There was no embrace or handshake, just a nod and a warm smile. "May the gods keep you both safe. And if by chance they turn their gaze from him, then I trust your eyes to be upon him. Ensure he returns to me. Value his life as if it were your own."

Quintus closed his eyes slowly; a deep bloom of embarrassment coloured his cheeks. "Jupiter send me strength," he mumbled. He buried his face in his hands, then dropped them to stare at Oscilius. "Oscilius, my good man, you would have him value my life, yet you mortally wound me with shame."

Oscilius raised his chin. "I would offer caution to see you returned whole and in good time, that is all." He looked to Kaeso then. "No offence intended."

Kaeso chuckled. "None taken," he said. Then he grinned at Quintus. "Are we leaving?"

"Yes," Quintus said, determined now. He walked toward his horse. "And everything Oscilius just said, you can strike from mind."

Kaeso laughed and hauled himself up into his saddle. "I will confess, I have never had a father figure warn me to be mindful with his son."

Quintus sat high on his horse and sighed. "Strike it from mind. I plead of you."

Kaeso laughed again, and with a final wave to Oscilius, they started for Neapolis.

THE RETURN RIDE from Oplontis to Neapolis was long, the carriage slower to move. Quintus had been mortified by Oscilius' paternal dressing down of Kaeso. He may as well have said, "Cause harm to him and see it returned tenfold," and though he had asked Kaeso to forget it was ever said, the smile on Kaeso's face told Quintus is would not be struck from memory any time soon.

Quintus let out a long sigh. "Break words, rabbit. Speak the thoughts that have seen you smirk for half the day."

Kaeso chuckled. "It does not concern Oscilius' thinly veiled threat should I break your heart."

Quintus rolled his eyes, ignoring his ludicrous grin, and sighed. "Then what does it concern?"

"I admit surprise to seeing two women in your selected ten," Kaeso replied; his smile remained.

"Why so?"

"Because you said men. Even after selection, you refer to your men."

"Your point?"

"They are not men. They are women."

"And yet still qualify to stand with my best ten."

"I am not in doubt of ability. I simply draw attention to your error."

Quintus stared at him. "My error?"

"They were not addressed correctly."

"I say men as a collective to simplify."

"And in doing so, stand to be corrected."

"Do you question my authority?"

Kaeso smiled. "No. I question your word choice."

Quintus was torn between wanting to pull Kaeso from his horse to punish him or to kiss him. "Do you recall my other word choice in which I asked you to speak your mind?"

Kaeso grinned still. "Yes."

"Consider it rescinded."

Kaeso laughed. "From where do they hail?"

"Who?"

"The two women about whom we argue."

"We do not argue."

"Because I am correct and you are not so. So yes, there is no argument here."

"You are insufferable."

Kaeso's grin widened. "Yet you suffer me well."

Quintus was smiling despite their banter being in Kaeso's favour. He enjoyed being challenged, and it wasn't often someone did. "I will see that tongue of yours put to proper use when we arrive in Neapolis."

"Another promise I look forward to holding you to." Kaeso shifted in his saddle. "You present visions to my mind of your cock to distract me from discussion."

Quintus laughed. "Discussion of what? Your incessant debate over word choice?"

"If word choice is of no importance, then Appias

remarking on my height last night should not have caused concern. Much less a threat to see him skinned."

Quintus glanced at Kaeso. "You heard what I said to him?"

"As did everyone who stood in the training square."

Quintus huffed. "That was different."

Kaeso laughed again. "If you say so."

"I do say so."

Kaeso made a happy sound, and Quintus could hardly be angry at him when seeing his spirits lifted caused his own to do the same. After a moment silence, Kaeso said, "You still leave my question unanswered."

"What question is that? This conversation has done more laps than the Circus Maximus."

Kaeso burst out laughing and the sounds echoed through the valley. "The women. From where do they hail?"

Quintus sighed, resigned. "From the lands south of Carthage."

Kaeso nodded. "I was unaware that women could even stand as gladiators."

"Gladiatrix," Quintus corrected. "They fight only other gladiatrices or wild beasts, not gladiators."

"You have valid reason for their selection then," Kaeso said. "For I doubt when we protect the senator at his ceremonial games that we will face enemies of women or wild beasts."

Quintus shot him a look. "Do you question my judgement?"

"No, Quintus. I do not. But granted, the senator will."

Quintus almost snarled. "Then the senator shall be taught a swift lesson. Perhaps I shall ask him to stand against target as Appias did last night."

Kaeso smiled, a keen glint in his eye. "How I would wish to see that."

Quintus let his flare of temper pass and they rode in silence for a short while. "Salonia," he explained, "the taller of the two, is with a spear as you are with a dagger. Fast and unequalled in aim. Varia can wield a hammer or axe, dagger or spear. Both are fierce, and even the men they train alongside at my ludus hesitate to stand against them."

"They are striking in appearance," Kaeso added. "Beautiful, even."

Quintus glanced at him, stunned, then looked back to the road ahead. "You take attraction to women?"

Kaeso couldn't help but laugh. "Not in the regard you think." Then he grinned. "Though you wear possessiveness well."

Quintus shot him a hard glare. "I wear no such thing."

Kaeso chuckled. "Do not take as insult. It is a side of you which appeals to me. And no, my eyes linger only on the form of men, yet I can admit appreciation for a deserving woman. Are there laws in Rome to forbid such a thing?"

Quintus scowled at the road ahead and mumbled under his breath.

Kaeso smirked at him. "Would you rather I admit appreciation for a man? Such as Helier, perhaps?"

Quintus turned to him then, his face and temper thunderous. "You will do no such thing!"

Kaeso chuckled. "I certainly would not. Strike him from all thought. I only mention him to taunt you."

Quintus fumed. "You would taunt the hornet's nest and laugh when stung?"

"Not likely. But I do raise a valid point of possessiveness."

Quintus took a deep breath. "By the gods, you test all patience today. Heed warning, it is stretched thin."

"Warning noted," Kaeso said lightly, as though it was noted but completely disregarded.

"Oh thank Jupiter!" Quintus cried, nodding ahead. "Never have I been so keen to set eyes upon Neapolis."

"If you would have me—"

"I would have you still your fucking tongue for the remainder of our travels," Quintus bit out. "And when we reach the villa, the only good use I will have of your mouth is for my cock."

Kaeso grinned. "That makes promises three. Heed warning, I am keeping count, and I shall collect."

Quintus growled at the sky. "Jupiter himself tests me this day."

Kaeso smiled, yet true to Quintus' request, he stayed silent for the rest of the ride.

THE TEN NEW guards stood in an inspection line in the courtyard of the villa under the late afternoon sun. Servius stood before them, appraising the choice Quintus had made, looking none too pleased. "These are the best you could offer?" he asked.

Quintus stood beside him, hands clasped behind his back, chin raised. "You will find no better men in Rome."

Kaeso quietly cleared his throat.

"Men or women," Quintus amended. Kaeso smiled from his line with the original six guards who stood in less threatening formation to the side.

"Hmm." Servius looked at Salonia and Varia, somewhat

aghast. "I can see that." Then he let out a tired sigh. "I assume you have valid reason for these two savages standing in place of two men."

Quintus kept his gaze straight ahead. "Valid reason and sound judgement. These two *women*," Quintus spoke through a clenched jaw, "honour my name with valour and skill unmatched. If you would like a demonstration..." He turned to Kaeso. "Kaeso, please fetch Salonia her spear."

Kaeso broke the line and ran off toward the stables, and Servius frowned, uncertain. "Demonstration not necessary. You asked for command and I gave it. Success, and failure, rests on your head."

Kaeso appeared before them holding a long wooden javelin taller than he. It was smooth wood with a flattened iron point. He bowed his head and held it out to Quintus. "Quintus."

Quintus took the weapon just as Servius said, "I see you have managed to teach your slave some manners."

Quintus gripped the spear hard, his knuckles white. Before he schooled Servius in manners, he thought it best to walk away. He handed Salonia her weapon of choice. Her eyes remained trained ahead, her face void of expression except that her full lips curved in the briefest smile.

"Salonia, there is a target at the back of the training yard. It is forty paces over your shoulder," Quintus said. "I would like you to hit it."

She bowed her head. "Dominus."

Then many things happened at once. Salonia bettered her grip, and the gladiators beside her stepped out of formation to give her room to move, and even Quintus stepped back. Because next, she spun and launched the javelin high into the air, then turned back to face the senator, and the gladiators moved back to their line next to her, as if nothing had happened. They moved as one, with military precision.

No one turned to see if the javelin had struck the target. They had no need.

Servius craned his neck and his eyes widened when he watched the javelin sail through the air to not only strike the target, but in its dead centre. He swallowed hard, then recomposed himself. "Well. As I expected."

"Do you have any other questions?" Quintus asked.

"I expect a full report at evening meal," Servius replied and turned on his heel to disappear into the villa.

Quintus couldn't allow his men—and women, he conceded with a mental nod to Kaeso—to see his frustration. "You are commended," he said to them. "I shall see you to the baths, to your rooms, and see that you are fed. Sleep well. Training begins at first light."

When he was sure his men and women were done and in their allocated sleeping quarters, Quintus followed his nose to where dinner was being served. He took his seat, Kaeso sat quietly beside him, and at least Servius let them eat before he began with his questions.

No, there was no trouble along the road. Yes Oplontis, the ludus and his house were all in order. The armour and uniforms for his new guards would arrive tomorrow after midday, and yes, a full day's training would be completed by then. Word had been sent to Roma, invitations included, for the Neapolis games to be held in three weeks. Tenders were already being taken from trainers of gladiators and wild beasts alike, so yes, things were moving along swiftly.

"And I have it on good authority from the consul himself, my appointment of promotion will be announced at the games," Servius said. His air of pomp and self-importance was suffocating tonight.

"I look forward to the announcement," Quintus said. "And I have given word to my house that I shall return after your games. We are contracted to attend the Capua games following your own."

Servius stared at him. "And if your obligation to me is still withstanding?"

"Then I shall see your men are trained for my absence."

"This was not part of our agreement."

Quintus wanted to smash his fist on the table, yet instead, he clenched his hands on his lap out of view of the senator. Though his tone hid nothing. "Our *agreement* was one-sided. I am simply adding weight in my favour to even the scales."

Servius' eyes were cold. "If you think to out manoeuvre me in political games, you will be mistaken."

The tension in the room was as thick as the humidity. What Quintus wanted to do was jump the table and crack the senator's skull open, but Oscilius' words snagged like a thread. The senator held all power—not just in wealth and status—but he held rightful ownership of Kaeso. And if Quintus angered the senator, to make Quintus pay, he could simply take Kaeso away from him. So maybe Servius was not wrong to call this a game. Maybe that's exactly what this was. Winner takes all. So instead of snarling at Servius, Quintus smiled. "I would not dare think I could beat you at political games, Senator—soon to be Prefect. I will see the threat upon you extinguished before your promotion."

Servius kept his gaze cool and distant. "I should hope so. I expect the games to be the height of danger, yes?"

Quintus nodded. "Agreed. You will be exposed to the public and to politicians, to any of the military by foot or boat who may attempt to seize opportunity on your life. If anyone possesses the balls to attempt it, they shall greet the Underworld with my blade through their neck and my foot up their arse."

Helier entered and, with polite apologies, handed Servius a note. While Servius was distracted, Kaeso leaned in close to Quintus. "Permission to speak?"

Quintus was stunned. Not that Kaeso had spoken, but that he had asked permission to do anything and showed subservience. It was a far cry from the man who had been loose of tongue and manners for the entire ride from Oplontis. Quintus fought a smile. "Granted."

"Should we seek invitation to inspect the arena before the games?" Kaeso asked quietly so no one else could hear. "For full advantage of strategy."

Quintus smiled, liking how close their mouths were. "Are you giving me instruction?"

Kaeso's big brown eyes widened. Even though Quintus was amused, perhaps he had misspoken. "I am not."

"Am I keeping you?" Servius barked.

Both Quintus and Kaeso turned to Servius, though it was Quintus who answered. "Of course not, Senator," he said graciously. "Though I would like to see the layout, points of advantage, and tunnels hidden under the arena. If attack is forthcoming, I would like to be prepared."

Servius nodded. "Sound strategy. I will see it done. Now, if you will excuse me, I have important matters to attend to," he said, holding the note. He stood from the table, and before he had even left the room, house slaves were clearing the table and cleaning.

Quintus stood and motioned for Kaeso to stand also. "Yes, I believe I have important matters to attend to also. In my quarters."

Kaeso smirked and ducked his head, then dutifully followed Quintus to his room.

Quintus stood beside his bed and pulled his belt from his waist with a sigh. "He's in an insufferable mood today," he mumbled. "Do not think I took credit for your idea that we visit the arena. If I had told him it was your idea, with his given mood, he would have made example of you."

Kaeso smiled as he moved a candle to the small table beside the bed. "I did not think anything of it. I could feel the anger toward him rolling off you. I merely proposed a distraction from the direction of conversation."

Quintus lifted one foot onto the bed and undid his boot. "So you give me advice on strategy and claim credit for directing our discussions?"

"I proposed a distracting topic only to stop you from wanting to part the senator of his tongue."

Quintus snorted and began untying his other boot. "The man provides a well of frustration. It brings no surprise someone seeks threat upon his life."

Kaeso chuckled. "Hush, or someone will overhear."

"Now you tell me to still my tongue?" Quintus dropped his now bare foot to the ground and stood to his full height. "Yet at the table you sought permission to speak!"

Kaeso shrugged. He aimed for diffidence though the sad reflection in his eyes gave him away. "I want the senator to believe you have taught me well."

"Have I taught you well?" Quintus asked. "Do not think I have forgotten your misdemeanours on the ride from Oplontis. Three times you needed correcting with the threat of a lesson hard learned."

Kaeso gave a poor attempt of a smile. "When it is just us, I can be me. I forget the collars around my neck and dare imagine I am free to be beside you."

Quintus sighed and put his hand to Kaeso's arm. "Apologies. Reminding you of your position was not my intent."

Kaeso's eyes met Quintus' in the flickering candlelight. "It is not you that bears reminder but the tin around my neck."

Quintus ran his finger along the metal collar. "If my words hold any worth to you, know that when I look upon you, I see the man and not the reminder." He pulled his hand away, his mood weighted down like the very collar Kaeso wore.

Kaeso grabbed Quintus' hand. "I see the man you are as well. Not the man the senator employs. If my words hold any worth to you."

Quintus pulled Kaeso in close and planted a kiss on his lips. "More than worth," Quintus whispered.

Kaeso smiled and ran his hand over Quintus' arse. "Good. Because I seem to recall the promise of three lessons tonight."

Quintus snorted. "Is that correct?"

Kaeso pulled his bottom lip between his teeth. "Once to find good purpose for my mouth, and twice to fill me with your cock."

Quintus ground his hardening cock against Kaeso. "I begin to think you would antagonise me only to reap reward."

Kaeso chuckled, his whole body warm with what he knew was to come. "It is my sole purpose. Goad you until you threaten to fuck me, then collect on what I am owed."

Quintus pulled Kaeso's tunic off over his head. "Be careful what you wish for," he murmured, capturing Kaeso's mouth with a bruising kiss. While their mouths were fused,

Quintus untied Kaeso's subligaculum, and once it had fallen away, he gripped his cock, making him groan into the kiss. Quintus pulled his mouth away. "Lesson one. Get on your knees and open your damn mouth."

CAPITULUM XIV

WHEN QUINTUS HAD TAKEN his limit of Kaeso's mouth, he reluctantly pulled out. "You will bring me undone too soon," he said, his voice gruff and coarse.

Kaeso's lips, wet and swollen, curved in a victorious smile, and he rose to standing. "I would not complain about swallowing, yet for the ache to have you inside me, filling me, fucking me."

Quintus pulled him close, rough and demanding, and took his mouth much the same way. "You were sent by the gods to punish me, I am certain of it. I lose all wit and reason when you lay tongue to such lurid words."

Kaeso slid his hand between them and gripped Quintus' throbbing cock. "Then see me on your bed, spread and oiled, for lesson number two."

Quintus gasped, his whole body shivered. He turned Kaeso around and held him tight, letting Kaeso feel his cock against his arse. Quintus leaned down and whispered in his ear. "Kneel on the bed."

Quintus pulled his tunic off and was rid of his subligaculum by the time Kaeso was in position. Quintus took the small vial of oil and let a few drops run down the crack of Kaeso's arse. Then, with a broad hand on his shoulder, he bent him forward so his arse was a beautiful display. He rubbed a slicked finger into Kaeso's tight body. More oil and a second finger, and Kaeso was rocking back on Quintus' hand. "Enough toying with me," Kaeso whined. He stretched his back and lifted his arse, his forehead to the bedding, rolling his hips, wanting, desperate. "You deliver me to the brink of despair. Quintus, I plead of you."

Quintus oiled his cock. He pressed against Kaeso's hole and paused. "You forget what you yearn for," he said, then gripped his hips and sunk into him in one long, hard push.

Kaeso grasped for the blanket, the mattress, the air in front of him. The strangled cry that escaped his throat became an elongated groan.

Quintus fought for control, the lure of desire overwhelmed him. He wanted to slam into him, fuck him hard, so if Kaeso ever thought to beg for his cock again, he would perhaps think twice. Buried to the hilt, he wrapped his arm around Kaeso's chest and pulled him up so he could whisper in his ear. "How does your memory serve you? Is this what you wanted? For what you pleaded?"

Kaeso whined and moaned. He was impaled, held up by Quintus' cock and one arm around his chest. And the sounds that escaped him were not tormented; they were not of regret or pain.

They were of pleasure.

"Yes, Quintus," Kaeso breathed. He let his head fall back onto Quintus' shoulder, and he gave himself to use as Quintus saw fit. He lifted his arms up, his hands finding purchase in Quintus' hair, and he moaned again.

"You crave this," Quintus murmured, rolling his hips, digging deeper inside him.

"Yes." Kaeso whined, long and loud. "By the gods, yes."

"You demand the pleasure of my cock like a drowning man begs for air," Quintus whispered. He wanted to embrace his climax. He wanted to wade into an ocean of pleasure, drown in its waves. He thrust harder, deeper, and Kaeso convulsed and his cock spilled onto the bed.

Quintus had not expected Kaeso to find such intense pleasure this way. He could not believe he had brought him undone like this. But Kaeso's rigid body went lax, and Quintus lowered him onto the bed, still inside him, then lay on top of him.

Kaeso was pliant and moaning as he lay there, smiling and dazed, and Quintus need only thrust a few more times before he spilled his seed inside him. It was an intense and powerful release, and while Quintus' tongue could not find the words to do it justice, his heart most certainly did.

It had never beat for another the way it did that night.

A bond had fashioned itself, stretched itself toward Kaeso's heart the way a flower searches for the sun. It gave warmth and life. A newfound purpose.

Quintus kissed Kaeso's shoulder. "Are you tender? Was I not gentle enough?"

Kaeso chuckled. "You ask unnecessary questions. My answer is sprayed beneath me. My spent cock sends its gratitude."

Quintus chuckled and kissed his shoulder again. "And your arse?"

He hummed and writhed a little. "Uncertain. Perhaps you should deliver your third lesson to guarantee your message is clear."

Quintus laughed. "Do you not have enough of me?" Then slowly, he moved and began to pull out.

Kaeso reached behind him and stilled Quintus. "Do not fucking move," he ordered. "You are where you need to be."

Quintus scoffed and thrust his hips hard, driving Kaeso up the bed a little. He whispered hot in his ear. "You give orders as if it is me who wears the collar."

Kaeso chuckled into the mattress, his knuckles white as he fisted the bedding. "And yet you comply."

Quintus rammed into him, making Kaeso groan. "I will give you your third lesson," Quintus added, "and see that tomorrow with each step you take, a sharp reminder swiftly follows." He thrust again, as hard as he dared, and Kaeso cried out.

Afterwards, when Quintus finally pulled out and rolled off him, Kaeso lay unmoving. Thoroughly had and twice sated, he stared—drunk on pleasure—he made no sound but his smile told Quintus all he needed to know.

With a laugh, Quintus pulled him in close so Kaeso could burrow in. "You always get what you want from me," Quintus said, followed with a kiss to his forehead. "Though you may not move too well tomorrow."

Kaeso made a happy sound and burrowed in deeper, and when Quintus looked down, he saw Kaeso was fast asleep with a gentle smile. Quintus tightened his arms around his sleeping rabbit, leaned over, and blew out the candle. And there, in the darkened room, Quintus' heart beat in time with Kaeso's as, Quintus was certain, it always would.

***

THE NEXT MORNING saw training begin before the sun was fully risen. Quintus gave instruction and his men—and women—followed dutifully. He would have each guard's duties tailored to their specific skill, overlapping strengths to hide weaknesses in what he hoped was a fabric of a new guard that could not be unravelled.

Kaeso trained as the others did, though Quintus noticed him wince a time or two. He was dedicated to his efforts, never taking pause or resting but when they broke for cups of water, Quintus pulled Kaeso aside. "If you have discomfort, I could set you another task. My leather strand around your neck grants you privileges not afforded to anyone else."

Kaeso shot him a hard glance. "Your leather strand around my neck is the reason I shall not be treated with favour. How do you expect I shall be viewed as equal amongst them if I do not carry the equal weight and responsibility?"

"You are not equal to them."

"A slave is but a slave."

"You are more than that," Quintus hissed.

"My collar begs to differ."

And to that, Quintus had no reply. Instead, he looked away and spoke with petulance. "I could insist you stand aside."

"You could. Yet you will not."

"And why wouldn't I?"

"Because I do not wish it so." Kaeso looked down to the cup in his hand. "I am part of the cohort you construct, and I would ask to train alongside them."

"Cohort? We hardly have the number of a cohort."

"*Cohort praetoriae,* is it not?"

A band of armed imperial bodyguards. "I guess it is."

"Then allow me to do what I do best."

"And what is that?"

"Fight."

Quintus was again short on reply. "My first concern was for you. If you had pain—"

"Strike it from your mind and do not raise the subject again," Kaeso said. There was no bite in his tone. "Quintus, how can these guards respect me if they think I am a favoured pet?"

"A pet?" Quintus almost laughed. "You raise your hackles too often to be a pampered pet in my bed."

"I raise my hackles to you and you alone, when it serves a purpose," Kaeso shot back. "Now if you ask me to fight alongside these guards, to trust them to defend your life, then I would ask you to allow trust and respect to form."

"It is not my life you defend," Quintus said.

Kaeso almost smiled. "I could care not if the senator were struck from this world, but if anyone dare raise a weapon to you..." He let out a long breath. "They will wish they had not."

Quintus stepped in closer. "Do not let anyone else hear you utter such words. Do not speak them again. If Servius were to hear you... My collar around your neck might afford you certain grace, but treason against him will see your head removed. And as you are my charge, my head would follow yours."

Kaeso's eyes flashed. "I would not permit such a thing."

"So still your tongue and strike such thoughts from your mind, or see us both dead." Quintus spoke through clenched teeth. "Stand back in the training yard and set your mind to your task. As you so request, you will train harder than the men alongside you."

Kaeso grinned. "And women."

Quintus took a breath in vain attempt to calm his temper. "Do not test me."

Kaeso raised his eyebrows as though he had just been

challenged; his smile became a smirk. "Would punishment be lesson four?"

Quintus pointed his finger at him. "Consider this a final warning, and may the gods grant me fucking strength."

Kaeso took a mouthful of water and tossed his cup into the open barrel of water. "They did. They granted you me."

Quintus snorted out a laugh. "They granted me you, to mock me and test me."

Kaeso stepped in close and looked up at Quintus through his long eyelashes. "If you wanted mediocre, you could have had Helier when he was offered. To say you do not crave the challenge would be false."

Quintus fought a smile and nodded to the training yard. "Take your practice sword to hand and set foot upon the sands." Then Quintus grinned to Salonia and called out for all to hear. "Salonia, Kaeso here needs swift reminder of my thoughts on *mediocre*. Train against him as you would me. Do not spare him."

Salonia gave a bright grin and moved with her usual fluid poise. She held her small round shield in one hand, a wooden sword in her other, then she lowered her stance, finding her centre of balance. Kaeso was a full head shorter than she, but he eyed her with a keen smile as he mirrored her in stance and weapon.

"Let us see what the gods make of you," Salonia said as they began to circle, vying for first attack.

Kaeso grinned. "What the gods make of me is between but them and me. Yet Quintus favours your odds against me, so let us see what the gods make of that."

Salonia attacked first, Kaeso countered easily, then Kaeso struck and Salonia parried, and so it went on. Each gaining little ground or advantage; Salonia had a longer reach but Kaeso was faster. Salonia took a hit to her arm.

Kaeso wore a strike to the cheek. Both grinned as they squared off again.

After a time of equalled skill, Salonia struck left. Kaeso deflected, and upon seeing an opening in her defence, he launched at her. He grabbed her shoulder and flung himself up onto her back. He held the wooden sword, and if it had been a battle and a real sword, he could have easily ended her. Then she somersaulted, landing him in the dirt, and they rolled, only when he was on top, Salonia used her feet to launch Kaeso off her. They both scrambled to their feet absent weapons and squared off, ready to attack, again.

"Enough," Quintus called. He shook his head, amused at the two in the yard, both covered in dirt, sand, and sweat. Both were smiling as if they could fight as long as the day allowed. "Enough games. Everyone to their position on the sands. Now we practise outnumbered combat." He split them into four groups of four, then had each take turns being the one against three.

Kaeso agreed to be the first in his group to stand against the other three, and when Quintus called for practice to begin and as his three attackers struck at once, Kaeso's laughter rang loud and clear.

What Kaeso had told Quintus had been correct. Quintus could have had Helier in his bed, at his feet if he wanted. He observed Helier as he followed on the heels of Servius through the courtyard, impeccably subservient and obedient, his movements like that of a dancer. And yes, Helier would have agreed to every whim Quintus could put his tongue to, his body to be used however Quintus desired. Helier was soft of voice and touch, scrubbed clean, and refined.

Or he could have Kaeso. A man who questioned every-thing he said, who raised his voice and temper, who spoke to him like no other slave would dare. Kaeso challenged him at every turn, and Quintus could not remember calling upon the gods for patience more in all his days than he had in the last three weeks. He could also not remember being this happy, this taken. And as he stood at the yard fence and watched as Kaeso, covered from head to foot in dirt and sweat, fought off three men, striking one, kicking another, all while laughing, Quintus was certain. There was no choice at all. Helier simply could not compare.

Quintus had been with delicate men before, and he had rather enjoyed their gentle ways. But Kaeso was in bed how he was out of it: stubborn, argumentative, defiant, and rough. The mere thought of having to prove his dominance over Kaeso in bed made his cock start to thicken.

Yet the most valid reason Quintus chose Kaeso was because Helier would lie with him because he was obligated to do so. Kaeso lay with him because he wanted it. Kaeso had had his free will removed when he was enslaved to Servius, yet Quintus had offered him this choice. No consequence, no obligation. Quintus would not take what was not freely offered, and Kaeso had freely given it. By the gods, he had even begged for it.

Again, his thoughts caused his cock to harden. Needing distraction from carnal memories, he turned his attention to the other teams of fighters, and soon the delivery of uniform and weapons arrived. It was diversion enough from his thoughts to see him busy until the descending sun brought an end to the day. Quintus ordered Kaeso to go ahead and bathe while he saw his guards fed and to their sleeping quarters.

When Quintus finally went into the baths before the evening meal, Kaeso was done and dressed. "I shall meet you in my quarters. I will not keep you long," he said, dismissing Kaeso so he could bathe alone.

He made short work of it, not wanting to be absent at the table with the senator. And when the plates were cleared away and Servius had his attention drawn to his wife, Kaeso lightly nudged Quintus. "Have I done something to displease you?" he whispered.

Quintus turned to him. He sat back a little from the table, as slaves did, his hands folded in his lap, his eyes down. "Not at all," Quintus murmured in reply. "The opposite, it would seem."

Kaeso glanced up, his eyes bright and questioning, then looked back to his hands. "Apologies. I know not what you mean."

Quintus leaned and whispered, right in his ear. "You cause distraction. My eyes fall upon you and visions of you naked and beneath me last night wreak havoc on my mind. My cock then commands my mind."

Kaeso kept his face down, though he grinned. "My arse still feels it and would feel it again if you would have it."

Quintus bit back a groan. "Suggesting such in present company is not wise. I ordered distance from you after training because I cannot trust myself. My desire erases all rational thought."

"Quintus," Servius called.

When Quintus turned to the senator, he found the whole table watching. He had not realised they had held an audience. "Senator," he said with a slight nod.

Servius' stare flicked to Kaeso for a brief second before falling hard on Quintus. "I see your slave has acquired clothing."

"Yes," Quintus answered. "A tunic, already worn."

Servius raised one eyebrow and hummed an unhappy

sound. He didn't need to give further comment. His tone and the displeased look on his face said what he did not. Yet Quintus refused to offer explanation or apology. "We received the armour and weapons today," Quintus said politely. "Gratitude."

"I am yet to decide if the coin is worth the cost of the service," Servius replied.

"I would not put a price on your life, Servius. A purse of silver is pittance to pay for your safety, is it not?" Quintus sipped his wine. "And at any rate, once you are promoted to prefect, Rome will cover the cost of your new military guards. So perhaps consider it a down payment for the cost to see your promotion achieved."

Servius appraised Quintus with a cool indifference. "Continue to offer such words and I would think you favour odds as a politician."

Quintus chuckled. "Never. My place is my ludus, and it will happily forever be."

The disposition at the table was lightened, as was the senator's mood, and he soon announced he had other matters to attend and bade the room goodnight. The house slaves began to clear the table, though Quintus saved his goblet of wine and offered it to Kaeso. "Drink."

Kaeso looked around them to see who might have noticed. Upon seeing no one paid them any mind, he smiled. "I cannot drink your wine," he said.

"You can if I permit it. I do not care for wine, so if you do not want it...," he teased.

Kaeso snarled playfully at him and took the wine. He sipped it first, then savoured a hefty gulp. "Not as sweet as Iberian wine."

Quintus laughed. "Of course it is not. I could offer you

the nectar of the gods and you would reason it tasted better in Iberia."

"Because it would," Kaeso said, his smile sweet and free. "Though I offer my gratitude for the drink. Dare I say it might dull the pain of what you might do to me when you take me to your room?"

Quintus bit his lip. "Do not tempt me, rabbit. I have fought the ache in my cock half this day."

"Then let us retire for the night, and I will see you rid of all aches," Kaeso murmured.

They were leaning toward each other, their foreheads almost touching, their eyes only for each other. Quintus sucked on Kaeso's earlobe, then whispered, soft and low, "I would not cause you more discomfort. Perhaps a night to abstain would save your—"

Kaeso pulled back just enough so Quintus could see his eyes flash with offended indignation. "Abstain from me?" Kaeso breathed. "I dare you to attempt it, and I will have that ache return tenfold until you beg."

Quintus quickly grabbed Kaeso's chin, holding it tight. "Your tongue beckons trouble. Perhaps I will see it put to better use." Quintus stood, keeping his finger and thumb clamped on Kaeso's chin. He rocked his hips forward, almost bringing Kaeso's face into contact with the ridge of his hard cock underneath his tunic. Kaeso eyed the bulge and smiled, and when he gazed back up to him, Quintus was unsure which of them was getting what they wanted the most. Quintus slid his thumb from Kaeso's chin, over his lip, and into his mouth, making Kaeso suck it. "My room. My bed. Now."

Kaeso leapt to his feet and disappeared before Quintus could clear his thoughts enough to walk. He strode with determined purpose to his quarters, pulled back the curtain, and slid inside. Kaeso was kneeling on the bed and Quintus could see his erection tenting his tunic. "I was unsure how you wanted me."

Quintus walked directly to him, grabbed his face with both hands, and pulled him up for a deep, deep kiss. When he felt all resistance leave Kaeso's body, when he surrendered into him, Quintus pulled back. "Tell me, rabbit, why I should not bend you over this bed and bury my cock in your arse?"

Kaeso gasped. "Because my tongue beckons trouble," he replied breathily.

Quintus smiled at him. "Did you speak out of turn so I would shove my cock in your mouth?"

Kaeso smiled but shook his head. "Of course not."

Quintus laughed and drew him in for a brief kiss. "I do not believe you. Now undress me and put your mouth to task."

Kaeso pulled up Quintus' tunic, then undid his subligaculum, revealing his hard cock. Kaeso looked up at Quintus and smiled. "My mouth's purpose is for your completion. You will give it to me or see what trouble this tongue can truly beckon."

Quintus was about to caution him, but Kaeso opened his perfect lips, flattened his tongue, and took him into his warm, wet, mouth.

THE NEXT DAY, Servius summoned Quintus to his office. Quintus entered, and as always, stood two paces from the desk, feet parted, hands clasped behind his back. "Senator."

Servius looked up from his papyrus and set his stylus

aside. "You requested inspection of the Neapolis arena, and I made it so. You will have access, two days hence."

Quintus nodded. "Gratitude, Servius."

"I assume the training of your men is going as planned?"

"It is."

"And it has been said you grow fond of my slave." Servius gave a sneer. "The defiant one."

Quintus' blood ran cold. "Your slave? Does he not also wear my collar?"

Quintus realised he must not have hidden his reaction too well because Servius' sneer grew smug. "For the time being."

"For the duration of my service," Quintus reminded him.

"Indeed," Servius said, changing to pleasant and obliging in that Janus-faced way he did. "He's yours for the duration of your service, of course." He picked up his stylus and turned back to his work. "What purpose he will serve me when you are gone will remain to be seen."

Quintus felt wrong in his body, both hot and cold at once, like he could be taken ill at any moment or burst into a fire of rage. He could not even form words to address the senator as he departed. He simply clamped his jaw shut, fisted his hands, and walked out.

CAPITULUM XV

KAESO KNEW something was wrong as soon as Quintus appeared at the training yard. He had spent the morning giving strict instruction but with good humour and open expression. Yet upon returning from words with the senator, Quintus stood with his arms crossed, jaw set, and waves of anger rolling off him.

Even Salonia saw the difference in him, eyeing him with curiosity and caution. "He is not pleased," Kaeso said as they exchanged weapons and shields.

"I would pity the soul who crosses him today," she replied. "I have seen that look in him but once before."

"And how did it end?" Kaeso asked, fixing the shield to his forearm. "I have only heard him offer hollow threats."

"Not well." Salonia made a face, then her eyes pierced his. "Be warned. His threats are far from hollow. If he issues a warning to whip a man to ribbons, he will do it if pressed for a reason. I have been witness."

Kaeso made the pretence of fixing a strap on his armour. "Reason?"

"A new gladiator swung for the doctor."

"Oscilius?"

Salonia gave a nod. "Quintus flogged the man until he begged for death, then sent him to the mines. No one dare think about provoking Oscilius after that, much less with a weapon."

"You two!" Quintus roared at them, bringing all training to a halt. Salonia and Kaeso stared at him, struck by fear at his tone. "You would stand and break words? Or should I take up a weapon and give you both a fucking lesson in duty?"

Salonia bowed her head. "Apologies, Dominus." She quickly took her place in the training yard, and Kaeso followed.

Quintus grumbled at them, though he began to pace, barking orders at someone else, and Salonia and Kaeso continued to train without another word between them until their day was done. Quintus gave orders for them to clear away their weapons and be ready for the baths as he turned on his heel and stormed into the villa.

Salonia let out a breath and shook her head at Kaeso. "I thought perhaps he might spare you from threat, given his favour toward you. But I was mistaken."

Kaeso picked up a pile of shields and carried them to the stables. Salonia took practice swords and walked beside him. "I should not have pressed for questions. Apologies," Kaeso said.

As soon as they entered the stables and were hidden from view, Varia took hold of Salonia's arm. "What foolishness causes Dominus to question you?"

"The foolishness was mine," Kaeso said.

Varia glared at him. "Dominus will not punish you as he would one of us."

"How so?" Kaeso bit back at her. "I am one of you."

"You sleep in his bed. You sit beside him to eat," Varia hissed back at him. She wasn't as tall as Salonia, but her glare was fierce.

"I stand with you as a guard," Kaeso snarled back at her. "Stripped of free will, the same as you."

Salonia put her hand up and tried for calm. "It was foolish on both our parts. A mistake that will not be made again." Then she turned to Varia and stroked a gentle finger along her cheek. "Apologies to you."

Varia's voice cracked. "Give him reason to part us and—"

"Shhh," Salonia whispered.

"He will not separate you," Kaeso said quietly. "He said as much. It is why you are both chosen for this purpose. He could not take one without the other."

Salonia tucked Varia under her chin and shot Kaeso a look. "Those were his words?"

Kaeso nodded. "As true as I stand here."

Salonia grinned and Varia closed her eyes with a sigh. Kaeso moved to the door to leave them alone in the stables. "Now I must go and attempt to soothe the beast," he said, looking up at the villa.

"May the gods be with you," Salonia said.

Now Varia smiled. "A poet would fare better odds at soothing a volcano."

Kaeso chuckled, but with a duck of his head, he made his way to the villa. Salonia's words gave him pause. She had seen Quintus flay a man of the skin on his back, then send him to the mines, a cruel and certain death. Admittedly, the man had raised a weapon at Oscilius, and Quintus loved Oscilius like a father; it seemed a fitting punishment. But to hear it and to see Salonia's reaction to Quintus' anger... Kaeso could not reconcile the kind and gentle man he knew with the one he saw and learned of today.

He had to wonder what lay at its cause. What could the senator possibly have said to him to warrant such a reaction?

Kaeso checked Quintus' room but found it empty. There was no sight or sound of him in the villa, so Kaeso assumed he was on important business. He bathed the best he could, using oil and a scraper, and when he was re-dressed and the evening meal was served, Kaeso found Quintus already seated.

He had not come for him, to check on him, to collect him for their meal. Quintus had not looked for him at all.

Kaeso sat beside him, seated back a little, and he couldn't see the senator through Quintus, though he heard him bumbling on with his matters of importance that Kaeso could care less about.

Quintus was quiet, save some subdued replies to questions asked, and the senator—and the night around them—droned on and on. When the senator left and the table was cleared, Quintus turned, reluctantly it would seem, to Kaeso and sighed. Yet, without a word spoken between them, he stood from the table and walked away. Kaeso scrambled to follow, and when Quintus slipped into his room and sat on his bed, Kaeso took position on the floor at his feet.

"Quintus," he said, his head bowed. He attempted a determined voice but couldn't find the strength. "Have I offended you?"

Silence.

"I offer humble apologies if my behaviour at training was anything less than desired. It was not my intent to show disrespect, and it bears no reflection on you but on myself and myself alone. It was not Salonia's doing. She cautioned me to silence, yet I pressed for questions."

"Kaeso," Quintus said, his voice weary and worn. "Look at me."

Kaeso raised his head and saw the voice matched the man. "You are troubled."

"I am," he said. He let out a sigh and ran a hand through his hair but offered no other words before he sighed again. "It is honourable of you to take blame from Salonia."

"Fault and blame both lie with me," Kaeso said, looking down to the floor again.

"To which questions did you press her for answers?"

Kaeso looked up then, and seeing a sadness on Quintus' face, he knew he must speak the truth. "I saw you were angry after meeting with the senator," Kaeso whispered. "She said she had seen you wear that rage once before. When a new gladiator raised a weapon at Oscilius."

Quintus closed his eyes. "Yes." He sighed again, and when his gaze met Kaeso's, he said, "Both times people have threatened what is mine."

Kaeso blinked in surprise, then whispered, "The senator threatened you?"

Quintus scrubbed his hand over his face and shook his head. "It was thinly veiled and indirect, but a threat nonetheless."

Anger burst in Kaeso's blood. "We shall—"

"We shall bide our time and deliver a swift lesson when least expected," Quintus said. He reached out and ran his thumb along Kaeso's chin. "I did not mean to cause distance between us. I only needed time to gather my thoughts and direction."

"Tell me what to do," Kaeso said, looking up at him with

his big brown eyes for which he knew damn well Quintus held a soft affection. "Name it, and I will see it done."

Quintus held out his arms. "Come up here, rabbit."

Kaeso was quick to follow orders and crawled onto his lap, finding warmth and comfort. He put a hand to the side of Quintus' face and looked into the depths of his eyes. "Whatever you need from me tonight, it is yours."

Quintus drew back on the bed and pulled Kaeso with him so they lay down, nestled in each other's arms. "Just to hold you," Quintus whispered. "For tonight, that is all I ask."

Kaeso clung to him and burrowed in like he always did and planted a kiss on Quintus' chest. "I would lie here until the gods called you home, Quintus."

Maybe it was the worry, maybe it was how hard he had trained all day, or perhaps it was the warmth and refuge of Quintus' embrace and the beat of his heart against Kaeso's ear, but sleep came easily. Though he couldn't be certain, whether it was real or a dream, though he swore he felt the press of Quintus' lips to his head and a solemn and fervent vow whispered, "I vow it, no god or mortal man will take you from my arms."

QUINTUS FOCUSED on training and attempted to strike sullen thoughts from his mind. His guards trained hard and not a word was spoken amongst them. He felt guilt for raising temper and voice at Kaeso and Salonia the day before. They *had* been talking, but his anger was misdirected.

He should have voiced issue at the man deserving of his

anger, but threatening to split Servius' skull if he attempted to keep Kaeso from him would get him nowhere.

And, Quintus reasoned, his display of foul temper had given his guards new focus. They pushed harder, they had found new vigour, they saw more tasks completed than any day prior.

They also fell to the sands, exhausted, when Quintus called it a day. "You honour me with your dedication today," he told them. "I will see the culina serves larger portions and cut fruit after the bread."

He received a round of grateful smiles and murmurs of gratitude, and Kaeso rewarded him with a fond gaze. Quintus chewed on his lip so he would not return it in front of his men. *And women*, he added mentally, then sent Kaeso a mental jab and found himself smiling.

Quintus recaptured his thoughts and announced, "Tomorrow we will conduct inspection of the Neapolis arena. Gallio, Oppius, Salonia, Varia, Kaeso, and myself shall attend. The rest of you will remain and train. Phaidon will take charge, and you will answer to him in my absence."

Quintus gave a pointed gaze to Phaidon, and he received a determined hard nod in return. Phaidon had been with him for years, and he knew the routine, and importantly, Quintus trusted him.

They were dismissed, and as Varia and Salonia brushed past Kaeso, Varia smirked at him. "You can calm the beast," she whispered, though Quintus heard, "Evidence is apparent from his manner today."

Quintus watched as Kaeso bit back a grin as the other guards disappeared into the baths. Then he turned to Quintus, gifting him a warm, almost shy smile; a welcome sight in the fading sunlight. "Shall we clean up before we are called to eat?" Kaeso said as he neared.

"We shall," Quintus replied. "Or would you prefer a private scraping down in our quarters?"

"I fear our absence at the evening meal might raise concern," Kaeso replied. "I can assume that look in your eye to mean you intend to do more than scrape me down."

Quintus grinned. "You can read me that well?"

"As clear as the sun in the sky, Quintus."

He laughed. "Though you might be correct. If we start anything now, we will be sure to miss a seat at the senator's table."

"Agreed," Kaeso added, his smile wide.

"Then we shall save it until we have retired for the night."

"Is that a promise?"

Quintus licked his lips, and the grin he fought won out. "Do not doubt me, rabbit."

"You know I hold you accountable for your promises."

Quintus laughed and nodded toward the villa. "To the baths and see yourself clean. I will see the culina to keep my promise for more rations for my men."

"And women."

Quintus growled at him, but all in good humour. "Be done before I find you naked in the baths and you will regret the lack of oils at hand."

Kaeso smirked and turned to the villa. "It would be no regret on my behalf," he said as he walked away.

Quintus took a calming breath and headed in the opposite direction. He found the house slaves in the culina and requested, with all his charm and dashing smiles, to provide extra food and cut fruit for his men.

And women.

By the gods, Kaeso was as infuriating as he was infatuating.

Quintus gave Kaeso ample time to be done in the baths and when he entered the humid room, he found him clean and re-dressed. Kaeso appraised Quintus for a long moment, with heated eyes and a lick of his lips as though Quintus was a tasty display of roasting meat and Kaeso a starving man. He swallowed hard, then lowered his gaze. "I should give you privacy," he murmured before leaving.

Quintus watched him leave and let out a breath. His body wanted Kaeso; his cock longed for the warmth of his mouth or arse; his arms longed to hold him. He wanted to taste and kiss him, but he knew he had to show patience. He had to sit through an insufferable meal with Servius first, then he could savour every moment with Kaeso after.

And suffer through the meal with Servius he did. Quintus understood the mounting pressure that Servius had found himself under, though his short temper had all his house slaves on their toes. Helier, usually the most accommodating who didn't dare put a hair out of line, sent a few well-aimed glares at Quintus and Kaeso as though they were the cause of conflict.

Quintus could feel the rumble of a growl in Kaeso's chest each time Helier looked their way, and he put a settling hand on his knee under the table.

Or maybe it was being in the vicinity of Servius after Kaeso knew the senator had threatened Quintus in some way. Quintus had not explained to Kaeso what Servius had implied because he knew Kaeso would react in a way that would end far from favourably.

After the senator had ordered Quintus be ready to depart for the arena after the morning meal, he left with a flourish, and his body slaves quickly followed. Quintus watched them leave, and when he was sure they were out of earshot, he leaned in and whispered to Kaeso, "Hold your temper in their company. Raising your hackles at your dominus or his favoured slave will see you beckon stern reply to us both."

He huffed. "I do not care for the way they cast eyes upon you."

Quintus fought a smile. "Redirect your anger and see it reap reward."

"Reward?"

"I believe I am in debt a promise," Quintus murmured. "I will see a thorough end to your anger."

Kaeso smirked. "Thorough. A second promise to collect." He stood, then paused. "Do you find purpose in delay?"

Quintus laughed and got to his feet. "I dare not or fear the wrath of the one who waits."

Kaeso chuckled as he stood aside for Quintus to lead the way. Quintus walked to his private quarters and held open the curtain for Kaeso to enter, then followed him. Kaeso went to the bed and wasted no time in pulling his tunic over his head, then untied his subligaculum, letting it fall away to stand completely naked. His cock hung half-hard, his eyes dark, his lips wet from his tongue.

"You waste no time," Quintus said.

Kaeso looked up and down his still very-clothed body. "And yet you delay." He collected one of two new vials of oil and raised an impatient brow at him.

"You found more oil," Quintus said, slowly pulling off his belt.

"When you insisted we bathe apart, I put my time to good use," Kaeso explained. He laid the corked vial on the bed, then went to Quintus' feet and began to untie his boots. "I found Petilia and requested more oil. She offered one, to which I explained you were gifted with a horse cock, so she supplied a second vial."

Quintus blanched. "You did not!"

"I did," Kaeso said, laughing. He pulled off Quintus' second boot, then still on his knees, he lifted his tunic and began untying his subligaculum to reveal the cock in question. He nudged the hardening length with his nose and sucked it briefly into his mouth. "And I told no untruth," he said before taking him in again.

Quintus pulled away from the warmth of Kaeso's mouth and lifted him onto the bed. He made good on his two promises, and Kaeso was so thoroughly met with pleasure, he could not even raise his voice in gratitude. He opened his mouth as if to speak, raised his hand, but let it fall heavily back to the bed, and sighed.

Quintus laughed and pulled him into a sated embrace, and neither man moved until morning.

SERVIUS WAS ESCORTING Quintus to the Neapolis amphitheatre, so Servius had requested Quintus and the guards accompanying him wear full armour. Not because he thought the threat of attack on this day was possible or even likely, but because he wanted the grandeur of his presence on full display.

Kaeso grumbled as he fixed his helmet, making Quintus laugh. "The look suits you," Quintus said, earning a murderous glare from Kaeso.

"I look like a prized bird dressed for public slaughter."

Quintus inspected the red plume of feathers atop Kaeso's helmet, trying not to smile. "The red of Rome suits you."

Kaeso's murderous glare threatened to pierce Quintus' skull. "You can strike that fucking thought from your mind. The day I stand as a Roman will be the day the Underworld greets me."

Quintus was still smiling when he lifted Kaeso's chin with one finger so their eyes could meet. "I care not on which lands you stand, only that you live. Cast all mention of the Underworld from thought. The very notion that your heart might stop beating causes mine to ache, so mention it no more."

Kaeso's eyes widened at Quintus' declaration. "My heart as well, should you be the one to go."

Quintus leaned down and attempted to steal a kiss, but the nose guards of their helmets met instead. He tried again, head tilted, but met only the clang of metal. He growled, and Kaeso laughed, reached up, and cupped Quintus' jaw in his hands, and brought their helmets together. Foreheads and nose guards pressed as one, he stared into Quintus' eyes. Not a word was broken between them, just silence and an unspoken acknowledgement that their declarations of heart and purpose were true.

Voices outside their quarters startled them apart, and upon inspection, they saw that Servius and his entourage were ready to leave, save Helier, who tended to the perfection of his master's toga. "You are ready?" Servius asked.

Quintus nodded and looked to Gallio, Oppius, Salonia, and Varia who stood armed and armoured. "We are."

"Then to the arena," Servius said. "But first a stop in the forum."

"The forum?" Quintus pressed. Why had he not mentioned such a visit before now?

"For business matters that are my own," Servius said. "This concerns you?"

Quintus wasn't sure how the senator would fare walking through an open market filled with citizens, fleet men, and slaves, none who seemed to hold the senator in good favour. He would be an open target.

Quintus smiled. "No concern at all."

CAPITULUM XVI

THE FORUM of Neapolis was a grand market. A large open square with its centre open to the skies, lined with taverns or stores selling breads, meats and fish, oils, shoes, and wool. Filled with Neapolis' finest citizens wearing delicate threads and elegant jewels, out for a stroll and immersed in polite conversation. Or slaves, wearing threadbare cloaks scurrying with their wares back to their masters. Soldiers and fleet men from the docks came for women and wine, staggering in the alleys after too much of both.

It was an eclectic populace, and Quintus ignored the stares and scorn. He cared only for any threat against the senator and his men, and the political issues the citizens had with Servius were of no concern to Quintus.

Servius cared not that some people sneered at him. He simply raised his hand as if greeting dear friends and announced, "I bring to you the Neapolis games! I will see to more bathhouses! I, Servius Atrius Augendus, Magistrate-elect, do this for you, for the good people of Neapolis!"

A simple walk through the streets had become a political campaign, and Quintus had to admit, it worked. Sneers became curious ears, and after promises of a better city, the scorn was all but gone. Not all, but mostly; a few citizens still lingered with barely concealed loathing on their faces.

They entered the forum square and Servius waved to the public as though he stood as the emperor himself, and Quintus assumed the brief detour to the forum was for public viewing, but then Servius made for the far corner to the basilica, where city officials kept their offices. There were stairs leading up to a second floor, and when Servius met the first step, he turned to Quintus and said, "No need for you to join me. Stand here and be sure no one enters."

Shocked but obliging, Quintus gave a nod, and the senator disappeared up the stairs with Helier on his heel. Quintus didn't miss the smug look Helier gave him and Kaeso as he followed his master dutifully. He also didn't miss the low growl that came from Kaeso.

"Keep a civil tongue," Quintus murmured gently.

Kaeso's helmet did little to hide his contempt. "He behaves as a pompous fool."

Salonia, who stood behind them, said, "Which one?"

Kaeso snorted. "Both." He and Salonia smiled, and Quintus found it hard not to join them.

"Still, our purpose remains," Quintus said. He had Salonia and Varia stand guard a few steps up, hidden from view, and Gallio and Oppius stood at the foot of the stairs. And so they waited. And waited some more.

Quintus eyed the vendors' stalls, as he did the people in them. He already had the exits surveyed and he monitored anyone who seemed a likely threat. And still they waited. Kaeso stood beside him and Quintus noticed how his gaze kept returning to a particular stall across the square. "What do you see?" Quintus asked. "Someone watching us?"

"Not that I see," Kaeso replied.

And yet he still looked. "Something else caught your eye?" Quintus asked. The stall in question sold a range of goods, herbs mostly.

"Something from my homelands," Kaeso murmured. "Something I have not tasted in a lifetime."

Quintus turned to Gallio and Oppius. "Hold position," he ordered. Then to Kaeso, he nodded toward the stall. "Show me. We have stood here half a day already in this unforgiving heat. Come show me what you long for."

Kaeso walked to the stall in question and he grinned at Quintus. "The smell takes me back to my mother."

The market was filled with different aromas, not all of them pleasant. But this was. "What is it?" Quintus asked as they neared. He could see a man stirring a pot, and he could now smell what Kaeso talked of. It was sweet. "Is that honey?"

"It is," Kaeso replied, his smile wide now. "Dates, stuffed with nuts, then rolled in salt and cooked in honey."

"What is it called?" Quintus asked him.

He grinned. "My mother called it 'only one, take only one, Kaeso' as I would take two and run into the fields."

Quintus laughed. "I like your story very much." Then he turned to the man cooking. "How many *sestertii* for two?" He held up two fingers but then turned back to look at his guards still standing at the stairs. "Wait," Quintus corrected, "how many sestertii for six."

Kaeso's eyes widened with his smile. "Quintus? How can you…?"

Quintus took a purse from his belt and gave the man his money in exchange for six small treats in a reed basket. When he took the basket, he found Kaeso looking up at him, his eyes full of wonder. "I would pay ten times the coin just to see that smile upon your lips," Quintus replied quietly.

Kaeso blushed and he blinked rapidly. "I am without adequate words... I, I, Quintus, I cannot ever repay you."

"You owe me nothing." Quintus gave him a shy smile; then he almost laughed. "I am rumoured to be one of the most hardened trainers of the best gladiators in all of Rome, yet you cast me that look but once, and I stand a fool."

Kaeso laughed and ducked his head, embarrassed, before meeting Quintus' gaze. "And I once swore to the gods I would leave Rome, but now I... I have reason to stay."

And as the market swarmed around them, they stood oblivious to it all, aware of only each other. Their smiles, the hint of promise in their eyes.

"Apologies," a woman said, trying to get to the stall. "If I could trouble you to step aside."

"Oh," Quintus replied, startled. "Of course."

They walked back to the stairs, and Quintus held out the basket. "Only one, take only one, Kaeso," he said, repeating the words from Kaeso's favoured memory, earning him a special smile. Everyone was stunned and unsure what to make of this gift, so Quintus explained. "Fault lies with Kaeso. A treat from his childhood, the aroma begged for purchase."

They each took a honeyed date and bit into it, their reactions mirrored around the six of them. Wide eyes and groans of pleasure. Even Oppius mumbled, "By the gods above us," as he hurried to eat the remainder.

Everyone laughed and chewed—Quintus had never tasted anything like it—just as a voice sounded atop the stairs. Servius was coming down! Each guard took their post, standing tall and stoic, except for subtle swallowing and sly smiles. Salonia motioned to Varia to wipe a drop of salted honey from her lip, and she wiped a panicked hand over her mouth as Servius descended the stairs.

He stopped, looked at each of them, then to Quintus. "Everything in order?"

Quintus gave him a nod. "Awaiting your instruction."

"Then to the arena," he said, back on display, waving his hand to the people as he walked.

Quintus fell into line and risked a glance at Kaeso, who sucked a sliver of honey from his thumb. And with that, Quintus had to make himself not smile the entire walk to the arena.

QUINTUS HAD BEEN to the Neapolis amphitheatre many times. Though he was familiar with the elaborate underground *hypogeum*, the tunnels and caged rooms beneath the arena floor, he was not so familiar with the access and stairs to the higher-level tiered seats.

As they walked into through the Grand Entrance—may the gods forbid the senator use an entrance reserved for the public—Servius turned to Quintus and waved his hand as though he had designed and built the amphitheatre himself. "Which areas are you most concerned with?"

Quintus ignored his pompous tone. "I am quite familiar with the hypogeum," he said.

Servius made a disgusted face. "Yes. I would think so."

Quintus ignored that remark as well. "I would like to see where you will be seated during the games. I would also view the entry gates close to and around your viewing balcony."

Servius sighed but waved his hand and led the way to the large arch that he and other senators—and the emperor

—would use. Stairs led to a short hallway, all elaborately decorated of course, then to a large room that opened out into the arena.

The room was of carved stone and marble tiles, painted plaster walls, with elaborate seating, and no expense spared. The opening to the arena was a large window, fitting two rows of six seats across, with *velarium* sails to shield the biting sun.

"One entry point," Servius said, pointing to the door. As though his insight was superior to Quintus'.

"Correction, Senator," Quintus said. "There are two entry points, two escape points. The door we entered through, and—" He gestured broadly at the massive opening to the arena. "—this."

Servius blinked. "You assume one could scale a stone wall to reach this balcony?" He leaned and peered down to the arena floor. "It's twice your height."

"Scale it, not likely," Quintus said. "Though perhaps I could ask Salonia to stand in the arena and aim her spear?"

Servius looked at Salonia, then back to Quintus. "A display not necessary."

"I could stand down there and launch any weapon if my target made my task easier," Quintus said.

"Easier?" Servius repeated.

"Yes, easier," Quintus replied. Then he stood at the balcony window and raised both hands, waving them as the senator would to any crowd.

"I must address the people," Servius barked defiantly. "It is my duty!"

"And seeing you live to take your desired promotion is mine," Quintus shot back in a tone Servius was not accustomed to. "You must use precaution, or instead of your wife choosing silks to wear to your inauguration, she'll be choosing fabrics for your funeral shroud."

Servius stopped at that as realisation quickly doused any flame of argument. His indignation replaced his anger. "Then by the gods, pray tell, what do you suggest?"

Quintus sighed as he gave it thought. "We move the seating to leave a walkthrough in the centre. You stand one step back for your speech and will have a clear retreat path if required. We have shields behind the balcony, out of view from the people." Quintus walked to the side and looked over at the next private senators' room. "Find out which dignitary will take the rooms closest to yours, and tell me, would you call them *amicus* or *inimicus*? Do they have their own agendas? Do they see you as a threat?"

Servius was not so indignant now. "Yes. I will press for information. Forgive my temper; it raises with this insufferable heat."

"There is nothing to forgive," Quintus replied. "Though if you are feeling ill-effects from the sun, perhaps Oppius and Gallio can see you returned to the villa, post haste. I and the three remaining guards can go over our steps in the arena. We will return as soon as we are done."

Servius gave pause, then wiped his forehead with the back of his puffy hand. "Yes, I think perhaps that would be wise." He clicked his fingers at Helier, who quickly took his arm as though Servius was suddenly without the ability to walk unaided.

Quintus resisted rolling his eyes, but he, Kaeso, Salonia, and Varia all stood in silence until no sound of Servius and Helier remained. It was Kaeso who spoke first. "I do not care for how he speaks to you."

"Strike it from mind," Quintus replied. "Voicing such concerns with him would be a fruitless effort. He speaks with little concern for others because he *has* little concern for others."

"Still," Kaeso countered. "Your temper would outmatch his on every front. It would be a swift lesson in manners on his behalf should you be willing to teach it."

Quintus snorted out a laugh. "To take aim at a senator is to take aim at Rome. At least, that is how he would see it." Then, he stood at the balcony, hands resting on the ledge, and overlooked the arena. He gave Salonia a quick smile. "Ever seen the sands from this perspective?"

She shook her head slowly and stood beside him. "And I am not likely to again."

Varia stepped next to Salonia. "This view belies its size," she said gently. "It looks so small from here."

Quintus took a moment to take it in; then he smiled at Kaeso. "Have you ever seen a Roman arena?"

Kaeso shook his head. "Never."

Quintus pointed to the huge gates at one end. "That is the Gate of Life, where gladiators enter and parade to the emperor or hosting senator." Then he pointed to the gate at the opposite end. "And that is the Gate of Death."

"Where the fallen leave the arena," Salonia finished.

Varia said, "The gods demand blood, and it is here they receive it."

They stood in a respectful silence until Quintus spoke. "Come. Let us take a look in the belly."

"In the belly?" Kaeso questioned.

"Under the arena," Quintus clarified.

Quintus noted the entry arches, the stairs, the vantage points, the exits. And the first thing he noticed when they took the entrance to the underground was the smell. Even though he had stood amidst it a thousand times, he would never get used to it.

"What is that foul stench?" Kaeso asked from the gate, his forearm pressed beneath his nose, barely keeping from gagging.

Quintus smiled at him. "That is the smell of blood, shit, and piss. The smell of animals—goats, bulls, wild pigs—used for the games. Gladiators and convicts are not the only ones to die in the arena." He sighed, long and loud. "The deaths of all living souls seep into the sand, and it cannot be erased."

"It is a reminder of our purpose," Varia said.

Salonia shrugged. "You should be down here during the games. When every room and stall is full. The noise, the stench, the screams..." She looked down the long tunnel before them and shook her head. "If you think it is a cruel life on the sands, you've yet to live beneath them."

Kaeso shook his head, his voice quiet. "I cannot even imagine."

Quintus clapped him on the shoulder. "Let us keep at task. We dare not be late back to the villa." He led them through the long and lightless corridors with a familiarity that was years in the making.

Kaeso did not enter. He stood, as if struck with fear.

"Kaeso?" Quintus asked. "Is something amiss?"

He opened his mouth but appeared without ability to speak. "I... I cannot..."

"You cannot what?"

He swallowed hard and grew pale. His eyes met Quintus', full of panic. "The darkness... it brings memories I cannot relive."

Quintus was stunned to silence for a moment. "Then we shall fetch light," Quintus replied, and he only need send a glance toward Salonia before she raced down the darkened corridor and returned swiftly with a lit torch. One or two always remained aflame in the hypogeum so the halls were not crypts of utter darkness. She handed it to Quintus, who in turn held it out for Kaeso.

"Take it, and find yourself without darkness," Quintus said.

Kaeso stepped forward and took the torch, and Quintus could see him flush with relief. He took a moment to collect himself and gave a nod when ready. Quintus could not remember Kaeso being in complete darkness before, he had always had a candle or oil lamp, and Quintus would press for words on the memories which caused Kaeso such fear—when they had a private moment—but for now, they would set mind to their task.

"Come," Quintus said with offered smile. "Let us see our purpose met."

KAESO TOOK a calming breath and solace in knowing Quintus was near. They started along the long corridor. "You know these walls," Kaeso said.

"Yes," Quintus admitted. "I have been here many, many times. The arena in Pompeii is closer to Oplontis, but it was closed for ten years after rioting. It is reopened now, but Neapolis was the next closest to us. We travelled the roads to here and stood within these walls more times than I could count."

Quintus stopped at a particular cell, and Salonia reached out and touched the iron bars. "Even empty of men, it yet looks familiar," she said.

"Can you hear the roar of the crowd?" Quintus whispered.

Both women smiled, and Varia raised her fist to the roof.

"Let them open the gates and unleash the Underworld," she said.

"And we shall bathe it in their blood," Salonia finished.

Quintus laughed and raised his fist. "You honour the gods and they shall welcome you with glory."

Without asking, Kaeso understood he was witnessing a pre-ritual battle cry. He stared at them in the flickering light of his torch. "I start to question the presence of wit."

Quintus laughed and put his arm around his shoulder. "Come this way, let me show you something that even you will not question." They began to walk further down the corridor. "Though you do question my every move."

"I question only that which needs it," Kaeso replied. His voice held more confidence now. "Which is most everything you do."

Quintus stopped at a set of stairs that led up to a metal gate, and beyond the iron was the blue of the sky. "Behold, rabbit. Are you ready to stand upon the sands of the arena? Where gladiators and mortal men become gods!"

Kaeso looked at him. "Are you ready to break the iron gate? Because it appears locked."

Salonia laughed beside them and took the stairs two at a time. She hefted the iron gate on its hinges and swung it open. "These gates are not locked. Only a fool would dare break in lest he wishes to find himself thrown to the sands in front of the cheering crowd."

Quintus and Kaeso walked up the stairs, and Kaeso slipped the torch into the iron brace upon the wall, then they stepped out onto the arena. The stands were empty of people, but imposing nonetheless. Quintus outstretched his arms as though a crowd roared his name, and when he turned to Kaeso, his grin was huge.

Kaeso shook his head. "You have lost your wits," he said,

though Quintus' smile was contagious. He did look glorious in full armour, huge and commanding. "Even the sunlight bathes you in gold as though the gods know power when they see it."

Quintus laughed, and he turned in the sun as if on parade. Kaeso watched the three of them walk the sands, looking up into the stands, and he wondered what they saw. Did they see past victories? Did they imagine crowds screaming their names? Or did they see their fallen? People they trained with, lived with, called gladiator brothers under the Ludus Varus name?

"What do you see?" Kaeso asked no one in particular; perhaps all of them.

"I see honour," Salonia said.

"As do I," Varia echoed.

"Your blood spilled is an honour to my name," Quintus said with a quiet reverence. Then he took a moment. "I see my life to this day. I was born of this. I was forged from these arenas. My name, my father's name, Varus, knows no other way."

Kaeso looked at Quintus, and for the first time, he saw him with different eyes. In Kaeso's view, Quintus was a Roman bodyguard, not a lanista. He had not known him at his ludus in Oplontis, as the man he was before the senator summoned him to Neapolis, and now faced with this version of him, he wondered if he knew him at all.

Oblivious to Kaeso's inner turmoil, Quintus slipped his arm around his shoulder once more and said, "Come. Let us finish this task and set our sights for the villa."

Kaeso claimed the torch once more, and they went down the stairs from which they had entered, then turned the way they had not yet been. They passed more cages, more pens, more corridors. Quintus showed Kaeso where all the armour was held, explaining that to leave men, gladiators, slaves, criminals, and Christians armed without strict supervision would be carnage of a different kind. Quintus watched Kaeso's reaction. "You are not impressed?"

"I do not know what to make of it," Kaeso replied. "It is a world unknown to me, and one I do not wish to learn."

Quintus frowned at that but raised no further words. Instead, he led them toward the far gate, directly opposite to the one they had entered through, but as they rounded a corner, they were startled by an intruder.

Quintus, Kaeso, Salonia, and Varia all drew their weapons and stood ready to defend and attack. It was but a young slave boy who screamed in fright as he fell back on his arse. His eyes were wide, his face drained of colour, startled beyond all response.

They lowered their weapons and stood at ease, and Kaeso noticed the boy was holding a large iron pin. "What do you have there, boy?" Quintus asked, obviously having noticed as well. His size was frightening enough, but in full guard uniform, even more so. His deep voice boomed through the darkened stone corridors. "Stand up. You will not be harmed."

The boy scampered to his feet. He couldn't have been more than ten summers old, and he trembled as he held out the iron pin. Quintus took it, and studied it before he stared at the child. "Whose orders do you follow?"

The little boy shook his head, too afraid to answer. "I was promised a bronze coin," he managed to say, fighting tears.

"You were promised a coin to unlock the gate? For what purpose?" Quintus pressed.

The boy shook his head. "I do not know. I dared not ask. He promised a bronze coin to see the lock removed. And this," he said, reaching into a fold at his belt. In the palm of his hand sat two amber balls of gum.

Mastic gum.

"Tell me, child," Quintus furthered. He crouched so he met him at eye level. "Did the man who gave you such an order have a scar on his face?"

The boy nodded, still frightened, and pointed to above his eye.

Quintus took out his purse and gave the boy one bronze coin. "Be on your way, boy."

The boy took the coin and ran, and Quintus rose to his full height. Just around the corner was the gate to the far exit, now unlocked. The four of them stood in the open daylight, for which Kaeso was eternally grateful. Though a stone path led to a road, not far from a large cave entrance with a road beneath.

"What is that place?" Kaeso asked.

"The crypt of Neapolis. A tunnel that joins Neapolis to Puteoli," Quintus replied. "A tunnel, which could hide men waiting for a signal to attack, a direct path to the senator." He held up the pin. "Through a now unlocked gate to the arena."

"You know who this man is?" Salonia asked. "With the scar the boy spoke of?"

Quintus nodded, though he and Kaeso answered in unison. "Tiberius."

CAPITULUM XVII

QUINTUS WALKED INTO SERVIUS' office and, without explanation, put the iron pin on Servius' desk.

The senator looked at the pin, then at Quintus. "What is this?"

"The lock pin from the far gate to the hypogeum, near the tunnel to Puteoli. An easy place to hide a band of men with intent to cause you harm; direct through the belly of the arena to your balcony, and an easier way for them to escape after the deed is done. With that gate unlocked, it would mean certain attack."

Servius floundered a moment. "What does this...? How do you know the removal of a lock is an aimed threat at me?"

"We found a boy paid to see it done," Quintus replied. "He could give no name to the man who paid a bronze coin for his trouble, but his description was enough."

Servius looked horrified. "And?"

Quintus smiled. "A man who chewed on mastic gum and bore a scar above his eye."

Servius scowled. "Tiberius."

Quintus nodded. "Agreed."

"He would put a plan in motion for an attack on me? At the games?" Servius looked around the room, bewildered, and wiped his brow. "I assumed threat would come from another senator, not the praetorian guard!"

"He either constructs a plan of his own intent, or he follows orders," Quintus allowed.

Servius' wide gaze shot to his. "From the emperor himself?"

"I would like to think not," Quintus said. "I believe the emperor to be a good man. Tiberius, I believe, has ulterior purpose."

Servius sat in silence for a long moment. He appeared tired. The lines of worry and unrest showed on his face, something Quintus had not truly noticed until now. Then, as he was wont to do, Servius' entire demeanour changed. Gone was the horrified, startled man, and in his place was the cold and calculating politician. "What would you have me do?"

"See the gate is forged shut," Quintus replied.

"And that is all?" Servius asked, stunned.

Quintus raised his chin. "Merely a start. We will see to other means."

"I would see to having Tiberius questioned!"

"And risk blame for plans yet seen? It would be Tiberius' word against that of a slave boy." Quintus countered. "Let him attempt his plan, and he shall be caught in a failed attempt. Let him speak his untruth to the emperor and see him executed at your games. It will be an exhibition they'll not soon forget."

Servius' eyes gleamed. "Yes, the crowds would love it. It shall be the talk of Rome, a lesson for those who think to stand against me." His smile turned sinister. "See it done."

Quintus gave a nod and walked out, finding his men—and women, Quintus allowed with a humoured sigh to Kaeso—finishing their training. It had been a long and fruitful day, and he longed to bathe and see his worries washed away.

He sought out Kaeso through his band of guards and found him at the wooden pole practising his strikes and blows with a rudis. He was focused, and his attack bore more strength than was necessary. From the pinch of his brow, Quintus could tell Kaeso's mood was dark.

"Are you not yet done?" Quintus asked. "One would think the pole offended you and you set yourself the task of teaching it manners." He was aiming for humour, but Kaeso did not smile.

He simply sagged and let out a harsh breath. "Apologies. Though a decent practice eases troubled thoughts."

"Strike Tiberius from your mind," Quintus said. "I long for a hot bath and your company in it."

Kaeso dropped his rudis with the others and walked, without another word, to their baths. Quintus watched as Kaeso sunk into the water, his shoulders relaxed, though from the pinch of his brow, Quintus knew his mind still worked.

"Oscilius says an onus shared is an onus halved," Quintus murmured, breaking the silence. He offered a small smile to Kaeso. "I fear it is more than Tiberius that weighs upon your mind."

Kaeso sighed. "Perhaps yes, or not. I am... Today has had moments of both light and dark, and I struggle to find words to explain."

"How so? Was it the matter of darkness and memories that put fear upon your face? Would you share that with me?"

Kaeso shook his head. "I would rather not speak of it, for the memories will swiftly follow. I would have you not ask, though please know you showed such kindness in providing a torch, and that shall not be forgotten."

"If you do not wish to speak of it, how can I see what troubles you set right?"

"I do not wish to speak of it. Not this day."

"Is that not what troubles you now?"

Kaeso shrugged and looked away. "I should not cause you further concern. Strike it from mind and I shall attempt the same."

"How can I?" Quintus asked. "I assumed your worry was over threat of Tiberius or the fear of darkness, but now you say there is another?"

"I should not have spoken out of turn," Kaeso whispered. "Please accept my apologies and speak of it no more."

Quintus sat, silent and stunned. The only reason he could fathom that Kaeso would not speak his mind was because his worry involved Quintus. Eventually he said, "Part of me would see your wish for silence granted, yet another part of me could order you to speak your mind."

Kaeso's gaze shot to his. "You would order me?"

"Do you forget the collar around your neck?" Quintus said, followed swiftly by a sharp dart of regret.

Kaeso's nostrils flared, but Quintus could easily see he held back the words he wished he could say, and Quintus let out a sorry sigh. "Kaeso—"

Kaeso spoke over him. "How can I forget I wear the collar of a slave when you so cruelly remind me?" He stood up and stepped out of the bath, not stopping to dry himself. He simply wrapped his subligaculum around his waist and was gone.

Quintus was left alone to wonder where he had gone wrong. Not the mention of the collar—that was evident—but where he had gone wrong earlier that day. Kaeso had been in such high spirits in the forum; he had eaten the honeyed treat and had declared Quintus was reason enough for Kaeso to want to stay in Rome.

But then Quintus thought back to Kaeso's face when he stood in the arena, absent smile and humour, his fear of dark and closed quarters. Something had changed for Kaeso. Something weighed heavy upon his mind. And Quintus was tangled in it somehow.

He could force Kaeso to speak; it was his collar around his neck after all. But Quintus lacked the patience to play such games.

Yet this was Kaeso.

His Kaeso. His rabbit.

He deserved so much more than to be reminded of his slavery. It was bad enough he had had his free will stripped away, but to be reminded, and to be reminded by Quintus, the one and only man he trusted...

Unease twisted in Quintus' gut, and regret squeezed his heart. His ribs felt too tight, and he knew, like he knew the sun would rise, what he must do to fix it.

He found Kaeso in his room, standing at the bed and wearing only his subligaculum. The tunic Quintus had given him was laid out on the mattress, and Kaeso was staring at it. He turned when Quintus entered but didn't speak. The soft glow of the candle deepened the shadows on his face.

"Is something amiss with the tunic I gave you?" Quintus asked. It wasn't what he intended to say, but it was a place to start.

"The tunic, no," Kaeso murmured. "I am grateful for it."

"Yet you will not wear it?"

"I am conflicted."

"How so?"

"Perhaps it is a conversation best left for after the evening meal..."

"Perhaps," Quintus allowed. "Perhaps I should apologise for my earlier words. It was not my intent to remind you of the collar you wear."

Kaeso's shoulders lifted, as did his chin. His defiance was back. "And yet you remind me again."

"I state a fact. A truth I cannot change," Quintus said. He stepped closer and didn't miss how Kaeso flinched. "A truth I would see undone if I were able."

"Would you?" Kaeso asked. He turned so Quintus could not see his face.

"See my collar taken from you? Yes," Quintus answered. "Yet one collar would still remain, and that is not in my power to remove."

Kaeso's shoulders sagged again. "If wishing it not so made it true... I never asked for this."

"I know."

"I have found myself stripped of freedom and my own will."

"And I wish to see it returned," Quintus said. "But for as long as the senator's collar is around your neck, I would have mine join it. You fare better under my keep than you would under his."

Kaeso looked up at him then and opened his mouth to speak, when someone cleared their throat at the door. It was Petilia. "Dominus has requested you at the evening meal," she said gently, then backed away.

Quintus hurried to dress for company, and they made their way to the table. Servius had every intent of keeping

Quintus for discussions on strategy, though the conversation was so one-sided, Quintus wondered if his attendance was even required.

It didn't help that he was distracted with matters of Kaeso. The fact was, when his time in Neapolis with the senator was over, his time with Kaeso was as well. He was half tempted to ask Servius outright if he could take custody and pay whatever sum he demanded for Kaeso's purchase.

But Oscilius' words played on his mind. If he showed this intent—this weakness—the senator would use it against him. So instead, he said nothing. He would simply need to bide his time. Not an easy feat with pressures closing in around him.

When Servius was blessedly done, Quintus bid him goodnight and went through the darkened villa to his quarters. His bedroom was lit by one small candle, and Kaeso sat on the bed. He looked as worried as he had earlier.

"Kaeso? I expected you to be asleep," Quintus said. "Apologies to have kept you. You know how Servius likes to hear himself speak."

Kaeso almost smiled. "Sleep eludes me."

"You have worries unshared."

"And I fear to speak my truth, Quintus," he whispered. "Yet I must. Forgive what I say, though please know it comes from my heart."

A creeping dread filled Quintus, slowly at first, then all at once. Realisation dawned on him that Kaeso was about to deny him. Not just his body. In that moment, Quintus could not care less for carnal needs. He was denying him his heart. And fear struck him like the ice of winter. He quickly sat beside him and took his hand. "Kaeso, I would not dare to ask Servius to remove his collar from your neck. To show him my weakness for you when treachery beckons from all sides would be foolish."

Kaeso blinked and his brow furrowed. "The collars I wear and the threats you speak of are not what concern me this night, Quintus."

Now it was Quintus who was confused. "Please break words of what weighs upon your mind, Kaeso. If you no longer wish to share my bed, I would not lie to say it would not wound me, but I would rather you say it than to pretend. False affection would inflict a deeper wound."

Kaeso shook his head. "There is nothing false about my affection, Quintus."

"Then what is it?"

"Today, in the arena," Kaeso said, his voice barely a whisper. "I looked upon you with unfamiliar eyes. I thought I knew you, but to hear your words of honour and death... I wonder now if I know you at all."

Quintus pulled his hand from Kaeso's. "Honour and death?"

"Yes." Kaeso's eyes were wide and pleading. "The Quintus I know treats a slave as he treats a freedman. He is kind and fair, and he expects no more than he expects of himself. The Quintus I have seen here, and the Quintus that showed himself in his own villa with Oscilius. Slaves, yes, but a family also. That is the Quintus I know." He swallowed hard. "But today on the sands of the arena you were different. You were a lanista, a trainer of gladiators, and Salonia and Varia were not guards on equal footing. They were once again slaves, to stand in an arena and fight for their lives. You said their blood spilled was an honour to you. That is what you said."

"Kaeso," Quintus said, truly stunned. "I do not follow."

"If it is my blood that spills to honour the gods and you,

is that all I am worth?" Kaeso's eyes filled with tears. "You speak of affection for me yet tell your other slaves their death brings honour to your name. There are two sides to you, and I cannot make sense of it, Quintus."

Quintus tried to keep his voice down. "I am a lanista. I train gladiators. That is what I do. It is who I am, and my father before me. It is all I know. You speak of equal footing, and that is what I give. To take a man who has no honour, no worth, and teach him how to stand with his head held high before thousands, and to stand tall before the gods and all of Rome."

Kaeso's response was swift and laced with temper. "You train these men to partake in their own death."

"I train them to die with honour!" Quintus cried. He stood and paced, then turned back to Kaeso. "Every man must face his fate, and I would hope for my men what I would hope for myself. To meet fate on equal footing. It is all a man can ask for."

Kaeso clearly did not agree. "I do not wish to meet the gods as an equal. I would rather meet fate around the fire with those I hold dear, our voices raised in song. We might raise our drink to welcome death, and it might join us a while, to sing and call upon cherished memories. To be struck from this world a freedman. A free man, Quintus. That is all one can ask for."

Quintus pulled at his hair in frustration. "I cannot change who I am, Kaeso. I was raised on the arena sands. I was born Roman. Am I not the product of lands forged from the fires of war, discipline, and death?"

"And I was raised in the fields of Iberia. I was born to a different way of life. Am I not the product of a quiet life of tending goats and soil, of peaceful days and nights of pleasant dreams?" Kaeso sighed, exasperated. His next words were quiet, his fight gone. "And you say that slaves have no honour or worth. That is the untruth, Quintus. It is absent within them because it is taken. My freedom was removed, my free will stripped away, and with it my honour. Not by *my* choice."

The tears that escaped Kaeso's eyes burned in Quintus' heart. He went to him, sat, and pulled him into his arms. "My vow to you, Kaeso, I swear to the gods that I will see your collars removed."

"Do not make promises you cannot keep," Kaeso murmured. He sounded defeated, exhausted, though he allowed himself to be held. "I fear my heart cannot take it."

Quintus lay back on the bed, taking Kaeso with him, and kissed the side of his head. "I will see it done. While there is still breath in me, I will see it done." Kaeso burrowed in, as he usually did, and Quintus took this as a good sign. "I am a Roman lanista; you are a captured Iberian. I know not how to mend the concerns that ail you, but what I do know, my rabbit, is that we will find a way. The gods will make it so. For it was them who brought us together on this path. It is them who shall make it so."

Kaeso sniffled and nodded into Quintus' chest and Quintus tightened his embrace, and that was exactly how they woke in the morning.

KAESO WAS quiet the next day and the next days that followed it. He didn't turn from Quintus. How could he? His heart would not allow it. Yet he was still torn. His affection for the man was true, there was no denying it. Yet the perception of Quintus valuing a slave's life—his life—as no more than a blood offering to the gods was a currency Kaeso struggled to accept.

Three days after their trip to the arena, Quintus was summoned to the senator's office, so he gave the order to break from training. They took their cups to the shade of the courtyard wall and sat.

Salonia tapped Kaeso's foot with her own. "You are distracted," she said. "Does our dominus not please you enough?" Her bright smile and shining eyes made her suggestion and humour apparent.

Everyone around them chuckled, and even Harpax added, "Perhaps he pleases too much. I heard it whispered that Kaeso here boasted our dominus is gifted with a horse cock."

Bursts of laughter erupted and faces filled with shock and disbelief. Kaeso, though he found it hard not to smile, shook his head. "And if he hears you speak such words, he would see you part with yours," Kaeso said. Yet, while he held an audience, he thought it best to use it. "I have a question to ask of all of you, if you would be so kind as to answer." Kaeso took a deep breath and looked at his fellow guards in the eyes. "I am not a gladiator. I know not what it means. Though I try to grasp understanding, it is lost to me. What does it mean for you to walk into an arena, to be called gladiator? And what does it mean to stand as such in Quintus' name?"

No one smiled now. Kaeso perhaps had not realised the weight of his words until he had spoken them.

Appius spoke first. "It is not just the glory and coin. The crowds roar my name to the gods, and I fight so the gods will hear."

"There are many other gladiator schools," Pellio added. "But to be chosen for Ludus Varus, to call Quintus my dominus, is a blessing. Some lanistas are terrible. They treat their men like shit and piss. Not Quintus."

"We respect him because he has earned it," Arruns said. "He shows us respect in return."

"If not for him, I would be in the mines," Messenio said. "He has given me new purpose."

"And for me," Lars added. "New purpose, new life. It is an honour to fight for him."

Pellio snorted and shook his head. "You assume we respect him because we call him *dominus*? No. We fight because we respect him, what he gives us."

Appius looked toward the sky, then to Kaeso. "There is not a man here who would not offer his life for our dominus," he said. "And that speaks of Quintus more than it speaks of us."

Everyone nodded and murmured their agreement, and when conversation turned to the coming games, Salonia nudged Kaeso's foot once more. She spoke so no one else but Kaeso and Varia could hear. "You question Quintus' intent?"

Kaeso shook his head. "Intent, no."

"You gathered insight on our trip to the arena," Varia noticed.

Kaeso gave her a small smile and a nod. "I assumed to know him, yet to see him in the arena and say your death would bring him honour..." He sighed. "The Quintus I know would do all he could to see you live."

Salonia laughed. "And he does. It is why he trains us so hard, to see that we do live. Before Quintus, there was certain death for all of us. Or a life so terrible we would wish for death to find us. He does not take our voice. He but gives us an arena so we will be heard."

"He gives us purpose," Varia said, her hand to her heart.

"Something another dominus would strip us of. But not Quintus. These lands in these times are not an easy life. People of Rome die with empty bellies and unheard voices. Free as the wind, yet slaves to an empire that does not care. I know which I would prefer. I would stand for Ludus Varus, for Quintus, this day and any day that follows."

"As would I," Salonia said.

Kaeso considered their words. "If given your freedom, would you take it? Would you not want to see the lands of your home south of Carthage?"

Salonia gave a saddened smile. "Wishing for such things will break men more than it will give them hope."

"Sometimes hope is all a man can cling to," Kaeso said, not exactly sure why.

Varia shook her head. "Cast thoughts of home from your mind. Set your sights on your new purpose. Your life is here now, and your heart too, it would seem."

"My heart?" Kaeso asked, pretending ignorance.

Just then, Quintus walked out of the villa and headed toward them. They watched as he searched the guards until he found Kaeso, and saw the set of his shoulders relax.

Salonia nudged Kaeso once more, and she laughed. "You will find no better man in Rome than the one who has eyes for you," she said as she got to her feet.

Kaeso stood also. "Eyes for me?"

Salonia dusted herself off and gave Kaeso a gentle smile. "I have borne witness to him being many things, but the way he looks upon you, never."

Quintus, who now stood before them, clapped his hands together. "Do we rest? Or do we fight?" he called out.

The response was immediate and in unison. "Fight!"

Quintus grinned at them, and Kaeso saw it then. What he rallied in his men.

It was as they had all said. Respect and purpose. He coaxed it out of them. He brought the best out of them. He was a true leader. He urged them to train harder so they would fight harder. So they would live.

Yes, he was a lanista. He trained these gladiators to fight, to stand before thousands and scream for blood, and in doing so, gave them honour and purpose. He was a product of his birthright, as all men were.

Kaeso felt a fool for questioning him, because this was the Quintus he knew. This was the Quintus he cared for.

When they broke for the day, Kaeso was sweating and breathless. Quintus went to him, smiling. "If I knew pushing you to new limits would earn me that smile," he said.

Kaeso laughed. "Not so much the orders but perhaps the man who gives them."

Quintus eyed him for a long moment. "Something is different in the way you look upon me than it has been in recent days."

"A reminder from those who know you best, of the integrity I overlooked," Kaeso replied. "I was a fool to doubt you. A mistake I will not make twice."

CAPITULUM XVIII

QUINTUS COULD TELL Kaeso had questions. His eyes gave too much away. "Speak your mind, rabbit."

"You were summoned by Servius," Kaeso said, not so much a question, but he awaited an answer all the same.

"Yes," Quintus replied. He let out a sigh. "His order for the rear entrance gate to the arena to be sealed is done. I asked that it be checked the day before the games, and he gave me permission."

"You are to make an inspection of the arena?" Kaeso asked.

"*We* are to make inspection," Quintus clarified with a smirk. "We shall make final inspection the day prior and see if everything is in order. I would have Salonia and Varia accompany us, perhaps Appius and Phaidon also."

Kaeso nodded. "Sound plan."

Quintus grinned. "Of course it is. I made it."

Kaeso rolled his eyes, though his smile showed his humour. "You are in high spirits today," Kaeso said.

"Yes. Because the sadness has left your eyes," Quintus

murmured. "You said you were reminded of my integrity. Do I want to know what my men said in my absence?"

Kaeso chuckled. "I fear to feed the ego, should it grow too big a beast to tame." Then his smile turned shy, his voice lowered. "They reminded me that perhaps the shadow cast over you simply needed new light. I saw you from their eyes, and all shadow of doubt was removed."

Quintus smiled and lightly touched the side of Kaeso's face. "I do not wish for shadows between us."

Kaeso blinked those big brown eyes. "Nor do I."

Quintus inhaled deeply, filled with new elation. Then he looked up at the sky and scowled at the sun. "This day has delivered heat from Helios. Let us bathe and retreat to our quarters where the air is cool."

"Where we are afforded privacy," Kaeso hinted.

"You read my intent well," Quintus said.

"Yours or my own?" Kaeso said as he started for the baths. He stopped and turned to find Quintus standing, unmoved, yet smiling. "You would do well not to make me wait."

Quintus laughed and walked toward him, slinging his arm around Kaeso's shoulders as they continued toward the baths. "There he is, my rabbit who thinks himself a commander. Oh, how I have missed thee."

They stopped before the bath and Kaeso stripped out of his armour and boots. He stepped right in close, looking up at Quintus. "Do not pretend you will not obey my orders," Kaeso murmured.

Quintus raised an eyebrow as he pulled off his belt. "You would be so brave to give them?"

Kaeso smiled at the challenge. He pulled his subligaculum off, standing naked before Quintus. "Tonight, I will have your cock inside me, as many times as you are able."

Quintus smiled as he took off his tunic. "An order I will gladly obey."

Kaeso hummed happily as he stepped into the warm bath; he sat and closed his eyes. "And you will deliver me to the gods every time."

Quintus lowered himself into the water and smiled at how Kaeso's closed eyelids and his long eyelashes gave him a beautiful, boyish look. "You are not shy to make such demands," Quintus said. "For a rabbit."

Kaeso opened his eyes and Quintus did nothing to hide the heated challenge in his gaze. Kaeso took the linen cloth and washed himself, a quicker bath than was habit, but there was clearly somewhere else he would rather be. He stood up and stepped toward Quintus, his hard cock near Quintus' face.

"I will have it once before the evening meal," Kaeso said, his voice gruff and full of want. "So you best not be long." He simply stepped out of the bath, wrapped his subligaculum around his waist, and not even pausing to dry himself, walked out.

Quintus was out of that bath before Kaeso crossed the villa. He dressed, still wet, and followed, finding Kaeso lifting his knee onto the bed.

"Do not move," Quintus ordered from the door. Kaeso smiled over his shoulder and let his subligaculum fall away, and Quintus' ribs tightened and his cock ached. The sight before him stole his breath and moved him in ways he had never known. He strode toward him, shedding his clothes as he went. Kaeso stood at the bed, one knee resting on the mattress, his bare and beautiful arse made Quintus' cock pulse. "To see you like this," Quintus said, running his hand down Kaeso's back and over his arse cheek, pressing a fingertip inside him. "Will have me undone before I am inside you."

Kaeso arched his back as he stroked himself. "Then waste no time in seeing me ready," he whispered. "The oil, use it, and see my demands met."

Quintus smiled at Kaeso's urgency. But he took the oil and slicked his cock with it, then applied it to Kaeso's arse. Kaeso turned to raise question, but Quintus held him still and pushed his cock against his hole. "Always quick with commands when fraught with desire," Quintus whispered in his ear.

Kaeso squirmed, his back to Quintus' front, pushing his arse back against him. "Then end your games and see it done," he hissed at Quintus.

Quintus chuckled now. "You become desperate," he breathed in Kaeso's ear. He had one arm wrapped around Kaeso's chest, one held his hip. "Your words give order, yet your tone is a plea."

Kaeso nodded, still stroking his own cock. "Please, Quintus."

Quintus pushed inside him in one hard, tight thrust. Kaeso sucked back a breath and let it out in a strangled whine. He arched, then struggled, yet Quintus held him fast. "Breathe," he murmured in his ear.

Kaeso breathed.

"This is what you begged for," Quintus said, his voice strained. Kaeso was so tight, so hot, he thought he might succumb already. Kaeso whined again, then he was panting. "Breathe," Quintus whispered again.

Kaeso breathed, and this time he relaxed. "I will beg for you, always," he mumbled as he took long strokes of his cock. All Quintus had to do was roll his hips, and Kaeso moaned. So he thrust hard, his completion drawing ever closer, and Kaeso let his head rest on Quintus' shoulder as he gave himself over to the pleasure.

"Where are your demands now?" Quintus grunted as he gripped Kaeso's hip and fucked. "You begged for my cock."

Kaeso groaned, long and loud. "Now give me your seed."

And, as though he were a slave to Kaeso's orders, Quintus did.

———

THE DAYS that followed were filled with training and strategy. The warm afternoon breeze brought little relief from the summer sun, yet Quintus' focus remained. Servius' attention was buried in papers and meetings with officials and men of importance regarding the upcoming games. Quintus insisted his men train in his absence so he was able to attend the meetings with Servius. Not for his input or opinion, only to stand and observe. He would know who was expected to be where within the arena and who, by elimination, would not.

He also discovered who would occupy the rooms adjacent to the senator's in the arena. Of course, it was the one senator who held contempt toward Servius, Marcus Maternus on one side, the emperor on the other.

News that did not please Quintus.

"You could allow the emperor to take your room," Quintus suggested. "Tell him it would be an honour to gift him with the best room in the arena."

Servius was horrified. "And by removing myself, hand Maternus a golden opportunity for elevated position beside the emperor? I think not!"

"By removing yourself, you also remove the threat from both sides," Quintus argued. "Maternus on one side, Tiberius on the other. You position yourself exactly where they want you!"

Servius' cheeks went red with anger, and he stood and thumped his fist on his desk. "I will not give up my room beside the emperor. Perhaps you do not grasp political manoeuvre, but this is the purpose of these games! Political promotion!"

"And perhaps you do not grasp tactical manoeuvre," Quintus countered. "For political promotion is void if you do not live to see it."

Servius stared at him. "Then you best be as good as you claim to counter any attack."

Quintus took a breath to calm his temper. "And risk the death of my men for your promotion in a vain attempt?"

Servius' reply was cold. "That is what you are paid for."

Quintus wanted to reach across the desk, take Servius' head in hand, and crush his skull. Instead, he took a step back and raised his chin. "Tomorrow my men will accompany me through Neapolis to the arena. They shall become familiar with exits and hidden routes to return, should any of them need to escort you back to the villa undetected."

Servius blinked and struggled to appear unbothered by the fact Quintus implied Servius *would* come under attack. "Very well."

"We shall leave after the morning meal and should not be expected back until the last meal of the day."

Servius' glare hardened. "To plan routes, yes. But I gave no such permission for a day of leave."

"Then it is just as well I require none," Quintus replied. He gave Servius no time for rebuttal, he simply turned on his heel and left.

"THE MAN IS A FOOL," Quintus whispered. He and Kaeso were lying on their bed; Quintus was on his back, Kaeso tucked into his side with his head on Quintus' chest. The room flickered with the gentle light of a small oil lamp, the villa all but asleep.

"Shhh," Kaeso whispered. "These walls have ears."

Quintus didn't care. "His ego will see him slaughtered," he added. "And he gives little thought to my men sworn to protect him. Political manoeuvre to what end? There is no honour in a title if it is ill-gotten."

Kaeso hummed. "Yet the title will remain, and the coin and pageantry to go with it. I would guess his purpose is to further manoeuvre. He is ambitious."

"It is not ambition that fuels him. It is greed." Quintus growled in frustration. "I trust none of them."

Kaeso leaned up then, so he could see Quintus' face. "None of who?"

"Any of them. Servius, Maternus, Tiberius."

"Do you think there is more to what we know?"

"I would stake my life upon it."

Kaeso frowned at that. "Who strikes a greater threat?"

"If I were to ask who had the most to lose by Servius' promotion, who would you answer?"

"Maternus, perhaps. Given such a promotion granted to Servius sidesteps him."

"And should I ask who has the most to gain by Servius' promotion?"

Kaeso frowned again. "You believe threat beckons from either outcome?"

Quintus nodded. "And Servius refuses to see it. He is blinded by his own purpose."

Kaeso put his head back to Quintus' chest, and they were silent for a moment. "I would be more inclined to be cautious of a snake closer to the nest."

"Who?"

"Helier."

Quintus made a sound in the back of his throat. "He is but a body slave."

"He is but closest to the senator. He knows his secrets and his future plans. He has very likely stood in on all the senator's secret meetings, and he has access to any part of the villa he chooses. The senator's office or, more pointedly, the senator's desk and reports." Kaeso let out a sigh. "He is also a man deeply troubled."

Quintus considered that. "Deeply troubled? He appears more arrogant to me."

"Maybe I misread him," Kaeso allowed. "Perhaps his glare is aimed at me and me alone. Rumour has it Helier was intended for your bed and was disappointed when you were not obliging."

Quintus snorted at that and rolled to his side so he could wrap Kaeso up in his arms. "Strike him from mind. He is not the one who caught my eye, and you are all too aware of my stance on being offered something that is not mine to take."

Kaeso chuckled into Quintus' chest. "How can I forget? You denied me at first because you will not take that which is not freely given."

Quintus kissed the top of his head. "And yet here you are."

"I would offer it freely again right now, if you are able."

Quintus laughed. "How can you not have had enough? Perhaps I should state that you are the one to demand and take from me."

Kaeso smiled on a sigh. "And by the gods, you give it well."

Quintus nuzzled into him, smiling and happy, despite the worries that plagued him. "Sleep, rabbit. Tomorrow comes early."

AFTER THEIR MORNING MEAL, Quintus met his men —and women—in the training yard. "I have unexpected plans for you all today," he said. "We will ascend to the arena. Full uniform, no weapons. It is an exercise in practice only. You will honour me with your discipline, am I clear?"

"Yes, Dominus," came the unified response.

Quintus looked to the original six guards. "Gallio, Oppius, Mettius, Lucan, and Decius," he said. "You will remain here and protect the senator in my absence. No one enters the villa unless under instruction from Servius himself." They nodded. Then Quintus glanced at Kaeso. "You are with me."

Kaeso smiled and Quintus ignored the small smirk from Salonia. Instead, Quintus took a rudis and drew a circle in the sand, then a rectangle one pace away. "We are here," he said, pointing the wooden sword to the rectangle. "We will divide into three and each take a different approach to the arena." He pointed to the circle. Then he drew three connecting roads. "One direct, one high, one low."

The three groups would be led by Quintus, Salonia, and Appias. "Look for concealed alleys, places of refuge, or exposure. I will take the lowest road near the docks, being the most likely to encounter trouble. It is also the longest road, so the first two groups to arrive will also do a full perimeter patrol of the arena." He drew an outer circle of the arena. "Look for any open gates, broken locks, anything out of place." Then Quintus stood to his full height and gave them all a grim look. "If Salonia's or Appias' team does not appear before the sun is directly overhead, wait for my arrival. If my team is compromised and does not make the arena by the midday sun, you return to the villa at once."

They each nodded. "Dominus."

And so they donned full uniforms and set off. Harpax, Phaidon, and Kaeso, of course, made up Quintus' team of four. They took the cobbled road to the bay and headed toward the docks, while noting high stone walls and vantage points, possible ambush points and escape routes.

The docks were busy, not only with fleet men and Rome's navy, but with merchants arriving with goods and produce to sell. The stalls and shops were doing a roaring trade, the inns and brothels as well. "The senator was right about one thing," Quintus noted. "Neapolis swells with travellers and visitors alike, and the coin they bring with them."

But it was the naval ships that caught Quintus' eye. There were six *quinqueremes* at port alongside other merchant and grain ships. Kaeso seemed to notice at the same time. "Is it common for that many naval warships to be in port at the one time?"

Quintus frowned. "I wondered this also."

Phaidon gave a long side-glance to Quintus. "Would you have me find answer?"

Quintus smiled. "I would."

As they neared an inn, where fleet men fell about with clay bottles in hand, drunken and loud, Phaidon took off his helmet and threw it to Harpax with a grin. He neared the inn, lined himself up with the drunk fleet men, and sang along with them. After a few loud and mumbled lines, he took an empty cup from one of the men, raised it into the air with them, then ducked inside the inn.

"Should he enter?" Kaeso asked, concerned.

Harpax snorted. "If anyone can act the part of drunken fool and strip a fleet man of information, it is Phaidon."

Quintus laughed. "Remember that time in Pompeii? He acted the drunk at an inn before a contest and came out with full detail of who we were set to fight against." He leaned against the stone wall and studied the flat roofline of the buildings opposite. They would make a sound escape option, if needed. The roofline followed the street all the way to the docks, and they could see the ocean and the coastline that followed it as far as the eye could see.

"The eye searches for home," Harpax said, looking at the same view.

"As does the heart," Quintus replied. "The mountain, the ocean, the fields in between. Soon we shall return there, and this will be a distant memory."

Kaeso clearly didn't have the patience for waiting. He fidgeted and kept his eye on the inn. "He takes too long. He might have found trouble."

Harpax turned his ear to the inn. "Do men scream in pain?"

Kaeso shook his head, alarmed. "Not that I can hear."

"Then he is fine," Quintus replied with a smile. "Patience. He will return when his task is complete."

Kaeso pressed on. "He is outnumbered."

Quintus' smile remained, not concerned at all. "Send in another ten men, and they would still be no match for him."

Just then, the door opened and Phaidon spilled out, cup in hand, amber liquid slopped to the ground. He was still singing, and he aimed for the drunken fleet men who he had met on the way in, handed them the full cup, then simply walked back to where Quintus stood.

His smile was gone, an edge to his eyes. Harpax threw his helmet to him and he fixed it on as he spoke. "Six fleet ships is not too uncommon, given the unrest in the Britannia. Of more pressing concern is the three more fleet ships to arrive in coming days. A total of nine fleet ships have not seen this dock at the same time since the battle against the Batavians."

"Do you know their intended destination?" Quintus asked. "Once they are laden with soldiers and supplies, which direction do they set sail?"

"The fleet men did not know. Some say Caledonia, some say Syria-Palestina," Phaidon replied.

"They do not know?" Harpax questioned.

Phaidon shook his head and met Quintus' gaze. "What they do know was under whose orders they sail."

Quintus was certain he knew the answer, yet he asked anyway. "Who?"

"Senator Servius Augendus."

Quintus felt a cold prickle run down his spine. "If he can give such orders, I can only assume he has the navy commander's ear."

Kaeso scowled. "Or his purse."

Harpax gave Quintus a look of worry. "I fear the senator's intentions are not what they seem."

Quintus nodded. "Let concern of his ill-intent fall to me. I count the days until we see this task over and return to my ludus, striking all memory of this from mind." He let out a sigh. "We will continue to the arena and see our purpose met. The sooner the better."

CAPITULUM XIX

WITH NEWS of the senator's command to see part of the naval fleets return to Neapolis, Kaeso's wariness of the situation he found himself in continued to grow. And now, hearing Quintus speak of returning to his ludus brought with it additional worry.

Quintus was free to leave at any time.

Kaeso was not.

He did believe Quintus' affection for him to be true. He knew deep in his heart that Quintus was not the kind of man to lie about such matters, and he wouldn't use Kaeso as a prop for this political game.

Servius would though, without a second glance. Servius would use him and throw him away as he would a broken cup.

But he had to believe, in his heart of hearts, that Quintus would find a way to keep them together. He had to believe this. Otherwise, what else was there? What purpose remained?

The rest of the walk to the arena was uneventful. No words were spoken as each of the men studied their path, keeping a keen eye for anyone who might pose a threat of attack. The streets were busy, much busier than Kaeso was accustomed to, and many of the people gave them a curious glance coupled with a wide berth, and soon enough they weaved their way to the arena.

They met Salonia and Appias and their teams under the huge entry arches. "The rear door to the underground remains tarred shut," Salonia said.

"Yet the main gates to the underground stand wide open," Appias added. "We did not enter without your order."

Quintus gave a nod. "Good. Let us see who lurks through the belly."

Kaeso didn't want to admit that he was not keen to see under the arena again, but all of Quintus' men, and Quintus himself, were at ease with it. The darkness and the feeling of being cornered and caged were bad enough, but add the horrendous smell, and Kaeso would be happy to never set foot underground again.

Yet without prompting or making point of it, Quintus handed Kaeso a torch to carry. He let out a relieved breath, stood beside Quintus, and followed his lead into the hypogeum. He would rather enter the bowels of the arena beside Quintus than go in alone; that was certain. The many tunnels made a labyrinth, and to save time, Quintus split their group into two. "Appias, take the lower path," he said, and without question, with only a small nod, Appias led half the men down a darkened tunnel.

Quintus and Kaeso led the others further along, and soon they were at the large caged-off area called the *armorum,* where all the weapons and armour would be stored. The gate was open, and inside stood an old man, a ratty shawl draped over his shoulders, and he started when he realised he had company.

Until he saw who it was. "Quintus Varus?" he asked, looking Quintus up and down. "Do you dress for an exhibition game?"

Quintus laughed. "Otho!"

The old man came forward and held out his gnarled hand. Quintus took it and greeted the man warmly. "Ignore the costume," Quintus said. "We serve Senator Augendus as guards, but only until these games pass."

"Will you not be attending the coming games with gladiators?"

Quintus grinned at him. "Oscilius will bring my remaining men. We have yet to be absent from any games."

Otho nodded. "I always liked you Quintus. You would make a decent guard, but a better lanista."

Quintus chuckled. "Keep well, Otho." Then, as if he had a second thought, he said, "Oh, by chance are you alone down here?"

Otho shook his head, and he grumbled. "Earlier, some imperial guards came through. But they pay no mind to me."

"How many were there?" Quintus asked.

Otho held up three fingers. "They went that way, then a short while later, they left. Not long from now as one barked orders, cursing about the gates being sealed with tar."

Quintus bowed his head. "Gratitude. Keep well, and I will see you during the games."

Otho gave him a smile and went back to his work, and Quintus looked down the darkened corridor. "Imperial guards. I need not guess who," Quintus murmured.

Kaeso need not guess either. The only guard to

complain that the gate had been sealed would be the one who ordered it opened.

Tiberius.

Quintus turned to his guards, put his finger to his lips to remain quiet, then pointed down the tunnel. They continued to the end of the arena without a sound. When Quintus asked for quiet, he got it. Kaeso found their collective silence a little eerie, not a footfall, not a breath, and it was only more silence they found. The corridors were empty. Appias and the guards with him soon joined them and confirmed the same.

They continued to check the underground, then the rooms which Servius and the emperor would occupy. No one of any threat lingered, and nothing was out of place. Not at the arena anyway.

"If it was Tiberius who Otho saw," Kaeso said, "what brings praetorians here from Roma?"

"Orders from the state," Quintus said with a shrug. "Or from the emperor himself."

Kaeso conceded a nod, though he didn't agree. "Perhaps we should scout the docks again and see if anything strikes as odd. There are more ships expected and the emperor's guard is here. I would guess these things are not coincidence."

Quintus met his gaze for a long moment. "Agreed." He turned to his guards. "Return to the villa, same way in which you came. Harpax, Phaidon, you are with me."

Kaeso blinked, his heart squeezed. Was he not required? Did Quintus want him to return to the villa? He took a step back and made to leave with Salonia, when Quintus' voice stopped him.

"Kaeso." He stood, head cocked, clearly confused. "Where are you going?"

"You did not call for me," Kaeso murmured. "I assumed I was not required."

Quintus stared at him, as though unable to make sense of something. "Assume your place is with me, always."

Salonia nudged Kaeso with her elbow as she left, and he could see her smile as she led her team from view. Kaeso turned in time to catch Quintus' eye. "Does something about me amuse the two of you?" Quintus asked with a smile.

"No," Kaeso lied.

"You are a terrible liar."

"She cautioned me not to doubt you," Kaeso said. "That is all."

"She would be right." Quintus narrowed his eyes. "Wait! You doubted me?"

"A reflection of me, not of you," Kaeso said. He glanced at Harpax and Phaidon. "A conversation for another time perhaps."

Phaidon rolled his eyes. "Not required. We see how Dominus searches for you and how he holds his breath until his eyes fall upon you. We all see it. A far cry from the dominus we knew just one full moon ago."

Then Harpax snorted and pointed his thumb at Quintus. "Yes, this one smiles."

Kaeso laughed, and Quintus glared at the three of them. "Are we done? Perhaps a swift reminder of your place is required? Absent Oscilius' whip, I should have you assigned to clean the latrinus."

Harpax and Phaidon both grimaced. "Apologies, Dominus."

Kaeso laughed again, then coughed when Quintus turned his glare at him. "I think your punishment will be dealt later."

Kaeso smirked up at Quintus and he raised an eyebrow. "Gratitude, Quintus."

Phaidon almost laughed but cleared his throat and kept his gaze to the floor. Resigned, Quintus sighed and turned, and both Phaidon and Harpax's shoulders shook with their barely concealed laughter. Kaeso gave them a grin before falling into step beside Quintus, and the four of them started toward the docks.

Their good humour was short-lived, however. Upon reaching the docks, Quintus approached the naval command post, seeking entry. "Under whose authority?" the officer asked. He looked over their uniforms, looked twice at Quintus' height and size, but remained stoic.

"Senator Servius Augendus," Quintus replied, his voice stern, his back straight, chin raised.

The officer hesitated, but their attention was taken by raised voices coming from the next tent. The red and gold banners and the two dressed guards by the door told Kaeso the tent was for someone important, and who should come out of it but Tiberius.

"See it done, or see the consequences," he barked back into the tent, then stormed off. He didn't see them. He didn't even spare a glance into the entry post. He scowled, red-faced, as he strode off; two of his fellow praetorian guards followed quickly. Then, not a moment later, a naval commander, Kaeso assumed from his uniform, stepped out of the tent. He wore a chest plate with an embossed ship, pteruges, and a red cape over one shoulder, fastened to his chest plate with gold buckles.

He too was red-faced, though more from fear than anger. He watched Tiberius leave, scowled at his back, then turned and marched off in the opposite direction. The two guards who had stood at the door followed on his heels.

The four of them watched the whole encounter, though it was Quintus who spoke. "Who is that?" Quintus asked, nodding toward the naval commander who marched down the docks.

The officer said nothing, so Quintus turned to him and glared. He seemed to get larger when he fumed. "I asked a question!"

The officer flinched and stammered. "Jovian," he said. "Commander Jovian. He commands the port, under order of the emperor."

Quintus hummed. "And if one wishes to meet him?"

The officer glanced at Quintus, then looked straight ahead once more. "The senator is free to meet him at any time."

"It is not for the senator," Quintus replied casually.

The officer blinked but nodded. "Oh. The commander only meets with officials of rank. If it is a civil matter—"

Quintus raised his hand. "I will have the senator arrange it," he said.

"Very well." The officer nodded. "Though the senator was here just yesterday, if he—"

"Yesterday?" Quintus interrupted.

The officer paused for half a beat, realising he had divulged information he was not at liberty to give. "Your name?" he asked, trying to gain control of the conversation.

"Is not your concern," Quintus snapped. "I will confer the matter with the senator."

The officer wisely shut his mouth and Quintus gave his farewell with just a nod, and the four of them departed. When they were out of earshot, Kaeso said, "I thought the senator did not walk through the city unattended by guards."

Quintus was clearly not happy. "As did I."

"What does this mean?" Phaidon asked as they walked.

Quintus' jaw ticked. "It means not all is as it seems." He shook his head and growled in frustration, or perhaps anger. Possibly both. Kaeso couldn't tell which. "It means we set our focus to task and see this done."

The people of Neapolis gave them a wary berth, given the mountain of fury that was Quintus as he led them back to the villa. Only a fool would dare step in his path. Even Helier looked to raise question with him until he saw Quintus' face. He promptly shut his mouth and stepped back. Kaeso couldn't help but smile at that.

He might have been biased against Helier. Quintus thought him harmless, but Kaeso couldn't even stand to cast eyes upon him. And it wasn't that Helier had been offered to Quintus; this was not jealousy. Something of unease sat under Kaeso's skin when he saw him. Helier wasn't imposing physically: he was not much taller than Kaeso and more slender-framed. Kaeso was without doubt he could best him if it came to a fight. But his eyes missed nothing, and Kaeso likened the way he moved to a snake. He slithered without sound around the villa, cold and calculating.

But Helier was no fool. He recognised Quintus' anger and backed away, so Kaeso took his helmet off and paused in front of him. "If you have words to break..." Kaeso said.

Helier's gaze shot to Kaeso and he glared. "Words which do not concern the likes of you."

Quintus stopped and spun back to him, his voice fortified with fire and fury. "The likes of what, slave? The likes of what?"

Helier's eyes widened and he paled. "I have misspoken. Apologies."

Quintus' hands were clenched into fists. "You will

speak to him as you would to me. Do you take issue with that, slave?"

Helier shrank down, his gaze to the floor. "No issue. Apologies. My words come from a place of worry with the pending games."

Quintus stared at him and something changed. He shook his head and waved him off. "Be gone."

Helier needed not to be told twice. Quintus stomped into his quarters and threw his helmet onto the bed. "I would have you in the baths," Kaeso murmured. "I will ask for privacy and see your worries erased."

"My men—"

"I will see to them," Kaeso said. "I will have them tend to their weapons. It will be no day wasted. See yourself to the baths, and I will join you."

Quintus took a deep breath and he sagged on the exhale. "You give me orders again."

Kaeso smiled. "Which you would do well to obey." He left Quintus there and found the guards in the training yard. Harpax and Phaidon had themselves an audience, obviously repeating what they had seen. Kaeso told them he delivered Quintus' order to sit in the shade and tend to their weapons, both wooden and combat metal. Sharpen, tighten, oil; they needed no instruction. When they were done, they could retire early for the day.

Without one utterance of complaint, without hesitation, they did as asked. Though Salonia cast Kaeso a curious look, he returned a small smile to ease her worry, then made his way to the baths to ease Quintus of his.

Quintus was untying his boots when Kaeso entered. "I seem to have fallen into habit of taking your orders."

Kaeso smiled. "I would ask one more of you yet."

Quintus kicked off his boot and raised an eyebrow at Kaeso. "And that would be?"

"You are not yet naked, and you are not yet in the bath. I would see both wrongs righted."

Quintus finally smiled. "You become bold."

"It is not for my pleasure that I make such requests."

"I beg to differ," Quintus said. "Your pleasure precedes mine, every time. Does it not?"

Now it was Kaeso who smiled. "Quintus?"

"Yes?"

"Your tunic."

Quintus' smile widened, but he did pull it over his head. Then he pulled at his subligaculum. "And this?"

"Most definitely off."

Quintus removed the cloth undergarment so he stood, naked. Gloriously so. His cock was half hard, hanging heavy and full, and Kaeso could barely take his eyes from it.

"Kaeso?" Quintus asked.

He startled. "Yes?"

"You are not yet naked," Quintus said, repeating Kaeso's words back to him.

Kaeso allowed himself another moment to appreciate the man before him. "It is as though the gods themselves carved you from stone. Or perhaps you should stand amongst them."

Quintus scoffed. "You will anger them should they hear you speak such things."

Kaeso pulled at his boots. "Not at all. They would cast eyes upon you and be in agreement with me." Then he pulled off his tunic and nodded toward the bath. "You are not yet in the bath, Quintus."

"I would wait until you join me," he murmured. "I would see you stand before me, as I stand before you."

Kaeso pulled off his subligaculum, and he watched as Quintus' blue eyes darkened. "I stand before you," he whispered. "For you."

Quintus took two large strides and closed the distance between them. He put his huge hand to Kaeso's jaw and tilted his face up towards his. It was this moment, before their lips met, that stole Kaeso's breath and made his legs weak. Then Quintus whispered against his lips, "And I for you."

And Kaeso thought his heart might gallop from his chest. He struggled to breathe, and it made him laugh. "Now step into the bath before I take you to the floor and have my way with you."

Quintus chuckled. "Your argument for a bath is lacking when the floor is more appealing." He gripped his hard cock and stroked it. "An ever-present concern when you are near."

Kaeso groaned; the heady scent of arousal filled the air. "Take to the bath or you will be seeing to your own needs."

Quintus laughed. "You give orders well," he said, stepping into the bath. "If Oscilius ever hands in his whip, he should hand it to you."

Kaeso raised an eyebrow. "Would you like my orders delivered with the sting of a whip?"

Quintus sank into the water and chuckled. "On second thought, perhaps not."

Kaeso followed him into the bath and stood at his back, beginning to knead the hard muscles of his shoulders. Quintus let his head fall forward and he groaned, a low, obscene sound. "You have the touch of a god," he mumbled.

"As you have said before," Kaeso whispered. He continued to dig his thumbs into Quintus' shoulders. "You carry your worries here. Let me help you lighten the burden."

Quintus eventually lifted his head, but Kaeso could see he kept his eyes closed. He smiled serenely. "When you said you would see to my worries, I assumed you had something else in mind."

"I do have something else in mind," Kaeso said. "I will see your whole body's needs are met."

Quintus opened his eyes and looked upward, smiling up at him, then turned to admire Kaeso's cock in the water. He licked his lips and looked up to Kaeso again. "A taste?"

"My purpose for this bath was to see your needs met," Kaeso said, though his cock jerked at the thought of Quintus' mouth.

"What I need is to taste," Quintus said. He gripped Kaeso's hips, looking up at him for permission.

Kaeso nodded and Quintus lifted Kaeso so he sat on the tiled edge of the bath, and Quintus knelt in the water. He licked and sucked the head, then took his whole length into his mouth.

Kaeso threaded his fingers through Quintus' short, curly hair, lifting one leg onto Quintus' broad shoulders. By the gods, if anyone were to see them now... Slaves were rarely pleasured *by* their masters; it was always the slave's duty to pleasure their master. If someone should walk in and see them...

Quintus took him into his throat and fondled his balls, and Kaeso could hold back no more. His tenuous grip on pleasure slipped through his hands, and he gave himself up to it. Quintus grunted as he swallowed, and Kaeso's back arched until he could give no more.

Quintus pulled off his mouth and stood, and as though Kaeso was weightless, boneless, Quintus flipped him over and bent him over the edge of the bath. He grabbed the bath oils, and still spinning with his release, Kaeso was barely aware of the sound of slick skin, and then Quintus was pushing against him, pushing inside him.

Kaeso gasped and attempted to stand. Quintus kept one hand on Kaeso's hip, holding him still, and wrapped his other arm around Kaeso's chest. He didn't thrust, allowing Kaeso to adjust to the size of him inside him, and he whispered, hot and rough, in Kaeso's ear. "Breathe."

Kaeso exhaled and took in more air, and he relaxed with the reminder.

"That is it," Quintus murmured. "This is what you crave."

Kaeso whined. He couldn't deny it. He did crave it. He was so full of Quintus, every part of him he could take, he took. Then Quintus pushed him back over the tiles and thrust in harder, making Kaeso groan with pleasure.

Quintus leaned over him, his forehead pressed to the back of Kaeso's head, and he continued to thrust. "I want to last forever, but you bring pleasure too fast," Quintus mumbled. Then his grip tightened, and he reached up to take hold of Kaeso's face, pressing his forehead to the side of Kaeso's cheek. "I will have you twice. In our bed when the night is ours, I will have you again. Would you like that?"

"By the gods, yes. Quintus, yes," Kaeso said between thrusts.

Quintus thrust hard one last time and Kaeso could feel his seed pulsing into him. Quintus made a strangled cry, and he collapsed on top of Kaeso, panting and rocking, murmuring sweet nothings. Then he slowly pulled out, collecting Kaeso in his arms as he sank into the bath with him.

Kaeso rested in his lap, encased in Quintus' strong arms

like a child. Kaeso buried his face into his neck and closed his eyes, and for one single moment, he could pretend everything was removed, and this—them alone without a care—was their life.

Then someone cleared their throat, and Kaeso opened his eyes to see a very subdued Helier standing by the door. "Apologies for the intrusion," he said meekly.

"What do you want?" Quintus' voice rumbled through his chest against Kaeso's ear.

Kaeso looked over at Helier and smiled. He didn't care if he saw this intimate moment between them. In fact, he was glad he did.

"The senator would have you join him for the evening meal."

Helier backed out of the room and Kaeso laughed. He crawled up and planted a kiss on Quintus lips. "Do you think he heard us?"

Quintus chuckled. "I think the gods heard us." Then he gripped Kaeso's face and deepened the kiss before eventually slowing and pulling his bottom lip between his own lips. "Did I hurt you?" he asked quietly.

Kaeso smiled and pecked a sweet kiss to his lips. "A little. I may show bruises for your efforts."

"Apologies, Kaeso," he murmured. "I get so taken with you I lose control."

"No apology required. You take me the way you know I like."

Quintus stroked Kaeso's hair and trailed his fingertips down the side of his face, searching his eyes. "I do not like causing you pain."

"Fear not. If I require your apology, I will be sure to tell you."

Quintus chuckled. "I am sure you will."

"You made a promise though, to have me again in our bed when the night is ours," Kaeso said smiling. "I will hold you to it."

Quintus hummed and shook his head, though his eyes sparked with a fire of wonder. "Perhaps you crave more than I can give."

Kaeso slid his arms around Quintus' neck and smiled against his lips. "Perhaps you should not doubt what you can deliver. Because you *will* deliver."

Quintus drew him in for another kiss, cupping Kaeso's jaw and drawing him to his chest. It was an intimate embrace, one of possession and emotion. Their tongues met in a tender dance, and Kaeso began to grind on Quintus' lap once more until Quintus pulled back with a laugh. "We should stop," he said, lips swollen and cheeks flushed. "Let us see what Servius has to say over our meal, then we can continue *this* conversation—" He thumbed Kaeso's bottom lip. "—in our bed."

QUINTUS COULD TELL by the way Servius shifted in his seat and eyed him across the table that he had words to break. Yet he fussed over his wife and over the other slaves, and normally Quintus would ask him outright to speak his mind.

But not this night.

Instead, he paid the senator no mind and found himself drawn to Kaeso. He urged him to sit forward at the table, not back a little as he was prone to do. Quintus wanted him to sit as his equal, so he took Kaeso's plate hostage until he complied. Kaeso chuckled, with heated cheeks, but he scooted forward and Quintus leaned into him. "Your place is beside me," he whispered. He slid his plate back to him and nudged him gently. "Eat. You will require the sustenance later."

Kaeso smiled and nodded toward Quintus' untouched meal. "I would caution you the same."

Quintus chuckled, and he felt all eyes at the table upon them. Perhaps it was foolish to show his affection for Kaeso so boldly—Servius would be inclined to use it against him, as Oscilius had warned—yet he found himself unable to hide it.

His affection for Kaeso had become something else. As if a seed of ember had taken hold in his heart and bloomed into a warmth he had not seen the likes of before. A fire, if he was being truthful, and every glance, every look, every time they touched, kissed, fucked, Kaeso fanned the flames.

Quintus was helpless to simply let the blaze consume him.

Servius cleared his throat and sipped his wine. His eyes were aiming for pleasant, yet the wariness seeped through. "Your expedition to the arena today," he hedged. "Unearth anything worthy of my attention?"

Quintus swallowed down his mouthful, and it gave him pause to consider his answer. From his words and his nervousness, Quintus assumed Servius knew something, but he could only guess what. "The praetorian, Tiberius, is in Neapolis," Quintus admitted.

Servius blinked, stunned. "You laid eyes upon him yourself, or you heard rumour?"

"We saw him," Quintus admitted. "At the docks."

Servius swallowed hard and his features grew cold. How he could change, as though flipping a coin, was unnerving to witness. "And you spoke to him?"

"No," Quintus said. "We remained undetected."

"Do we know his purpose here in Neapolis?" Servius gave Quintus a cool stare. "He does not tend the emperor, as I would know if he himself were here."

"It would not appear he is here on instruction, yet who gives the orders is unknown. It was only him and two other guards," Quintus replied. "We saw him leave the docks, cursing and foul-tempered."

"You did not follow him?" Servius pressed.

"No. I believed an altercation between us would be fruitless."

Servius gave pause and seemed to consider this. "I believe you are right." He sipped his wine and swallowed. "Anything else?"

Quintus held his stare, and it surprised him how easy it was to lie. "No. Uneventful. The arena is being prepared, the rear gate is still sealed."

Servius smiled and his pleasant face was back. "Very good then."

"The games draw near," Quintus added. "Just eight days hence."

"I trust you have everything in order," Servius said, smiling now.

"Oh, yes," Quintus answered. "I trust you do too."

KAESO HAD NOT SPOKEN for the remainder of the evening, and Quintus knew as soon as they were alone the questions would be fast and forthcoming. He wasn't wrong.

"You lied to the senator," Kaeso hissed; Quintus barely heard him. They stood in their barely lit room, facing each other. "We saw Tiberius argue with the naval commander, who we learned the senator met with just two days ago. We know he has ordered warships returned to port. When he asked if there was more to your findings, you said there was not."

"I withheld information," Quintus whispered in reply.

"To lie to a senator is treason," Kaeso hissed again, his eyes wide and frantic. "Quintus, to what end does this serve? Do you wish to see your head parted from your neck? Because I do not."

Quintus pulled Kaeso against him. "I assure you that will not happen. Strike such worries from your mind—"

"I will do no such thing," he said, looking up at him. He attempted to pull away, but Quintus held him close. "You cannot lie to him, then say there is no cause for concern."

"I have my reasons," Quintus said calmly.

"Explain them to me," Kaeso said. "For I fail to see any."

Quintus brushed Kaeso's face and held his gaze. "Trust me, rabbit, when I say I cannot tell you. I would not have you implicated."

"Quintus," Kaeso started.

"Do you trust me?"

Kaeso stared back at him, his dark eyes imploring. "I do."

"Then I would ask you to hold onto trust and know I have your best interest at heart."

"And if the senator should ask me what I saw?"

"Tell him you saw a town swelling with people and coin," Quintus said. "Tell him the games are a welcome reprieve, and the people will not forget it or the senator who made it so. Plump his ego; you know as well as I do how he likes that."

Kaeso sighed. "I do not like this, Quintus."

"I know you do not."

Kaeso was quiet again, though Quintus could feel how Kaeso's pulse quickened with his breaths. "What is it, rabbit?"

"You ask for my trust, and you have it," he replied. "So if you wish to know from where my dislike of the darkness stems..."

"Only if you wish me to know."

"It is not easy for me to speak of it." He swallowed hard, and Quintus gave him time to find the words he needed. "On my journey to Rome, I was thrown in the cargo hold of a leaking ship. It was old and it would creak and groan, and we had water at our feet. I feared a stronger leak would see us drown." He looked up at Quintus. "Like the darkness of the hypogeum, only surrounded by sea and a darkness so black... Day or night made no difference. The darkness scares me but for when I am in your arms." His breath shook, and Quintus cupped his face, letting him get the words out that haunted him. "But that feeling has returned. Of being trapped and absent light. Only the situation we find ourselves in with the senator and Tiberius is the ship, and we were taking on water, Quintus. That is how I feel. One more leak, one more wave to crash down upon us and we are drowned."

Quintus wrapped his arms around him tight and held him until he could feel the tension leave Kaeso's shoulders. "I am sorry you suffered through that," he murmured. "I wish it otherwise. I wish it all was different. I wish we were at my ludus, in the orchard under the stars without worry. I wish for so much it makes my heart ache for it. But I promise you this." He pulled back and brought his forehead to Kaeso's. "I promise you I will see it so. After these games, just eight days from now, I will see it so."

Kaeso nodded sadly. "I do not see how it is possible," he whispered. "Yet I trust you."

Quintus kissed him softly. "I owe you a promise made," he murmured. "If you lie on the bed, I will make good on my debt."

Kaeso gave him a sad smile. "I would ask for something else," he said. "If you're agreeable."

"Anything."

"Just lie with me. Hold me in your arms and let me hear

the beat of your heart in my ear. I would sleep in your arms if you would have me."

"If I would have you?" Quintus asked with a smile. "Ridiculous rabbit. I would not ever have anyone else."

———

THREE DAYS LATER, Quintus broke from training and made his way to Servius' office just as the senator appeared to be leaving. He wore his formal toga with a scroll of papyrus in hand, and Helier stood with him.

"You are leaving?" Quintus asked.

Servius blinked. "No, whatever gave you that idea?"

"Your shawl," Quintus replied. "It hides the senatorial stripe, and Helier is wearing shoes." Quintus smiled and held his stare. "I can prepare an escort in a moment's notice."

Servius knew he had been found out. "Not required. The matter is a private one."

"But I insist," Quintus said coolly. "The streets and marketplace swell with strangers and unseen threats. It would be unwise to go unaided."

"Caution is well-advised, but I insist on your absence. I carry with me a private matter of Roma, entrusted to me by the emperor. I shall not be swayed from duty."

Quintus conceded a slow nod, almost a bow, and he stepped aside. "Apologies. Please proceed." Servius and Helier slithered past, but as they got to the door, Quintus said, "Though I would ask one thing?"

Servius stopped. "And what is that?"

"Simply to know when to expect your return. Should you be late, then I will know to raise the alarm."

Servius considered this for a moment and finally

nodded. "Very well. I do not expect to be later than midday. Should you have cause for concern."

Quintus simply replied with a nod, and he watched as Servius and Helier left the villa. Quintus went to the training yard and called a pause to training. "Kaeso, Salonia, Varia, Harpax, and Phaidon," he said. "You are with me. Appias, resume command."

The five of them followed Quintus toward the stables where the weapons were stored, but also where he could speak with no one listening. "We need to move quickly. We cannot be seen or heard. Conceal your weapons."

"Weapons?" Kaeso asked.

Quintus nodded, and they each took a small blade and slid it into their belts. "To be used only if your life depends on it," Quintus whispered. "Salonia and Varia, take to the roofs and follow us. Harpax and Phaidon, take the lower roads and stay hidden. Kaeso and I will take the main road. I assume our destination is the docks."

"Whom do we follow?" Kaeso asked.

"The senator and Helier. We see whomever it is they intend to meet and, if we are able, what is said." Quintus looked each of them in the eye. "Let us move with haste. The senator already has time and distance on us."

They slipped out of the slaves' gate at the back of the lot, and exactly as Quintus had ordered, Phaidon and Harpax disappeared down the street, and Salonia and Varia were already out of view. He couldn't see them, yet he knew they were there. He kept to the wall of stone, and Kaeso was close behind him.

It wasn't lost on Quintus that the only one to question him was Kaeso. The others simply took his orders without hesitation; whatever he asked of them, they would see it done. And it wasn't that Kaeso questioned Quintus, it was his curiosity, his need to know the stratagem before he stepped into the fight. He would fight without question, his blades would always find their mark; he simply needed to know his targets before he began.

Quintus was the same. He had a tactical mind, and it helped to see the desired end before the first strike. Quintus liked this about Kaeso. That he would question the manoeuvres and the wit of the one who gave commands. He was no fool; his mind was sharp. He had the eye of an eagle and the tongue of an asp: fast and fierce.

Quintus had no doubt that tongue of Kaeso's would find him in trouble in coming years and he looked forward to it. Quintus was acutely aware that Kaeso was the only one to raise his hackles at him, question, and confront him. He had spent his life after the earthquake that stole his parents, and even just a child himself, as a dominus. No one dared question him. Except for Kaeso, and Quintus liked it. And the coming years, where he and Kaeso would spend days together at his ludus, were so close, Quintus could almost taste it. They would have endless nights and—

"Quintus!" Kaeso hissed, grabbing the back of his tunic.

He stilled and realised he had almost walked out into the open. He could have blown their cover if Kaeso had not stopped him. "Apologies," he mumbled.

"Where is your mind?" Kaeso whispered.

Quintus pressed himself against the wall, hiding in shadow. "Years from now, when this is far behind us. When I will pick apricots from my orchard for you, and you will laugh as you catch fish from the shore. When our biggest concern is time." He sighed. "That is where my mind is."

Kaeso sighed. "A favoured thought, and one I would cherish. Yet perhaps we should live through this day first."

"Sound advice," Quintus mumbled. He chanced a look

around the corner and saw Servius talking to a merchant. He looked frustrated, and Quintus was of the opinion that the merchant had stopped him, not the other way around. The merchant held rolls of vermillion and was trying to convince the senator to buy. Eventually he bought a swathe of the fabric and he handed the folded parcel to Helier, and the merchant very happily pocketed the coin.

Servius marched on with a more determined gait, so Quintus waved Kaeso along, and on they went. Servius strode past the markets and rounded another corner before taking the last street to the docks.

Quintus and Kaeso were concealed mostly by the crowds of people in the streets. Well, Kaeso was easily hidden, though Quintus had to duck his head a little as he stood well taller than most people. Broader too, and if he was being sought, he would have been easily found. He wore his standard tunic and not his armoured uniform and helmet, thankfully. Even Quintus could admit he was a formidable sight in full uniform. Helpful against any attack. Not so helpful when trying to hide.

But Servius wasn't keeping an eye out for Quintus or anyone else. He walked at a pace that Helier struggled to keep up with, as though he was now late meeting someone. And Quintus and Kaeso took refuge in the doorway of a *taberna* and watched as Servius and Helier slipped straight past the naval command post, past the guards at the tent of Commander Jovian, and disappeared inside.

Two things were very clear to Quintus; Servius and Helier were expected, and they did this often enough not to raise even an eyebrow from the best naval guards.

Then he saw Phaidon and Harpax walk by the command post as if they had every civilian right to do exactly that. They looked the part, wearing basic tunics, and

Phaidon boasted loudly of a feigned brothel conquest, earning not even a second glance from any passers-by. They disappeared from sight perhaps, Quintus realised, to gain access from behind the tents. Quintus saw a flicker of fabric on the roofline opposite, and then it was gone, and he knew Salonia and Varia were watching as well.

And they waited.

Not long afterwards, Servius appeared at the doorway to the tent. He was in conversation with someone, and Quintus expected it to be Helier who followed him into the sunlight. But it wasn't.

It was Tiberius.

Both men smiled and spoke, and even though Quintus could not make out their words, it was obviously an amicable exchange. Quintus bristled at what he was seeing, though it wasn't until Helier appeared behind the two, salacious smile in place, that Kaeso let out a growl.

Suddenly, all three turned to the roofline, and Quintus feared Salonia or Varia had been discovered. His heart stopped and he held his breath, and then a flurry of birds squawked and took flight from the roof. The three turned back to their conversation and Quintus finally breathed.

"By the gods," Kaeso whispered. "That was too close."

"Agreed," Quintus mumbled.

It looked as if Quintus and Tiberius were nearing the end of their meeting. Tiberius now held the scroll of papyrus and he nodded his gratitude toward the senator. "We must take our leave," Kaeso urged.

"No. We follow again and see in which other lair the snake makes its bed."

"How do we—"

Quintus took Kaeso's hand and pulled him into an alley. They earned the interest from both beggars and prostitutes, but when Quintus pushed Kaeso up against the wall and kissed him, they were quickly left alone.

Quintus was not careful or polite; he took Kaeso's mouth as a drunkard might take a whore's. He pressed Kaeso against the wall, his huge frame holding Kaeso in place with just his body, his hands pinned above his head. Though Quintus also leaned and hid Kaeso mostly from view, should any curious eye seek them from the street.

Eventually Quintus had to draw breath. "Have they passed?" he asked.

Kaeso blinked, his eyes unfocused, his lips swollen.

Quintus moved back enough so Kaeso could slide down the wall. Still unable to form words, he did manage a smile. Quintus chuckled, then was startled by three sharp taps above his head.

His gaze shot upward, and he saw Salonia's hand tap the tiles on the roof, then her long finger pointed to the direction the senator had gone.

"Now we take our leave," Quintus said. "Are you able to walk?"

Having regained his wits, Kaeso snarled at him, and the sound of laughter, as light as the breeze, rang out overhead. Quintus grinned. "Let's go."

THEY MADE it back to the villa before Servius and Helier. They stopped nowhere else, and it was only the fact that Servius was stopped in the street that gave Quintus and his men the advantage to get back to the villa before him.

They slipped through the slaves' gate at the rear of the villa and were in the training yard throwing knives when Servius came to the courtyard steps. "Quintus," he called.

Everyone paused, and Quintus gave them an order. "Break for midday meal." He left them and approached Servius. "Grateful to see you have returned without incident."

Servius sighed. "Yes, well. Advice given will be heeded in the future. The streets are overflowing. Good for Neapolis, though it slows my purpose."

Quintus feigned alarm. "Were you accosted?"

Servius waved him off. "Nothing I could not manage, but in two days I will be tasked with giving a speech at the forum to precede the games. I should expect greater audience and the threat which accompanies it."

"Then you will not be without guards," Quintus said.

Servius huffed and took off his cloak and threw it to Helier. Servius dabbed the back of his hand to his forehead, clearly affected by the heat. "No. I would not think so."

"As opportunity presents itself," Quintus said. "A full uniform practice before the games."

"Very well," Servius said as he turned to leave. "I shall be in my office."

"Before you go," Quintus said. "Tomorrow, my men will practise the parade to the forum, then seek the fastest route to return you to the villa, if required."

Servius sighed again. "Agreed," he said reluctantly, as though his mind was elsewhere, then turned and walked away with Helier following dutifully.

Quintus returned to the training yard to wary eyes. Kaeso went straight to him. "Does he suspect you?" he whispered.

"Not at all," Quintus replied. Then he spoke loud enough for all to hear. "Tomorrow after the morning meal, we make for the forum with full uniform and weapons as a practice run for two days hence when the senator is due to declare the games."

This was received with serious nods and obedience, as Quintus expected, until his eyes met Kaeso's. He smiled. "You have questions?"

Kaeso gave a nod. "Of course. Why does he declare the games three days before they begin?"

"To welcome travellers to Neapolis and to give a gentle reminder to his people to be gracious for the coin travellers bring." Quintus smiled. "Anything else?"

"How long are the games expected to last?" Kaeso asked.

"Three days," Quintus said. "Sometimes longer."

"And on which day do the gladiators take to the arena?"

Everyone's gaze leapt from Kaeso to Quintus and back again with each question and answer, and Quintus fought a smile. "Usually the last day, as it is what the public come to see, though it will depend on who they bring to fight."

Murmurs of Appias' name were followed by some claps on Appias' shoulders, and he raised his right hand as he would in victory. "If they roar my name, I shall gladly answer," he said, and all the guards laughed.

Except for Kaeso. "When does the emperor arrive from Roma?" he asked.

"I expect he will arrive the morning of the first day. The games will not start until he is there," Quintus answered. He was curious now as to Kaeso's line of thought. "What is your purpose in asking?"

"And when is Oscilius expected with your remaining gladiators?" Kaeso asked.

"The day before," Quintus answered. "Kaeso, where do these questions take you?"

Everyone now stood in silence and waited for Kaeso to

answer. He looked around to see no other ears were listening. "I can't help but wonder why the naval ships are to dock on the same day as the emperor arrives. And if those ships are expected to return from the Britannian battles empty. Or if they bring soldiers. We can perhaps hold off an attack from a handful of enemy guards, but Quintus, we cannot hold off a legion."

Hushed murmurs whispered of soldiers swarming the arena to attack the emperor. Was this the senator's bidding all along? Not to take promotion, but to take Rome? Had he acquired Quintus and his men to help safeguard this treacherous manoeuvre?

Quintus felt a coldness caress his skin, and it seeped inside and twisted in his gut. He stared at Kaeso as everyone else stared at him. "Then tomorrow, I shall meet with Fleet Commander Jovian. And we will see once and for all whose arrows are aimed at who."

CAPITULUM XXI

COMMANDER JOVIAN WAS A TALL MAN. Not as tall as Quintus but taller than most. He was perhaps in his fourth decade, maybe fifth, and he had short brown hair and dark rings around troubled eyes.

He had possibly been a proud man once, and if his rank had been in the army, he would have been feared and renowned throughout all of Rome. But the Roman navy lacked the reputation of its land-based military forces. Quintus wasn't sure why; in his opinion, the navy worked just as hard protecting Rome from invasion, on rough seas in grand ships, no less. If the navy had not transported soldiers and supplies to all far-reaching places, Rome would never have grown and conquered as much as it had. But still, the navy was never held in the same regard as the imposing Roman army.

Naval officers, men such as Jovian, were considered inferior officers compared to their army counterparts, and as such, they weren't always accompanied by guards or lower-ranking officers.

And it was by this good fortune that Quintus and Kaeso

found Jovian darting through the crowded streets unattended. Quintus had sent half his guards to the arena to scout for any developments and the other half to the forum, while he and Kaeso went to the docks. They had not even reached the timber piers yet when they saw Jovian hurrying toward them. He appeared focused on his task. And worried. He looked even older than he had just a few days prior. Something was definitely weighing on his mind.

Quintus gripped Kaeso's arm, stopping him in his tracks, and Quintus nodded to Jovian who scurried past without even looking up. They quickly fell into step beside him and swiftly ushered him into an alley, which turned out to be lined with pens of goats and sheep—the smell wasn't exactly pleasant—and Quintus pushed them into an archway out of passing view.

"What do you want?" Jovian hissed, his fear apparent.

"No need for concern," Quintus said. He slid off his helmet so he was less imposing. "I am Quintus Varus, and I am guard to Senator Servius Augendus."

Jovian's eyes widened. "I have delivered the order," he said quickly. "I cannot do any more."

"Calm yourself," Quintus urged him and glanced around to see if anyone was listening. No one was. "What order do you speak of?"

Jovian's face drained as though he had given himself away too easily. "A p-private matter," he stammered.

"A private matter that involves the games two days hence?" Quintus asked. "Perhaps he has warships return to Neapolis while the city's eyes are averted to the arena? To ambush the emperor, perhaps? Is that his ploy?"

Jovian's eyes widened, and his mouth fell open. "What? No, never!" Then he whisper-hissed, "You do not speak of such attack on the emperor, or I will—"

"You will tell me what the senator is planning," Quintus growled. "You will tell me what lies and treachery he beckons from secret meetings with the fleet commander and praetorian guard."

Jovian sagged. "To imply his meetings with me are in my favour is a lie. He threatens me—"

An outburst of bleats and foreign commands interrupted him, and they paused to watch a herder wrangle his goats past them down the alley.

Jovian edged away while Quintus was momentarily distracted. Quintus quickly grabbed his arm. "I cannot be seen," Jovian mumbled, fearful. He leaned in and whispered urgently, "The ships that return are not warships; they carry no soldiers. They leave empty and return laden with riches only to leave again at the senator's doing. You want to know what treachery he beckons, look to the praetorian." Jovian sneered. "They circle like wild beasts. I know not whose bite I fear the most, but know this. If either smells blood, they will both attack."

And with that, Jovian was gone.

Quintus' mind swam with all that Jovian had said, and when he met Kaeso's eyes, he saw a flicker of fear. "Look to the praetorian?" Kaeso whispered. "He means Tiberius?"

Quintus sneered and swallowed down the metallic taste of anger on his tongue. "Confirmation of what we already suspected," he murmured. "Servius and Tiberius move toward a mutual end."

"Against the emperor or Rome?" Kaeso asked.

"They are but one and the same." Quintus moved to walk back onto the street.

"Quintus, wait," Kaeso said, pulling his arm. He looked up into his eyes, imploring brown to furious blue. "I know you would move to stop them, but this is not our fight."

Quintus stared, unblinking. "How is it not? How is a threat against Rome not a threat to each man who calls himself a Roman?"

"I am not a Roman man," Kaeso snapped back.

"I beg to differ." Quintus had to rein in his temper. "You stand in front of me, on Roman soil, wearing the uniform of a Roman guard. You are Roman."

Kaeso kept his voice down, though his anger hissed through. "The soil on which I stand and the uniform I wear do not speak for what is in my heart."

Quintus smartened. "And what is in your heart?" he asked quietly, afraid to ask, and equally afraid not to.

"A foolish man who is blind to a land, to an empire, that would quicker see him dead than hear him accuse a senator or praetorian of treason."

Quintus wasn't sure which part of that to pull apart first. "Foolish?"

Kaeso sighed with frustration. "Just because you are an honourable man, do not expect all others to be. Servius and Tiberius would put a knife in your back without second thought." Kaeso jabbed a finger into Quintus' breastplate. "Do not lay down your life for someone who would step over your dying body for financial gain."

"So am I foolish or honourable?" Quintus asked. "Because you seem—"

Now Kaeso pushed his chest, hard. "It is not just about you. Not anymore. You have men who need you. I need you, Quintus. *I need you!*" He took a deep breath and appeared to calm his temper. "If you start speaking of treason without a proper plan, it will be your head that falls. Do you think Servius and Tiberius would be so foolish as to have no counter-plan? If ever questioned, they would bring false reports or paid witnesses, and you would lose your fucking head."

Quintus bit back his anger. He was furious that Kaeso dare speak to him like that, but angrier still because he was right. "What would you have me do? I cannot stand idle."

"Construct a plan to best them. Construct many plans in case we are thwarted at each turn." Kaeso shook his head. "I do not know. But tell me this, when you send your gladiators into the arena, do you brew a plan first or just send them in and hope their anger will see them through?"

Quintus huffed with indignation. "Of course, we have plans. Tactics, manoeuvres, counterattacks. A gladiator can win when he uses his body, but he will be a champion if he uses his mind." His words ran out of momentum as he saw Kaeso's purpose.

Kaeso smiled. "Then set your mind to the task, and only when all anticipated moves can be foiled, then see it actioned."

Quintus stared at him for a long moment. "I am not certain I can. Given how foolish I am."

Kaeso rolled his eyes. "I make no apologies for calling you foolish. Be grateful that was all I put my tongue to."

Quintus scoffed. "There was more? Please, let us hear what you really think of me."

"I was going to say you had an insufferable temper."

Quintus narrowed his eyes. "As do you."

Kaeso smiled. "And you have the impatience of a spoilt child."

Quintus gasped. "I seem to recall many a time in bed where my patience easily bested yours."

Kaeso's nostrils flared. He had not seemed to notice how Quintus had cornered him against the wall or how close they now stood. "I also called you honourable."

"Now you flatter?" Quintus asked. "You also called me a horse's cock."

"Correction," Kaeso murmured. "I said you were gifted with a horse's cock, not that you were one."

"Your mouth will see you punished," Quintus added.

Kaeso spoke through clenched teeth. "Do not threaten me to win an argument."

"It is no threat," Quintus said. "But I do make one promise."

"And what is that?"

"I will punish you tonight," he murmured. "And you will beg me for it."

Kaeso smirked. "That was two promises."

"Your insolent mouth," Quintus growled. "I would have you on your knees right here lest it strike fear into the goats."

Kaeso laughed and glanced at the pens with the stock animals. "Gods forbid we scare the goats."

Quintus gave a half smile, and after a long moment, let out a sigh. "Gratitude," he mumbled. "I could have done without the insults, but you remind me of my truths, and I am grateful."

Kaeso looked up at him and smiled. "I will deliver your truths and insults as required. Now those sent to inspect the arena should have returned to the forum, let us collect the men and get back to the villa. We have a plan to forge, and you have two promises to make good on."

"And women," Quintus said.

Kaeso stopped. "What?"

Now it was Quintus who smiled. "You said 'let us collect the men'. I was correcting you. Men *and women*."

Kaeso sighed. "I will find purpose for your mouth as well."

"A promise I shall hold you to."

Kaeso growled and shoved him. "To the forum and on to the villa, then we shall see which of us is the first to beg."

Quintus chuckled, and they made their way to the forum. The guards were obediently standing post in practice for the next day, and Quintus ordered them home. He had discovered much today. Not just about Servius and Tiberius, or Jovian, but about himself and how well Kaeso could read him. Kaeso knew him like no one else. He saw Quintus for the man he strived to be. Quintus had allowed himself to be vulnerable, exposed like a wound to Kaeso, and was met with only kindness in return.

Kaeso also met him with fierce temper and never hesitated to question him or rebuke him. Quintus was like a stallion yet to be broken, yet Kaeso could pull on the reins with the gentlest of hands and turn Quintus on his heels.

Quintus knew he would have seen Servius and let his temper get the best of him, but with a reminder from Kaeso, he collected himself. He wouldn't roar and demand answers, as he was wont to do. Instead, he would set into motion a plan where Servius and Tiberius would reveal their own hands.

He just had to put his mind to the task, for he knew to lure snakes out of their lairs, he had to first provide the bait.

***

"WHAT TROUBLES YOU?" Kaeso asked. They were lying naked on their bed, their bodies spent, but sleep eluded their minds.

"A question better asked is what does not trouble me," Quintus answered with a sigh. He kissed Kaeso's forehead.

"For what troubles me is the world outside this room. I wish it would all fade away and all that remained was us."

Kaeso burrowed into Quintus' chest and sighed when Quintus tightened his hold. "Let us pretend. So in our dreams at least, we can have peace. When we are in this room, in this bed, there is only us. Strike all else from mind, Quintus. Morning comes early, and I would have you well rested for tomorrow." Kaeso kissed Quintus' chest and settled in finally to sleep.

Quintus hummed, his eyes closed. "Yes, and you also."

Only sleep didn't come easily. In fact, it barely came at all. Quintus had closed his eyes but for the briefest moment before he started awake. Horrors of having Kaeso ripped from his arms played in his mind, so vivid he thought them real until he realised Kaeso was still sleeping safe beside him.

He settled back down, his heart hammering like stampeding hooves. He didn't dare close his eyes again. He cradled Kaeso in his arms and stared at the doorway until dawn.

QUINTUS WAS AGITATED. Kaeso could see how he clenched his jaw, his fists. His gaze was piercing, his words short and clipped to match his temper.

Kaeso noted the wary looks from the other guards, how they eyed Quintus, how they could see something wasn't right, but how they kept their heads down and listened to his orders.

"Stay alert. Protect the senator. Protect each other. If we come under attack, get the senator back to the villa." He swallowed hard. "Do me proud today, as you do all days."

Then he walked over to where Kaeso waited. "You are tired," Kaeso said.

"A heavy mind," he murmured. Then he waited for someone to walk past, and when his eyes met Kaeso's, he said, low and just for him, "Stay beside me this day. I would have it be all days, but this one to start."

"Does your plan unfold today?" Kaeso asked quietly.

"My plan, no. Yet what lurks unforeseen, I cannot tell," he replied. "I would have you near. I can't protect the senator while I search for you at the same time."

"I can mind myself," Kaeso replied. "How about you watch Servius and I watch you? But fret not, Quintus. I will not be but a few steps from you. My heart would not allow it."

Quintus gave him a weary smile. "Gratitude."

They waited for Servius to be ready, took formation, and began the long procession to the forum. They had taken this path several times; they were familiar with the cobbled streets and high walls. People overflowed, excitement filled the air taking the edge off the summer heat and humidity.

Servius waved and paraded to the public, and Kaeso was grateful that his helmet hid most of his loathing for the man. To hear Quintus order his men to protect the senator was not easy. He understood why Quintus was maintaining the façade—to tell them of Servius' treachery would endanger them all—but still, the idea of protecting him made Kaeso's skin crawl with unease. He would rather step aside and let the blades find their intended mark, and he would certainly rather Quintus did the same. The very thought of Quintus being harmed while protecting that lying sack of shit and piss made Kaeso's blood boil.

And now, knowing Servius was linked to Tiberius and they were deceiving not only Quintus but all of Rome made

Kaeso even more wary. Threat wasn't now only from a jealous senator, or an angry civilian, or a naval commander pushed too far. Threat could now be the emperor and the entire Roman fucking army for all Kaeso knew.

And one thought plagued him as they entered the forum: now that he and Quintus knew something was rotten in the senator's plan, did that make them complicit?

It was no wonder Quintus had not slept.

The forum filled to bursting. Civilians, travellers, fleet men, and everyone in between embarked into the large square, and Servius stood on a wooden platform at the rear. He raised his arms and called for silence, and a hush fell over the crowd.

Quintus stood to the side, keeping an eye on the audience in all directions. He had guards posted in every corner, at every other column. Kaeso stood a few paces behind Quintus, watching the crowd, watching Quintus, watching Servius.

The senator welcomed people to his city, then proceeded to boast of himself mostly for the rest of his speech. If his intention was to make it known that he was to thank for the coming games, then he succeeded.

Before the heat became too much, before he lost the interest of the people, Servius concluded with an exaggerated welcome. Kaeso's contempt for the man grew with each treacherous word he spoke. Not that he knew the extent to which Servius was untrue, but now that Kaeso saw him with tainted eyes, everything he did was awash with it.

When Servius bid the crowd be well and promised to see them two days hence, he also promised them a spectacle not soon to be forgotten.

Kaeso smirked at that, but not for the reasons Servius hoped. It'd be a spectacle, that was certain. Kaeso wasn't sure what Quintus was planning, but he trusted him to expose Servius to the world.

If it all didn't unravel at the seams before then.

When Servius stepped down from his stage, Quintus was right there, and Kaeso was half a step behind. "I have a matter to tend to," Servius said. "In private. Though I would have you stand at the foot of the stairs and by its end"—he waved his hand in distaste to the crowd he just spoke to—"our return path might be clear."

Quintus gave a nod. "As you wish."

Servius dabbed the back of his hand to his forehead, grumbled at the sun, then disappeared in the corner of the forum to the stairs at the basilica with Helier on his heels. It was the same place he had gone before, the day Kaeso remembered as the day Quintus bought a honeyed date treat for him; a whim from his childhood, but the gesture from Quintus had forged so much more than that.

Quintus had said he would buy ten if Kaeso smiled as he had that day.

And that was why they had to see this plan to its end. They had to see Servius brought to justice; they had to find a way to break Kaeso from the bindings of Servius' collar. They had to live through this, and they had to be together on the other side at its end.

Kaeso couldn't imagine a life without Quintus would be worth living.

So they stood in formation at the stairs as they had before. Quintus stood at the entrance, his jaw clenched, his eyes a fierce blue. "Stay here," he whispered, then disappeared up the stairs.

His silent steps belied his size, and Kaeso thought he might lose his mind waiting for him to return. After what felt like the longest time, Quintus came down the stairs as quietly as he had gone up them. He stood, chin raised, staring straight ahead, then after a long moment, he finally glanced at Kaeso.

"We will return here later, when night is on our side," he said. "The man he meets holds the proof we need."

Soon after, Servius came down the stairs with the noise of an entire procession with Helier, as always, dutifully following after. Kaeso noticed Helier held a scroll of papyrus, and from Quintus' quick glance at him, he saw it too. The guards all fell into formation, and they began the trudge back to the villa. The crowd had dissipated somewhat, though people still filled the streets and Servius was back in public mode, waving and touching the adoring hands of the people.

Quintus and Kaeso stood at his sides, helping him move forward and keeping the crowds from swarming. By the time they reached the villa, it had been an exercise in patience more than strategy. And no sooner than they had walked through the villa doors, Servius announced he had more important matters to attend to in his office and he wasn't to be disturbed. Helier scurried off behind him, and Kaeso was glad to see the backs of both of them.

"Insufferable," Kaeso mumbled.

"Quite," Quintus agreed. He ordered his guards to the back courtyard, to strip out of their armour and store their weapons, then sit in the shade and drink water. They smiled gratefully and did as they were bid, but Quintus asked Salonia and Varia to remain with him. He waited until no other ears could hear. "Tonight, with the cover of darkness, we return to the forum. The man Servius meets there is an *actuarius* or perhaps a *quaestor*," Quintus murmured.

"A quaestor?" Kaeso asked.

"A magistrate who manages the treasury of the army and senate," Quintus answered. "Or in this case, I assume the navy. If Servius partakes in transactions against Rome, this man will know."

Kaeso grinned. "Then let us hope he can help us balance the scales."

Quintus, Salonia, and Varia all stared at him. Salonia tilted her head and Varia squinted her eyes at him and Quintus sighed. "Your attempt at word play falls flat," he said gently.

"Oh, come now," Kaeso said. "Do you not admit a smile, at least?"

Salonia gave Quintus a hard stare. "Does he inflict such wounds often?"

Quintus chuckled. "No, gods willing."

"Oh, you raise a smile at that," Kaeso said, duly offended.

Salonia laughed. "We will join you tonight," she said. "And if the quaestor refuses to part with information, perhaps we could subject him to Kaeso's jocular attempt as torture."

Varia's laugh, and her accompanying grin, was huge as they walked to the courtyard, stripping off their armour.

Kaeso glared at Quintus. "There is little wrong with my play on words," he grumbled. "Though I question your ability to comprehend."

Quintus slung his arm around Kaeso's shoulders and chuckled as they walked to the courtyard. "You bring welcome relief for a worried mind. Gratitude."

"Glad I have at least one purpose," Kaeso grumbled.

Quintus laughed some more and pulled Kaeso into his side as they walked out to the courtyard. Kaeso was smiling by the time they reached the yard where everyone rested in the shade. Quintus sat with them, so Kaeso joined him and listened as they told stories and laughed. Oscilius and the other gladiators would be arriving tomorrow, and there was an excitement in the air. Their ludus family would be reunited once more.

The excitement, the smiles and laughter, the feeling of belonging was contagious. And as the warm afternoon became evening, the culina called for the evening meal, and for a moment, no one moved. They all looked to Quintus, not for him to give the order, but for something else.

Of course, he noticed. "Tomorrow our brothers come to Neapolis. We shall see them at the arena. A few more nights and we shall eat, reunited together, under Oplontis' skies. I will have Cythereia cook a feast and we will celebrate our victories and we shall celebrate being returned home." He inhaled as though his chest filled with their joy. "I know what I ask of you here is not what you train for in the ludus. I offer my gratitude; you honoured me today."

"And we will honour you tomorrow," Appias said.

"And the day after that," Salonia added.

They all agreed with hollers and claps, and Quintus waved them toward the villa. "Go eat, and rest well."

Kaeso waited for the last of them to leave, and he offered Quintus his hand to help pull him to his feet. "If I ever doubted you," Kaeso said quietly, "doubted you as a lanista or as a dominus to those who wear your collars, I was a fool. They may honour you, but you see it returned. You honour them, and they know it."

Quintus lifted Kaeso's chin with gentle fingers and pressed their lips together. "Your words are well received. I wasn't aware how much I needed to hear them."

"Promise me, Quintus."

"Anything."

"The family you speak of," Kaeso murmured. "The family in your ludus, make me a part of it."

Quintus' smile rivalled the beauty of the sunset. "Kaeso, silly rabbit. You already are." He took his hand. "Come. We will eat with our brothers and wait for dark before we leave for the forum once more."

Kaeso was familiar with the house slave quarters, but he had not seen where the guards had been eating before now, but it was a long, crude table where they all fit facing each other. They all sat with their bowls of fish and beans, heads down as they ate. Quintus said, "Could you spare room for two?"

Everyone grinned and moved up one space on either side of the table, two more bowls were served, and they ate, still telling stories, still laughing.

As a family.

CAPITULUM XXII

ONCE THE VILLA WAS ASLEEP, in the dead of night, Quintus, Kaeso, Salonia, and Varia slipped out through the slaves' gate at the rear of the lot. The streets were empty, save a rat or two that scurried away, though a few errant hollers or bursts of laughter sounded as they drew closer to the forum, to the docks and brothels. They stayed pressed along the tall walls cloaked in darkness and silence and entered through the forum doors unseen.

The large square forum was eerie at night, Quintus thought. The columns appeared to move in the moonlight, casting shadows that made Quintus look twice. They stayed in the darkness, moving along the walls and not running across the open square, until they reached the stairs at the basilica.

"Stand guard," Quintus murmured to Salonia and Varia, and he and Kaeso took the landing to the room above. It was a lone room; there were no other corridors or doors to other rooms.

"It is locked," Kaeso whispered.

Quintus lifted the iron bolt and lock, then studied the door itself. "Not to fear. I have the key."

Kaeso eyed him curiously. "You do?"

Quintus grinned, took one step back, and lifted his boot. "Affirmative." He then proceeded to kick the door with his heel.

"Do you wish to be discovered?" Kaeso hissed at him.

Salonia appeared behind them, her eyes wide and furious. "You have the tact of a ballista," she whisper-shouted.

Quintus grinned at them both. The door had budged but not opened, so he kicked it again with more force, and the door splintered around the lock and it gave in. Quintus caught the door before it clanged to the floor, and he set it aside.

The room was small and dark, and Quintus could see Kaeso tense. "Fear not. There is a door for easy escape," Quintus whispered. Kaeso nodded with determination and stepped inside.

There was a desk and a chair, a long shelf on one wall with stacks of papyri, and not much else. Quintus grabbed the first stack of papyri and put it on the desk. It was lists of financial records, similar to those he kept at the ludus. He could not make much sense of the lists of public revenues and taxes; it was a lot of names in some kind of order he assumed made sense to the man who wrote them.

Kaeso had grabbed the second pile and was leafing through them. "What are we looking for?"

"Anything that might tie Servius or Tiberius to each other. Anything that has Jovian's name, or any naval inventory," Quintus whispered.

He found nothing in the first stack, or the second. Kaeso was also on his second stack, shaking his head as he read through the pages. "Nothing."

Quintus stopped his fruitless search. "Agreed." He sighed. "There has to be evidence. A snake cannot slither without leaving tracks in the sand."

"Perhaps we search the wrong office," Kaeso murmured.

Quintus tapped one scroll where the quaestor had signed. "Rufus Dinia. We have a name. It isn't much, yet it is more than we came with."

Kaeso straightened his back and ran his hand through his hair, and he tapped his foot as though trying to vent his frustration. Only, the floor made a dull echo in reply. Both Quintus and Kaeso looked to his feet, to the floor, and found a square tile ever so slightly misaligned. The lack of light was deceiving, and Kaeso must have thought the same because he dragged his boot across the tile, and his toe caught on the slightly raised lip of it.

They went to their knees and dug at the tile with their fingers, but to no avail. Then Kaeso took out his dagger and edged it between the marble tiles and levered it up. Quintus gripped it by the sides and lifted it easily, despite its weight, to reveal a small compartment. Inside were papyrus sheets, laid flat and pressed by the tile that concealed them.

Quintus only had to read the first three lines.

Senator Servius Augendus.

Praetorian Tiberius Hirrus.

Commander Linus Jovian.

Quintus snatched up the find and slid them into his breastplate. They slid the tile back into place and left the room. Salonia and Varia needed no instruction, they simply fell into step, keeping to the darkest shadows. Quintus had chosen them to accompany him tonight, not only for their fighting skill, but also their ability to move without sound. They could also kill with no more noise than the wind through the leaves on a tree.

So when Salonia tensed and put her finger to her lips to urge for silence, Quintus stilled. They were close to their escape but not close enough. He put his hand on Kaeso's arm, and he didn't dare to even breathe. They pressed themselves up against the wall in complete darkness and two figures entered the forum and headed for the far corner. To the office they had just raided.

They weren't careful or even trying to be quiet. "The next ship to dock," one of the men said. "Should be the last for a time. Too many people grow curious."

Kaeso recognised the voice at the same time as Quintus. Kaeso let out a hiss and slid his dagger from his belt. Quintus put his arm across Kaeso's chest to stop him, and he shook his head.

"Tiberius," Kaeso breathed the word.

The two men, one of whom was unmistakably Tiberius, approached the stairs, and Quintus knew they had but moments before they found the door had been kicked in, so as soon as they had made the first step, Quintus pointed to the exit.

The four of them slipped out of the forum and ran up the street and had barely reached the first crossroad before they heard a bang—a door being slammed—and a rough voice cut through the night. "Find who did this!"

But the four figures, shrouded in shadows, were long gone. They stayed in the darkest paths below tall stone walls, and without being sighted, they slipped in through the slaves' gate, and only then did they pause to breathe.

Quintus leaned against the wall near the stables and Kaeso rested his hands on his knees. Salonia and Varia were breathing hard as well. "Too close, Dominus," Varia said, panting.

Quintus nodded. "Agreed. Let us not do that again."

Salonia chuckled. "Feel alive though, do we not?"

Kaeso looked at her as though she had spoken in tongues. "Have you lost your mind?"

Quintus grinned, his body thrumming. "We are not safe yet. Return to your quarters and let us not speak of this again."

They nodded and disappeared through the courtyard. Kaeso watched them go. "How do they move without sound?"

Quintus almost laughed. "Remarkable, is it not?" He took Kaeso's hand. "To bed."

They walked quickly to the villa steps and in through the atrium toward their room. Quintus pulled back the curtain to enter when Kaeso halted. Quintus turned in the doorway to see what had caused him to freeze. He followed his line of sight to find a lone figure, half hidden in shadow, half lit by the lamp he held.

Helier.

Futuo!

Quintus pretended to be a little unsteady on his feet and held up his hand. "I sought a drink and found one too many," he said to Helier.

Kaeso quickly caught on. "I shall see him to his bed."

"You shall see to more than that," Quintus added and proceeded to step backwards into their room, pulling Kaeso with him. Kaeso laughed so Helier would hear, then once they were away from view, they fell quiet.

Too quiet, and Kaeso groaned loudly as though they were in bed. Quintus raised his eyebrow. "You act too well," he whispered. "Do you act that way with me?"

Kaeso laughed out loud, then as part of their theatrics, he moaned again.

Quintus pretended to be taken aback. "I shall now

doubt every sound you make," he murmured and pulled Kaeso onto the bed with him.

"I am yet to pretend any sound you elicit from me," Kaeso said. He stared down at Quintus, tracing his eyebrow. "Do you think he still listens?"

Quintus smiled. "Perhaps we should give him a performance."

Kaeso laughed and Quintus cut it off with a hard kiss, which grew with heat and urgency. Maybe it was the rush of running through the streets, at being caught, at possibly being found out, but their bodies were quick to rouse, and they were even quicker to fall lost to desire.

If Helier stood on the other side of the door, he got more than a theatrical portrayal, but neither Quintus nor Kaeso were in any frame of mind to care.

BEFORE THE SUN WOKE, Quintus was up and reading through the papyrus records. What he had was everything he would need. Jovian had said there was treachery threaded between Servius and Tiberius, and now Quintus had the accounts to prove it.

Quintus had not even been sure what Servius and Tiberius were guilty of shipping into Neapolis, but now he knew: riches that were shipped back to Rome from Britannia, secured from the far reaches of the Roman invasions, and Servius and Tiberius were pilfering them.

Not enough to perhaps cause notice from Rome but skimming mostly gold and silver items and coins. Items that could be melted, rendered unidentifiable from the original, yet retaining their worth when made into bars or coin, or even into jewellery and then sold to merchants.

Quintus' mind raced with just how far this went. Who was implicated? Just how far did Servius' claws reach?

"You are worried," Kaeso said, his voice thick from sleep.

Quintus afforded him a smile. "How long have you lain watching?"

"A moment." Kaeso stretched out on the bed though kept his eyes on Quintus. "A favoured view while it lasts."

"While it lasts?" Quintus scoffed. "You think I will age so terribly to lose the face you look upon?"

Kaeso shook his head and sighed. He took a while to put tongue to his thoughts. "Or perhaps this is the last morning I shall wake next to you."

Quintus blinked, stunned. "Why do you say such things?"

"It would not be my choice," Kaeso said. He sat up and rubbed Quintus' back, then scratched his fingers at the back of Quintus' head. "Cast it from your mind. We have other pressing concerns, do we not?"

Quintus frowned and looked to the reports he still held. "Servius lines his purse with the coin of Rome."

Kaeso's eyes widened. "From the ships that return?"

Quintus nodded. "I assume he seeks promotion to further his reach."

"And lessen the eyes who see," Kaeso added. He scowled, then eyed the room with caution. "We must find safe keeping for those," he said, nodding to the papyri in Quintus' hand.

Quintus nodded. "But where?" In their room was only a bed and a small table. "I would hide it with my men. By the gods no one would search their room from the smell alone, yet I would not have them implicated."

Kaeso stood up and lifted the thin straw mattress. "Under here?"

Quintus shook his head. "Too easily found," he grumbled.

Kaeso pursed his lips. "Then where?"

Quintus sighed and slid the stack of papyri under the mattress. Kaeso gently lowered the mattress back into place, then sat down and gave Quintus a hopeful smile. "Let us gather the guards. Today Oscilius arrives. Sunshine on an otherwise darkened day, yes?"

Quintus smiled at that. "Agreed. Gratitude for the reminder of our true purpose."

Kaeso gave him a blank stare. "True purpose?"

"Home. To meet with Oscilius and prepare for our journey back to Oplontis."

Kaeso was slow to smile, a reaction Quintus didn't quite understand. "Yes," Kaeso said. "A bright day indeed."

WHEN THE SUN was well past its highest point, the streets around the arena were bustling, the way they always did the day before the games. But it was the belly of the arena, hidden from the streets, where the most action was. Lanistas from all over Rome were getting their gladiators settled into their cells, the animal trainers doing the same with their troops. Quintus noticed Kaeso taking in all the people with a look of wonder and perhaps a share of anger. He paused to stare at a carriage with two lions.

"You favour them?" Quintus asked.

"They are remarkable," he murmured. One lion hissed and took a swipe at someone who dared get too close. Kaeso flinched. "What is their purpose here?"

"They have a few," Quintus explained. "Sometimes they are free to roam in the arena and are hunted. Other times they are held in a pit and some poor soul is thrown to them."

Kaeso turned to stare at him, horrified. "For sport?"

"Criminals, usually," Quintus replied. "It is over surprisingly fast, though not a pleasant or honourable death."

Kaeso still stared. "And you approve of this?"

Quintus sighed and stared at the caged lions. "It has always been done. I have not thought to question it before."

Kaeso's jaw ticked before he turned back to the lions. "I was transported in a similar carriage when I was stolen from my home. Much like this lion, I would imagine. Have you thought to question that?" Kaeso turned to him then. "You were raised above the need to question it. A fault not your own, yet I would hope, if you hold my life in any regard, you might question it now."

Quintus felt the burn of indignation that Kaeso would dare speak to him in such a way, swiftly followed by a rush of shame. Kaeso's right to question him in such a fashion was the very meaning of his words. "I begin to see things in a different light," Quintus admitted. "You have opened my eyes."

The corner of Kaeso's lip twitched in the beginning of a smile. "You have never questioned your freedom because you never feared to lose it," he said. "A fault not your own, yet a lesson also to newly opened eyes perhaps."

Quintus gave a nod just as Harpax interrupted. "Dominus, Oscilius arrives."

Quintus turned to find a carriage, and a familiar face holding the reins... Not one familiar face, but two.

"Why does Cythereia ride with him?" Harpax said, voicing Quintus' concern.

Quintus watched them approach. "I do not know." As they drew near, Quintus couldn't help but smile. By the gods, he had missed them. In all his years, he had never been absent from them for this long. "You are a welcome sight," Quintus said when they could hear.

All of Quintus' guards surrounded the carriage, and they reached through the bars to welcome their gladiator brothers with warm greetings and wide smiles. Oscilius was quick to step down and Quintus embraced him. "I have missed you," Quintus said.

Oscilius pulled back, taking Quintus by the shoulder with his one hand. It was obvious Quintus' warm greeting was a welcome surprise. "It is good to see you again as well."

Then Quintus looked up to the carriage seat. "And Cythereia, a pleasing surprise, though not expected."

She moved to step down from the carriage and Oscilius beat Quintus to offer his hand to help her. It was a kind gesture, normally afforded by a suitor or husband, and when Cythereia smiled at him, Quintus felt he was invading a private moment. Had they become close in his absence? Had they a newfound affection? Quintus was so taken aback, he was lost for words. It was Kaeso who broke the silence. "I trust your journey was not too harsh in this heat," he said.

"It was fair. I knew not what to expect. The men take this journey often, yet this is my first." Cythereia took Kaeso's hand and smiled up at Quintus. "And to cast eyes upon you both is most welcome."

"And you," Quintus finally said.

Cythereia and Oscilius both smiled at each other, then

at Quintus. Oscilius spoke first. "Gratitude. Cythereia can stay with me. She will be no burden."

Quintus put a hand on each of their shoulders. "Nor could she ever be. Let us get the men out of the carriage. They will need to stretch weary legs, and we have much to discuss."

"Of course," Oscilius said. "Anything you desire to know."

Quintus went to the back of the carriage to open the latch. "First, the men. Then second, you can tell me when you and Cythereia first cast such smiles toward each other."

Cythereia blushed and Oscilius smiled, but Quintus' attention was soon turned to the men climbing down from the carriage. He clapped each of them on the back and called them by name, and they returned with, "Dominus."

Kaeso stood next to Oscilius, and Quintus didn't dare hide how happy he was to be reunited once more with his men. They stood and broke words, stories and laughter from training and lessons, and each of the newly arrived gladiators laughed at the guard uniforms on their ludus brothers. Quintus listened to them, his longing for home growing with each story. Yet all too soon it was time for them to enter the hypogeum. The day was getting long, the sun almost at the horizon.

Quintus took them to their cell and ensured they were fed and watered, while Salonia and Phaidon checked the corridors and that the far gate was sealed shut. When they returned and confirmed it was, Quintus stood at the bars, facing his gladiators. "You have trained for this day that comes. You will honour yourselves, and you will honour me. Rest well tonight, and sleep knowing I am grateful."

Quintus rarely let sentiment colour his words, but he wasn't afraid to let it show.

"To have you here after all this time means my days here are at an end. Let us see these games won so we can return to better days at home."

He left with their loud cheers in his ears and smiled as he walked with Kaeso to where Oscilius and Cythereia awaited him. "I would have you stay with me tonight at the senator's villa," Quintus told them.

Oscilius bowed his head. "The offer is generous, but I will stay with the men."

Quintus smiled fondly at him. "I assumed you might say that." Then he looked at Cythereia. "And you?"

"I will stay with Oscilius, if you would please," she replied, her cheeks staining red.

Kaeso chuckled and he took a step back. "I will survey the senator's room and leave you to discuss familial matters."

Quintus laughed and nodded to the other guards. "Take them and see nothing is amiss."

Kaeso gave a hard nod, and upon giving the guards brief orders, they set off at a pace into the arena. Quintus smiled after them, and Oscilius said, "It lightens me to see him still at your side."

Quintus smiled at that. "For all time, if the gods allow it." Then he eyed both of them. "Not that I complain, it brings me great joy to see you, Cythereia. But what brings you to accompany the men?"

Cythereia's face fell, and she turned to Oscilius as though he might find the words she lacked. "She would not stay behind," he said.

Cythereia shook her head, her eyes tearful, and it struck at Quintus' heart. "What concerns you?" he asked.

"The ground rumbles, more than we are accustomed to,

but it's the birds, Quintus" she said, her lip trembling. "They are without song."

A cold dread ran down Quintus' spine. "The birds are quiet?"

"There is a quiet, a stillness not felt before," Oscilius added. "It is not just the birds. There are no fish in the sea, even the fields are absent dormice, and even locusts are gone."

She nodded. "The orchard, as you know, usually full of birdsong, is silent. It began yesterday, and Quintus, they have only been silenced once before."

No one spoke, and Quintus tried to gather his thoughts. He knew what this meant, and a cold, hollow realisation settled into his bones. He swallowed hard so he could speak. "The only time, once before, the birds were absent song," he whispered, "was the day the earth shook, and the death of my parents swiftly followed."

KAESO WAS happy to leave Quintus to have a private moment with Oscilius and Cythereia. It was clear to Kaeso from Quintus' reaction when he saw them how much he felt their separation. They were his parents. Not by blood, but they had raised him and shaped the man he had become.

It made Kaeso long for his own parents. It made him long for a home he no longer had, that he no longer called his own. It made his heart ache for a path different from the one he found himself on. Yet the gods had delivered him to Quintus, and Kaeso knew no matter what the coming days brought, he would fight to stay by his side.

He and the other guards inspected the senator's room and the rooms the emperor and other senators would occupy during the games. They were the very opposite of what he had witnessed in the hypogeum. The belly of the arena, as Quintus had put name to it, was cramped, dark, overcrowded, and reeked an unspeakable stench. It painted a picture of slavery, poverty, and of woeful deaths.

Whereas the upstairs, the private rooms for politicians

and wealthy Romans were white marble, clean, and spacious. There were jugs of clean water, vases of scented herbs, padded seats, and silks draped on the walls. The contrast between the wealthy and the poor was baffling to Kaeso.

He stood at the balcony and watched as slaves tended to the sand in the arena, raking it even in readiness for tomorrow, and he was lost in his thoughts. "Kaeso," Harpax said from behind him. "All is clear."

Kaeso gave a nod and sighed. He gazed back out across the arena, his thoughts pensive. "Tomorrow, the emperor will stand right here," he said. "Where a slave stands now."

Harpax came to stand beside him and watched the men who tended the arena sands. "It brings a new perspective to see it from this view," he said.

"Do you wish to fight down there in the coming games?" Kaeso asked. "Or do you prefer the duty of a guard?"

"I do this to serve my dominus," Harpax answered.

Kaeso considered the weight of his words and all they implied. "Do you wish for freedom?"

Harpax gave him a saddened smile. "I have long cast those thoughts from my mind, and I would urge you to do the same. Nothing good can come from wishing for impossible things." Then Harpax raised his chin and nodded to himself. "I will do as my dominus, as Quintus, bids me to do, as would any in his ludus."

Kaeso smiled despite the lump of unease in his chest and clapped his shoulder. "As would I."

"Then we should return to him," Harpax said. "Before he comes in search of us."

Kaeso nodded and they met the other guards under the arches. The sun was almost gone, and he watched as

Quintus said farewell to Oscilius and Cythereia and turned, scanning through the crowds, and he smiled as soon as he saw them.

Some of the guards chuckled. "Rest easy, all," Appias said. "That look is cast for but one of us." He playfully shoved Kaeso's shoulder and the others laughed. It did make Kaeso smile, and Quintus gave Appias a pointed glare, though it lacked any heat.

"The arena is clear," Kaeso told Quintus.

He nodded. "Then let us return to the villa for food and rest. There's no saying what these next days will bring."

Kaeso nodded, and a shiver ran down his spine. Quintus had just voiced what Kaeso couldn't, and Quintus didn't miss Kaeso's reaction. Thankfully, he waited to question him. The rest of the guards formed two lines and began the march back to the villa; Quintus and Kaeso stayed at the rear.

"Break words of what concerns you," Quintus murmured.

Kaeso let out a rough breath. "I cannot, because I do not know if it is pressing concerns that the senator brings upon himself or if there is true concern of possible attack tomorrow? I would like to think that is all there is to this unease I feel."

"But?"

"You might question my presence of wit."

Quintus' gaze narrowed, and his reply was immediate. "Never."

"I cannot shake the feeling that a darkness lurks." Kaeso shook his head at how foolish he sounded.

Quintus put his hand to Kaeso's back to urge him to walk behind the other guards. "You are not alone," he said. "Cythereia spoke of the same. It is why she accompanied the men. She claims the birds are absent song. Oscilius said the fish have left the sea."

Kaeso's gaze shot to Quintus'. "A sign to what end?"

Quintus gave him an uncertain glance and shook his head. "I... I would like to say I do not know..."

"But?" Then Kaeso remembered something Quintus had told him once, and his sense of dread solidified. "You have witnessed this before."

Quintus nodded. "I have. The day the earth shook and walls fell." He gave Kaeso a worried look. "Cythereia claims the earth rumbles. A warning of worse to come."

Kaeso could not fathom it. "I know not words to offer as comfort," he said as they walked. "Yet I am happy she did not remain behind."

Quintus gave a smile that was brief at best. "As am I. But our task here is upon us." He frowned ahead and set his jaw. "If the walls of the villa tumble, then we rebuild. We have done it before; we can again. As I said to Cythereia, my home can fall to ruin. It is the people I hold in my heart who matter."

Kaeso nodded, and they let a silence fall between them. Kaeso had shared his worries, yet that didn't lessen their weight. Now it seemed they both carried twice the burden.

AS ALWAYS, the guards entered through the slaves' gate at the rear of the property and Quintus ordered them to eat, bathe, and retire for the day. Morning would come early, and he needed them well rested, though Quintus doubted sleep would come easily for himself or Kaeso. He was about to suggest the baths to help them relax when they heard voices coming from Servius' office.

Familiar voices, arguing. "Lower your voice and watch your tongue," Servius said.

Another man. "Do not caution me. I need not remind you who I answer to." That voice was unmistakable. Tiberius.

Quintus met Kaeso's eyes before he raced for the office. He took the stairs two at a time and met the two guards at the door. "What is this?" Quintus asked.

"The senator allowed it and instructed privacy," Gallio said, though he had paled.

Quintus barged into the room, and he found Servius and Tiberius standing, facing each other with the desk between them. "Senator," Quintus said, though he glared at Tiberius as he spoke.

Servius raised his hand and seemed to take the interruption as a moment to gather himself. "No need for concern, Quintus."

Quintus kept his eyes on the piece of shit, Tiberius. "Does he need assistance to the door?"

Servius waved his hand again. "No, of course not. He was just leaving."

Tiberius sneered at Quintus, though his eyes barely hid his contempt. The air between them was thick with mutual loathing. Quintus stared down at Tiberius, thrumming with anticipation that the piece of shit might make a move against him. He itched to rip him apart. All he needed was one reason...

Tiberius turned to Servius. "We shall resume our conversation at another time."

Servius waved him off with an impatient scowl, and Tiberius turned on his heel and walked out. Quintus took a moment to collect his temper, willing himself not to aim his outburst at the senator. Traitor or not, Quintus had to be patient.

Then he heard a scuffle and an abrupt, "Halt!"

Quintus burst out of the door, and it seemed that the sun stilled in the sky with what he saw. Tiberius had Kaeso pinned to the wall with a hand to his throat and the two guards, Gallio and Oppius, stood with their blades drawn at Tiberius, but clearly uncertain of what to do.

Before Quintus was aware he had even moved, he barged through and took hold of Tiberius by his neck and held him off the ground. "Touch him again and I will split your skull open to the gods," he growled. Tiberius' eyes were wide and he made a choking sound, so Quintus squeezed harder.

"Enough!" Servius yelled from beside them.

Quintus let Tiberius drop to the floor. "He threatened Kaeso," Quintus ground out. "A punishable offence."

Tiberius managed to stand but he held his throat. "You would hold a slave's life over a praetorian guard?" he rasped out.

"A man is yet a man," Quintus replied through clenched teeth and he crowded him against the wall. He shot a quick glance to Servius. "How would you have me punish him?"

And it was there; they all saw it. That one moment where Servius considered it. He weighed his options, the scales of favour if Tiberius were taken out of the equation. But then he blinked and shook his head. "No, let him be. I will not have trouble in my house. He is leaving; let him go and let us move forward. The games are upon us and tensions are high."

Quintus glared at Tiberius, not moving back at all so Tiberius had to slide out from the wall. Once he was back one step, he laughed a menacing sound. "So, we finally see what draws reaction from you," Tiberius said, glancing quickly at Kaeso, then back to Quintus. "It is not a threat upon the senator or even yourself. But a worthless slave."

Quintus bristled and clenched his fist, ready to strike Tiberius, but Kaeso's hand on his arm gave him pause. "He baits you for reaction," Kaeso said. "Ignore him."

Tiberius laughed and took a step back. "Now I know where to strike you to inflict the greatest wound."

"Tiberius, you are excused," Servius barked. "I would ask you to leave before blood is spilled on my floor. I will not have it in my house!"

Tiberius nodded his head to Servius. "Tomorrow then," he said, then sneered at Quintus as he left.

Quintus wanted to smash, rip, and tear Tiberius apart. He wanted to hear bones snap and pop, he wanted to feel flesh sluice, and he wanted to hear Tiberius scream for death. "I will see his end," Quintus whispered, trying to contain his rage. "And deliver him to the afterlife in pieces."

Kaeso slid his hand along Quintus' arm and he turned to face him. It was then Quintus saw the red marks on his neck, and he growled. But with deep breath, he traced a gentle touch along Kaeso's neck. "He hurt you."

"Not at all," Kaeso whispered.

Quintus sighed, lowered his hand, and dropped his head. Kaeso's denial was a vain attempt to soothe him, and it only served to anger him more. He turned and took a step toward Servius, his rage barely contained. "When this agreement is over, my obligation is met and your coin is paid, Kaeso comes with me."

Servius took a small step back in fear and opened his mouth to reply. He floundered. "A discussion for another time, perhaps. When the flames of tempers are not freshly fanned."

Quintus seethed, his fists clenched. He seemed to grow taller with his wrath. His voice boomed as if delivered from the gods. "There is no discussion!"

Servius paled and glanced quickly at Gallio and Oppius who were also wide-eyed. Servius stood as if struck still. It was Kaeso who soothed the moment. "We will take our leave for the night. We rise early tomorrow and will see the senator to the arena at first light."

Kaeso pulled on Quintus' arm and he relented, following him to their quarters without another word. Quintus pulled his helmet off and threw it to the floor; his chest plate swiftly followed. He pulled at his hair and growled through his frustration.

"You said you would not ask Servius yet," Kaeso murmured. "Now he knows you have one weakness."

Quintus sighed. "Servius is no longer a concern to me. Yet I have shown Tiberius my one weakness, and now he aims for you instead. Tiberius now knows if you are struck from this world, much like if my own heart were pierced, that I would not live through it."

Tiberius wasn't going to aim for Quintus. Why would he? He would be bested in every way. Why battle the biggest threat when he could take a smaller threat and watch the bigger man fall at the same time? As a puppeteer would sever the strings to watch the puppet crumple, his own life was tethered to Kaeso's, and Tiberius would take full advantage.

Kaeso reached up and cupped Quintus' cheek. "We have proof. The emperor cannot question the evidence." Then he went to the bed and lifted the mattress, as if producing the papyri would bolster his argument. Only when he turned back to Quintus, his hands were empty, his face drained of colour.

"The records, the proof," he whispered. "Quintus, it is gone."

Quintus felt like the gods mocked him, like the room was absent air. He watched as Kaeso upended the mattress, frantically pulling at the bedding, finding nothing. "Do you think Tiberius knew to search our room? Is that what he and Servius argued about? Oh, by the gods, Quintus, do they know we stole the records from their quaestor?"

Quintus had no reply. Kaeso sagged and his legs folded underneath him as though unable to hold the weight of this discovery. He looked up at Quintus from the floor. "What do we do now?"

Quintus sat on the bed, slumping with the burden of it all pressing down on him. "I do not know."

LATER THAT NIGHT, while the villa was asleep and silent, Quintus awoke with a vivid horror of Kaeso being ripped from his arms and slain before his very eyes. He sat up in their bed, gasping for air, his heart thundering, only to find Kaeso gone.

Quintus flew out of their room and into the atrium, unsure of where to search. If any harm had come to Kaeso, Quintus would rip the world apart to find those responsible. If Kaeso lived no more, Quintus would see the streets of Rome filled with blood. Panic rose in his throat, his hands shook, his mind scrambled to search in the darkness, and then he saw him.

Out on the courtyard steps, Kaeso sat. Lit by only moonlight, he cast a lonely figure. Quintus' lungs screamed for air and he finally sucked back a breath. The blow of relief almost knocked him from his feet, and he had to put his hands on his knees until he could regain composure. Then, with slow and cautious steps, he went to him.

"Kaeso," he whispered so as not to startle him. Kaeso turned to look at him. "I thought you gone."

Kaeso smiled. "Was it relief or alarm that woke you?"

Quintus sat beside him, took Kaeso's hand, and put it over his hammering heart. "Your answer." He took another deep breath, not yet fully recovered. "And I'd have you not joke of such things. My heart will not survive it."

Kaeso's smile became saddened. "Apologies. I did not mean to cause worry."

Quintus sighed and stared up at the stars. "Sleep eludes you?"

Kaeso gave no answer to that. He simply looked up at the night sky. "The moon mocks me. It makes its way to the horizon, the sun soon to rise. I wish I could hold them at bay. I wish this new day were a thousand days from now."

Quintus looked at his profile, magnificent in the silver light of the moon. "If I could stop the sun from rising and have the night for always, I would."

He met Quintus' gaze then. "You would hold back the sun for me?"

"I would. So we could have countless more nights, endless days."

Kaeso shook his head and searched the sky once more. "Perhaps if I were able, I would take us days from now so this is all behind us and only days of summer breezes and apricots from your orchard are before us."

"A pleasant picture you paint," Quintus replied gently. "I would have that life for us as well." A silence fell over them, and when Quintus cast his gaze upon Kaeso once more, he saw his eyes welled with tears. "Is that all that weighs on your mind, rabbit?"

Kaeso blinked and swallowed hard before he gave Quintus a sad smile. "Talk of a life with you is almost too much to bear. I fear my heart cannot take it."

He took Kaeso's hand. "Why? Speak of your fears and I will see them slain."

"Quintus, how can you not see?" Kaeso's tears threatened to fall. "How can you not know when it hangs around my neck like a weight I can barely hold. This tin collar burns with the heat of a thousand fires. How can you not have considered this? For after this day, your collar is removed and his remains." A single tear ran a solitary line down his cheek. "I am but a slave to him, bought and owned like a trinket to throw away when he no longer finds value in it."

Quintus took Kaeso's face in his hands and pressed his forehead to Kaeso's. "I promise to you, with every truth I am, I will see his collar from your neck. Trust in me to find a way." Quintus wiped away Kaeso's tears with his thumbs and kissed his lips. "I will rip the life from any man who dares attempt to part us."

Quintus sighed and asked something he had not wanted to give voice to, but now seemed it felt unavoidable.

"Kaeso," Quintus whispered. "If you give me one thing, give me honesty and answer me this."

Those big rabbit eyes implored. He nodded.

"When Servius' collar is gone, if I were to remove the leather strand around your neck, the collar which binds you to me, would you return to your homelands or would you stay by my side?"

"I know not what you ask."

"Speak the truth. If you cannot look upon my face and

give honest answer, for all we have endured and for all we have done—for what we have shared—for what lies ahead, then at least honour me with silence. For there is always truth in words left unsaid."

Kaeso was quiet a long moment, then, "Quintus, I..."

He raised his hand and made move to stand. "Your lack of answer is answer enough."

"What would you have me do?" Kaeso asked, grabbing his arm. "I was stolen from my homelands, made slave by Roman hand. By you—"

"My choice far removed!" Quintus hissed.

"Still your tongue and let me speak!" Kaeso whispered right back at him. "You took a slave, and you gave him purpose when he had none. You gave him trust and honour when he had none." Kaeso's voice cracked. "You gave him reason to live when he had none."

Quintus put his hand to Kaeso's face, and it squeezed his heart to see those wide rabbit eyes well with tears.

"I was taken from my people." His voice a whisper. "Roman soldiers demanded my father's crop for half the coin, and when he argued, they slayed him where he stood, then my mother..." He swallowed hard. "I fought them the best I could but was easily outnumbered. They took everything from me and bound me in chains. Fate could have handed me to savage men who whipped or beat me or broke my bones for sport. Yet the gods gave me to you. I thought they sought to punish me; instead they gave me the gift of a good man. Strong mind, sharp wit, bravest I have ever had the honour to witness. Gentle hands, kind heart. His body would rival Jupiter himself."

Quintus gave in to his smile, but Kaeso was not done with words. "If there comes a time unseen from now, when your collar around my neck be removed, I would ask it to remain."

"You would keep it?" Quintus dared not believe it.

"I would be yours for all time, Quintus. My loyalty does not lie with Rome. Nor would you find it in Iberia. My loyalty is to you." He closed his eyes and leaned into Quintus' palm. "Do not doubt where my heart is."

"As mine is with you," Quintus murmured and pulled him in for a kiss. "I would not have my collar upon your neck. I would have you stand beside me, equal in all things."

Another tear escaped Kaeso's eye. He nodded and leaned his face into Quintus' touch. "I am afraid of what this day brings."

Quintus pulled him into his arms and kissed the side of his head. "As am I."

CAPITULUM XXIV

QUINTUS AND KAESO dressed in silence. The sun was yet to rise, their moods as dark as the sky outside. They wore trepidation like their armour, fastening buckles so leather and anxiety fitted like a second skin.

Shin guards, wrist guards, leather pelmet skirts, shoulder guards, and helmets. Quintus would have taken a moment to appreciate Kaeso's form in his uniform if he did not feel the weight of uncertainty bearing down on him.

He could not shake the sense of foreboding. Something terrible would happen today. He could feel it in his bones. Without the accounts they had stolen from the office at the forum—the proof of Servius and Tiberius' theft, proof that Tiberius had undoubtedly stolen back—all Quintus could hope for would be to see the games end. Then he and Kaeso, and all their men, would return to Oplontis and put this behind them.

Yet the ominous sense of coming darkness clung to him like the red cape he fixed to his shoulder.

"You have a troubled mind," Kaeso noted. "Share with me and see troubles halved."

Quintus nodded. There was little point in denial. "I fear the gods will seek retribution."

Kaeso met his gaze for a long moment, then raised his chin. "We have done no ill toward them. Let them reap grievances with those more deserving. I care not for greed or treachery. I just ask to see these days through to their end and still have you by my side."

Quintus finally smiled. "Your fire of defiance lights a spark in me. Let us get this day started, and if the gods seek quarrel, they will have their hands full with you."

Kaeso smirked at that. "I would not quarrel with the gods. I would merely speak my mind until they saw reason."

Quintus chuckled, then gave Kaeso one long look, his smile slowly fading. "No matter what happens this day, stay beside me. You have all your blades?"

Kaeso turned his wrists to reveal two small blades concealed in each wrist guard, then one in each shin guard. "I am armed as much as I dare. And for what it is worth, I would have you stay beside me so *I* can protect *you*. Do you have your weapons?"

Quintus lifted his arm to reveal his dagger sheathed in his belt, then nodded to where his small round shield leaned against the wall. "And my shield. It is all I need."

Kaeso raised one eyebrow. "Is that so?"

Quintus rolled his eyes. "And you, rabbit. My blade, my shield, and you."

"Then let us gather our men," Kaeso said.

"And women."

He smiled. "And let us see this day through."

All the guards were in the courtyard dressed in full armour with weapons and dour faces. Servius appeared in his finest woollen toga with circles like bruises around his eyes, which suggested lack of sleep.

Quintus was well familiar with the feeling.

Servius could not meet Quintus' eyes, and it fuelled his distrust of the man. Helier appeared to stand behind Servius dutifully and other slaves quickly followed, and when they were ready, the guards fell into position, and so the procession to the arena began. The sun was barely breaking over the horizon, yet the streets were already buzzing.

Quintus knew all too well that games were granted so the peoples would forget their poverty. Open to the public, free to all citizens, swells of people already filled the streets, making their way to the arena.

The lightening skies were cloudless, and a cool breeze was a welcome reprieve from the crowds. Their mood might not be pleasant when the heat of the sun baked their patience. Quintus hoped Servius had well-planned games for these three days. If there was a lack of blood offered to the gods, citizens already fraught over increased taxes and decreased food would be the least of Servius' worries.

Servius would be deserving of riots, Quintus thought. Let his name and reputation be worth the shit and piss he would have thrown at him. Quintus could only hope he, Kaeso, and their men would be back in Oplontis by the time that happened. And it *would* happen. The path he and Tiberius were on could only have one destination; treachery in Rome meant certain death. Quintus could only hope they would bring about their own demise, long after he was gone.

The arena was already almost at capacity and the sun was barely up. Servius played his role with his usual pomp and flair, waving to the people, smiling and announcing that he, and he alone, was responsible for this gift of games. The gods would be pleased and reward them all, he told them. Quintus kept them moving through the crowds, not allowing anyone to touch or get near. Kaeso did the same from the other side, though with the procession of uniformed guards, most people gave them a wary berth.

The columns and arches of the arena towered over the swarms of people vying for best position in the stands. Quintus led Servius through the unnumbered arch to the private rooms for Rome's more elevated society. The senator's room was clear, and slaves soon began filling trays with fruits, dates, and nuts, and filling jugs with water. Servius sat on a cushioned seat, and Helier and Petilia began to fan him with feathers and fronds.

"This heat," Servius complained. "The sun is yet to climb the sky and already it punishes."

Quintus paid the senator no mind. Instead, he positioned Decius and Mettius at the balcony and ordered Harpax and Phaidon to go into the hypogeum and see that Oscilius and their gladiator brothers were well. Appias and Pellio were sent to ensure the sealed gate remained so. Quintus ordered all others to find their positions around and throughout the arena as he had instructed prior.

For now, Quintus and Kaeso would not dare leave the senator. Not for his protection, but to ensure his agenda could not be furthered. Not in their presence anyway.

The arena was filling quickly, the excited buzz filtering up to the senator's balcony. Quintus had always been inspired at the sound, yet this time was different. Dread, ominous and expanding, sat cold in his belly.

Senator Marcus Maternus was next to arrive. He entered Servius' room with his slaves at his heel. He was without bodyguards, and Quintus was uncertain if the man was naïve or a fool.

Or perhaps his confidence stemmed from knowledge Quintus was not privy to?

He wore his official senatorial toga and an insincere smile as he extended his hand to Servius. "Gratitude for these games," Marcus said. "You shine a light on a city otherwise cast in a shadow of worry. The people, like myself, extend their gratitude. Your name will be well remembered."

Servius nodded and smiled despite Marcus' jab about his people being shrouded with worry. "An offering for the gods," Servius said.

Marcus returned Servius' hypocritical smile, knowing all too well that Servius' agenda served no one but himself. "May they be pleased and reward accordingly."

Quintus had lost all patience and palate for politics. The respect he once carried for the power of Rome was diminishing.

Just then the emperor appeared at the door, and seeing the two senators, he paused. "Ah, good men of Rome," he said as he entered, his guards at his flank. Everyone bowed upon seeing him, though both senators were quick to take his offered hand. Quintus searched the faces of the praetorian guards, finding Tiberius did not stand among them. His relief at his absence was short-lived; one should be most concerned about the enemy he could not see.

"An honour to have you attend," Servius said, and Quintus' stomach rolled with the deceit that spilled so smoothly from the senator's tongue. How dare he meet the emperor's eye when he steals from him!

Quintus took a breath to calm himself when Appias and Pellio hurried into the room, their faces etched with worry. "Quintus, a word," Appias said.

Pellio had more presence of mind to notice the imperial

purple in the room. He eyed the emperor and his guards warily, then looked to Quintus. "The gates to the hypogeum are open."

"Not just opened," Appias said. "But fucking removed."

Appias had no manners for the company of elevated men, yet Quintus could not bring himself to care. "Removed?" Quintus clarified.

"Open like a whore's—"

Quintus raised his hand. "Picture painted well enough. I would remind you of the company in which you stand."

Appias and Pellio both eyed the emperor and senators who now stood watching them. "Any pressing matters?" Servius asked, his tone light, yet his eyes cautioned Quintus to carefully consider his reply.

Quintus gave Servius as pleasant a smile as he could muster. "The gates you ordered sealed have been reopened."

Servius stared, his features schooled, though it was clear the news surprised him. "Perhaps the keepers of the hypogeum had them opened for air."

"Yes. Perhaps it is nothing," Quintus replied with a nod. "Apologies for the interruption."

"Ah, Quintus Varus," the emperor said. "The nova praetorian! I did not recognise you in uniform. I must say, it is a look you wear well. A formidable sight in full armour. You should be careful, Servius, or I might insist he join my guards."

It was as if the room stood still. Not because Quintus was stunned by the emperor's words, but because Tiberius stood in the doorway. He had heard what the emperor said and made no attempt to hide his loathing.

The emperor paid Tiberius no mind. He simply continued his conversation with the senators. "I was saddened to hear of the passing of Rufus Dinia. A terrible tragedy; a callous murder the state will investigate until the one who took his life is brought before Rome."

Servius blinked. "Rufus is dead?"

All eyes fell to the emperor. "As I was advised upon my arrival by Tiberius. His office torn apart, the door kicked in. Perhaps a lowly thief was unaware a quaestor merely reported income and taxes. His office held no coin."

Servius cast a surprised look to Tiberius, his face drained of colour. "A tragedy, indeed," he whispered. "Has anything been said about his demise?"

"He found a watery death at the docks, his throat cut," Tiberius said, his gaze boring into Servius as he spoke.

Quintus was struck cold, and the world started to fall away when he realised what was said.

The quaestor, the man who accounted Servius and Tiberius' treachery, had been found dead. The upending of his office was not the murderer's doing. It was Quintus who had kicked in that door above the forum. It was Quintus who had stolen the accounts to prove of treachery.

The reports that, in turn, had been stolen from him.

Quintus had no doubt, not for one moment, that Tiberius was responsible. Then he was struck by another realisation. Jovian was a man marked for death if he wasn't dead already.

And now that Quintus was absent physical proof, Fleet Commander Jovian was also the only man who could prove that Servius and Tiberius moved against Rome.

Quintus knew with sudden clarity that he and Kaeso were now implicated. If it could be proved that he and Kaeso had stolen the reports, the finger of guilt for Rufus' death would point toward them.

The only way to prove their innocence was to prove with whom true blame lay.

"Quintus," Kaeso whispered beside him.

He met his gaze and saw his fears reflected back at him. Quintus nodded to him. "I know." Then turned to Servius. "We will see to the first concern," he said, then pulled Kaeso, Appias, and Pellio to the far side where listening ears could not hear. "Go to the docks. Find Jovian and return with him."

Kaeso shook his head slightly. "I will not leave you here," he said, his gaze darting to Tiberius and Servius before meeting Quintus' once more. "Not when wolves circle."

"That is the very reason you must," Quintus urged him. "Jovian is the only one who can clear our names."

Kaeso's brow furrowed. "I do not like this."

"Neither do I."

"You gave the order to remain beside you, and that is where I will stay," Kaeso said.

"Consider a new order given," Quintus said. "I trust no one else to see our purpose met. Go, and return to me."

Appias and Pellio moved to the doorway, and for one moment, Kaeso remained. His jaw clenched, and fury burned in his big rabbit eyes. Then he turned on his heel and the three of them disappeared.

Quintus returned his attention to the emperor and the two senators who had watched their entire exchange. And Tiberius, of course.

"They will see the opened gate guarded," Quintus lied.

Marcus frowned. "And the smaller man defied your order?" he asked. Then he pursed his lips at Servius. "Not something I imagined you to tolerate."

"The smaller guard is Iberian," Servius replied as

though that was explanation enough. "I thought it at first a waste of purchase. Yet Quintus here has managed to tame it."

It.

Quintus smiled through clenched teeth. "Not so much tamed but given new focus," he said, the most diplomatic way of correcting the senator in front of the emperor. What he wanted to do was cut out Servius' tongue for speaking in such a way of Kaeso. Instead, he followed with, "The Iberian has a fire in his belly." He was passionate in all things—training, fighting, sex—though Quintus would not admit that to present company. "That defiance you see as troublesome, I see as an asset. When faced with almost certain death, other men might turn and flee, but not him. The defiance that burns in him will see him rage forward when others would stand in fear."

Servius and Tiberius stared, their expressions evidence that Quintus' subtle warning against threatening Kaeso was heard.

"He is too defiant to die?" Marcus said with a laugh, easing the tension. "Typical Iberian."

Quintus forced a smile only to be interrupted again, this time by Harpax and Phaidon. Quintus could tell by their faces that something was wrong, and Quintus was acutely aware of Kaeso's absence. "Apologies," Harpax said, bowing his head to the emperor and senators. Then he stared at Quintus. "We would have words."

"Another issue," Marcus said, giving Servius a raised eyebrow. "These games appear cursed before they begin."

Servius glowered and gave Quintus a pointed glare that insisted he see the issues amended. Quintus turned to his men. "What comes at me now?"

"Oscilius gives unexpected news," Phaidon said.

"Speak of it," Quintus urged, the dread in his belly pooling like spilled blood. "Has he been harmed?"

"Not harmed," Harpax replied. "Though word from the editor at dawn proclaimed these games to now be a *primus*."

A primus?

Quintus's chest felt too tight, and the ominous shadow that had hung over him all morning darkened. His omen of bad things to come was now a reality. Threats now came from all directions.

He turned to Servius. "Senator Augendus," he said, addressing him formally. "These games are now a primus? Our original agreement was exhibition battles only. None of my men were to fight to the death today."

Servius sighed and waved his hand with a flourish as though he could simply brush away Quintus' concerns. "I would think the gods are deserving of blood, are they not? I would please the gods so the people of Neapolis are rewarded." Then his eyes turned cold in the way they did when he revealed his true nature. "Fear not, Quintus, if I have them sacrificed, you will be paid their worth in coin."

Quintus felt a chill all over his skin, yet a fire roared within. He wanted to cross the room and break Servius' jaw with his bare hands. He wanted to rip his tongue from his head.

A low burst of laughter drew Quintus' attention to Tiberius. He found the dishonourable, sacrificial death of Quintus' men amusing? Yet his smirk was more than telling. He knew about the primus. In fact, Quintus would guess it was Tiberius' idea.

Tiberius had convinced Servius to see Quintus' men slaughtered. Again, if he couldn't strike a blow against Quintus, he would set aim for those he could reach.

Quintus knew he had been thoroughly outmanoeuvred

by Tiberius. He even felt cornered, his hand forced. But Tiberius had angered and threatened the wrong man. There would be blood offered today, Quintus vowed to the gods. He smiled at Tiberius, and the flames of ice and fire raged inside Quintus.

Oh indeed, there would be blood spilled on the sands today. And Quintus would enjoy killing Tiberius. Very much.

CAPITULUM XXV

KAESO RAN. He was faster than Appias and Pellio and he led their charge the entire way. Swarms of people were still vying for entry to the arena and Kaeso could only hope the games would not start yet. They had to fight against the flow of crowds; their guard uniforms could not outweigh the sheer number of people.

As soon as the emperor had announced the death of the quaestor, Kaeso had known. He had known at whose hand Rufus had met his end. He also knew Tiberius had found the reports under Quintus and Kaeso's bed, and such proof would easily tie them to the murder.

Seeking out Jovian and returning him to the arena made sense. Kaeso knew Quintus was right. He knew his reasons and he would never doubt him. But he trusted Tiberius to do harm more than he trusted Quintus to be able to prove what he knew.

Tiberius had the ear of the emperor, and he had the ear of Servius. And while Quintus stood for Rome, he was also apart from Roman men; he would side with his slaves before he took the word of a Roman man blindly.

Quintus was now in a room with both Tiberius and Servius, without Kaeso. Being half a city away may as well have been half a world.

And it was for Quintus that Kaeso ran.

As they gained ground from the arena, the crowd thinned to the point where Kaeso assumed all of Neapolis was at the arena. They eventually came upon the docks and found the tents of fleet guards empty. Kaeso took a moment to catch his breath and waited for Appias and Pellio to join him. "The post is absent guards," he told them.

Pellio breathed hard. "Could all attend the arena?"

Appias, the biggest of all of them, took longer to find his breath. He shook his head. "Surely a fleet guard's duty is at his post. Not a soldier of the army, granted, but still a soldier."

Kaeso looked down the pier and noticed the row of tents from which he had once seen Jovian walk out. It was the same door he had once seen Tiberius and Servius walk out from. "If they left freely, they would not leave doors open," he said, walking slowly toward the door. Appias and Pellio followed behind him. "Guards? We come on behalf of Senator Augendus," Kaeso announced, hoping if anyone lurked behind the door, he would draw them out.

Only silence replied, so Kaeso paused at the door and drew his daggers. Appias and Pellio took formation in the manner for which they had trained, weapons at the ready, and Kaeso pushed the door open with his foot.

The tent was dark, but there was no sound, no surprise of anyone lying in wait. There was, however, an overturned chair and papyrus scrolls on the floor. "We are too late," Pellio murmured.

Kaeso shook his head. "No. There is no blood, no body." He picked up the scroll and opened it flat on the table. It was a map of the oceans, showing lands as far as Britannia and Greece. Kaeso saw the name of his beloved Iberia but dared not dwell on it now. "This is Jovian's office, I have no doubt. More pressing concern is where is Jovian?"

"Perhaps we should turn our attention to the waters," Appias said. "To see if he met his end there."

Kaeso nodded. "Agreed."

"I will search the tents," Pellio said.

Kaeso and Appias raced along the pier and began to scout the depths in search for something afoul. Ships were docked, yet the absence of people was eerie, until Kaeso spotted a lone figure at the far end of the dock. They made toward him and Kaeso could see the man wore an old tunic, and with a pot of tar and a brush, he was sealing the side of a boat. "You, there," Appias called out, and the man turned. "Where would we find fleet men or naval officers?"

The man was long in years: his skin had seen too much sun and not enough kindness. "I care not to guess," he said. "The arena, most likely. Or where the drinks and whores cost no coin."

Appias growled at the man's reply, but Kaeso put a hand on his arm to calm him. "Are these fishing boats returned of this day already?"

The old man shrugged. "No boats went out today," he said. "No fish. Not a one. This day or the last. The gods should seek to punish the men who thieve and call it taxes, and let the poor man eat."

No fish, no birds. Kaeso recalled Quintus' words echoed from Cythereia and Quintus' unshakable certainty that something bad was coming.

"We need to get back to the arena," Kaeso said. "Let us find Pellio and not waste time in our return."

They turned back to go the way they had come when

they saw Pellio walk out from one door, only to turn to look at them. "Come!" he yelled out, then he turned to the next door and kicked it in before he disappeared inside.

Kaeso and Appias ran after him and raced into the darkened room to see carnage piled upon the floor. Bodies, blood, slit throats, and unseeing eyes. The fleet guards, who stood post in the tents, now lay absent life on the floor. Kaeso counted five in total, Jovian not amongst them.

"The same scene will greet you in the room next to this," Pellio said, his expression awash with fresh horrors.

Appias crouched to the closest body and put his hand to it. "Cold. They met their end long before now."

Kaeso felt as though the world was crushing down on him. "Jovian remains unfound, and there is nothing to be done for these men. We must keep to task."

Appias stood to his full height, his brow deepening under his helmet. "Who would do such a thing? To strike down a Roman soldier..." He shook his head.

"I can guess whose blade inflicted such wounds," Kaeso said, nodding to the pile of bodies. Both Appias and Pellio stared at him, waiting for him to divulge. "Praetorian Tiberius. He and Servius line their purses with stolen Roman coin. Quintus and I uncovered their truth to unravel their treachery." Kaeso looked at the pile of bodies. "Though it would seem Tiberius is tying off loose ends."

They both stared at him. "Tiberius?" Appias growled. "Who is in the company of Quintus while we stand idle?"

Pellio nodded. "I do not like this. We should return to Quintus."

"Agreed. Though this attack lacks thought," Kaeso said, trying to see reason where there was none. "These men would have been found, if not this day, then tomorrow."

"So?" Pellio asked. "To what end?"

"Precisely," Kaeso replied. "It would mean Tiberius cares not of consequence. That whatever plan he has to this end, it ends today."

"More reason for us to return to the arena," Appias said.

Kaeso nodded. "Without delay."

They turned and made for the door. The sun was above the horizon now, barely, and a huge cheer burst from the arena. And without another word broken between them, they ran. Only when they reached the end of the docks, a man stood in at the end of a gangway that brought them to a complete stop. He was covered in blood, blade still in hand. He was pale, with madness in his eyes.

Jovian.

THE ROAR in the arena drowned out all other sound. A sound Quintus had loved all his life, until now. The stream of gladiators paraded for the emperor to cheers that surely could be heard by all of Rome.

The emperor stood in the centre of the balcony, with Servius and Marcus either side of him. They had been caught in conversation when the procession started and had not yet gone to their own private rooms. Quintus knew this was not uncommon, but it left the room crowded, and it also left Tiberius closer than Quintus would have liked. Quintus took his place behind them, and Tiberius was only a few paces to his right. He could feel Tiberius' eyes boring into the side of his head and he could hear the putrid sound of him chewing the mastic gum.

The emperor gave a wave as the last of the gladiator parade left the arena and Servius raised his arms to quieten the crowd. "The city of Neapolis welcomes one and all," he yelled to another round of raucous applause. "I am Senator Servius Atrius Augendus, and I am the patron of these games. Three days of games to honour the good people of Rome, and enough blood to honour the gods!"

More deafening cheers, and Servius revelled in it. He incited more applause, winning the crowd over, and Quintus hated the man more with every breath he took.

"I am seeking position of Magistrate to bring more people, more wealth to Neapolis. My people of this great city have spoken, and I have heard your pleas. I will sit with the people, for the people. More jobs, more baths, more coin!"

The roar of the crowd shook the arena, and Quintus was so lost in his own loathing for Servius, he had not noticed the emperor come to stand beside him. "He lives for the adoration," the emperor said.

He would die for it, Quintus thought. "So it would seem," he answered more diplomatically.

"You were unaware the games were a primus," the emperor noted.

"It would seem Servius is a man of many secrets."

The emperor frowned for the briefest moment before schooling his features. "How have you found the adjustment from lanista to this nova praetorian role?"

Quintus smiled at that. "It has been an honour to serve Rome, but I look forward to the day I return to Oplontis. A ludus and twenty gladiators are more to my liking."

The emperor smiled. "Not a fan of politics?"

Quintus shook his head. "At least with gladiators, I know from where threat beckons."

The emperor nodded at that. "This is true. Though I

think you are more cut out for politics than you realise." And it was then Quintus noticed his age. The concerns of all of Rome creased the corners of his eyes, his brow, the worry in his eyes. Quintus did not envy him at all.

"Spend one summer day in my villa and you will see why my heart belongs there. Apricots and pears fresh from the orchard while the sea takes your troubles, carried off on a breeze."

The emperor looked into his eyes. "Is that a formal invitation?"

Quintus saw a good man with a burden he could not imagine. "No invitation required. You would be welcome any day."

The emperor gave him a genuine smile, and it was then Quintus noticed Tiberius watching them. He had cold eyes and his jaw clenched tight, not even attempting to hide his glare, and Quintus returned it with equal fervour. "Ah, Servius draws his speech to a close," the emperor said, and Quintus turned back to find that, indeed, Servius had called for the games to begin.

Quintus prayed Kaeso would not keep him waiting much longer. He had been loath to send him on an errand that would part them, but he trusted Kaeso. If there was any man who could see his demands met, it was Kaeso.

Quintus felt every moment of his absence.

The emperor and both senators took seats at the balcony's edge and the first two gladiators entered the arena. Quintus recognised one immediately. It was Paullus, one of his newer gladiators. He had promise but would need more fights to find proper form. Quintus could only hope his opponent was of equal or lesser standing.

Servius gave the signal to start, and the roar of the crowd went to the heavens. Not even the clang of metal swords meeting on the sands could be heard over the sound of it.

Tiberius moved in beside him to stand behind the emperor, though he spoke only to Quintus. "I would hope you were not attached to your gladiators," he said with a sneer. "Given their odds of dying today. Though you have a fondness for slaves. One is noticeably absent." He glanced around the room as though searching for someone. "The bed-slave whore you dress as a guard. Where is he?"

Quintus clenched his teeth. He refused to entertain his line of question. Instead he asked his own. "I trust you have enjoyed your time in Neapolis these last days. I thought your duty was in Roma, yet you are seen around this city as though you claim it as your own."

The emperor cocked his head, turning his ear. A movement neither Quintus nor Tiberius missed. He had clearly heard what Quintus had said, and from his curious expression, it was news to him.

Tiberius scowled at Quintus. "Official business that does not concern the likes of you."

"Concerning as the death of Rufus Dinia. Loose ends can unravel the richest of brocades," Quintus countered. "Would you not agree, Tiberius? Even the best fabrics are only simple threads when they are undone."

Both Servius and the emperor turned at this exchange. Servius' expression was urging caution, and the emperor wore a look of curious confusion. Though raucous cheering drew their attention back to the arena.

Paullus had bested his opponent and stood over his lifeless body. A strike to the throat had been a quick death for the man, and Paullus raised his sword to the sky and the cheers of the crowd grew louder.

Servius shifted in his seat. Feigning excitement, he

gestured broadly to the blood pooling on the sand. "A decent offer to please the gods with the first battle of many," he yelled. They watched the dead man be dragged through the far gate, then Servius stood and raised his arms to the people. "Bring more blood!"

The arena exploded with cheers, and two more men entered the arena. They wore no armour and Quintus didn't recognise them. He exhaled his relief slowly as cages were wheeled in and two wild boars were let loose.

The crowd cheered, for beast or man, Quintus couldn't guess. And before Tiberius could break more words with Quintus, a frightened cry from a slave made everyone turn.

Appias now stood in the room, his chest heaving, covered in sweat and dried blood, his helmet gone. But that wasn't what had the room's attention. He was carrying a man over his shoulder. All Quintus could see was the leather pelmet skirt and boots and red cape, and for one heart-stopping moment, Quintus thought it was Kaeso. When Appias set the man onto his feet, Quintus almost collapsed with relief to find it wasn't. His relief was quick to be replaced by horror when he saw who it was.

Commander Jovian stumbled backwards, his hands shaking, his face absent colour and reason, and suddenly everyone in the room was on their feet.

"What is this?" Quintus barked to Appias at the same time the emperor asked, "What has happened here?"

Everyone awaited Appias' reply. "We went to the docks, as ordered," he said. "We found all fleet guards dead, locked in dock offices with their throats cut. We left to return and found the commander. He speaks little sense but of horrors witnessed."

"Where is Kaeso?" Quintus asked.

Appias swallowed, still breathing hard. "He sought

further proof and ordered me here. He swore to return to you. He promised."

Then Commander Jovian wailed and flailed his arms. It was apparent he was lost to madness. His eyes were wide, he was smeared in dried blood, and then he seemed to realise where he stood. He took in the faces looking at him, and when he saw one in particular, he scampered back as though he had seen a haunted spirit.

"No, no! Not you! Be gone. Slayer of innocent men. So much blood," he cried. He began to shake as he pushed backwards, his gaze unwavering from one man.

Tiberius.

Then Jovian produced a dagger, and Quintus moved in front of the emperor to protect him. But Jovian dropped it as though he had never laid eyes on it before. The dagger clanged to the marble floor and Quintus could see what it was.

It was a Roman-issued pugio. The dagger used by praetorian guards, the leather handle marked with the insignia of its owner.

The emperor sidestepped Quintus and went to Jovian, who had slid to the far wall and sat on the floor, with wide eyes and ashen face. "Speak of what happened?" the emperor urged him. Quintus knelt also and picked up the blade to show the emperor the insignia. "My guardsman," the emperor murmured.

Jovian raised a shaking hand and pointed his finger to Tiberius and then to Servius and back to Tiberius. "So much blood. He took the lives of my men. He screamed to find me, so loud," Jovian whispered musically, like a madman.

The emperor stood slowly and faced Tiberius. "Give explanation or face the fury of Rome!"

Tiberius waved a dismissive hand at Jovian, who was now crying. "He's absent wit and reason. Look at him! He knows not what he is saying!"

Servius was ashen, panicked and scared, and he looked upon Jovian with fake pity. "His word surely cannot be held against ours."

Quintus saw the emperor consider this, and he could no longer stand idle. "Emperor, I have seen with my own eyes, Servius and Tiberius move against Rome. They line their purse with the wealth of ships returned from war, carrying coin and gold. I have seen them meet. I have seen the ledgers from the quaestor's hand. Jovian himself told me he was threatened to comply."

The emperor's face reddened, and he turned his fury toward Tiberius. "Is this true?"

Tiberius sneered and chewed on his mastic gum. "This man is of no worth, and I would hold his opinion in the same regard."

The emperor picked up the dagger with the end of the shawl, still glaring at Tiberius. "Who owns this dagger? And how was it found covered in the blood of Roman soldiers?"

Tiberius shook his head. He covered well considering the charges against him, and Quintus could see that Tiberius still thought he would walk away from this. "I cannot give answer," Tiberius said. "Perhaps it was stolen!"

The emperor moved his head to look past Tiberius, to one praetorian guard who had taken a step back. He appeared particularly unwell. "You!" the emperor demanded. "Speak!"

He shook his head and retreated another step. Then he looked at Tiberius and said, "It must have dropped from hand. It was dark and—"

Tiberius stepped toward him, fist raised.

"Enough!" the emperor yelled, his face red with anger. Tiberius stilled and recoiled at the emperor's rage. The emperor turned to Servius. "And what say you, to the charges Quintus claims against you? You would dare to steal from Rome?"

Servius shook his head but words failed him. "Th-th-there is no proof of this," he stammered, looking as though he might take ill. He was deathly pale, and the sweat at his brow had little to do with the heat.

The emperor seemed to grow taller, realisation and rage filled his chest, and he bore down on Tiberius. "You took Rufus' life? You ended his life in a vain attempt to conceal your crimes?"

Before Tiberius could form reply, Helier stepped around Servius. He had his head bowed and Quintus noted how his hands trembled. "Mighty Emperor," he said, his voice meek and uncertain. "Permission to speak."

All eyes in the room were on him. A slave would dare approach the emperor? It was utter madness! The emperor cast him a cautious look, knowing whatever he had to say must be important enough for him to come forward. "Granted."

"I am but a slave to Senator Augendus, my word holds no value, yet I speak only the truth. I have witnessed his meetings. I have heard how he and Tiberius pose to strike against you. Wealth is not the only thing they seek to steal from you, but your title also."

Servius' face darkened as he set his gaze upon Helier. That coldness Quintus had witnessed many times was now on full view for all to see. "You worthless slave, I will have your head for this!"

The emperor raised his hand to silence Servius. He

studied Helier, who still had his head down. "My title? They would take Rome?"

Helier nodded and finally raised his chin. "You seek proof, and I have it," he said, then reached into his garment and pulled out a roll of papyrus and handed it to the emperor.

The records Quintus had stolen from Rufus.

The emperor's expression turned livid as he read the inventory records of Servius and Tiberius' treachery.

Quintus could not believe it. It wasn't Tiberius who had taken them from his room, but Helier. He stared at the slave. "You took these?"

The emperor turned to Quintus. "You knew?"

"To provide as evidence," Quintus replied. "We knew the senator and Tiberius moved against Rome, but not how deep the well of deceit ran."

When Quintus looked back to Helier, Helier's eyes were full of tears and pleading. "Do you know what happens to the slaves of a man guilty of treachery?" he asked. "They meet the same fate, even when the treachery is not theirs. The emperor can decide my fate as he chooses, but I sought evidence that might spare the lives of the other slaves of his house. They have had no part in this."

The emperor read each leaflet, letting each feather to the floor as he read the next. "This amount of wealth..." He looked up, glaring at Servius. "To what end? You would see the citizens of Neapolis starve while you grow fat on the coin of Rome. For what purpose does this amount of wealth serve you?"

Servius could only shake his head, frightened and pale. His game of deception was up, and he knew it. Tiberius, on the other hand, still stood defiant, and he quickly stepped forward. "He offered coin to the praetorian cohorts to form an army to stand against you," Tiberius said. "He threatened me to abide his demands. If the praetorians could manoeuvre him to the throne of Rome."

Servius' mouth fell open as he stared at Tiberius. "Liar! It was you who first came to me." He shook his head vehemently and grabbed for Helier. "Tell him, Helier. Speak the truth you were witness to. Was it not Tiberius who arranged such a meeting?"

Helier took a step closer to Quintus, closer to the emperor, and stood opposite Servius and Tiberius. "They agreed to such conspiracy together."

Servius' fear turned to rage, and he lunged for Helier. Quintus intercepted him, shoving him to the floor. "You will threaten no one again as you threatened me to stand as your guard!"

"He threatened you also?" the emperor asked.

Quintus gave a nod. "The life of my men if I did not agree. He assumed I would defend him while he slithered into Rome. He assumed wrong. I stand for the good of Rome, ruled by what is right and not by coin."

"You concerned yourself with matters not your own," Tiberius seethed. "You and your filthy Iberian slave."

Quintus turned to Tiberius, his vision tinting red with pure rage. "Still your fucking treacherous tongue, or..."

"Or what?" Tiberius goaded.

"Or I will see it ripped from your head," Quintus replied. He stepped closer, his fists clenched at his sides. "Emperor, give order, and I will see it done."

The emperor stood beside Quintus. "We shall have lesson made of him, of them both, so all of Rome can see what becomes of treasonous men." Then the emperor waved to the other praetorian guards. "Seize them, Tiberius and Servius. Seize them both and take them to the sands of the arena."

Servius shook violently, pleading for his life, and Tiberius might have been fearful at first, but the guards beside him didn't move.

"I said seize them!" the emperor yelled.

When they did not move again, Tiberius smiled. His men stood with him, loyal to the dog that would sooner bite them than defend them. Quintus assessed the room: there were ten armed praetorian guards flanking Tiberius; Servius, who was unarmed and no threat in a fight; a handful of slaves stood scared in the corner; and Jovian, who now wept silently on the floor against the wall. Helier stood behind him; he was not armed, but Quintus had no trust in him, and he would rather not have anyone at his back. "Stand with the other slaves," Quintus said to Helier. There was only him and Appias, and Decius and Mettius at the balcony. Not the best odds but he would not back down, and he would not retreat. Quintus stood in front of the emperor, to defend him at all costs, and drew his sword. "Make attempt on the emperor, and it will be your last," Quintus said.

Tiberius raised his chin and must have assessed the room as Quintus had done. "You are outnumbered," he sneered.

In that moment, Harpax and Phaidon raced into the room. They froze at the standoff before them but were quick to stand on Quintus' side of the fight. Quintus smiled at his increased odds, but Harpax shook his head. "Praetorian guards flood the tunnel, Quintus," he said. "Too many to count."

Servius gasped, clearly not aware of this double cross. Tiberius laughed at him. "A hundred men come through the tunnel to see me take the position of emperor. For me, not you. Did you think sealing one door to the arena would stop us?" He laughed again at that. Then he turned to Quintus. "You would need an army to stop me."

A voice from behind Quintus spoke, loud and without falter. "Just as well he has one."

AS SOON AS he saw Jovian, saw him ramble madness as he dropped bloodstained coins onto the docks, Kaeso knew what he had to do. Jovian spoke of hiding with the hidden, and Kaeso could not make sense of it.

"Who did this?" Kaeso asked. He held Jovian's arms and looked into his eyes. They held no focus. "Who killed your men?"

"Scorpions of gold," he whispered. "They came in darkness with talons of blades."

By the gods, the man had lost all wit.

"Scorpions of gold," Pellio said. "Praetorian guards have golden scorpions on their armour."

Mention of the guards sent Jovian into a panic, and Kaeso knew, even in his madness, it had struck a nerve. He held his arms tight to stop him from flailing. "Tiberius," was all Kaeso had to say and Jovian was stricken, and Kaeso knew it to be true.

"I hid with the hidden," he whispered again. "Where he would not think to find me."

"Where? What is hidden?" Kaeso demanded.

Jovian held out his hand with the blood and more gold coins. "Where they hide the coin to pay their army," he answered, his voice almost musical. Then he waved his hand toward the closest ship, but then he seemed to notice the blood on his hand and fell into his mind's horrors once more. He began to ramble and sob without making sense.

Kaeso turned to Appias, the only one of them big enough. "Take him to Quintus. Carry him if you must. Hurry. He speaks no sense but could yet prove Tiberius the snake he is."

Appias took Jovian's arm, then stopped to look at Kaeso. "And what of you? If I return absent of you, Quintus will—"

"Tell him I seek further proof to clear his name, and I will return. I swear it." He put his hand on Appias' shoulder and looked into his eyes. "I swear it. Now, go."

Kaeso watched as Appias scooped up Jovian to carry him on his back and began his way back to the arena, then turned to Pellio. "Come with me." He ran along the gangplank to the ship Jovian had pointed to, and his stomach squeezed. He didn't need to question where Jovian had come from. There was a trail of bloodied gold coins showing the path to a hatch in the deck.

"I cannot," Kaeso started. "I cannot go in there." A wave of sickness rolled over him. "I was held in a ship like this, down there..." He shook his head, trying to shake vivid reminders. "I cannot see it again."

Pellio nodded as though he understood, and he pulled the hatch back, revealing a dark void below. The stench threatened to make Kaeso ill, and he put his hand to his mouth and stepped back. Pellio met him with a determined gaze. "What do I search for?"

"Gold. The coins Jovian held." He let out an unsteady breath. "Gratitude, Pellio."

Pellio grinned at him. "For Quintus," he said, then jumped into the belly of the ship.

It seemed to take an age. Kaeso felt he waited on the deck of that ship for a lifetime waiting for Pellio to surface. He heard him curse the darkness, he heard him curse the placement of hard objects against stubbed toes. He heard him mutter about the smell, the filth, then after a long pause of silence, Kaeso grew worried. "Pellio?" he called. "Pellio?" He gathered his courage and peered down into the hatch, only to have Pellio appear.

He struggled to hold a sack. "Take hold, and help lift my burden," Pellio urged. Together they heaved the sack up onto the deck and followed it, clambering out unaided. He knelt at the sack he had carried and pulled it open to reveal its contents.

Coins. Gold and silver, and a lot of them.

Pellio grinned up at Kaeso. "There is yet more where this came from. Crates of it."

"We need to bring this to Quintus," Kaeso said. "If Tiberius or Servius attempt to blame Quintus, we now have proof of whose hand truly moves against Rome."

Pellio nodded and closed the sack. "Then let us hurry."

Kaeso took one corner of the sack, Pellio the other, and together they carried it off the ship and onto the docks. Kaeso was grateful the streets were empty. He looked to the sun and could not believe it was still early morning.

"Time has stood still this day," Kaeso said.

Pellio nodded in agreement. "And it is far from over."

Kaeso swallowed hard as he glanced up the street leading toward the arena. It seemed so far away and an impossible journey to make. Quintus may as well have been on the other side of Rome. "Quintus spoke of bad omens for this day," Kaeso said as they walked. "That it would not end well."

Pellio smiled. He had a sort of handsomeness about him despite his scars from arena battles, and Kaeso wished he had had more time to know him better. To know all of them better.

"He sees the future now?" Pellio asked, his grin widening. "Or he speaks directly with the gods now? Rumour has it you said he had the cock of a god, not that he broke words with them."

Kaeso snorted out a laugh. "A horse. I said he has the cock of a horse. Not a god, though Priapus surely shined upon him. Yet I wish if I am to be quoted, it could be with some amount of accuracy."

Pellio burst out laughing. "I will do well to remember that." They continued to walk some more in silence, the sack gaining weight with every step, before Pellio spoke again. "It is a genuine affection you have for him, is it not?"

Kaeso cast him a wary look. "Why would you ask such a thing?"

"My concern is for my dominus," Pellio replied. "We all see how he casts eyes upon you. I fear a broken heart would leave us with a dominus different to the man he was before you."

Kaeso blinked and changing his grip on the sack to give him a spare moment to think. "You fear if I were gone, he would become cruel in his training? Then you do not know the man I know. He is a man like no other, and it is not only he that would risk his heart." Kaeso shook his head, feeling foolish discussing such matters with him. "He holds my heart also, so if you would be willing, I would have you still your tongue and set your mind to this task so I may return to him. If that piece of shit Tiberius has made threat upon Quintus' life, I will see the skies rain with his blood."

Pellio grinned, impossibly huge. "I see why he favours you. You threaten death and violence as he does."

Kaeso smiled at that, and together they carried their heavy sack toward the arena. Only when they drew near, a few people scurried away from the arena with deep concern etched on their faces. "Why do you leave?" Kaeso called out to one man.

"The emperor's guards come to take the arena," he said as he raced away.

Kaeso and Pellio stopped and watched as a few more people raced away from the arena. "Pellio," Kaeso said. "Find all our men and bring them to the senator's room. We protect Quintus at all cost."

Pellio shoved the sack of coin into Kaeso's chest. "I will see it done," he said with a determined nod.

"Watch your back," Kaeso said.

Pellio met his gaze. "And you yours. I will not be the one to tell Quintus you are no longer of this world, do you hear me?"

Kaeso nodded and the two men parted ways. Pellio raced into the belly of the arena without pause, and Kaeso struggled to find an easier hold on the sack. He had never dreamed of so much coin, and now that he had it, surely the gods mocked him by making it too heavy for him to carry.

Yet he pressed on, up the stairs to the unnumbered archway and along the narrow corridor. He had to rest against the wall a moment, and he could feel the arena itself hum with the roar of the crowds, but over that, there was shouting. All he heard was a booming "Seize them!" and it struck Kaeso into moving. He took the last flight of stairs and he ran past the emperor's room only to find it empty.

His heart was pounding out of his chest, and he feared he was too late, and as he ran through the doorway, he saw the room divided. Tiberius and his men on one side, Quintus and the emperor on the other. Appias, Harpax, and Phaidon were there, and Mettius and Decius too. Senator Marcus Maternus stood with them also. Servius stood in the middle, horridly pale and sweating, and Jovian was slumped against the wall, crying silent tears.

Kaeso had no idea what had transpired here, but he could guess well enough. Then Tiberius sneered at Quintus. "You would need an army to stop me."

Kaeso would allow no one to threaten Quintus. No one. "Just as well he has one," Kaeso said. Everyone stopped and turned to see who had spoken. He let the sack of coins drop to the floor and some of its contents spilled onto the tiles. "Coins taken from Tiberius' and Servius' stowed shipment," he explained, picking up a handful of coins and handing them to the emperor. Then he looked directly at Quintus. "You asked for proof. See it provided."

"These are not true Roman coin," the emperor said, his face growing dark.

But for one moment, despite the standoff in the room, Quintus stared at Kaeso. Quintus' smile at seeing Kaeso was warm and immediate, but Tiberius had grown impatient. "Ah, the filthy Iberian arrives," he spat. Then he directed his gaze to Quintus. "The nova praetorian has nothing but a common bed slave to stand beside him! And you would call that an army?"

Kaeso turned to face Tiberius as he unsheathed the blades from his wrist guards. "I never said I was the army. Did you think for one moment that Quintus brought his men here to defend the senator?" Kaeso barked out a laugh. "He surrounded himself with his men as soon as he sniffed out deceit. Men who would stand to defend him, and for good reason it would seem."

And just then, Pellio led a barrage of red Roman guards into the room. Salonia and Varia at the fore, weapons at the ready. They now outnumbered Tiberius and his guards in the room by more than two to one.

Yet Tiberius still smiled. "I will be Emperor, you can mark my words."

Quintus took a step closer. "You will be dead before this day is over, you can mark my words."

Tiberius outstretched his arms. "A uniform on a filthy gladiator does not make him a guard. Nor does it make him of any more worth. You will need the gods themselves to sway me from my path."

Then, like the gods had heard and answered, a resounding boom broke the silence.

Everyone stilled at the sound, distant yet far too close, and glanced around for the cause. Kaeso noticed the quiet of the crowd at first, then someone screamed. Then Kaeso noticed people in the arena were pointing, faces stricken.

He followed their lines of sight and saw their cause for concern. Before he could speak of it, someone else said, "Vesuvius. Look at Vesuvius!"

And there it was, the mountain in the distance, the peak that towered over all of Campania had awoken. A pillar of dirty white smoke plumed skywards. It appeared peaceful at first, as though the world had turned to admire it.

Then men in guard uniforms, crested with gold scorpions and plumes of blue feathers and capes, swarmed the arena sands. There were too many to count, and Kaeso realised this was what had sent people fleeing earlier...

The entire arena was silent, and no one in the room dared move.

Then the screaming started. And chaos swiftly followed.

IT WAS like the sun stood still in the sky and time was forbidden to move forward. Quintus could not believe his eyes. A cohort of guards filled the sands and stood in formation facing their balcony.

One of the guards tossed a severed head onto the sands and the people in the arena saw this for what it was. This was no exhibition, no theatrics.

Tiberius turned to Servius. "You have exceeded your usefulness. I will choose my own fate, and—" He glanced toward Quintus. "—let you fall to yours."

Then Tiberius ran and leapt off the balcony. The drop to the arena was twice as tall as Quintus, yet Tiberius rolled into his landing and sprung to his feet unharmed. The guards he left on the balcony, in the room with Quintus, panicked.

One jumped from the balcony, only to scream upon landing; a bone had broken the skin at his knee. Tiberius walked over to the suffering man, took his dagger, and sliced the man's throat.

No one else attempted to jump. Instead, they turned to face Quintus and his men, weapons raised. It was over quickly. Quintus took care of three men; Kaeso claimed two; Salonia and Varia, one apiece; Appias, Pellio, and Harpax managed one apiece also.

"I am Tiberius Hirrus. Heed my name," Tiberius yelled from the middle of the arena sands. The crowd gave pause to watch, to listen. "Your emperor rules no more. I have acceded his place, so from this day forward, I am the new emperor of Rome."

The crowd was silent, stunned.

Quintus picked up the closest body by one arm and one leg and tossed the dead guard over the balcony as a clear message to Tiberius and to the people of Neapolis. All eyes were now on him at the balcony, a mountain of a man wearing armour and a helmet with the red colours of Rome. He had addressed many arenas and he knew how to win a crowd. He raised both hands for their attention. "The true emperor yet lives and stands beside me," he said, giving them full view of the emperor. Then Quintus pointed both fingers to Tiberius. "This man, Tiberius, claims false title. He is guilty of treason, along with any guard who stands with him, and Rome will pay ten thousand denarii to any man who brings me his head."

Tiberius stood in the arena for two long heartbeats, in absolute silence. His expression slack with the realisation of what Quintus had just done; he had put a public bounty on Tiberius' head.

And then, in a display of violent poetry, the arena dissolved into chaos.

Some scrambled to leave, while other men leapt from the stands onto the sands. Some guards moved to defend Tiberius; some became targets themselves; some dropped their shields and deserted Tiberius' cause. Unarmed civilians fought against swords and daggers, taking heavy toll and drowning the sands in blood.

Quintus turned to face the emperor. He was pale but still stood tall, his shoulders set, his eyes determined. "Trust me and my men to defend you," Quintus said. "Wear this," he said, as he took off his helmet, then his chest guard, pulling straps and lifting it over his head. He slid the chest guard over the emperor's head. "And see yourself protected."

Then Quintus took one of the dead guards' daggers and shield and handed them to the emperor, then one of each to Senator Marcus. Quintus looked him dead in the eye. "You will protect the emperor with your life."

Marcus swallowed hard, but he nodded. "I am no soldier, but I swore my life to Rome; my oath still stands."

Quintus nodded. "Good man." Then he put his hand on the emperor's shoulder and met his gaze. "Do not attempt to make for Rome," Quintus urged. "The roads and tunnels would be a certain ambush. Stay here until no threat remains, and I will see you return alive."

The emperor nodded quickly, but Quintus gave him no time to speak. He turned to his men, his voice deep and resounding. "You will protect the emperor as you would me. Do not leave his side. Do not leave this room. Imagine this to be a fight to the death on arena sands and protect your leader. Defend, defend, defend, and kill anyone who makes an attempt on his life."

Then Quintus pointed to Servius, who was now sitting propped against the wall looking as vacant as Jovian. "And if this man," Quintus barked, "this treasonous sack of shit and piss moves, *at all*, kill him."

Then he turned to Salonia and Varia. "Find Oscilius and Cythereia and have them get my men out. Tell them to leave without delay."

Salonia nodded, her gaze fierce. "Dominus." Then they dashed out the door.

Finally, Quintus turned to Kaeso. "You are with me."

Kaeso held his gaze. "In all things."

Quintus went back to the balcony to see the carnage he had

set in motion. There were slain bodies everywhere, blood pooled and sprayed in a gruesome shrine to thankless gods. Many guards in blue remained, some actively striking civilians, some encircling Tiberius, defending him, and they were moving toward a gate while some of his men were trying to open it. Desperate civilians still attempted to best the guards but were no match. Quintus threw his shield onto the sands below. Then with a final smile to Kaeso, he leapt down into the furore.

KAESO WATCHED as Quintus rolled and sprang to his feet. In one swift movement, he collected his shield, unsheathed his sword, and struck at the closest guard.

"Futuo!" Kaeso swore.

He slid his daggers into his wrist guards. "That impossible man! He thinks himself immortal." Then he collected all the daggers from the dead guards and tossed them over the balcony, followed by a shield or two, and when he straightened up, he found everyone watching him. He pointed to Harpax and Phaidon. "Follow him to the sands as fast as you are able. Slay any blue guard who stands in your way."

Harpax nodded, but Phaidon gave pause. "And what of you?"

"I swore to stand beside him," Kaeso replied. "Foolish or brave, that is yet to be decided." And with that, he ran for the balcony, put two hands on the ledge and, in a fluid jump, followed Quintus into his quest of madness.

He landed with ease, a childhood of jumping from tree branches well spent. He rolled, and by the time he righted himself, he had assessed where Quintus was, and his closest threat. He was half the arena away, a trail of blue guards in his wake, and he was battling with another guard, his shield raised in one arm, his sword in the other. Though Quintus was moving forward, his opponent on the back foot, and Quintus almost had him beat. But another guard was running toward him from behind, sword ready, his gaze focused on Quintus.

Kaeso took his smaller dagger from his wrist guard, and in a swift flick of his wrist, the blade cartwheeled across the distance and struck the guard under his arm. In that small space where his chest plate bore straps and no leather, the blade pierced his heart. It was a perfect kill shot. The man fell, his sword nearing Quintus' foot. Quintus glanced, seeing the guard, then seeing Kaeso. He offered a brief smile, then turned back to his opponent. He smashed the man with his shield, then buried his sword in his neck. He pulled it clear and started on the next guard.

But from behind his wall of guards, Tiberius had sighted Kaeso. "Kill that man!" he screamed as he pointed. "That filthy Iberian slave. Give me his fucking head!"

Blue guards then turned to face him, and Kaeso scrambled in the dirt for the daggers he had thrown from the balcony. He found one, then two, and spun on his knees, launching both blades at the same time.

The two guards fell.

Kaeso found another two daggers in the sands and dropped another two guards as they ran toward him. But other men kept coming and the other daggers were out of reach. So he took his last dagger and dodged a sword as it swung for him, and while the guard fell into the follow-through of his swing, Kaeso buried the dagger into his throat.

And then another.

But then another readied his sword, and Kaeso didn't

have time to duck away. The guard stood over him, his strike imminent, and all Kaeso could do was watch. But then the guard's face changed, from rage to surprise, and in that split second, Kaeso rolled out of the way. The guard fell forward with Quintus' sword in his back.

Quintus smiled at him, red sprays of blood flecked his skin. "Returning the favour," he said.

Kaeso saw a blue guard running for Quintus's back, and he launched a side-throw to drop the guard mid-step. "I would suggest you keep your back from the enemy," Kaeso said. "Should you wish to live through this."

Quintus smiled as he turned around to the guards and smashed another with his shield. He now stood in front of Kaeso. "And I would suggest you find more daggers," Quintus said as he thwarted another attacking guard. "Should you wish to live through this."

"When this is done," Kaeso said, scampering over a dead guard and relieving him of his sword and also a smaller dagger. "We shall have words of your leaping into a hundred guards."

Quintus chuckled as he swung at another guard. "And of your following me."

Kaeso threw the dagger and stopped a guard who began his approach toward him. Then he stood with a heavier sword poised to attack and defend, but the guards across the arena had broken through the gate, and one by one—Tiberius amongst them—they disappeared into the belly of the arena.

"We must stop them!" Quintus growled before charging after them.

"Wait!" Kaeso cried. He dropped the heavier sword in favour of two smaller daggers from fallen guards, then looked toward the open gate. "I cannot bear the cramped darkness in there."

"Stay beside me," Quintus replied. "I will guide you through." He ran to the darkened entryway. "All you must do is follow. And kill any guard wearing blue."

Kaeso rolled his eyes, took a deep breath, and followed Quintus into the darkness of the hypogeum. The stairs leading downward were free of threat, though it took a moment for Kaeso to grow accustomed to the dark, to the stench. To the memories. To the horrors he had endured while held captive on that ship. Torches now hung on all the walls yet offered little reprieve.

But he wasn't afforded time to adjust or prepare his mind. For just then, a guard dressed in blue came charging up the stairs, shield and sword at the ready. Before he drew too close, his mouth and eyes opened wide and he slowly fell forward, a sword in his back.

Salonia stood at the bottom of the stairs but spared no time for greetings. "They have gone toward the far gate. The gate ordered to be sealed."

"Toward the crypt. The tunnel that leads to Puteoli," Quintus murmured.

They stepped into the corridor and Kaeso found more torches lighting the way. He couldn't describe the relief; he almost sagged with it.

Of course, Quintus noticed. He put his hand on Kaeso's shoulder and squeezed but made no point of it. "Let us make short work of this."

Kaeso had never agreed with anything more.

Their number now at four, they edged along the corridor with Quintus at the front, Kaeso behind, then Varia and Salonia at the rear. Their path would have been quicker if it weren't for the scores of unarmed gladiators being led out by dominus and doctor.

Quintus grabbed the arm of one. "Ovid," he called him by name. "Have you seen Oscilius?"

The man had to look twice. "Quintus?"

"Oscilius, have you seen him?"

The man shook his head. "They did not pass here. Though you should turn back the way you came. Guards, different to these," he nodded toward Kaeso and Varia. "They vowed death to anyone who stands in their way."

Quintus snarled at the corridor ahead. "Then we are on the right path. Go well, Ovid. Get yourself and your men to safety." And Quintus began to move again at a faster pace, and after a turn or two, soon they came to a caged room familiar to Kaeso.

It was the armorum, and it was locked, full of weapons yet absent the man who would tend them.

"Otho!" Quintus called. "Otho!"

There was no reply, only a man who led three shackled prisoners down the corridor.

"Everyone is abandoning," Salonia said. "Perhaps Otho did as well."

"Perhaps," Quintus conceded. "We could have done with more weapons."

"Quintus?" a weak voice asked. And there, behind a crate, Otho appeared. He looked more feeble than Kaeso remembered. "By the gods, man. I heard screaming and panic. What brings such madness?"

"Treachery against Rome. Indiscriminate murder."

Otho blinked his wide eyes. "I saw the guards before. But they wore no uniform familiar to me, so I hid. They tried to get through my gate."

"Then you were wise to stay hidden," Quintus replied. "I must ask a favour."

Otho nodded.

"Weapons. Smaller daggers for Kaeso, spears for Salonia. Any you can spare. I will see you paid."

Otho scrambled to pass through four daggers to Kaeso and two spears to Salonia. Varia took a sword. "Consider payment made," Otho said.

"Gratitude," Quintus said. "We must hurry."

And so they ran.

The stench was unspeakable, and if he had had time to pause, Kaeso surely would have retched from it. They passed a man with lions in a cage yelling orders in a foreign tongue. They passed another with a chain line of criminals or slaves, Kaeso couldn't tell which. And then the corridors grew lighter, the air cleaner, and he knew the opened gate was near.

Yet Quintus did not slow. As he did in all things, he simply charged into the sunlight, into the fray without fear of what lay beyond. Of course, Kaeso would follow, as would Varia and Salonia; none would leave him to face the unknown alone.

And he ran them all right into a trap.

CAPITULUM XXVII

QUINTUS KNEW BETTER. He had ingrained into his gladiators never to charge blindly into battle. A clever gladiator, a gladiator who bested all others, was one who put strategy into play. He assessed his opponents and sought a weakness, a ploy to see their shortcomings be their downfall.

Quintus had said a hundred times that the first strike made in error, to be caught unaware would be any gladiator's first and last mistake.

And he had done exactly that.

The outside of the arena was a flat area with a cobbled path, which led up to the road that became the tunnel and road that lead to Puteoli. The road was blocked with people, horses, carts, and carriages trying to leave, and half a *centuriae* of blue guards attempted to push their way through.

It wasn't their number that Quintus noticed. It was the two red guards being dragged with them. Harpax and Phaidon struggled against their hold but were outnumbered and pummelled with fists into submission.

"Tiberius!" Quintus roared.

The blue guards stopped and turned, coming back around in formation. They had the higher ground, they had the numbers, and they had two of Quintus' men. Tiberius appeared in their centre, smiling. "Predictable as the sun rising," he said. "I thought to hold your two men to draw you out. I knew you would come for them."

Quintus didn't think Tiberius expected to find them so soon. He might not have planned to have their meeting come to its end here and now, but this setting was definitely in Tiberius' favour.

"So these men are of no value to me now," Tiberius said. The guards who held Harpax and Phaidon brought them forward, and Tiberius grabbed Harpax by the hair. "Their purpose has been met."

Before Quintus could demand Tiberius let them go, a blue guard raised his dagger to Harpax's throat and Quintus expected to witness his death. Then time slowed beyond reason. Kaeso somersaulted out from Quintus's side, and in the blink of an eye, he flicked two daggers toward the guards.

One guard took a dagger to the throat, the other to his cheek. They both staggered back, and Harpax and Phaidon took their chance to turn and fight. Phaidon kicked his other guard in the side of the knee, snapping his leg at a wrong angle, and when he fell to the ground, Phaidon wrested his sword and ended the man's screams. Harpax was still struggling—his guard was bigger and stronger—so Phaidon swung the sword into the man's arm.

Tiberius stumbled back. "Take them! Give me the Iberian's head!"

The blue guards launched forward, swords raised, and Quintus and Varia deflected sword with sword, the clang of metal echoing loudly. Salonia attacked with her spear, and Kaeso sliced with his dagger. Phaidon and Harpax, both with bruised and bloodied faces, joined them with swords.

But there were too many blue guards. They had the advantage of higher ground, and they began to circle around them. "Do not let them flank us!" Quintus yelled as he smashed his shield into one guard, the wet snapping of bone crunched against the metal.

But he knew. He was certain, this would be their end. They had taken down many guards and had not yet lost one of their own, but they could not maintain this fervour. They would tire eventually; he would fight until he could no longer hold the weight of his sword, but the blue guards would simply keep coming.

And with that, Quintus' mind cleared, his thoughts becoming serene. Despite the carnage, despite the blood and the stench of death, despite the violence and brutality, he would meet his end with a sword in his hand, fighting for Rome with Kaeso by his side. If this was his path, if this was what the gods had decided, then he made his peace with that.

There were less honourable deaths than this.

It wasn't how he wished it all to end. He had a life yet to live with Kaeso. Of summer breezes through tall fields, of stolen kisses and warm laughter, of nights that met the dawn all too soon. If he was granted one more day, he would tell his men how they honoured him, how he loved them like brothers. If he had but one more day, he would take Kaeso in his arms and never let him go.

Yet there were no more days. Quintus knew his path in this world would end here. Perhaps he would meet his parents in the afterlife. He would introduce Kaeso and they would welcome him with open arms, and there would be sunshine and peace, not blood and death.

Quintus struck a guard's throat and used his foot to push the body off his sword, just as Kaeso ducked a swinging blade. He parried and struck the man under the ribs as Quintus met another guard's attempted strike.

"I will find you in the next life, my rabbit," Quintus said as the guard he fought bared down on him. "My promise to you."

Kaeso swung away from a strike at his head and buried his dagger in the man's neck as he turned. "I am not done with you in this life," he snapped. Then he launched himself at the guard who was pushing Quintus backwards and stuck his dagger in the base of his skull. "Speak again of defeat and you will meet my wrath."

Quintus swung his sword at a man who came for Kaeso, taking him in the jaw and removing half his head. His sword grew heavier with each strike, as did the weight of their fates. "We are still outnumbered."

Then an unholy roar came up behind them. Quintus glanced back quickly, knowing if it was more blue guards, it meant certain death.

But they weren't guards.

They were gladiators. Men in gladiator armour, carrying axes and spikes and clubs. Not just any gladiators, but *his* gladiators. The men who had come with Oscilius: Lars, Artamo, Messenio, Paullus, Arruns...

They charged upward, weapons raised, and the blue guards all watched in horror as the odds were turned against them. Gladiators without fear, without mercy, tore into the blue line, slaying as they went.

For one brief moment, Quintus let his sword droop to

the ground and drew in a much needed breath. As did Phaidon and Harpax, and Salonia and Varia. He met their eyes with a smile and a nod before lifting his sword once more.

"Tiberius!" Kaeso cried. "He yet escapes!"

Over the sea of blue capes drenched in red, Quintus could see Tiberius attempting to squeeze into the crowd of people fleeing.

"Stop him!" Quintus cried.

Kaeso bounced his dagger in his hand, then threw it with such force, such accuracy, it stuck Tiberius in the back of the thigh. He dropped with a scream, the people pushing away from him. Tiberius reached around and pulled the dagger out. Blood ran quick and thick from his wound, but he staggered to his feet, limping, his face etched in pain and anger.

"Filthy fucking Iberian!" he screamed and threw the dagger back at Kaeso. Quintus leapt to hold up his shield in front of Kaeso, but the dagger fell woefully short. It bounced off the body of one of his guards and skittered onto the cobblestones.

Tiberius couldn't even do that right.

Artamo and Lars finished off the last two guards, and Tiberius knew he had met his end. He stood, shaking, frantic, but defeated.

"You dare to call him filthy," Quintus said, walking toward him, "when it is you who is shit in squalor." Tiberius took a step back as Quintus approached. "You are a pitiful traitor, bested by slaves."

Tiberius was pale, the blood from his wound now pooled at his foot. "...worthless fucking slaves."

"They are each worth a hundred of you!" Quintus

roared, furious. His vision tinted red and he made to grab Tiberius by the throat and rip his skull apart.

But an almighty crack boomed through the air and the ground shook beneath their feet.

Everyone turned at the sound to see Vesuvius explode. The white smoke was gone, replaced by a grey, black, and red cloud pluming skyward. Larger than the gods themselves, fire clouds spewed upward, as if wrath and fury had taken physical form.

Quintus had never seen anything like it.

It was... *monstrosum*.

People screamed and wailed, and the swell of the crowd pushed toward the tunnel. It was chaos and disbelief, panic and confusion.

And in that moment of madness, Tiberius disappeared into the swarm of people, heading down toward the bay. His leg was dragging, his blood loss severe. He wasn't going to get far, yet for as long as the snake had life in its body, it would attempt to slither away with venom still in its bite.

"Salonia!" Quintus called.

Salonia knew what he was asking. She took her spear, and then looking to where Tiberius was limping through the crowd, she took three long strides and launched her weapon.

Any other person would have missed. Any other person would have killed an innocent civilian. But not Salonia.

The spear struck Tiberius in the back, dead centre, piercing his spine, through to his chest.

People screamed and gave a wide berth. Tiberius went to his knees, then fell forward, Quintus and Kaeso ran toward him and Quintus grabbed him by the hair. The spear protruded from his chest, he gargled a breath and blood bubbled from his mouth. People were trying to scurry past or stood watching on in horror. Quintus looked into Tiberius' eyes and said, "A dishonourable death for a traitor." Then Quintus pointed to the rising cloud of ferocity spewing out of Vesuvius. "See this? The goddess Discordia comes for you. She will drag you to Tartarus where you will spend eternity begging for mercy."

And with those final words, Quintus watched the light dim in Tiberius' eyes until he lived no more.

He should have felt relief. He should have rejoiced in victory. But with another glance toward Vesuvius, he knew it was far from over. He pulled the spear free and handed it to Kaeso, then grabbed Tiberius' boot and dragged his lifeless body back to the others. "We must go. Back through the belly to where the emperor waits."

Without question, Messenio grabbed Tiberius' other boot and helped to drag him, and they set off back into the darkness. Quintus waited for Kaeso to go first—he did not want him out of his sight again—and they ran along the now abandoned corridors.

Quintus looked to Messenio. "Your arrival to our aid was most welcome."

Messenio grinned at the praise. "Ovid found Oscilius and told him where he had seen you. He gave us weapons and orders to follow you."

"You saved us," Quintus said. "I have no doubt of that."

Messenio nodded, his pride evident in his grin. "Yet it is I who stand honoured."

The darkness of the tunnels soon gave way to light, and they came out upon the other side. Tiberius' face thudding on each step was a satisfying sound, as was the sight of smeared blood that followed.

Oscilius and Cythereia ran to meet them on the street.

"Oh, praise the gods," Oscilius said, using his one arm to embrace Quintus.

Cythereia wept openly. "I thought you dead," she cried. Then she raised a shaking hand to point to across the bay to the mountains. To the volcano that raged, a blackened cloud now as high as Vesuvius itself. "Quintus," she sobbed. "Word has come, people who fled, who have seen it with their own eyes—" She couldn't speak.

Oscilius finished for her. "Oplontis stands no more."

Quintus blinked. He couldn't make sense of what Oscilius was saying. "What?"

"Oplontis, the town, the villa, the ludus are all gone. Rivers of burning pumice and ash, they said." He shook his head, his eyes filled with tears. "Took all in its path."

<hr>

KAESO WATCHED AS QUINTUS' face drained of colour. "Our house, our orchard..."

"All gone," Cythereia sobbed.

Everyone stood without words, faces ashen, and they looked to Quintus, but he had turned to face the bay. And across in the distance, beneath the billowing clouds of smoke, a trail of fire and ash led to the sea.

Where Oplontis once stood.

Quintus swallowed hard and regained his wits. He looked at Oscilius and Cythereia and then his gladiators. "Stay here until I return. All of you. I ask that you stay. I promised the emperor..." He shook his head, and words seemed to fail him.

"You rebuilt once before, then we will rebuild again," Kaeso said, putting his hand to Quintus' back.

Quintus stared at Kaeso, as if seeing him again for the

first time. He slid his hand along Kaeso's jaw and rested his forehead to his. "My clarity, my reason," he whispered.

"Come," Kaeso said. He glanced to the darkening skies burgeoning above the volcano. "Time is against us." He picked up Tiberius' boot and began to drag his body to the entrance of the arena. Quintus hurried to join him, taking the other boot, making lighter work of it.

The arches were now empty, and they made their final way to the room where the emperor waited. Kaeso almost expected him to be gone yet was surprised to find him there. Still wearing Quintus' armour, still surrounded by Quintus' men. They all let their weapons fall when they saw who it was, and a cheer went around the room when Quintus dropped Tiberius' lifeless body onto the tiles.

"Emperor," Quintus said, meeting his gaze. "Threat against you has been removed."

The emperor's gaze narrowed. "And his men?"

"Dead. All of them dead," Kaeso said.

"Emperor," Quintus said. "Vesuvius... Oplontis is lost. People are fleeing, and the skies grow dark. You must make for Roma."

"I will be expected," the emperor agreed.

Senator Maternus nodded. "And I as well. I offer any help."

Quintus nodded at him, then turned to Appias and Mettius. "You two, take my collars from your necks and assume lead guard. Defend these men with your life on their return to Roma."

Appias gaped at him. "We are no longer gladiators?"

Quintus put his hand to Appias' shoulder. "If you want. You are free to choose. If you consider yourselves praetorian, act as such and seek the title and pay that accompany it."

Appias looked to Mettius, and they both nodded. Praetorian guards were paid more coin a year than a gladiator could hope to see in two lifetimes. Along with the best food and, most of all, freedom.

Quintus looked at his other guards. "Anyone else is free to join them. Remove the collars from your necks with my one request: you will honour the emperor as you have honoured me."

Gallio, Oppius, Pellio, Arruns, Lars, and Caius all nodded and moved to stand beside the emperor. Quintus took a moment to look them each in the eye. "You are good men. You have made me proud today." Then he moved to Appias and looked him in the eye. "Return to the senator's villa. Take the horses, mine included, and see yourselves to Roma."

Then Quintus turned to the emperor. "Your nova praetorian. I swear you will not find better men. Honour them as such."

The emperor gave a solemn nod.

"What about me?" Servius said, clambering to his feet. "I can repay—"

Quintus turned on his heel and pointed his blood-covered sword at the senator. "One more word from you and I will sever your fucking tongue."

Servius paled and fell back to his spot against the wall, and when Appias handed Quintus the leather band he had worn as his slave, Quintus smiled. "It shall fit a man more deserving of it," he said, then stomped over to Servius. He took the collar and clasped it around Servius' neck. Servius wailed pitifully and clawed at the leather. Quintus stood over him. "Attempt to remove it, and you will meet the Underworld absent your hands."

Then Quintus ripped his senator's shawl from around

him and tossed it to the floor. He pointed the sword at Servius in warning, but with one heavy swipe, he hacked off Tiberius' head.

Servius screamed and cried, trying to scramble away. Kaeso pushed him back with his foot, and Quintus wrapped the head in Servius' white and purple cloak. Then he tossed it into Servius' lap. "Carry your fate back to Roma," he said with a sneer. He gave a nod to Appias. "Make the traitor run behind the horses. Drag him for all I care."

Appias gave a nod and walked over to Servius and pulled him to his feet, and the nova praetorians, the new guards, stepped into formation. The emperor raised his hand to pause. "You do not join them as my lead guard?"

Quintus paused; everyone in the room awaited his reply. "I cannot. My men..."

The emperor smiled. "I owe you a great debt," he replied, bowing his head. The emperor... bowed to Quintus... "Name your price, and I will see it done."

Quintus looked up, then around the room. "I have but one request."

The emperor cocked his head. "Just one?"

Quintus nodded. "These slaves," he replied, nodding to everyone in the room. "See them freed."

The emperor blinked, stunned. "You could have anything in all of Rome, and you request freedom for a handful of slaves?"

Quintus smiled. "One above all others, but all of them, yes."

The emperor glanced at Kaeso, and Kaeso felt his cheeks heat under his gaze. "See it done."

Quintus scooped up handfuls of gold coins from the sack that still lay spilled across the floor, filled a smaller sack that had contained bread, passing it to Lars, who stood clos-est. "If you require a horse for your travels, or food. Share the coins with your brothers."

And with a nod, the emperor and Maternus moved out with Servius scurrying behind, still crying. Kaeso doubted he would make it far.

Then Quintus looked to the slaves who huddled in the corner. They had once been Servius' slaves but now stood free.

Quintus had them tear Tiberius' tunic into shreds to make linen pouches and handed them each enough coin to see them safely into new lives. They all cried and nodded their thanks before slipping out of the room. Helier stood, his coins in his hands, his head bowed.

Kaeso knew Quintus had no time for Helier, but Kaeso saw him differently. He saw him as a fellow slave, as an equal. He didn't trust him, and he didn't particularly care for him. Yet, Helier had done what he had to do to survive, and Kaeso could not begrudge anyone that.

"Gratitude," Helier whispered. "If deserving—"

Quintus raised his hand. "You stole the scroll of papyrus from my quarters. An offence that should have your head." He took a deep breath. "Yet you did it for reasons not your own. You secured the life of your fellow slaves, despite your master's crime."

Helier nodded, and a tear rolled down his cheek. "Gratitude," he murmured again. Then he met Kaeso's eyes. "Gratitude."

Kaeso gave him a nod, and Helier hurried out the door.

Quintus picked up the sack of remaining coin and nodded to the men who remained. "Oscilius awaits outside."

They nodded dutifully and followed, leaving Kaeso confused. Had Quintus not just freed them? Were they not included when he said all slaves? Or did they respect him so much that they would follow his orders, slaves or not?

Kaeso looked around the room, at the pristine marble, at the luxury of it all, now strewn with dead bodies and pools of blood. He would be all too glad to never see the likes of it again.

Jovian still sat slumped against the wall, pale and lost. He had been so quiet, Kaeso had almost forgotten he was there. "Jovian," Kaeso asked.

Recognition flashed in his eyes, but he appeared lethargic. His mouth opened, though he appeared without the ability to speak.

"I will help you leave," Kaeso said, helping the older man to his feet. "You should not stay here." He had witnessed too much death already.

Jovian went willingly, now babbling again, a sure sign his mind was gone. And when Kaeso got him down the stairs and out into the streets, Jovian saw the might and fury of Vesuvius for the first time. "The gods have abandoned us," he mumbled. "The gods have struck Rome at its heart."

Kaeso tuned out his ramblings to hear what Quintus was saying. His men stood around him, and he was handing them handfuls of coin until the sack was almost empty. "I have no home to give you. I have no ludus," he said.

"We can rebuild it," Salonia said. "We will all see it rebuilt."

Everyone nodded, but Quintus shook his head. "You have given me more today than I had the right to ask. I would see the collars from your necks and bid you to start a new life away from the arenas, away from the bloodshed."

"What will you do?" Decius asked. "Where will you go?"

Quintus turned in search for someone, and upon seeing Kaeso, he sighed and smiled. "Start a new life away from the arenas, away from the bloodshed." He took in a deep breath. "Go and know that a piece of my heart goes with each of you."

They reached to remove the leather strands at their necks in silence. An odd moment of solace as Vesuvius wreaked havoc in the distance. They nodded and put their hands to Quintus' arm before they turned and walked away.

Yet not all would leave. Salonia and Varia, Harpax and Phaidon, and Oscilius and Cythereia of course. "We go with you," Salonia said; they all nodded.

"You are granted freedom," Quintus said. "You can return to the lands from which you came."

Varia raised her chin. "If we are free to choose, then we are free to choose to go with you."

Quintus looked at each of them until they all smiled. Kaeso chuckled as he unclasped the tin collar from around his neck and tossed it away. "Where do we go?"

Quintus smiled at Kaeso, the kind of smile that caused his heart to race. "If it were my choice, I would head for Iberia."

"Iberia?" Kaeso asked, stunned.

"I am done with Rome. I am done with greed and politics and bloodshed. I would choose somewhere no senator or emperor would look to find us," Quintus replied. "So if we are to choose a new place to call home, then let it be where one of us already does so."

Then he turned toward Vesuvius, at the darkness, at the clouds of fire and ash falling across the bay. "We may already be too late," Quintus said. "I do not even know how to get there, and I am out of coin," Quintus added, holding up the empty sack.

Salonia held out the coins he had given her. "Take mine."

But Kaeso stilled her arm and grinned. "Follow me."

CAPITULUM XXVIII

"WE CANNOT DELAY, or we will have more than time against us," Kaeso said, then he began to run toward the docks, against the flow of people fleeing, and Quintus had no choice but to follow. They all ran after him, though Quintus helped Cythereia and Oscilius as they were the slowest.

When they got to the docks, Quintus found Kaeso speaking with a man Quintus had not cast eyes on before. The man was older, wearing a rag tunic covered in tar and arguing somewhat, but Kaeso barked orders. Quintus smiled, knowing the brunt of what Kaeso's temper was like. "I do not care if another ship is faster, we are to take this one," Kaeso pointed to one ship in particular.

"That is a fleet ship," the man said.

Kaeso glowered at him. "Look at us! Do we not wear the uniform of Roman guards? We are under orders from the emperor and we must leave now."

The man mumbled something Quintus couldn't hear, but Kaeso hurried over and took the coins from everyone

Quintus had given them to. "Trust that I know what I am doing," Kaeso said. "I promise your coin returned."

"You are not going to kill that man once he delivers us, are you?" Cythereia asked in a hushed whisper.

Kaeso smiled. "Not unless he gives me good reason."

"If you are leaving," the old man called out. "We leave now. The water is dropping."

Other people scurried about to other boats and ships, with cloaks over their heads to escape the falling ash, and it wasn't until they were on the ship that Quintus could fully take in the horror of Vesuvius. Kaeso gave the old man all the coins they had, more coin than this man had perhaps seen in his life, and soon after, he had a team of men rowing them away from the docks.

And their small group, all that was left of the Varus Ludus, stood on the deck and watched the sky. It was as though the sun had been stripped from the heavens. Darkness loomed, clouds of dust and ash sparked with fire and lightning high above the volcano. It was like nothing Quintus had ever seen before.

"It is as if the gods are at war," Salonia murmured.

Everyone nodded. It was exactly what it looked like.

The ship had to sail downward to round the landform before it could head outward to Iberia. They gained some distance from Vesuvius, but it gave them a clear view of Oplontis. Or where Oplontis should have been.

What was once green fields between Pompeii and Herculaneum was now smouldering ash and fire. "Oh, fuck the gods," Harpax mumbled.

"When they said all was gone," Oscilius murmured, "they told no untruth." Cythereia began to cry again, and Oscilius put his arm around her. "What is important yet lives," he said.

"Oscilius is right," Quintus said. "We have lost much, but what matters the most stands on this ship."

Salonia put her cape across her face. "The air grows thick."

"We should seek cover inside the ship," Quintus agreed, just as a small lump of smoking pumice landed on the deck. A bigger one fell to the sea right in front of them. Quintus put his arm around Kaeso and they moved to the hatch.

Oscilius went first, then he helped Cythereia inside. Then Salonia and Varia, then Harpax and Phaidon. Quintus held the hatch opening. "Kaeso, you are next."

Kaeso shook his head, his face pale, his eyes wide. "I cannot... the dark, the sounds of it. The smell. Quintus, I... I came to Rome on a ship like this. I will seek shelter up here," he said, looking around the deck.

Quintus had spent weeks with Kaeso. He had seen him defiant, he had seen him angry, and he had seen him happy. And he thought he had seen him scared, but nothing had prepared him for the look Kaeso wore. The fear on his face squeezed Quintus' heart. "Oh, my rabbit. I did not think..."

Kaeso shook his head quickly. "I would not have suggested the ship if it did not mean sure escape, but Quintus..." He shook his head again. "I cannot go down there."

Another lump of pumice smashed onto the deck, scattering red sparks across them.

"Kaeso, you cannot stay up here."

And another lump, in size larger than Quintus' fist, hit the deck. It was smouldering rock this time. The old man yelled at the galley men below deck to "Row faster, row faster!"

"Kaeso, I beg of you," Quintus said. "I will stay with you. I will not let you go. I promise you." Then Quintus yelled down into the hatch, "Find a torch and set it aflame."

Salonia grumbled back that she was trying to do just that, and after a moment, a faint glow illuminated from the hatch. Quintus held out his hand. "You won't be alone. You will not be out of my reach."

Kaeso swallowed hard, took Quintus' hand, and lowered himself down. Quintus quickly followed and pulled the hatch shut. The inside of the ship was small, and Quintus had to duck his head to walk. The others were huddled in the far corner, surrounded by crates and boxes. Cages stood empty, and when Kaeso saw them and froze, Quintus didn't need to ask. "You are safe with me," he whispered, rubbing Kaeso's arm. "I am weary and would like to take a seat with my people," Quintus added. "And I have you in my arms."

That seemed to strike something within Kaeso because he shook his head as if waking from sleep, and he nodded.

Quintus fell to the side of the ship and slid down to sit between Harpax and Oscilius. Kaeso sat between Quintus' legs and Quintus pulled him against him.

Covered in blood, drenched with sweat and ash, no one broke words for a long while. The ship lurched in the water, creaking, and the occasional bang of falling pumice lessened as they drew further away.

But Kaeso shivered and shook with every sound, and he turned his head into Quintus' chest. Quintus could see the questioning look from Cythereia and Varia. "He came to Rome on a ship such as this." He nodded to the empty cage. "In a cage such as that." He put his hand to Kaeso's face and tightened his hold on him. "There was no light for days. And it haunts him still."

Quintus might have expected a varied reaction, but they all frowned sympathetically. Harpax reached over and squeezed Kaeso's fingers. "As did I."

"And me as well," Oscilius said. "Many years ago."

Quintus let his head fall back and he closed his eyes. The cruel hand of Rome, the weight these men had carried... He had never thought to ask before. He had never thought to care. Until Kaeso.

His whole world was different now.

How he viewed these men was different now. *And women*, he thought, and almost laughed out loud.

Quintus had always treated his men well. He demanded respect, but he gave it in return when it was earned. But now he saw them as men. Men, like him, only born to a different fate. It could have very well been him if, after the death of his parents, Oscilius and Cythereia had not cared for him and guided him. A lesser person could have thrown him to the streets and taken his ludus. But not them. They had raised him like a son.

A tear escaped the corner of his eye, and he gave no care to who saw it.

These men—and women—would not judge him. Quintus was with his family, not a drop of blood shared between them. Not their own, anyway.

Despite their lineage, despite the tiers of Roman society based on wealth and breeding, these people were of no less importance, no less value.

They were his equals.

Kaeso had opened Quintus' eyes to what he should have seen all along. That the worth of a person was not decided by a collar. For sometimes those who bore the burden of slavery were worth the entire world.

Quintus tightened his arms around Kaeso and let exhaustion claim him.

KAESO SAT atop a large crate on the deck, watching the ocean, enjoying the fresh air and daylight, enjoying the sun on his skin. He pulled his chest guard off and his shoulder guard, revelling in the freedom of having them removed. His freedom.

He had awoken to find himself in darkness, as though his mind had tricked him to think he was back in the cage.

Quintus held him tighter but didn't fully wake, and he wasn't surprised. The man had hardly slept at all the last week. So Kaeso had slipped out and left him to sleep.

Behind him, some great distance now, the sky still bore the mark of Vesuvius. As though the mountain had grown ten times its size and set itself on fire. Dark clouds of smoke and ash could still be seen, even from such a distance.

Kaeso wondered if any of Rome still stood. He wondered if the gods were angry at the greed of Roman man and had decided to end them all. Not that all Roman men were fuelled by greed, but Kaeso did not care for all the political manoeuvring and the covert agendas that seemed to lurk at every turn. He did not care for the belief that a man could be bought and sold like a mule. That *he* had been bought and sold like a mule.

Kaeso cast those memories from his mind. It was behind him, much as Rome was now. Burning to cinders, for all he cared. He set his sights over the front of the ship, over the waves and endless sea. To Iberia, to his home.

Not long after, Quintus pulled himself out of the hatch and Kaeso could see him relax as soon as he saw him.

"You were gone," he said. "I thought I would find you where the light is brightest."

"And the air is sweeter," Kaeso added with a smile. He extended his arm. "I would have you sit with me a while."

Quintus smiled as he walked over. "Just a while?" He

stood between Kaeso's legs and they embraced. Quintus held Kaeso against him and Kaeso wrapped his arms around him, and for the longest moment, Kaeso allowed himself to enjoy just being held.

Their fight was done, their struggles behind them.

"I still cannot believe we aim for Iberia," Kaeso murmured.

Quintus rubbed Kaeso's back, then pulled back so he could meet his gaze. "My words hold true. I would have us far from the reach and eyes of Rome."

"Will you regret such a move?" Kaeso asked. "Will you long to return?"

"Return to what? My ludus is gone. After bearing witness to politics, I fear the Rome I knew is also gone. And all the people I hold dear are with me," he answered stoically. "The one I hold most dear is with me now."

"'I care not on which lands you stand, only that you live,' was what you once said to me," Kaeso said.

"See? I have always been wise."

Kaeso laughed, but his thoughts turned sombre. "When we fought Tiberius' men, you thought us defeated," he whispered. He looked up into Quintus' blue eyes. "You spoke of goodbyes."

"And you threatened to kill me," Quintus said with a half smile. "If memory serves correctly."

Kaeso snorted. "My words hold true."

"Must all my words be aimed back at me?"

Kaeso smiled. "If they need repeating." He pointed to his own lips. "If you need to be silenced, find your mouth a better purpose."

Quintus smiled and leaned down to kiss him. A gentle, lingering kiss. A kiss Kaeso felt in his bones. Before they could lose themselves, Salonia lifted herself out of the hatch, all long limbs and slender frame, with the grace only she could manage. "Oh, apologies for the intrusion," she said, catching them in a tender moment.

"No apologies required," Quintus replied. "Do you travel well?"

She nodded. "Well enough. Varia sleeps yet."

"She fought well," Kaeso said. "Such bravery."

Salonia's smile tinged with pride. "I would have no other stand beside me." She turned then to see the mark Vesuvius yet made upon the sky. "I cannot imagine the horrors we left behind."

Quintus gaze narrowed at the horizon and he frowned. "May the gods be merciful."

They let a moment of silence pass between them, and it was Salonia who spoke first. "I came seeking permission to scout this ship for food and blankets. There are crates worth a closer eye."

Quintus smiled at her. "Permission no longer required," he said. "Or have you forgotten your freedom?"

She blinked in surprise, her hand absently finding her neck now bare. "Oh. A habit long ingrained."

"A search for fresh water would be appreciated," Quintus said. "I shall aid you."

"You shall remain in the arms I found you in," Salonia said, nodding to Kaeso with a smile. "And return to the task I interrupted."

Kaeso laughed and tightened his arms around Quintus. "A wise woman, you will do well to obey," he said, smiling up to Quintus. Then as Salonia returned to the hatch, he called out, "Oh, I believe some crates hold more worth than others." Salonia stopped, giving him a curious eye. He laughed again. "You will know when you find it."

She disappeared through the hatch once more, and Kaeso pointed to his own lips again. "As you were."

Quintus chuckled and saw Kaeso's demands met. Kisses that led to no further passion, yet kisses that spoke of deeper meaning. Of more than words could say.

Quintus broke the kiss to rest his forehead to Kaeso's. His eyes were closed, and he held Kaeso's face. "I thought us dead," he murmured. When he opened his eyes, there were such depths within them. "I thought we had met our end, and I swore to the gods if I had more time with you... but one more day. Just one more day..."

Kaeso put his hand to Quintus' cheek. "We have more than one."

"I knew in that moment what mattered most," Quintus said. "It was not coin or reputation. And perhaps it lessened the blow of the news of my ludus, because in that moment when I was certain of death, it was not my ludus or my house that I longed for. It was you. I longed for you and days in the sun, in the breeze and long grass. I longed to see your smile, free of all concern."

Kaeso pulled him down for a sweet kiss. "And you shall have it."

Quintus grinned and pushed Kaeso onto his back on the crate and Quintus lay over him, and Kaeso's legs wrapped around Quintus' hips. "I shall have you," he said, with mischief in his eyes. He kissed Kaeso's mouth, down his jaw, behind his ear, and stopped when he got to his neck. He pulled back, frowning. "You wear my collar still."

Kaeso cupped Quintus' face. "And it shall remain so."

Quintus' eyes searched Kaeso's. "To what end? You are no longer my slave. You are my equal. To stand beside me, not a pace behind."

Kaeso smiled and ran his thumb down Quintus' cheek.

"I know, yet I would have it remain. I might not belong to you, but I belong with you."

"But—"

"Still your tongue," Kaeso cautioned. "Or I shall find something to fill your mouth with."

Quintus barked out a laugh. "Is that so?"

"Do not tempt me." Kaeso grinned. "I will have your collar remain if we are to draw unwanted attention in Tarraco. We may have roles yet to play." Kaeso traced his finger down Quintus' neck. "We could have the collar upon your neck and I act as master, yet I think that would cause more heads to turn."

Quintus laughed. "Once again you prove a pace ahead, rabbit."

Kaeso smiled and pulled him in for another kiss. "We will need a plan for our arrival in Tarraco," he said.

Quintus pecked his lips. "I would have you choose."

Kaeso froze. "What?"

"You are familiar with the city, are you not?"

"Some. Though I would move away from the city, where the valleys afford us privacy."

"Then you know more than me. Though we will need to find shelter and work so we can eat. But those are worries for another day. Set your mind to plan while I find other purpose," Quintus said, then claimed Kaeso's mouth with his own. The rock of the ship made time with the roll of his hips, and everything fell away but the hardness of Quintus' desire and the heat of his mouth.

"Quintus!" Salonia called from the hatch. "Quintus! You must see this!"

Quintus growled and pulled his mouth from Kaeso. He stood back and adjusted his cock. "I would have your plan consist of time uninterrupted, if you are willing," he said.

Kaeso laughed up at the sky and Quintus disappeared down the hatch. He didn't move from his spot, he didn't need to. He was sure he knew what Salonia had found.

There was the sound of scraping and hauling followed by loud cries of joy and shock. Quintus' head appeared in the hatch, his smile as wide as his eyes. "You knew of this! When you said you would see their coin repaid, this is what you meant?"

Kaeso laughed. "How many crates are there?"

"Two crates full of coin. Full! Enough coin to see out all our days," Quintus shook his head in disbelief. "This is the coin stash you brought to show the emperor as proof!"

Kaeso grinned. "Why did you think I insisted on this ship?"

Phaidon's face appeared next to Quintus', still bruised and bloodied but now grinning. "I would be inclined to kiss you if this one"—he nodded to Quintus—"would not throw me overboard."

Quintus's smile became a glare, but Phaidon only laughed and disappeared down the hatch. More laughter echoed up and cheers and excited talks of all they dared to spend. Quintus stared at Kaeso, then shook his head and smiled. "You knew."

"I do not think we have concern for shelter or food when we reach Iberia." Kaeso took in a deep, deep breath and smiled up at the blue sky from where he lay. "I do not think we have concerns for much at all."

QUINTUS STOOD in the orchard overlooking the green valley and smiled. He plucked a pear from a tree and bit into it, wandering back into the villa. They had so much coin, even split between the eight of them, even after paying the captain and crew double the fee, to see themselves worry free for many years.

Phaidon and Harpax had stayed a while but eventually ventured further into Iberia, and in their five years since arriving, had sent word that they had found themselves wives and had children.

Yet Salonia and Varia remained in Tarraco, owners of a boarding house and inn. Quintus and Kaeso saw them every time they travelled to the city, which admittedly was not often, but it gave Quintus true joy to see them thrive.

Oscilius and Cythereia remained with Quintus and Kaeso, and they had found a villa far removed from Roman roads and eyes. It was large enough so they could have privacy when required, yet small enough to feel like a home. It was in disrepair when they had bought it from an old man whose wife had left this world a year prior. He was happy to take his purse bursting with coin and live out his days in warmer climes.

It had taken some time and much hard work, but they saved the villa from ruin and now called it their own. There was an orchard and gardens for food. A yard for sheep and pigs. Cythereia used the fleece for cloaks and blankets, Oscilius tended the gardens, Quintus made weapons and traps, and Kaeso hunted their lands. They traded their wares and wild rabbits and ducks for grains and oils in the closest village.

Over the years, Quintus had trained himself to work with leather and animal hides, and Kaeso practised carpentry. They spent their days busy and never far from the other.

Mostly, they spent their days in peace.

Quintus saw Kaeso climbing the hill toward the orchard. He had hunted in the valley, and it was a steep incline. He was grumbling and frowning, with two rabbits slung over his shoulder. Quintus grinned upon seeing him, plucked another pear, and tossed it to him. He caught it, but it did little to improve his mood.

"You would be of more help if you carved steps into the side of the slope for me," he said, puffing. "After all these years, it gets harder to climb." He bit into the pear and stretched his back.

"If you wish for steps," Quintus said cheerfully, "I shall carve the whole mountain for you."

Kaeso took the dead rabbits from his shoulder and saw Quintus look at the rabbits and smile. "Say it and you shall share their fate."

Quintus laughed and said it despite hollow threats. "A rabbit for my rabbit."

Kaeso threw the pear at him and chased Quintus into

the villa. Quintus rounded on Kaeso, scooping him up in his arms, and pressed him against the table, discarding his half-eaten pear so he could focus on Kaeso. He was laughing, and Quintus knew Kaeso could never stay angry at him. He nuzzled into Kaeso's neck.

"You insist on calling me a rabbit when you know it galls."

Quintus sucked on that sliver of skin just under Kaeso's ear that made him squirm every time. "You are my rabbit."

Kaeso lifted his legs around Quintus' hips and arched his back. "You know my weaknesses," he said, gasping when Quintus thrust against him.

"And you know mine," Quintus replied, claiming his mouth.

Kaeso pushed him back. "Where is Cythereia?"

Quintus' eyes darkened. "They have gone to market."

Kaeso grinned. "And I suppose you would have us use our time wisely?"

"If you do not object."

Kaeso reached over and took the pear that was beside his head. "First, a request."

Quintus raised one eyebrow and pulled back a little. "Such as?"

Kaeso put the half-eaten pear to Quintus' lips. "Tell me the pears are sweeter in Iberia than they are in Campania."

Quintus laughed. They argued often about who had the best. He bit into the pear and chewed with a grin. "Everything is sweeter in Iberia," he replied. "Especially you."

"Then have me," Kaeso replied.

Quintus thought to pick Kaeso up, as he had many times before, and carry him to their room. But a vial of oil sat on the table... Cythereia's cooking oil, but Quintus could only grin.

"She will not be pleased," Kaeso began to say, but Quintus was desperate.

He freed his cock and snatched up the oil, hastily smearing his length with one hand and lifting Kaeso's tunic with his other. He pulled his undergarment to one side, held the base of his cock, and pushed it into Kaeso's tight warmth.

In one deep push, he buried himself inside him. Kaeso arched, his mouth open, eyes wide, gasping short breaths in that way he did when Quintus took him like this. Though Quintus was never fooled.

Kaeso craved it.

He wrapped his legs around Quintus and took all of him. He would beg for more, always more, and Quintus would never fail to give it.

Quintus would be forever amazed by how intoxicating Kaeso was. His body, his hands, his mouth. His mind.

And as he always did, he took Kaeso to heights of pleasure before taking his own. He would never tire of this. Every time was as though time anew. When they were done, Quintus collapsed on top of him, his face buried in Kaeso's neck, and Kaeso held him close. "When I think you have my heart already, you take more."

Kaeso sighed with content, tracing his fingers through Quintus' hair. It was a little longer now, and even curlier. "You have such a tender heart," he murmured.

"And it is yours. And not just my heart." Quintus pulled back so he could look into his eyes. "With every day that passes, I am more yours than the day before."

Kaeso smiled serenely. "As I am yours." He glanced to the top of Quintus' head. "I do prefer your hair at this length," he said, gently fisting a handful of his curls. "I can command you with my hand this way."

Quintus chuckled. "If you deem yourself brave enough to attempt."

Kaeso smiled and leaned up to kiss him. "We best straighten this table."

Quintus pulled away, helped Kaeso to his feet, and gestured to the evidence of their coupling on Kaeso's tunic. "I will see to the table," Quintus said.

Kaeso laughed at the mess of his seed and oil smeared into his tunic. "I will see to this." He disappeared to their room and soon after reappeared in a clean tunic as Quintus had the two dead rabbits on the table with a cleaver in his hand. "What is this?" Kaeso asked, snatching the rabbits off the table.

"I thought to stew the rabbits," Quintus said, taking the rabbits back.

"You will do no such thing," Kaeso argued, stealing them away once more. "If you wish for anyone to actually eat them, I will cook the rabbits. You can tend to the beans."

"I can cook them," Quintus argued and stole them back. "I am not so useless."

"Your tanned leather is better on the tooth," Kaeso snapped, snatching the rabbits back from Quintus.

"Neither of you will attempt to cook in my culina," Cythereia said, walking into the room. They had not heard them enter the villa. "Attempt to cook, perhaps. Attempt to clean, I have yet to witness."

Oscilius laughed as he slid a basket of grain onto the table. "You will do well not to upset the cook," he said.

"Now, all of you will find yourselves absent of my culina," Cythereia said with a smile. Then she snatched the rabbits from Kaeso. "Leave them. See to some wood for my fire, if you could be so kind."

Kaeso kissed her cheek. "As you wish."

"Before you go," Oscilius said, and both Quintus and Kaeso paused and faced him. "At the market, we had word from Rome."

Quintus paused. "And?"

"Last month past, much of Roma burned to the ground," Oscilius said. "The city, forum, houses. Many perished."

"The emperor?" Quintus asked. "Any word of him or his men?"

Oscilius gave a brief smile. "He yet lives. Saved by your men beside him."

Quintus let out a breath of relief. Appias, Mettius, Gallio, Oppius, Pellio, Arruns, Lars, and Caius had become formidable praetorian guards and saw many attempts on the emperor thwarted, and as a result, Rome had seen five years of peace and prosperity. A strong emperor who ruled with a fair hand. And Quintus was glad he had helped balance the scales in the emperor's favour for a better Rome.

"Do you wish to return?" Kaeso asked him quietly.

Quintus answered without hesitation. "The Rome I knew is gone. My life, my heart is here." Quintus lifted Kaeso's chin and pressed a soft kiss to his lips. "It matters not on which lands I stand when I stand with you."

"For all days," Kaeso whispered, his hand to Quintus' heart.

Quintus pressed his forehead to Kaeso's. "Aeternum."

FINIS

ABOUT THE AUTHOR

N.R. Walker is an Australian author, who loves her genre of gay romance. She loves writing and spends far too much time doing it, but wouldn't have it any other way.

She is many things: a mother, a wife, a sister, a writer. She has pretty, pretty boys who live in her head, who don't let her sleep at night unless she gives them life with words.

She likes it when they do dirty, dirty things... but likes it even more when they fall in love.

She used to think having people in her head talking to her was weird, until one day she happened across other writers who told her it was normal.

She's been writing ever since...

The Spencer Cohen Series, Book One

The Spencer Cohen Series, Book Two

The Spencer Cohen Series, Book Three

The Spencer Cohen Series, Yanni's Story

Blood & Milk

The Weight Of It All

A Very Henry Christmas (The Weight of It All 1.5)

Perfect Catch

Switched

Imago

Imagines

Red Dirt Heart Imago

On Davis Row

Finders Keepers

Evolved

Galaxies and Oceans

Private Charter

Titles in Audio:

Cronin's Key

Cronin's Key II

Cronin's Key III

Red Dirt Heart

Red Dirt Heart 2

Red Dirt Heart 3

Red Dirt Heart 4

The Weight Of It All

Switched

Point of No Return

Breaking Point

Starting Point

Spencer Cohen Book One

Spencer Cohen Book Two

Spencer Cohen Book Three

Yanni's Story

On Davis Row

Evolved

Free Reads:

Sixty Five Hours

Learning to Feel

His Grandfather's Watch (And The Story of Billy and Hale)

The Twelfth of Never (Blind Faith 3.5)

Twelve Days of Christmas (Sixty Five Hours Christmas)

Best of Both Worlds

Translated Titles:

Fiducia Cieca (Italian translation of Blind Faith)

Attraverso Questi Occhi (Italian translation of Through These Eyes)

Preso alla Sprovvista (Italian translation of Blindside)

Il giorno del Mai (Italian translation of Blind Faith 3.5)

Cuore di Terra Rossa (Italian translation of Red Dirt Heart)

Cuore di Terra Rossa 2 (Italian translation of Red Dirt Heart 2)

Cuore di Terra Rossa 3 (Italian translation of Red Dirt Heart 3)

Cuore di Terra Rossa 4 (Italian translation of Red Dirt Heart 4)

Natale di terra rossa (Red dirt Christmas)

Intervento di Retrofit (Italian translation of Elements of Retrofit)

A Chiare Linee (Italian translation of Clarity of Lines)

Spencer Cohen 1 Serie: Spencer Cohen

Spencer Cohen 2 Serie: Spencer Cohen

Spencer Cohen 3 Serie: Spencer Cohen

Confiance Aveugle (French translation of Blind Faith)

A travers ces yeux: Confiance Aveugle 2 (French translation of Through These Eyes)

Aveugle: Confiance Aveugle 3 (French translation of Blindside)

À Jamais (French translation of Blind Faith 3.5)

Cronin's Key (French translation)

Cronin's Key II (French translation)

Au Coeur de Sutton Station (French translation of Red Dirt Heart)

Partir ou rester (French translation of Red Dirt Heart 2)

Faire Face (French translation of Red Dirt Heart 3)

Trouver sa Place (French translation of Red Dirt Heart 4)

Rote Erde (German translation of *Red Dirt Heart*)

Rote Erde 2 (German translation of *Red Dirt Heart 2*)

NOVA
PRAETORIAN